These girls just want t̶[...]

Look for

✦

Irish Girls About Town

The smash international bestseller featuring stories from
Maeve Binchy   **Marian Keyes**   **Cathy Kelly**
and thirteen other Irish women writers

Scottish Girls About Town

Get ready for a Highland fling with the stories of
Jenny Colgan   **Isla Dewar**   **Muriel Gray**
and sixteen other Scottish women writers

American Girls About Town

A star-studded story collection featuring
Jennifer Weiner   **Lauren Weisberger**   **Adriana Trigiani**
and fourteen other American women writers

All available from
Downtown Press and Pocket Books

Irish Girls
are back in town

doWn tOwn press

New York London Toronto Sydney

DOWNTOWN PRESS, published by Pocket Books
1230 Avenue of the Americas
New York, NY 10020

Originally published in Great Britain in 2004 by Pocket Books,
an imprint of Simon & Schuster UK Ltd.
Published by arrangement with Simon & Schuster UK Ltd.

Library of Congress Control Number: 2004061751

ISBN: 0-7434-9926-3

First Downtown Press trade paperback edition March 2005

10 9 8 7 6 5 4 3 2 1

DOWNTOWN PRESS and colophon are trademarks of Simon & Schuster, Inc.

Manufactured in the United States of America

For information regarding special discounts for bulk purchases,
please contact Simon & Schuster Special Sales at 1-800-456-6798
or business@simonandschuster.com.

Contents

Foreword

Irish Girls Are Back in Town reunites some of Ireland's best-loved women authors as well as up-and-coming stars in an all-new short story collection to raise money for charity. *Irish Girls Are Back in Town* was originally published in the United Kingdom and Ireland, and a portion of the proceeds from each book sold was given to Barnardo's, the United Kingdom's leading children's charity, and to the Society of St. Vincent de Paul in Ireland, which works to alleviate the effects of poverty.

Barnardo's works with more than 100,000 children, young people, and their families in 361 projects throughout the United Kingdom. Its work with families covers a wide range of age groups and issues, including homeless teenagers, children with disabilities, children who have been excluded from school, and people who have decided to improve their surroundings through community development initiatives. For more information about Barnardo's, visit the website at www.barnardos.org.uk.

The Society of St. Vincent de Paul has more than one million members in 132 countries, where it works tirelessly in a wide variety of activities to alleviate the effects of poverty and exclusion. These include running breakfast clubs and homework clubs for schoolchildren, providing advice and counseling services, giving educational grants, running 120 "good-as-new" clothing and house-goods shops, and providing housing for the elderly. The Society in Ireland is also a major contributor to the development of public policy to eliminate poverty.

As with the U.K. and Irish edition, Barnardo's and the Society of St. Vincent de Paul will each receive a donation in connection with the release of the U.S. edition of *Irish Girls Are Back in Town.*

Irish Girls
are back in town

Spinning Sugar

Morag Prunty

S tanley looked up and saw two fat ankles squashed into a pair of cheap high heels. The woman's legs were firmly pressed together so that the shiny patent shoes glowered down at him like a couple of prim twins. The window was near the ceiling in front of his worktop, and it looked out onto the front of the shop where his cakes were displayed.

Passers-by were often arrested by the sight of his magnificent spun-sugar confections. Most stopped to look, some to shop, but few noticed the window at their feet or the small man buried in the basement whipping and creaming and dripping hot sugar, creating the pornography of pastries that drew customers into this exclusive deli.

The cheap stilettos had been there at around this time every day for almost a week now.

He went upstairs to arrange a row of lemon tarts in the window. He always arranged the cakes himself. He didn't trust Marjorie, the shop assistant. On one occasion she had dislodged a

1

raspberry from its rightful place on a cream fruit tart. He saw it sitting forlornly on the stainless steel less than an inch away from its rightful home. It looked like a severed nipple waiting to be sewn back on, and Stanley had felt unable to reach down and replace it as Marjorie would accuse him of being fussy.

"It's only a cake, Stanley. It won't taste any different because of *one lousy raspberry.*"

Marjorie was ignorant. The boss understood that Stanley was a genius in his field and he paid him well. Marjorie knew that, and that, Stanley thought, was why she was so dismissive. She was jealous because she was nobody and he was a master pastry chef. That helped him ignore her.

"She was in again today."

Stanley said nothing.

"The fat woman. She was in again today, just now."

Stanley noticed another chocolate cake was missing.

"That's four days this week, and a chocolate cake every day."

Stanley turned his head slightly away from the display counter to signal he was listening.

"Twenty-five euros a pop. That's a hundred quid this week. Must be loaded—or very fat."

Marjorie collapsed into a fit of giggles. Stanley hated giggling girls. He always felt they were laughing at him.

He mumbled something and went back downstairs.

The following day was Saturday, and the fat lady came again, this time she wanted two chocolate cakes, and there was only one in the window. The cakes were time-consuming to decorate, and expensive, so Stanley only ever had one on display at a time. He heard the thump of Marjorie's boots marching down the narrow staircase.

"She wants two."

She didn't ever give Stanley full information straight away. It was her way of forcing him into conversation. He ran a warm knife along the inside edge of a flan case and gave no reply.

"The fat lady was in and bought another chocolate cake. She wants you to make her an extra one—she's coming back at five. O-*kay?*"

Anger rose through his steady hand and the knife flicked, cutting a nick in the smooth custard.

"I said, is that o-kay?"

Stanley turned and gave Marjorie a fierce look.

"I heard you—now fuck off and leave me alone."

Marjorie's face registered angry shock—not that Stanley was looking.

He heard her mutter "deaf weirdo" as she stomped back upstairs to file her fingernails over the imported cheeses.

A moment later anyone passing might have looked down through the basement window, and seen an almost-perfect cheesecake land against it in a tragic mess.

"Someone to see you."

Marjorie shouted down the stairs. No questions today. She was still smarting from Saturday.

Stanley was prepping his day's creations and there was a pot of espresso sizzling on the stove.

He reached for a clean muslin cloth and sloughed the flour from his hands, allowing himself a small smile. He had known this was coming.

The fat woman negotiated the stairs with little grace, her legs manoeuvring their trendy metal curves with grumpy stumbles. Pretty? he thought. Maybe once. Stanley didn't notice women any more. He had had a girlfriend once. They had met at college and moved to Paris together when he was twenty-two. Stanley had thought that that was that. He hadn't had any particular longing for marriage and children, but he had assumed both were inevitable. Marie had just been there, and her background presence in his life had meant he could get on with the business of his further education in food. When she left he was briefly devastated; but the pain quickly transmogrified into a determination never to allow himself to become so distracted again. In any case, the business of acquiring someone to have a relationship with seemed to him tedious beyond belief and his solitary state was made all the easier by the fact that, generally speaking, Stanley found that women's foolish personalities got in the way of his feeling any sexual attraction for them. Women always diluted their physical attractiveness with gossipy conversation and complicated notions of relationships. If a woman could just be sweet and silent. Like a cake. Girls like Marjorie, he thought, were brittle and noisy, even when they weren't talking. Their purple nails scattered and snapped against worktops like busy cockroaches. The jingling of cheap earrings announced their arrival; their thin bodies squeaked like they were on hinges. They interrupted him.

She was inelegantly dressed in a large beige coat over a fat lady's uniform—leggings and a baggy shirt.

There was a moment's silence while she gathered herself after her arduous journey down the narrow staircase. Against the pristine stainless steel, the angular shapes of instruments, and the spotless whitewashed walls of this designer kitchen, she looked like a cheap, gaudy sofa. Then she did what most people did on meeting Stanley for the first time. She babbled nervously.

"Your cakes are lovely, really. Really delicious. I mean, the chocolate ones are *really* nice. I've bought one every day this week. Even though they're expensive, I mean, they're worth it. Not ordinary like . . . Not like the ones you get in other shops. It's just that, well, the one you made me yesterday, well, I mean one of the ones you made me yesterday. Well, it's just that it was *different* from the other one. Other ones. I mean, it looked the same but it tasted different. Maybe I'm wrong. Maybe it was the same, it's just that it tasted different. Orangey or something, I don't know. Not that it wasn't nice or anything, it *was* nice. It's just that it didn't taste the same and well, it wasn't what I was expecting. And well, I was just wondering why?"

Stanley began to bristle. She was using words like "nice" and "lovely" in a pathetic attempt to describe his indescribably beautiful work. He thought he had better say his piece and he blurted it out with prerehearsed precision.

"Why do you buy the same cake every day?"

The fat lady blushed, and for an instant she looked like she might cry. That she might disappear into her vast blouse—a giant turtle cowering beneath the glare of some tiny but aggressive adversary.

"Well, because I like chocolate."

Stanley was annoyed now.

"Clearly," he said, "you like it a little too much."

He had not intended to say it, and it was only in her reaction that Stanley noticed it might be misconstrued as a comment on her size. That she was fat was of only passing note to Stanley. That she was ignorant of the tender teasing treat of chocolate eaten in chosen moderation was an aberration.

She might have run up the stairs and never returned, had she had the agility to make a faster retreat. But she didn't. She just stood and reddened. Then she blinked and two tiny streams of tears negotiated the vast contours of her cheeks.

"How dare you?" She sucked herself in. "I have spent £150 this week in your shop . . ."

"It's not my shop, I just work here."

Stanley was struggling to find a diversion.

"Worse still. I shall write to the manager and complain. I

shall tell him what you said and I shall never come back into this shop again. Never . . ."

Before Stanley had time to take it in, she was in full flood. Crying. A customer crying in his kitchen. He felt out of control.

Coffee, he thought. Coffee. He went over to the side bench and got two cups. He put one in front of her, poured out the thick liquid and added two spoons of brown uncut demerara sugar. Then he got a chair, sat down and patiently waited for her to stop.

"I'm sorry," she said, "I didn't mean to make a fuss."

Stanley had never made anyone cry before. Or rather, never insofar as he'd had a sense that perhaps they hadn't deserved it.

The fat lady took a side road into embarrassed politeness.

"Do you work here alone? That is, do you work by yourself?"

He nodded.

"And you make *all* those cakes?"

"Yes."

"So I suppose it was a lot of work making that extra one on Saturday? Was that why it was different? Because you forgot and put in the wrong ingredients?"

Stanley was tempted into delivering a caustic curriculum vitae, but thought better of it.

"No," he said, "I did it deliberately. I wanted it to be different."

She looked and waited for him to continue. She was silent. A silent woman.

"I wanted you to notice that it was different."

"But why?" She was calm now. Listening.

"You ordered the same cake every day. Every cake is different. I wanted you to try something else."

"I still don't understand." Slowly. She was speaking slowly, quietly. Respectfully.

"I wanted you to expand," he said.

She smiled. A thorough, broad smile. She had curvaceous lips, he thought. No fruity giggle, no coarse laugh.

"I think," she said, "I've expanded quite enough already. Don't you?"

Stanley smiled back.

"I'm sorry," he said. He was slightly surprised to mean it. "I wanted you to expand your horizons, is what I meant. I wanted you to try something new, something different."

She looked at him quizzically.

"I wanted you to experience something new. Every cake has it's own special flavour, you see——"

"Like a USP?" she butted in.

"A what?"

"A Unique Selling Point. I did a night course in advertising."

"Yes," he said, "I suppose so."

Stanley shifted awkwardly in his seat and the fat lady knew that he had begun to draw back.

"Well, I won't outstay my welcome," she said. "And that's what I'll do then—if you'd like."

Sensing his increasing discomfort, she finished: "I'll come in every day and I'll buy a different cake. You're the expert, and if you think that's what I should do—then I will. How's that?"

A small thrill shot through Stanley, making him feel rather at odds with himself.

"Fine," he said. Then he got up from his seat and began fumbling around on his workbench as a clumsy signal to request her departure.

The fat lady trudged her way back up the stairs. She was feeling slightly shell-shocked after her strange encounter with the peculiar little pastry chef. Not bad, she thought, but a bit of an oddball. I don't know what came over me crying like that, she thought. Then decided to treat herself to a Big Mac and fries to settle herself down a bit.

Beverly kept her word. The following week she bought two fruit flans, of varying shape and type; a lemon sponge with an elaborate candied pattern carved on top, a cheesecake of indiscriminate type, and four individual créme caramels. She was having a "Chinese" week, and so every night after her generous takeaway and half a litre of Diet Coke, she settled down in front of the telly with a large pot of tea (low-fat milk, of course), and devoured one of Stanley's cakes. She didn't enjoy them as much as the chocolate ones she'd had the week before. Mostly, they were too light. The first half of *Coronation Street* was over—and they were gone. Beverly liked food that took its time, it helped her pace herself—made the experience last longer. She loved eating. Loved the sensation of chewing, then swallowing; chewing, then swallowing. She barely smelt the food, let alone tasted it before it was down and the next mouthful on its way in. She needed the full-up feeling it gave her. It was a kind of satisfaction she couldn't get anywhere else. When the cakes didn't satisfy, she filled up on bread. It seemed wrong, somehow, to load half a white loaf on top of those wonderful cakes. Seeing as how, she thought, Stanley had gone to so much trouble making them and they *were* so expensive.

Beverly hadn't always been this fat. For a time, in her early twenties, she had been simply voluptuous. She had had sex then. Her best friend, Karen, a skinny, funny girl she used to work with, used to make Beverly wear tight black dresses and push-up bras and red nail polish. They went to discos together and got drunk and picked up boys. Once they went off in a car with two rough lads from the northside, and the one with Karen had left her in the front seat and joined his friend in the back to look at Beverly's breasts.

"Look at the size of them—they're huge."

"Great," said Jacko.

"Go on, then—have a feel. She doesn't mind. You don't mind, do you love?"

Beverly didn't mind. Even today, the memory of lying back in the back seat of a battered Ford Capri and letting those two lads each suckle a breast like a couple of sleepy pups, stirred her. It had made her feel almost regal, giving them the permission of her indifference. Karen hadn't minded at the time, but then she had started dating the one called Jacko, and had ended up married to him. She never saw Karen now. Jacko had said Beverly was a slut. He must have been embarrassed after that night, although they were all very drunk and as he had said himself—Beverly hadn't minded.

Beverly stopped going out after that. She had no one to go out with. So she stayed in and pursued her one other pleasure—food. She missed Karen sometimes. Or maybe, she thought, she just missed going out. When she felt like that, Beverly just had another packet of biscuits and she felt better. She enjoyed her work. She had been with the advertising firm for six years, starting on reception and after two years being moved sideways into the administrative department. Unbeknownst to herself, Beverly had been the subject of a moral debate at a board meeting just prior to her move.

"She's too bloody fat and getting fatter. It's terrible that the first thing that people see when they walk into this building is that lump of a woman."

"Seems pointless commissioning that Knuttel for reception with her blocking the view."

Roars of laughter from the men. Snuffled giggles from the Managing Director's PA, Sinead, who recounted the comments with glee around the building.

"Can she type?" asked the Creative Director, the only female board member.

Sinead mumbled, "I think so."

"Fine—she can go into admin Monday morning. I'll tell her myself." Then, in reply to the incredulous stares, "You can't fire somebody for being fat. It isn't right." Thus Beverly was given a small rise and shifted to a back office where she could keep doughnuts on her desk without fear of reprimand, if not occasional bitchy comments from the other girls, which she chose to ignore.

Beverly had a good salary, she knew that she earned more than at least two of the girls in her department, but she never seemed to have enough money. She managed to put aside each month for her rent, electricity and phone, which she seldom used. She was horrified, at the Admin Department's Christmas drinks last year, to discover the price of a round, and vowed never to enter a public house again. She felt this vilified her limited social life. She wore the same black leggings until they wore out, and bought large men's shirts and jumpers from Dunnes Stores. "It's terrible," she used to complain at work, "that these shops do not cater for the woman with a fuller figure." Even if she could find them to fit, Beverly could never afford nice clothes. She considered the prices in Dublin's specialist outsize boutiques astronomical. She never once considered that the price of a smart suit from Big is Beautiful was less than her weekly food bill.

Stanley lived above the shop. It was best, he thought. The owner had given it to him as part of his package. After ten years of drifting, finishing his training in Paris, and working there for a while before taking up a position in one of London's more exclusive restaurants, Stanley realized how lucky he was to get a job back home in Dublin. He didn't care much about money, or where he lived. He didn't even really know why he had come back to Ireland. He had no friends there, and didn't get on with his family. He had just drifted back in the same way he had drifted away. The job, when it had been offered to him, had seemed ideal. A functional apartment above the premises where he worked six days a week, and enough money to save. Stanley thought one day he might open a place of his own, but he recoiled at the thought of having to deal with customers. Suppliers were all right. Once you were spending money, you were accorded a quiet respect. But the thought of gaggling rich housewives batting their eyelids and fingering his wares filled him with dread. He put the money aside anyway; he had nothing else to spend it on.

On Sundays, Stanley walked down to Marks & Spencer on Grafton Street and bought his week's supply of coffee and groceries. Food was never skimped on—he bought little and chose well. One small corn-fed chicken which he would roast with garlic and eat cold with chunks of his own flavoured soda bread would almost serve him for the week. The maturest Italian salami bought and paid for (much to Marjorie's amusement), from the delicatessen would be all he needed for a working lunch. Stanley ate a lot of meat. He felt he accorded the animals the respect their dead bodies deserved by savouring their flesh—appreciating it, enjoying it. He often thought that when he died, he would like to be cured, like a fine ham, then hung in the finest *boulangerie* in Paris and served at a premium price to those with an appreciative palate.

This very thought was upon him when a large arm reached in front of his face and five fat digits slid down the wrapper of a ready-cooked chicken, missed and sent a display of Italian garlic sausages tumbling into Stanley's basket, which was balancing on the edge of the fridge.

A plump giggle was accompanied by "Excusey . . . oh it's you!"

For the most part, Stanley kept himself to himself, and wandered around the shops cocooned in his own concentration. Lost in this cheery city where acquaintances need only the mildest excuse to stop on street corners for a chat, Stanley had a dread of meeting people in public. Now he found himself trapped at the cold-meat fridge with his best customer. He had, much to his own irritation, been over and over their last encounter in his own mind. Why, he didn't know. He felt like he was trying to wring some meaning out of it—some theory to satisfy his culinary intellect. When he would be doing some mundane task that required little concentration—beating a roux or thrashing egg white around a bowl until it rose up to greet him—Beverly's fat face dissolving into tears would come into his mind. She had become a source of a most annoying daytime fantasy. A nightmare. And now, she had him pinioned up against the wall with her packed trolley.

"I do so love M&S, don't you? So many scrummy things. I expect you appreciate quality, being a cook and all."

Stanley said nothing but looked at the contents of her trolley. Ready-made meals, the kind that executives buy for dinner parties. Special occasion biscuit boxes—gifts for maiden aunts, but Beverly planned to eat them all herself. The usual groceries, milk, bread—but in family quantities. Then he saw them. Two frozen ice-cream cakes. Manufactured by machine to imitate the flounciest efforts of an over-indulgent pastry chef on the cusp of a nervous breakdown. Promising every vice that earned its calories—"Smooth creamy ice cream, topped with rich dark chocolate on a crunchy biscuit base layered with caramel and nuts." That such a glamorous monstrosity should be sharing the palate—or even the fridge—with one of his own sophisticated confections, was a downright insult. He would ban her from the shop. He would put a cockroach in her next cake. No. She probably wouldn't even notice. She wasn't worth the trouble. She wasn't worth the head space.

"I'm not much of a cook myself," Beverly babbled on oblivious to Stanley's dark thoughts, "that's why I love the food here. It's like you cooked it yourself. You just pop it in the microwave, and there you are. I always put it on plates, mind you—I think it's *so* awful to eat out of the carton—don't you?"

"Are you planning to eat all this food yourself?"

This time he had meant it although, again, Stanley had regretted it as soon as the last word was out. The silence was awful. It seemed like someone had turned off the Muzak and the whole of Grafton Street was standing in awe of his rudeness. Worse, he thought Beverly was going to cry—again. Beverly thought about walking away, but then she thought, no—I've nothing to be ashamed of. I have a right to be here, just the same as him.

"Yes," she said. "All of it. It's my weekly shopping," and then fighting back an indignant tear, she looked Stanley straight in the eye—like she'd been taught in her advertising course about presenting an idea to a client that you think they won't like—and announced, "Have you got a *problem* with that?"

Stanley was not used to being confronted.

"Excuse me," he said and pushed his way past the trolley.

Beverly was mad now. She couldn't remember ever having been this mad before. Stanley was halfway down dried foods when she bellowed after him, "I said, have you got a problem with that, you weedy little creep?" Stanley was stopped in his tracks, pasta to his left, designer kettle chips to his right. His legs wouldn't move; his whole body was hunched up in distaste. Dignity was a distant memory. People were looking now. Delighted mothers stopped wheeling to stare. A supermarket brawl was rare enough entertainment, especially in Dublin 2.

She marched up to him, and stared him in the face. Beverly didn't care if people were staring. They stared at her all the time anyway. This time she looked like she really was going to cry.

"Would you like a cup of coffee?" Stanley quickly blurted out. It had worked the last time.

It was Beverly's turn to be shocked.

"Yes," she said, "that would be very nice."

They left their groceries behind. Beverly didn't worry that it was less than an hour to closing time, and she might not get the chance to revisit the supermarket again at such leisure before the week was out. They walked to a small coffee shop just off Wicklow Street. Beverly hadn't been there before. She noticed that they had lovely cakes in the window, but she said nothing. Stanley ordered a double espresso for himself and a cafe latte for Beverly. He laced his with sugar from a brightly coloured china bowl on the table. Beverly picked it up.

"I don't take sugar in coffee," she said, almost proudly.

Stanley said nothing.

"I'm sorry for shouting at you," she said. "I don't know what came over me."

"Why do you buy those ice-cream cakes when you can have anything that you want from my shop?"

He realized then that he felt insulted. Let down. He had wanted it to come out more aggressively than it had. Had wanted to sound confrontational; angry. Frighten her a bit. But he didn't. He sounded hurt. Let down.

"Oh." Beverly blushed. She knew somehow that his cakes were very important to him. More important than they were to her.

"Well, your cakes are lovely—but they *are* expensive."

"You still buy one every day."

Beverly was flattered that he had noticed that she visited the shop every day. She would have liked to have asked him how he knew. Made him say that he watched for her every day, then flirted with him a little. But the time didn't feel right.

"They are delicious," she said, struggling to find the route to say what was on her mind without offending him, "better than you get anywhere else. It's just that, well, they don't always fill me up." She blushed again as she said it.

Stanley was beginning to feel flustered. His cakes were special. Most people ordered them only for dinner parties and gifts. Here was someone who threw them into her like they were merely fuel for some kind of monstrous ship.

"Why do you eat so much?"

"I beg your pardon?" Beverly was grateful she didn't have a plate of food in front of her.

"Why? Why do you eat so much?"

Beverly intercepted the sick feeling that was coaxing its way up from her gut.

"Well, I enjoy it, I suppose."

Stanley huffed in amusement and shook his head—smiling.

"What? I do! I enjoy it!"

Then the miniature pastry chef threw his head back and he laughed.

"What's so funny? What did I say?"

He laughed and laughed until he thought he was going to explode. Then Beverly started laughing too.

"I don't know what you think is so funny," she said, but she was enjoying herself. A dour man laughing is a rare sight.

When Stanley composed himself, he held Beverly's bemused look and said, "No. You don't enjoy food. You cannot possibly enjoy something you don't understand."

"What do you mean?" She didn't know whether to feel offended or relieved.

"Food," Stanley said, "should caress your senses, not assault them."

Beverly looked at him blankly.

"Here," and he got up from the table and reached for Beverly to go with him, "come with me and I'll show you something."

They walked to a restaurant nearby. It was the sort of place that Beverly would never go to. The prices were outrageous, the portions small and she found she got better value eating at home. Her boss sometimes went there for lunch, and she had once been called in there to deliver some important documents that she'd left behind.

"I know this place," she said, hoping to impress him, but Stanley wasn't listening.

"You see these people. They eat here because it's the most expensive restaurant in Dublin. Some of them pretend to understand the food, but few of them do. I work for them sometimes; they buy from the shop. They spend up to a hundred pounds to eat the best food available and they come out of here the same way they went in—full of shit."

Beverly didn't really take in what he was saying, but she was quite stunned at his new-found verbosity.

"Are you hungry?"

"We're not going in," she said, horrified, but also a little thrilled at the prospect. "I'm not dressed or anything."

"No. Wait here," Stanley said, and ran down the stairs at the side entrance to the basement kitchen, leaving Beverly standing on the pavement. Just as she thought he was never going to come back, Stanley appeared at her side with two plates covered with heavy linen napkins. He walked her hurriedly up to Stephen's

Green where they sat on the first available bench and put the plates on their laps.

"Where's the cutlery?" said Beverly.

"No," said Stanley, "no cutlery. We'll eat with our hands."

Beverly thought she had never eaten anything so delicious in her life. They ate slowly. She was careful to eat at Stanley's pace and found herself tasting every morsel. The sweet roasted pepper slithering over her palate, the pungent aroma of the cured meat lifting up against the back of her mouth and exploding through her nostrils. When the plate was clear Stanley unwrapped a small slice of corn bread and encouraged her to soak up all the juice and fat from her empty plate until it was bone dry.

"I could eat that all over again," she said, "times ten!"

Stanley looked slightly confused, disappointed even.

"Are you still hungry then?" he asked.

For the first time in her life, Beverly thought about it and realized that, in actual fact, she wasn't.

———————

London-reared of Irish parents, **MORAG PRUNTY** edited several young women's magazines in London, including *More!* and *Just Seventeen,* before moving to Ireland in 1990 to relaunch *Irish Tatler.* She is now a full-time writer and lives in Ireland with her family. She is the author of three bestselling novels: *Dancing with Mules, Disco Daddy,* and *Poison Arrows.*

At Least There'll Be Diamonds

Martina Devlin

*C*rystal Dolan swept into the airport departure lounge with the air of someone expecting stares. Right on cue people gave her a second glance, some even batted her a third, for she had the gloss of a 1950s starlet. Hers was a polished glamour requiring constant maintenance but Crystal was permanently willing to invest in her appearance. It was, after all, her primary asset.

Despite the mild spring weather, which made it uncomfortably warm, a rabbit-skin coat dyed to resemble ocelot was draped around her shoulders. Its purchase had meant a straight choice between not possessing it or defaulting on the gas and electricity bills. Crystal hadn't hesitated: she knew looking the part was infinitely more important than any of that middle-class nonsense about paying bills as they were due. Her parents were like that, her father spent all his free time fretting about his pension, but thankfully she'd escaped such petty tyrannies.

Dangling from French-manicured fingers was a Prada handbag. It was divine, it was exorbitant, it was coveted by her friends, it was . . . not large enough to accommodate the detritus she needed to carry about on a daily basis. However, it was the latest model and had a waiting list of desperate would-be owners. Two women had already gaped at the bag with naked desire as she'd strolled through the duty-free shops and Crystal had revelled in it.

Terry had bought the bag for Crystal during their last weekend break, a jaunt to London when they'd stayed at the Ritz. Terry preferred more intimate hotels—but Crystal had pouted so winningly as she'd begged for the treat that it had been a foregone conclusion their limousine would purr its way along Park Lane. Understated didn't suit her at all, she craved opulence.

Her real name was Anne, changed by deed poll to Crystal on her twenty-first birthday. She had almost trained herself not to respond if old acquaintances or family members inadvertently used the despised former name. She had been saddled with that to ensure an inheritance from her Great Aunt Annie, but Meals on Wheels had ended up the recipient instead. Calculating, phoney Samaritans, serving up chicken casserole and apple crumble year after year to the old dear. Running her errands when she became housebound and making themselves indispensable. Opportunistic do-gooders.

Crystal nursed the accustomed ruffle of animosity for a few moments as she scanned the departure lounge; those Meals on Wheels-ers were spending money that was rightfully hers on nutritious dinners for geriatrics. Selecting a seat, she checked it carefully for stains before lowering her body into it.

She eyed the rabble with distaste as they milled around Dublin Airport. Why on earth airlines accepted passengers wearing shell suits she'd never fathom. Anyway, she thought, resting her Prada bag gingerly on her knee, at least Great Aunt Annie's senile decision to squander her money on outsiders, instead of keeping it in the family like anyone with an ounce of sensibility, had left her free to choose a more apt name. Crystal felt the revision suited her perfectly, with her ice-white sheet of hair, although Terry claimed that it also captured her aura of fragility. Terry was a shade blinkered when it came to Crystal. Even she acknowledged she was far from delicate. Eye-catching? By all means. Frail? Er, pass.

Despite her impeccably packaged attractions, at twenty-seven Crystal looked at least eight years older. This was not because of emerging wrinkles or crow's feet—she was zealous in her use of skin-firming lotions—but because, for all her designer-label fixation, she dressed with a matronly care for accessories. She had a weakness for matching bags and shoes, invariably wore pale colours and was defined by the fluttering scarves she tied around her neck.

One ex-boyfriend—who'd sneered that she was mistress material but a non-starter as a wife—had called her an air stewardess clone in those scarves. Brute. She'd wasted four months of her life on him, only to discover he had a wife and three children in Kildare. And he had no intention of trading in any of them. Pipsqueak magazine publisher. Crystal almost—but stopped herself in time because it wasn't ladylike—snorted. She'd taught him a lesson. All it had taken was an anonymous call to the tax office about a certain offshore bank account he'd visited during their trip to the Cayman Islands.

The loudspeaker pinged and a real air stewardess intruded on her reverie. "Aer Lingus is now boarding flight number E1602 to Amsterdam. Would passengers in rows one to sixteen prepare to take their seats and have their boarding cards ready for inspection?"

Crystal crossed her legs and banked down a niggle of annoyance. She was in row thirty, tourist class. But the next time she travelled it would be first class—or club class at a push. She'd requested an upgrade at check-in, but had been refused.

"Couldn't I at least sit in a row on my own then?" Crystal had persevered. "I get claustrophobic." Her blue eyes had been beseeching as she'd twined a strand of silken blonde hair around an index finger, lying glibly in the hope of avoiding some peasant's elbow nudging hers during the trip. However, the brisk woman at the check-in desk had said the flight was nearly full. "What can't be cured must be endured," she'd remarked—unnecessarily, in Crystal's view.

Terry would have paid for her flight, making sure she had the best seat money could buy, but Crystal had hesitated to hint that she might need help financing the trip. Terry would be picking up the bill wherever they went from now on. She didn't care to risk any eleventh-hour jitters about gold diggers.

At least she had an aisle seat. Crystal folded her Joseph coat carefully, lining side outwards, and stored it in the overhead compartment. She checked the rows in front and behind: good, no squalling babies. Just as she'd settled, hands laced demurely on the lap of her black and white checked suit—only Jigsaw but the colour was perfect for travelling because it didn't show the dirt—a shambling man in an ill-fitting navy blazer touched her shoulder.

"I'm so sorry, could I squeeze past?" he apologized.

An English accent. Home Counties, but not top notch, she guessed.

Crystal arranged her face into a mask of indifference as she unbuckled her belt and stepped into the aisle to let him through to the window seat.

As he passed, she wrinkled her nose in repugnance: he didn't use deodorant. Crystal turned her head to the side, trying to avoid inhaling, and noticed the glint of gold on the hand cradling a briefcase close to his chest. He was wearing a wedding band. How incongruous that he should be married: surely a wife would buy a can of something and order him to point and squirt. Going natural was downright unnatural.

Then she was distracted by the plane's engines as they emitted that whining blast signalling take-off, and had more pressing matters to concentrate on. Air travel was a necessary evil, but how she longed for the days of luxury liners and special carriages for the élite coupled onto trains.

"You can open your eyes now, we're airborne." The business-man's tone was sober, not a hint of ridicule. "It might also," he continued, "be advisable to start breathing again. I know the theory for the kiss of life but I've never been called upon to practise it." Crystal, the only passenger on board convinced the captain would have a heart attack at the controls and when his co-pilot took over there'd be engine failure, eked out a laugh. But from the plane's angle she knew it was still climbing, so she shouldn't relax her vigilance.

"My wife's a nervous flyer too," continued her neighbour, whose florid complexion was already beaded with pearls of sweat. "She always insists on an aisle seat and won't leave the departure lounge without at least one gin and tonic inside her. Preferably two."

"I had a Bloody Mary while I was waiting for the flight to be called," admitted Crystal. "I don't even like them." Her voice croaked, as though she'd just woken up. "It seemed the only drink I could decently ask for at 9 a.m., apart from a Buck's Fizz."

And she didn't believe in buying her own champagne, that was other people's function.

The businessman's shoulder was wedged against hers and she

had to keep moving her feet because they continually collided with his. These rabbit-hutch seats were not designed for portly middle-aged men. The curtain into business class was raised as a flight attendant whisked through and she had a glimpse of wide seats and drinks balanced on a tray. Crystal pursed her lips, discontented, then risked a peek through the window beyond her neighbour. Clouds, fluffy expanses of them. Her shoulders untensed and she leaned back against the headrest.

"It's only the take-off and landing that bother me—I'm fine with the in-between bit," she explained, nerves rendering her uncharacteristically conversational with a stranger who appeared to be neither well-heeled nor well-connected.

"That's not so bad, my wife is like a cat on a hot tin roof for the entire flight. If it weren't for the Channel Tunnel I doubt if we'd ever leave Sussex." He reached into an inner pocket of the jacket hooked to the seat in front and produced a wallet. It was flipped open and Crystal was confronted by a photograph of a sallow-complexioned woman with one hand shading her eyes from the sunshine, the other resting on the shoulder of a solid, cross girl with a fringe.

"She's fair too." He indicated his daughter.

What did he mean "too?" Crystal bridled. Her hair was a radiant shade of blonde, not a drab fair—platinum, if he wanted to be specific. Obviously that was beyond him. She haemorrhaged enough money into the most exclusive hair salon in town every six weeks to keep her mouse-beige roots at bay; the least that prying strangers could do was be dazzled.

He retrieved the wallet and continued chattering seamlessly, spewing out data. He was based in England but spent one day a week in Ireland in the Dublin office. Usually it didn't require an overnight stay, but he'd done some forward planning and had arranged to take a client out to dinner—Thornton's, had she ever been there? Crystal didn't deign to reply; naturally she and Terry had dined in Thornton's, as well as every other restaurant of note in the city.

The English businessman didn't notice the condescension curled around her upper lip, too intent on capitalizing on his captive market. After some very fine duck and a bottle of Châteauneuf-du-Pape apiece, rewarded by the promise of a contract renewal, he'd checked into a hotel near the airport. Since he had to fly to Amsterdam today, he'd reasoned that he may as well do it from Dublin as Heathrow. The passenger folded his arms in readiness for Crystal's murmurs of admiration over his time-management strategy.

Crystal was only half listening, marvelling at how many letters he could squeeze into the word no. There was definitely an a there, and a w, maybe an h too. She contemplated delving for the *Cara* in-flight magazine in the seat pocket in front of her as a deterrent, but the stranger seemed harmless. Normally she wouldn't tolerate his intrusion, she couldn't associate with just anybody, after all, but he had distracted her from her dread of— not death, exactly, but of entrapment. Every time her stomach flipped that somersault which coincided with take-off and landing, she imagined some catastrophe condemning her to an eternity in one of these slim cylinders—suffocating from lack of oxygen, gnawing her own arm when food supplies ran out.

Besides, her neighbour with the unruly nasal hair didn't seem to expect much in return for the barrage of information he was unleashing on her. An audience was enough.

What was it about the enforced intimacy of adjoining seats in a plane that prompted strangers to swap confidences? It was an impulse that moved only some people, she amended—Crystal had no inclination to spread her own life like a deck of cards. She had an ace in her hand and she preferred to keep it there, in a visor grip. She wriggled in her seat to reclaim some space and noticed the businessman's odour didn't seem so objectionable any more. Maybe his wife had simply become accustomed to it, as she was beginning to.

His pool of biographical details was hit by drought somewhere over the north of England and he began to inflict questions on her. Honestly, the impudence, you gave these people an inch and they took a mile. Crystal evaded them with practised ease, pretending to be engrossed in drinking the coffee served a few minutes earlier. But she grew agitated by the "fasten seatbelts" sign flashing and the cabin crew's precipitate removal of the refreshments' trolley. And Crystal let slip a nugget of information.

"I'm on my way to Holland to be married," she admitted.

"Congratulations. Is your husband-to-be Dutch?"

"No, Irish, but Terry has residency in Holland. For business purposes."

Just then the loudspeaker crackled and the chief flight attendant asked passengers to return to their places. Crystal fretted, imagining various Doomsday scenarios. Her neighbour reattached his seatbelt—Crystal had never removed hers—and continued to quiz her.

Instead of his questions, she concentrated on the flight attendant, attentive for any hint of panic in her voice. They'd hit some turbulence, the stewardess was explaining in that simultaneously placatory and upbeat tone peculiar to the profession. Nothing to be concerned about, she stressed. Crystal wasn't convinced.

Diamonds, she reminded herself, fumbling for distraction. Amsterdam was famous for diamonds. Terry had promised to collect her from Schipol Airport and take her shopping for an engagement ring. "Solitaires," she muttered. "Huge, pear-shaped ones. Or clusters. A cluster of glittering carats."

The businessman droned in her ear. Franchise opportunities . . . spreading the risk . . . expertise on tap . . .

She made no pretence at answering him.

Take it one stage at a time, she advised herself, courtesy of the self-help tape she'd listened to on headphones the previous night. You're beyond the take-off stage, that's the part you most detest, you're halfway through the journey, you only have landing to manage and then you're safe and sound. Think positive images. Imagine the plane landing on the tarmac at the airport, taxiing to a halt, ground staff scurrying out to attach those staircase things. Terry will be waiting for you at the airport: it's the beginning of a new phase in your life. You'll be a married woman with access to a joint bank account bursting with health and vitality. Don't blow it, girl, you're on the brink of achieving what you've worked towards for the past seven years.

The plane seemed to list to the left and Crystal's stomach tried to follow it. This self-help wasn't working. Even engagement rings had lost their sparkle.

"I don't want to live in Holland," she gasped. "Dublin is where I belong, with a holiday home in Cannes or Deauville."

The businessman slewed his eyes towards her. "Home is where the heart is," he suggested.

Crystal glared and he wilted.

Then she relented. "Would you like my biscuits? I'm not hungry."

He accepted the airline's complimentary packet of shortcake in a spirit of reconciliation and suggested they share a cab into the city centre. Crystal flourished Terry as her let-out clause.

"Lovely girls, the Irish," he remarked, sugar from the biscuits clinging to his lower lip. "You have a nurturing way about you."

Crystal was nurturing a desire never to see him again, as fear-fuelled irrationality consumed her and she blamed him for the bumpy ride. Another few minutes of turbulence and he'd be responsible for the fingernail which had splintered while she was zipping up her case, and the cab arriving fifteen minutes late and leaving her convinced she'd miss her flight. Her breathing was becoming progressively more shallow. If Terry were here she'd be in safe hands. Terry always knew how to allay her fears. "I'll order us a bottle of Dom P," Terry would say, and give her that intimate smile reserved only for Crystal.

Crystal had met Terry through a mutual friend. She'd gone along to the drinks' reception in the Ice Bar at the Four Seasons specifically hoping to bag a wealthy husband. It had been her ambition since the age of twenty, when she'd realized that she didn't enjoy working for a living. Not in the slightest. The self-financing state was overrated.

Furthermore, her job as the manager of a dress shop in Sandymount was never going to earn her enough money to facilitate the lifestyle she knew she deserved. It allowed her a useful discount on clothes and just about covered the rent on her apartment in Ballsbridge, but there was nothing left over. Even if Crystal could find someone willing to set her up in her own shop, it would entail more work than she was prepared to consider. She was a woman with other plans for her life, as determined as a force of nature.

"Is this your first trip to Holland?" asked the businessman, helpfully flicking up her table and hooking it under the lever on the seat in front.

Crystal closed her eyes and pretended to nod off, although she thought sleeping in public very déclassé.

She fantasized about her life when she'd be married to Terry. Crystal knew she'd have absolutely no difficulty filling each day as a lady of leisure. She'd start with breakfast on a tray in bed, brought up by the Filipina housekeeper, followed by a little light shopping. Perhaps there'd be lunch or afternoon tea with a friend, and then a Brazilian—painful, but you grew accustomed to it—or a manicure. Hands were always on show, but even the best-groomed women sometimes overlooked regular maintenance. Details, details. Crystal knew how consequential they were.

Now, let's see, what would she do after her salon visit? She might stop off at the travel agency on the way home for some brochures to plan their next holiday, for she intended to take trips away every couple of months. The daily routine could be so monotonous. She should probably squeeze in a couple of gym sessions every week—it was essential to keep herself fit and toned for Terry. She'd have to undertake some charity work too, but nothing strenuous—just a case of insinuating herself onto the committee of a couple of high-profile charities where she could help organize their annual balls. It would give her a profile, with a guaranteed name-check in newspaper social diaries, and it would all be useful for Terry's property interests. Networking in the right set was crucial in that line of business.

She wouldn't take Terry for granted, like some wives, as soon as the ring was on her finger. She'd always make sure her car—a convertible, she mused, perhaps a Mercedes SLK—nosed up the drive of their detached home in time to check the housekeeper had dinner under control. Naturally it would be a Dublin 4 home, there was no way she was staying in Amsterdam, whatever Terry's current intentions: together they'd face down the prudes, conservatives and stick-in-the-muds who didn't accept that she and Terry were a couple. Terry's relations would help. As one of the country's most distinguished families, with impeccable Fine Gael credentials, once they rowed in behind the pair everyone else would be obliged to follow suit.

Of course she wasn't an idiot. She knew some people would always disapprove of their marriage. They might even refuse to acknowledge it. But money talked in Dublin—and judging by the size of Terry's bank account, there were enough funds in it to keep them both in conversation for the rest of their lives.

A self-satisfied radiance illuminated Crystal's features as she remembered the reverential way Terry's eyes had lingered on her that evening a year ago when they'd first met. She'd realized instinctively that here was a big fish so willing to be hooked there was no need for bait: whatever Crystal had, it worked for Terry. She'd responded to the blatant admiration the way she always did when she encountered it, using her own studied blend of charm—a combination of flirtatious and imperious.

Strictly speaking, her other half was really not her type. She had never dreamed she would end up with someone quite like Terry White-Clarke, but Terry was single, besotted with her, and a millionaire property developer with office and apartment blocks in Dublin, Amsterdam and Manhattan, as well as interests in hotels in Cape Town and St. Lucia. That was enough for Crystal. With a portfolio as impressive as Terry's, physical attraction was irrelevant. Or, to put it another way, physical attraction could be simulated. She'd been faking it for a year with Terry. Then again, she'd feigned passion on nearly every occasion with her publisher boyfriend.

"You mentioned you were getting married but I notice you're not wearing an engagement ring." The businessman encroached on her reverie.

She sighed and fluttered open her eyes. He'd introduced himself to Crystal but she hadn't bothered trying to remember his name. She only retained the names of people who might be useful to her.

"Are you one of these fiercely modern women who disapprove of signs of 'ownership?' " He made flopping rabbits' ears with his fingers to signify quotation marks.

Crystal's face almost cracked into a smile, although she tended to ration these because someone had advised her once that staying expressionless was the best way to defer those appalling furrows and puckers you saw in older women. Before they went on a scalpel safari to South Africa, that is, and returned with face-lifts they attributed to the therapeutic value of a relaxing holiday. As though anyone in their circle was fooled for a second.

"I'm choosing my engagement ring today," announced Crystal. "We decided to leave it until we were together in Amsterdam because the selection of diamonds there is far superior to anything in Dublin."

"I borrowed the money from my dad to buy my wife her engagement ring," her companion reminisced. "She wanted a sapphire just like Lady Di's. I couldn't afford anything as big as hers, but we found something that pleased my Sandra and meant I wouldn't be in hock to my old man for the rest of my life."

No need for Terry to borrow money from anyone for her engagement ring, thought Crystal smugly. She could point out a rock the size of Gibraltar and Terry would reach over the black Amex card without so much as an involuntary wince. Terry's idea of economizing was to order Moët et Chandon instead of Dom Perignon.

"Ladies and gentlemen, we will shortly begin our descent into Schipol airport. Would you please ensure that your seatbelts are fastened and your tables are stored in the upright position."

Crystal stopped listening to her companion again, as sheer terror convulsed her. It would all be worth it, she reassured herself, when she saw Terry's thin, brown, supremely indulgent face.

Terry was waiting for Crystal as soon as she stepped into the babble of the airport arrivals' area, almost obscured by a mammoth bouquet of palest pink roses.

"You look gorgeous, darling," beamed Terry, breathless at the sight of Crystal.

"We aim to please," dimpled Crystal, accepting the blooms.

Terry stroked the exquisite blonde's face, taking care not to smear her make-up. "Everything's booked for the wedding, it's all set for the day after tomorrow. I can hardly wait."

Crystal linked arms with Terry and allowed herself to be led towards the exit, where a chauffeur-driven limousine awaited them.

It was all bordering on perfection. Except she wished some of her old school and work colleagues could be there to watch her being fêted. To see how Terry could refuse her nothing.

"If only we were getting married in Donnybrook Church with a reception at Powerscourt, instead of this cloak-and-dagger affair," she murmured.

A frown flickered across Terry's forehead. She unhooked the arm which clasped Crystal's, smoothing down her sleek, dark bobbed hair. "I'd give you anything money can buy, Crystal, but I can't manage that. Holland and Belgium are the only countries which recognize gay marriages, you know that as well as I do. It was either Amsterdam or Brussels—Dublin was never an option."

Crystal sighed, trailing a finger along the stem of one of the roses in her bouquet until it hit the first thorn. Then she rallied, slipping her hand inside Terry's, squeezing it until her fiancée's mouth relaxed into that smile of worship with which she'd met Crystal in the arrivals' hall.

There might not be any envious girlfriends on hand, but at least there were diamond shops.

Born in Omagh, County Tyrone, **MARTINA DEVLIN** now lives in Dublin, where she writes a column for the *Sunday Worlds* magazine. She won a Hennessy Prize for her first short story and has gone on to write three highly acclaimed novels: *The Three Wise Men, Be Careful What You Wish For* and, most recently, *Venus Reborn*.

Her website is www.martinadevlin.com.

Part-time Lover

Tina Reilly

Sunday. 14th February. And she'd forgotten the candles.

Abby cursed herself as she stomped up the road toward Rob's corner shop. On any other day it wouldn't matter. On any other day, she could go to the supermarket, but at seven o'clock on a Sunday evening, the only place open was Rob's.

She hated Rob's.

Besides being the most aptly named shop in Dublin due to its exorbitant prices, it was also staffed by a guy who fancied her rotten. He'd even sent her a Valentine card that very morning. Just shoved it in through the door while she was looking at the telly. She heard the letter box slam and thinking it was the local freebie newspaper she hadn't bothered to go out into the hall. And when she eventually did, she was taken aback to see a gi-normous pink envelope sitting on the floor. For one mad moment she thought . . . but nope, there was no way David would have sent it.

And ruling him out, Rob was the only other possibility left.

With a heart sinking faster than Michael Jackson's career, she opened it. The card was bear shaped and its awful verse read:

I love you here
I love you there
Please be my cuddly teddy bear
Cos then I can love you everywhere.

Underneath the rhyme, a big letter R was done in a sort of fancy calligraphy script.

Abby winced as she remembered. God, she couldn't face him. "Please don't let him be working," she half prayed as she pushed open the shop door. "Please don't let him be working. Please don't let him be—"

"How's it goin'?" Rob waved at her. "How's my favourite customer?"

"Great. Fine." She hopped from one foot to the other, hoping to appear in a mad hurry.

Rob didn't seem to notice. "I'll be with you in a sec," he said as he carefully added a packet of fruit polos to a polo mint tower he had built behind the counter. "There now—great display—what?"

"Yeah. Great."

"So," Rob came towards her, all dark hair and white grinning teeth. "Come to ask me out, have ya?"

"Nope." She didn't smile back at him. Smiling at Rob only made him want to keep talking. "I'm actually looking for two candles."

"Awwww." He feigned huge disappointment. Then grinning ruefully, he added, "Aw well, it's for the best really. I'd have had to say no. I'm booked up this evening but I could fit you in tomorrow, if you'd like?"

"Naw."

"Hey—don't spare my feelings by pretending to think it over."

Abby grinned without thinking. He never got offended. Though she guessed, with the prices he charged, it was his customers who ended up offended. "Candles?" she prompted.

"Oh, yeah, right." He ducked under the counter. "Don't tend to stock too many of them—I have a box here somewhere." There was a bit of shuffling and sounds of him moving things about before he placed a box of assorted candles in front of her. "So—d'ya get any nice Valentine cards?"

"Nope."

"None at all?" He looked surprised.

"Well, just one but it wasn't very nice."

"Ouch."

He grinned down at her and rather than hold his gaze, she turned her attention to the candles. What colour should she go for? She wished she could remember what colour they'd had the last dinner they'd had together, but it was ages ago and she couldn't. Her hand hovered over the reds.

"Have you a nice dinner planned?"

Nice would be stretching it. Cooking had never been her strong point. "Mmm."

"With?"

She swallowed hard. She never mentioned David, not even to her closest friends. If she told them about him, they'd think she was crazy. And if they didn't think she was crazy, they'd probably try to lecture her. They'd say things like, "But what's in it for you?" And "He can't give you anything." But it just showed how much they knew.

"Well?" Rob asked.

"Just a friend," she murmured. It didn't sound right, just calling him a friend. "A very good friend," she amended.

Rob's face fell and Abby felt a bit of a heel. Then she realized that in order to get Rob off her back, it was exactly the way to go about it. "I'll, eh, take white ones, please." She lifted the candles from the box. "How much?"

Rob waved her away. "I'll give them to you for half price if you go out with me tomorrow night."

"Give them to me for free and I'll think about it."

"Done."

Abby laughed. "Call you if I'm desperate," she giggled.

Rob groaned good-naturedly.

He wasn't so bad, she guessed.

The pasta sauce smelt very strange.

Well, more disgusting than strange.

"Ohhh God!" Abby dropped the candles and legged it towards the cooker. She'd left the sauce simmering when she'd gone to get the candles. Now she realized that maybe it hadn't been such a good idea. Instead of being a nice shiny runny consistency, what she had, in her saucepan, were lumps the size of apples surrounded by some nice shiny runny bits. "Shit." She pulled a fork from a drawer and began to mash it. It wasn't fair, David was making the effort to be with her and all she could do was wreck his dinner. One bloody night and she couldn't even get the dinner right.

Chances were, tomorrow she could cook the same thing and it would turn out fine. But there was no point thinking of tomorrow. Tomorrow would be extra horrible because she'd be so happy tonight. By tomorrow, he'd be gone and it would be ages before she'd see him again. He wasn't always able to visit whenever she wanted and it was only when missing him became too painful that he would come again. And his wide grin and handsome face would make her catch her breath, just like it had the first time she'd set eyes on him, and she'd know that he was right for her, the only man for her, and that she'd wait for ever if it meant being with him at some stage.

In the beginning, he'd come more often, sometimes once a week, but as time wore on, he came less and less. Abby thought it was because he didn't love her as much but he kept assuring her that he loved her more than ever.

More than ever.

And he always made a special effort on Valentine's night—they'd spent it together for the last seven years.

As she de-lumped the pasta sauce, she refused to think about the possibility of him not loving her. The possibility that maybe he wouldn't turn up.

"He'll come," she said out loud. "He'll definitely come."

She'd met him in a pub. He'd been over in the corner with a mate, having a laugh and drinking a few pints. It was his laugh that had made her turn towards him—such a bright sunny free kind of sound. And it was as if he knew she was looking at him, because he turned and looked at her at the same time. And she'd fallen for him, right then, fallen for his dark, shining eyes and his laugh.

Just before she went up to change, she inspected the dining room. It was as cosy as she could make it. She dimmed the lighting, bathing the room in a warm golden glow. Framed pictures of the two of them were on the mantelpiece. Her favourite one, the one taken four years ago, was in the centre. In it, David had his arm slung about her shoulder. Her head was nestled in the crook of his neck and her eyes were gazing up at him. She didn't know who'd taken the shot, some stranger that they'd asked, but this person had captured probably one of the happiest moments of her life. Abby ran her finger down the picture and smiled. She never tired of looking at it.

On the table, the cutlery gleamed, having been especially polished for the occasion and the crystal wine glasses threw shards of light onto the white linen tablecloth. She stuck the candlesticks into the holders and stood back, once again to view it.

It looked perfect.

Abby took her new dress from the wardrobe and winced slightly. Why had she bought the damn thing? It was more suited to a big posh bash than a stay-at-home dinner with de-lumped pasta sauce. But its colour had suited her eyes. She'd always had nice eyes. Lately, though, everyone had been telling her that she looked tired. "You look tired," her mother had snapped only last week. "Tired face, tired eyes. You should get out more."

Abby grinned as she stepped into the dress. Her mother was one to talk. Her mother never went anywhere, preferring instead to stay indoors and talk to anyone who visited her about her long-dead husband. Abby had loved her dad, but the way her mother seemed to have died with him had been hard for her to cope with.

The zip went up easily. The dress fell in soft folds about her thin figure. Her pale face stared back at her from the mirror and for a weird moment she didn't recognize herself. "That's me," she said to herself. "That's me in there."

But it still did no good.

Maybe if she shovelled on some make-up?

As she grabbed for her make-up bag, Rob's card fell from the bed onto the floor. Damn! Where was she supposed to put it? It was too big for the bin—David would definitely spot it. It wouldn't fit in any of her presses. Finally, she shoved it under the bed, resolving to throw it out the next day.

❖　　❖　　❖

David had only ever given her three Valentine cards. She still had them somewhere. Three Valentine cards in seven years. It just didn't seem that fair to her. In the beginning, it had made her angry. But her anger had upset David and almost spoiled their time together, so now she didn't talk about it any more.

By nine o'clock, the sauce was congealing nicely in the saucepan, the pasta was ready to go. Her hair was caught up in a French roll and she reeked of expensive perfume. Her face was hidden under a tube of Max Factor and her eyes were heavy with some clumpy mascara she'd found in the bottom of her make-up bag. Ginger, her cat, wound herself in and out of her legs and was making half-hearted attempts to jump up onto her lap.

David had bought her Ginger.

He'd thought it funny to call a black and white cat Ginger.

And so had she.

A pain in her heart.

Was he never going to come?

Miaow.

"Go away," her voice wobbled. "Stop, Ginger, it's my new dress."

The cat miaowed some more and she stared at it. Then the cat sort of shimmered and went out of focus.

"Damn!" Tears were eeking down her face. Her eyes were stinging now as mascara ran into them. David would think she looked awful.

If he came.

She crossed to the counter to get herself some kitchen tissue.

The tears were coming faster now. Her nose had joined in the act and had begun to dribble.

"Abby." David's voice getting closer.

She froze. He'd surprised her, like he always did. She hastily dabbed her eyes and blinked, holding on hard to the kitchen sink. God, she hoped he wouldn't know she'd been blubbering.

"Hiya, Ab."

Steeling herself, she slowly turned to face him. And he looked the same as always—tall and dark and smiling, the way she always pictured him in her mind. He wore a black suit and black shirt and tie. "Hiya yourself," she said, feeling shy. "You're a bit later than I thought."

"Have you been crying?"

"No. No. My mascara has turned to acid—that's all."

"Sure?"

She gulped. He had his worried face on. "You were just so late," she whispered. She sounded pathetic, even to herself. "It's not polite, you know," she added jokingly.

"I tried to get away earlier, but I couldn't. I'm awfully sorry, Ab."

"You'll be even sorrier when you taste your overcooked pasta sauce."

"Oh God, say you didn't cook!"

His anguished face made her giggle.

Ginger began to hiss and spit.

"And I see Ginger loves me the same as always," David half laughed.

"I'll put her out." Abby brushed by him as she bent down to pick up the cat. She felt self-conscious in her over-the-top dress.

"You look gorgeous."

"I know."

David laughed.

She cornered Ginger and opening the back door, shoved the cat out into the freezing rain, trying to ignore the offended look on the animal's face. "Sorry, puss." Then she turned to face David again.

"Come here." He held out his arms and she walked towards him.

He was cold. She welcomed his embrace though, the feeling

of his arms about her, the hard, firm body that always made her feel so secure.

"I love you," she whispered, her face upturned for a kiss.

He hesitated, just for a second, which caused her to panic. She didn't want to lose him.

"And I love you," he answered. "Much more than you know."

They held each other for a long time.

Then the sauce began to burn.

Fish and chips weren't what she had planned. The stink of them for one thing. The stench of grease and fat filled up the cozy little dining room. It'd take her weeks to get the smell out. Still they tasted great. She forgot about the heavy silver knife and fork on the table and ate with her fingers. She was starving; being with David made her ravenous—maybe it was the relief that he'd actually come.

David didn't seem to be hungry, he ate hardly anything. He just seemed happy to look at her. And he kept glancing at the table and smiling for some weird reason.

"Eat up, would you."

"I'm fine." He pushed his plate away from him. "So, tell me, how've you been?"

"Fine." She'd left the largest chip until last. Popping it in her mouth she grinned at him. "You?"

He shrugged. "Not too bad."

"And the two kids?"

He flinched. "They're fine too." He never liked her asking about the kids. It was better for her not to know things like that, he'd said. But she *had* to know. She didn't like that he had a whole other side she never saw.

"I'm glad."

"Yeah."

For the first time, she noticed how tired he looked. It was in his eyes. They didn't sparkle in quite the way she remembered; instead they were a dull sort of brown. She'd fallen in love with his eyes. Once again, the memory of how they'd met washed over her. She always seemed to be thinking of that lately.

She'd heard him laugh, turned and seen him, and then asked her friend Clara, "Hasn't that guy over there got lovely eyes?"

"What guy—where?" Clara shouted.

"Jesus!" she hissed. "Don't make it so obvious."

"Sure I don't even know who you're talking about," Clara hissed back. "How can I make it obvious?"

"The guy in the corner."

Clara's head had swivelled, exorcist-like, to view the corner of the room.

"Jesus!" Abby had moaned.

"Cor," Clara sniggered. "D'you mean the brown-eyed guy who's coming over here?"

"No!" Abby wanted to die. "He's not!"

"You're right, he's not," Clara cackled.

Abby grinned as she remembered.

"What are you smiling at?" David asked.

"Just remembering the first time we met," she admitted.

"In the pub?"

"Yep."

"When your mate Clara let the whole place know you fancied me."

She grinned. "Bitch—wasn't she?"

"She did me a favour." David studied her, his chin cupped in his palms. "Jesus, I couldn't take me eyes off you. I don't think any fella there could."

"Get lost!"

"Naw, serious—when you walked in, it was as if a light got switched on. You looked great—all mad colours, mad hair, this kinda cute grin. I fancied you like mad."

"I fancied you."

"Yep, so everyone found out."

They laughed. At least his laughter was the same, she thought.

"I never would've come near you otherwise," David admitted. "Jesus, I thought you were way out of my league. You were loud and colourful and there was boring old me, sitting in a corner nursing me pint."

"You were never boring."

"And me mate told me I was mental heading over to talk to you. Jesus, it was the most terrifying thing I ever did."

She flinched. "Don't say that."

"It's true. The nearer I got, the sicker I got. I can't even remember what I said to you."

"'Hi.'" Abby smirked. "You said, 'hi.'"

"See? Boring."

"Made my night."

"I kept thinking what would I do if you had a boyfriend."

"And what would you have done?"

"Had a duel over you, I reckon."

She smiled. "Awww, you wouldn't have had to—I would have left him for you anyhow."

David grinned. Then, haltingly, he asked, "And tonight—did you leave anyone for me tonight?"

"No." Abby stood up. She didn't want this conversation any more. "Of course I didn't. I've ice cream outside—d'you want some?"

"Ab—"

"Ice cream?"

He bowed his head. "Sure, yeah," he muttered, sounding dejected. "A small bit."

She took her time in the kitchen. She wished she hadn't snapped at him—the nights they had together were so few, she didn't want to spoil it. But he shouldn't have asked. How *could* he ask her that?

Ginger was stalking up and down outside the kitchen window, hissing like mad, her tail flicking this way and that. She was jealous. Normally on a cold wet night, she'd be curled up on the sofa, being rubbed and spoiled. Abby filled her dish with some salmon and put it outside the door for her. Guilt food.

Then she took the ice cream from the freezer and scooped some into two bowls.

David was looking at the photos when she got back. He didn't seem to hear her as she entered the room. He was looking at her favourite picture. Just like she had done, he ran his finger down it and smiled.

"I love that photo," she said as she set the ice cream down.

He didn't reply, just turned from the picture and stared hard at her.

"David, don't," she muttered.

"Don't what?" he said. To her ears, he sounded annoyed. "Don't tell you that you can see anyone you want?" He paused and added, "You can, you know."

"I only want to see you." She was staring at the tablecloth. There was a stain on it.

He crossed to her, knelt down and tried to peer into her face. "That isn't always possible—you know that."

"I don't care."

"But I do. I only come here because I love you, Ab, but I'm holding you back."

"No you're not!" She figured if she said it firmly and furiously enough that he would stop. "No—you're—not!"

"Yes—I—am." He made an attempt to hold her hand but she pulled away. "I can see it, you know. You don't go out any more, you don't party and it's because of me."

"I don't need to go out. I don't need to party. What's the point in going out if *you're* not going to be there." Oh God, she was going to cry.

"Abby"—he sounded panicked—"don't!"

But she did. Big fat tears rolled down her face and she wiped them furiously away. Why did she have to spoil the night? Why did he have to spoil it?

"You're spoiling the night," she hiccuped.

He put his arm about her and kissed her on the cheek. "Only because I don't want to spoil your life."

"Fuck off."

He looked hurt at that. A sort of bewildered look crossed his face and he studied his fingernails.

"Sorry."

" 'S OK."

But it wasn't. He still looked hurt. "Why did you have to bring it up, David?"

"Because tonight you look so good. Don't waste it on me—I can't give you what you want."

"Yes, you can. All I want is you."

"But you can't *have* me—you know that."

"I don't mind."

"But *I* do." He sighed and closed his eyes. When he opened them, he pinned her with his gaze. "Jesus, you deserve flowers and cards on a night like this, and what did I get you—nothing."

"Yeah, well, I only got you burnt pasta sauce and greasy chips."

He smiled.

There was silence broken only by Abby scrubbing her eyes.

Maybe now, she thought, he'd stop. Maybe they could just get on with having a good time.

David shoved his hands into his pockets and started to pace the room.

Abby watched him. He didn't look happy. And she'd always thought that she made him happy.

He crossed to the sofa. Patting it, he said, softly, "Come here, sit here, Munchken, I want to tell you something."

He always called her that. She didn't know why. It sort of warmed her inside. "I'll get some coffee."

"Forget the coffee, come here."

He was going to go at it again, tell her to get out more. She didn't want to hear it. They'd had this discussion before, a while ago, but she'd put him off. Now she knew that if she pleaded with him hard enough he'd stay in her life. He'd never been able to resist her. So she sat beside him and he wrapped an arm about her shoulder and kissed the top of her head, so softly, so gently that it made her want to cry again.

"You've left me behind, Ab," he said then, "whether you like it or not."

"What?" She hadn't expected that.

He indicated the table. "White candles. We never use white candles."

And it hit her. *Red.* David always bought red candles. Even when they'd eaten out, he always brought along red candles. Red for passion, was his joke. How *could* she have forgotten that? How *could* she?

"Plus you didn't kiss me the minute I arrived and you fought with me and—"

"That doesn't mean anything."

"It means you've got a life."

"No!" She tried to struggle out of his embrace. The anger inside her was running in rivers from her toes to her head. Waves and waves and waves of it. "It's you—every time we see each other now—you keep hinting that we should go our own ways— you just don't want to come any more."

"I don't want to *have* to come any more."

"Oh don't—"

"Can I tell you a story?" he interrupted. "Can I tell you how I got the courage to come over to you that night in the pub?"

"You already did." She folded her arms and glared at him.

"Naw, naw I didn't." He touched her face. Ran his thumb along her cheek. "I mean, you were gorgeous and everything, but when I looked at you, I mean, *really* looked at you, I felt that I knew you. And even though you were laughing and giggling with your mate, there was something sad in your face."

He took his hand away and she found her eyes filling up again. Some night this was turning out to be. "I *was* sad," she said, "you *know* that. Dad had just died and me mam was acting all weird."

David nodded. "Yeah. And I knew that if I could make you happy, then I'd have a chance with you—so I made you laugh and kept making you laugh."

"You rescued me," Abby nodded, smiling slightly.

David didn't smile back. "And Munchken, I'm still doing it. I think I've been rescuing you all your life. Only now it feels like I'm killing you. You just have to let me go."

"You're not killing me!"

"You won't go out," David said. "You won't date—"

"In case *you* come. I don't want to miss you."

"You'll end up like your mother if you're not careful."

The words were like a slap in the face with a cold wet cloth. "No. No I won't." But it sounded hollow. In horror, she realized that maybe she was already like her mother. Hadn't they both lost their husbands young? Hadn't they both grieved so badly? It hadn't been fair what had happened. Not fair at all.

A Valentine's day wedding.

A marriage which had lasted only a week.

Driving along in France, listening to some foreign music station and laughing at the sounds of the words. The sun had been spilling across the fields and the roads and a heat haze shimmered up from the tarmac in front of them. And, at first, they thought the car heading towards them was just some sort of heat haze mirage. By the time David realized that it wasn't, it was too late. Abby remembered the whole slow-motion crazy swerve. The way David was thrown forward. The way her seatbelt lashed her neck. She remembered him staring dazed at her before she screamed that her belt was stuck, that she couldn't get out. And she never knew if that's what galvanized him. He was suddenly out of the car and pulling her free. Rescuing her. And then he was over to the other car. A man, bleeding from the forehead was shouting something in French. Together he and David began pulling the doors of the car. One child was pulled free.

And then the explosion . . .

Four dead—two men and two kids.

It hadn't been fair.

Not fair at all.

"I pulled you free so that you could live," David was saying as tears slowly rolled down her face. "That's how you can best make me happy, Ab."

She gulped.

"I only come when you're sad, that's getting less and less now. And to be honest, I don't want to remember you always sad— you were my happy half."

"And you were my better half."

"And always will be," he joked. He touched his forehead to hers: "You've got the pictures, the memories—they're what keeps me here but still let you move on. Let's both move on."

He was right. Heart-achingly right. "But I'll miss you."

"You'll miss *seeing* me," he clarified.

She didn't say anything. Just let him hold her. And she fell asleep.

In the morning, she awoke, stiff. The smell of uneaten chips combined with burnt-out candles was heavy in the air. Abby rubbed her eyes. They were grainy and sore. And her face was breaking out in spots because she hadn't taken off her make-up. And her dress was crumpled and . . . David was gone.

The house was quiet.

Silent.

Empty.

And even though she'd agreed to it, it was as if her heart was hurting all over again. It was like losing him twice.

How would she start to live again? She'd forgotten how to, she reckoned.

Well, maybe clearing the table would be a good start.

She hauled herself from the sofa and froze.

In the centre of the table was Rob's card.

Beside the card was her mobile phone. The message was obvious.

Call him.

And at once, she knew that David loved her and would

always love her. He hadn't been able to give her a card himself, so he'd done the next best thing. Given her someone else's card.

So that she could move on.

And let go.

"Love you," she whispered.

And she fancied that a "love you too" came back to her from somewhere.

———————

TINA REILLY is the author of the bestselling *Flipside, The Onion Girl,* and *Is This Love?* Her new novel, *Something Borrowed,* has just been published.

She freelances for the *Evening Herald* and under her married name, Martina Murphy, she has published a number of teenage books: *Livewire, Fast Car, Free Fall* and *Dirt Tracks. Dirt Tracks* was shortlisted for both the Bisto Book Award and the RAI Reading Award, while *Livewire* won an international White Raven Award.

Tina runs a drama school and lives in County Kildare with her husband, two kids, and a cat.

Deep Throat

Clare Dowling

Maeve got Brendan a digital TV package for his birthday. Well, the evenings were getting dark already, and there seemed to be very little to watch after the children had gone to bed. Besides, he had been a bit down since Arsenal had been beaten in the Championship last year—"by *Everton,* for fuck's sake"—and she hoped the inclusion of nine dedicated sports channels in the digital package would cheer him up.

"So now I can watch them getting hammered nine times instead of one?"

"It's not just football." She opened the brochure. "There's a racing channel, and one with extreme sports, and a boxing one—"

"I don't like boxing." Brendan's ideas about what he liked and what he didn't like had grown more definite over the years. This lent their home life a degree of predictability—for instance they'd had fish and chips every Friday since 1994—but on the other hand you could look upon it as comforting, Maeve's married friends said. God knows after ten years of marriage things were bound to settle down a bit, they agreed, and she felt bad for complaining in the first place.

"Oh, look!" he said. "A dedicated high-speed-car-chase channel!" And there was a cookery channel, and shopping channels, and several music channels, and a wildlife channel for the children—Maeve hoped it wasn't too gory—and even a channel that showed nothing but a brilliant yellow sunflower swaying in the breeze that made Maeve half giddy if she stared at it long enough.

"Turn it over to the footie there, love, will you?"

After that it was hard to drag him away from the television at all. Every night the house was filled with the sounds of the Premiership and the play-offs and the European Cup. The minute one league was over another one seemed to begin. He began to watch Formula One racing too, and sumo wrestling—"he's got a backside on him like your mother"—and even swimming when there was nothing else on.

"Surely there's no football on at this hour?" She had just finished making the kids' lunches for the morning.

"I'm waiting to see the results of the American league," he said. "It's a different time zone."

He looked keyed up and excited, and she said impulsively, "I'd love a back rub upstairs." That was their little code. And it had been ages since the last "back rub." But that too was a consequence of being married a long time, Maeve's friends said, rather gloomily.

He said, "Ha? Oh, right—go on up so, I'll be up in a minute."

Eventually she fell asleep lying on top of the duvet waiting for him.

He began to stay up later and later watching sports. The back rubs all but disappeared. Often it was after midnight when he would crawl into bed, and he would fall asleep immediately, dreaming no doubt of goalposts and Beckham and Ireland winning the World Cup.

One night Maeve woke, cold and alone. The alarm clock on the locker said it was half past two. He must have fallen asleep in front of the blasted football.

She tiptoed down the stairs, careful not to wake the children, and quietly pushed open the living room door. Two things struck her at once: Brendan was not asleep, and there was no football on the telly. Instead, a young woman fondled her large bare breasts while a naked man bucked behind her. The programme makers had helpfully supplied English subtitles for those digital viewers in Ireland, but they were hardly needed.

"Uh, uh, uh, uh!" the man groaned in ecstasy, as his large, hairy bottom filled the screen.

Maeve's friends were all sympathy.

"Aren't they right bastards," Jacinta spat.

"I caught Harry with three Big Macs once, but *pornography . . .*" Niamh whispered, shocked.

"Disgusting," Anna denounced vehemently. "And after all we do for them, as well."

Maeve awkwardly stirred her cappuccino (they met for coffee on a Monday afternoon as a treat). She had been unaware until now that catching one's partner with pornography was the hideous crime it obviously was.

"So what are you going to do?" Jacinta demanded.

"Do?"

"About him watching filth!"

"I don't really know yet." That was true. Brendan had left for work at the crack of dawn and, after last night's fiasco, would undoubtedly be working late. She had the whole day to come up with a suitable form of retribution—which was obviously necessary, from what the girls were saying. But what was she to do—take away his digital TV? That would feel rather like taking sweets from a child.

Niamh pitched over and said, sympathetically, "It's no reflection on *you,* you know."

"I hadn't thought—"

"You're a very attractive woman. Just because he gets his jollies off watching Swedish sleaze—"

"German. It was German."

"It's no reason to beat yourself up about it."

"I'm not."

"Good. Good! That's the spirit." And they all gave her supportive little pats, spooned sugar into their coffees and fired up fresh cigarettes.

After a moment, Jacinta enquired, "How bad was it anyway? The stuff you were subjected to?"

"I didn't see very much, obviously." Brendan had scuttled for the remote control with a speed she hadn't thought him capable of. "But there was a man and a woman. The usual."

She didn't know why she'd said that; it wasn't as though she sampled pornography on a regular basis. In fact, the most racy thing she'd ever seen was a couple of tattered magazines of topless girls posing seductively with cream éclairs, that kind of thing, and a poorly lit video once, where the acting was so bad that it had been more amusing than anything else.

"Yes?" prompted Anna, and Maeve saw that the girls were leaning expectantly over their coffees. Possibly they were trying to assess the enormity of Brendan's crime.

She said, haltingly, "Well, there was a woman kind of feeling herself. You know, her boobs. And he was behind . . . doing the business."

She felt a bit warm at the memory of it.

"Yes?" Jacinta said. More detail was obviously required.

"Um, he was, you know, well endowed. He began to pick up speed. And *he* started to feel her boobs too, and she kind of encouraged him—in German, but it translated into, 'I really want it, big man,' that kind of thing."

"Oh!" Anna looked a bit red in the face.

"That *really* got him going. He put his hands on her bum and you could hear this slapping noise as he started to go at it really hard." Her voice had gone rather husky. "And she was panting now, moaning, calling him all kinds of things in German, and rubbing herself down there—"

"Jesus." Jacinta's knuckles were white on her paper napkin.

Maeve hardly heard her. "And she had to hold onto the bed rails because he was really into it now, grinding and thrusting"—a speck of spittle flew from her mouth and landed in the sugar bowl—"and then they were both moaning and panting, and then it kind of went to a big close up of him and he was shouting, 'Uh, uh, uh!' and then it was just all one big climax!"

There was an empty little silence, and Maeve realized that the snotty bistro waiter was standing by their table.

"Anything else, ladies?"

They all shifted and made a great pretence of looking into their coffee cups, and checking their watches.

"No, I'd better go collect the kids from school . . ."

"Me too."

"Tommy's teacher goes *mad* if I'm late."

They left a ridiculously big tip and left very fast, walking back out into the grey, drab day.

When Brendan finally arrived home at ten o'clock that night he found Maeve waiting on the sofa in her dressing gown, holding the remote control.

"Hi," he said. He wore the hangdog expression usually reserved for when he would stay out drinking half the night with PJ and the lads from work.

"Hi," Maeve said chirpily. "Have you eaten?"

"I grabbed something in the canteen." He looked wary now at this enquiry into his wellbeing.

"Great," she said. "I've just opened a bottle of wine."

He continued to stand just inside the door, hunched and defensive.

"For goodness sake, Brendan. You're letting a breeze in."

She poured the wine, held out a glass, and patted the sofa beside her.

He sat and took the glass, all the time watching her as though this were some kind of sick, masochistic game she was playing before snarling that he would find his clothes in bin liners outside and that her solicitor would be in contact with his.

"How was work?" she asked.

His eyes were like saucers. "All right."

"You're not too tired I hope?"

"No."

"Good."

"I suppose you want to talk," he said, gulping back his wine as though for fortification and putting the glass down on the coffee table.

"Talk? Lord, no."

"But . . . you must be upset."

"Why?"

He looked disbelieving. "Because . . . because other women would be upset!"

She began to feel a bit deficient again; that her reaction was somehow lacking. "Like who?"

"PJ's wife found his stash of *Hot Euro Girls* on the top shelf of the hot press and she went ballistic. She rang up the mail order company in Holland and said they weren't to send so much as a postcard to her address again—"

"What was in them?"

"Sorry?"

"The magazines. Were they, like, hardcore?"

She wasn't entirely sure of the difference between hardcore and softcore—was softcore even a category?—but she thought that perhaps hardcore involved more than one person. Surely Brendan would know?

But he just looked a little startled. "It was just girls," he said. "Naked girls. Anyway, PJ was only let back into the house recently, on the condition that the only magazine he buys is the *RTÉ Guide.*"

This seemed to Maeve to be rather extreme.

"Well, I'm not PJ's wife," she said, to reassure him. She picked up the remote control. "Now, what channel is it on?"

"What?"

"The pornography."

He pitched forward, and said, fervently, "I won't watch it ever again, Maeve. I swear. I didn't even know it was there until I went looking for the basketball quarterfinals! But I stumbled across *Fetish World* and I was hooked." He went on in a low, ashamed voice, "Then I began to stay tuned for the pole dancing, and *Bathtime Buddies.*"

"What's that?" Maeve was intrigued.

"Oh, it's disgusting—women in baths, spraying each other with water, having a great time." He rubbed a hand over his eyes as though in pain, and whispered, "Then one night I stayed up past the watershed—midnight. That's when they start to charge. *Dirty Weekend, Girls Together III,* a digitally revamped version of *Deep Throat* . . . I watched them all. I'm so sorry, Maeve."

His self-flagellation seemed a little excessive. "Yes, all right, Brendan—you didn't *murder* anybody."

"But I feel I've betrayed you, Maeve. Deceived you. Let you down!"

She was slightly irritated now. "Well, don't. Because I don't feel that way at all."

It was obvious he could hardly believe his luck, but he still exerted caution. "Do you not? Because I wouldn't blame you at all."

"Oh, let's not get into *blame* here," Maeve said.

"No?"

"Well, it's not very constructive, is it?"

He began to relax now, relief breaking out all over his face. "You're marvellous, Maeve, do you know that?" he cried. "I don't know of any other woman who would have been so forgiving!"

"It's not a question of forgiveness, Brendan. It's a question of improvement."

"Sorry?"

"This pornography thing—I think it's a great opportunity for us," she said brightly.

Brendan blinked. "Sorry, I'm not with you . . ."

"As a couple. You know, to spice things up, Brendan. To add a bit of excitement—maybe learn something new?" She plucked at her dressing gown (she was wearing a silky little nightie underneath).

For a moment he sat there, very still, and then he said, "You want us to watch pornography together?"

"Well, yes."

"*Pornography?*"

She couldn't quite understand his expression. "I'm not suggesting we put it on at teatime. I mean after the kids have gone to bed. In fact, just like you watch it now, only I'd be watching it with you. Imagine what we might get up to!"

To lighten the mood, she reached over and squeezed his thigh jokily, but he grabbed her hand and threw it off as though it had burned him. "That's sick!" he cried.

"What?"

"What kind of a man do you think I am? That I'd sit here and watch filth with my own *wife?* While my kids are asleep upstairs in bed?"

"Brendan—"

But he stood very stiffly and gave her a look of deep righteousness. "And, frankly, I don't know what kind of a woman you are to have suggested such a thing in the first place!"

Maeve began to watch pornography alone. Just the odd bit here and there, when Brendan would be on a night out with the lads. Guiltily, she would pull every curtain in the house and dim the lighting, just in case any of the neighbours saw. Then she would aim the remote control and women called Rita and Miranda and Debbie would fill her living room in various states of undress. There were no men involved before midnight—something to do with censorship rules about erect penises—but Maeve found she didn't really miss them. In her experience penises, erect or otherwise, weren't the be-all and end-all, no matter what the men thought. She rather preferred it when it was just Rita and Miranda and Debbie admiring themselves through chiffon scarves— and they *were* lovely—and giving each other what looked to be very soothing back rubs. Brendan's attempts at massage looked very amateur and brutish in comparison (not that there had been any of *that* recently).

"Well? What did you watch last night?" Jacinta asked. They were huddled over coffees one Monday afternoon. Maeve's viewing was being monitored very closely by the group, none of whom had digital.

"Topless darts. Very disappointing. It was just boobs wobbling whenever one of them threw a dart. It wasn't even erotic."

"Was there a prize?" Anna wanted to know. "For whoever won?"

"That's hardly the point," Jacinta said crossly. She hissed to Maeve, her face shiny and flushed, "When's the next viewing session?"

"Thursday. *Bathtime Buddies* is on, I checked the guide."

"*Bathtime Buddies!*"

"That sounds lovely," Niamh said enviously.

"We only have a power shower at home," Anna agreed.

Maeve said impulsively, "Why don't you all come over?"

There was scandalized sucking in of breath.

"We *couldn't.*"

"Why not?"

"To watch porn? Harry would have a fit," Niamh worried.

"Don't tell him," Maeve said bluntly.

"It's my night off, I suppose I *could . . .*"ventured Anna.

Jacinta was shredding a paper napkin again. "Just out of curiosity," she said.

"I'll provide the snacks," Maeve decided. "You lot bring the wine."

The week seemed to pass very slowly. Maeve found herself in a constant state of anticipation, which she was sure wasn't appropriate. To divert herself, she went through her wardrobe and filled a big bag for charity with all her comfy tracksuit bottoms and woolly jumpers. She got her hair done and, on impulse, bought a couple of new outfits in rather bold colours.

"What are you all dressed up for?" Brendan asked. "I thought it was just the girls coming over for a game of cards."

"That doesn't mean I shouldn't make an effort."

"I suppose not," he said, loftily (somehow, he had acquired

the moral high ground in all this, and was rather enjoying it—so much so, in fact, that he had stopped watching football even, and would tune in to a worthy BBC documentary on unstable South American countries before pointedly going to bed at half past ten every night). "Don't I look nice?" she asked, trying to be conciliatory.

"Well, yes, I suppose."

"And so do you," she said brightly (he had changed his stained jumper).

He looked at her suspiciously. "What's all this?"

"All what? Can we not pay each other a compliment any more, Brendan? For God's sake, is this *it*, for the rest of our lives?"

"I don't know what's got into you at all these days, Maeve," he said, very accusingly, and left for the pub, no doubt to complain to PJ about the unreasonableness of women.

The girls arrived soon after, giggling and half-shot from a couple of vodkas in Jacinta's house beforehand. They were dressed up too, and Niamh was wearing make-up, which she never usually did.

"I think Harry thinks I'm meeting a man," she confided breathlessly. "He kept asking what time I'd be home at. Imagine! He hasn't done that in years."

"I left Eamon making the kids' lunches for the morning," Anna confided. "He was really pissed off."

"Sssh! It's starting," Jacinta said.

And they all dived for the couch as Maeve dimmed the lights, and there was much shuffling and giggling—"mind my wine, Anna, you big horse"—and then there she was on the screen: Debbie, walking into the bathroom, as naked as the day she was born except for a long chiffon scarf artfully draped over her body. Oblivious to the camera, she began to apply the scarf to her own body—lightly running it over bare legs, stomach, brown but-tocks, nipples.

"I have a scarf like that—I never thought of doing that with it!" Niamh screeched.

"I never thought of doing that with my power shower either!" Jacinta cackled a minute later.

They were just nervous, Maeve knew. But the laughter soon died away when Debbie began to get down to the serious busi-ness of having a good time.

"Should we be watching this?" Niamh worried. "I mean, it might be immoral!"

"Do you want to go home?" Maeve said kindly. "Harry'll be glad to see you."

She watched as Niamh weighed up the threat to her moral conscience against a night spent on the sofa with Harry.

"I'll stay," she decided swiftly.

"Debbie has a lovely bottom," Anna said wistfully. "I wish I had a bottom like that."

"You don't have to have a bottom like that. You can still have a good time," Jacinta declared fiercely. "Look at Debbie, for God's sake!"

And they did. They stayed looking as Debbie got through bottles of bubble bath and gallons of water—"she must be clean as a new pin"—and even a different shower head—"this is *defi-nitely* immoral"—in her long, slow, bubbly search for pleasure. She squirmed and stroked and moaned, and at the very end, threw her head from side to side in a show of ecstasy that had them all on the edge of the sofa.

Afterwards Jacinta handed around cigarettes.

"I don't want to go home," she said with a sigh.

"After midnight we have to start paying," Maeve reminded them.

"Oh, I don't want to get into *paying*," Niamh said, obviously very concerned again about the moral implications of it all.

"We'll just watch the free stuff then," Anna decided. They all turned to Maeve. "When is Brendan's next night out?"

The town council observed that there was a fierce run on water in the locality that particular winter. And in school it was noted that a lot of the kids' lunches were very haphazard—Daddy had made them, the teachers were told, while Mammy was out. And some of the fathers were indeed looking tired and harassed, while the mothers concerned were turning up at the school gates very glamorous—sluttish even!—and wearing make-up. This had a knock-on effect on the *other* mothers, of course, who began to compete, until some days it was like a fashion parade out there, they complained in the staffroom.

There was a new kind of confidence about some of them as well, and it didn't go unnoticed how they would walk down the main street in their high heels, brassy as you like, and into that fancy bistro as though they were movie stars—even that Niamh one, who would never say boo to a goose! There were reports of long, boozy lunches, and that young waiter had apparently said that one of them had made a suggestive comment to him. They didn't turn up for the Women's Community Spirit project any more either, which of course shook the confidence of the *other* women members, who began to leave in droves to drink coffee in the bistro instead. There was something dark and evil at work, Fr. Ryan warned strongly from the pulpit one Sunday.

It wasn't long before the connection was made between this state of affairs and the girls' nights out in Maeve's house.

The town's husbands gathered in the pub.

"They're like demons when they come home!" Niamh's husband, Harry, declared.

Anna's husband, Eamon, agreed. "Ordering us about, criticizing us, making sexual demands!"

Jacinta's husband shuddered. "Every night she's sitting up waiting for me, demanding massages, and she's bought this range of body oils. The whole thing takes hours whereas before you could get it over and done with in ten minutes!"

"Shocking, shocking," the rest murmured. "And you having to get up and work in the morning!"

"And if she doesn't get what she wants, she goes and shuts herself in the bathroom for an hour and a half! Our immersion packed up last week!"

"Disgraceful."

And they all looked at Brendan very accusingly.

"Maeve says they just play cards!" he said, but the pieces were beginning to come together in his head. "And drink."

"Oh, there's far too much drink involved," Anna's husband said. "I think we should start to discourage these nights out in the strongest possible terms."

"I agree," Harry said, sucking in his gut (Niamh had made a crack last week about him being too fat, and he found himself drinking slimline tonic instead of his usual four pints).

"Leave it with me, lads," Brendan said, grimly.

The following Thursday night he left for his regular night out in the pub, only he secretly doubled back and hid in the rhododendrons in the front garden. After a while he began to get pins and needles, and spiders kept running over the back of his neck, but he bravely carried on. He owed it to the lads to get to the bottom of the matter before any more damage was done.

Soon they began to arrive, clutching bottles of white wine and packets of cigarettes. So cheap! Maeve admitted them one by one, dressed up to the nines and looking up and down the street

covertly like she was running some kind of a brothel. The ring-
leader! In the bushes, Brendan's blood began to boil.

Then the lights in the living room went off, and the curtains
were pulled over securely. Lurid music spilled out through the
open window, along with loud laughter. Brendan imagined that
they were laughing at him—at Harry, at all of them! Looking at
smut while their husbands were at home making lunches and
putting children to bed! (He forgot that he had in fact been on
his way to the pub.)

He crawled out from the rhododendrons, plucking twigs from
his hair, indignation quivering from his every pore. There was a
tiny crack at the top left-hand corner of the living room curtain,
where it had come off the rail, and if he climbed up on Mrs. Darcy-
next-door's wall, he should be able to lean over and see in . . .

He wasn't as agile as he used to be, and the wall was slippery
from the rain, and Mrs. Darcy's wall was higher than it looked—
the old bitch was paranoid about privacy—but he finally scaled
it, panting and cursing under his breath. He leaned over and
peered into his own living room.

It was just as he'd suspected: filth and smut and women flashing their bits (he would have quite enjoyed it had he not been on
a moral mission). And look at them, loving it! Giggling and joking on the sofa, their mini-skirts riding up shamelessly like they
hadn't a care in the world!

Just wait until he told Harry—and the others! In hours it
would be all over the town that these four had been watching
pornography. Skin flicks! They wouldn't be able to hold their
heads up at the school gates, never mind drink fancy coffee in
that bistro they had started to frequent. Oh, there would be no
more new clothes and make-up and sarcastic comments about
their menfolk. In fact, Brendan wouldn't be at all surprised if
there weren't a couple of divorces out of it.

Not him and *Maeve*, of course. Ah no, this was just some kind of very odd phase she was going through. Even though she was obviously the catalyst in all this, he believed that she was essentially good at heart. After a suitable period of repentance on her part, Brendan would forgive her. They might even renew their wedding vows—maybe abroad, on one of those beaches. And they would have to get rid of the digital television, of course. Well, it would be too much of a temptation to Maeve. Unless, of course, Brendan password-coded it, so that only he had access to that particular channel. Yes, that might be safer.

On this pleasant thought, he shifted on the wall. But his foot slipped right off the wet edge, and he toppled backwards into Mrs. Darcy's garden, giving her the fright of her life as she was settling down to television in her nightie and curlers.

Maeve left him a week later.

"But my leg is broken in three different places!" he protested, shocked.

"I know," she agreed. "That's why I've organized for the public health nurse to come around. And meals-on-wheels, and if PJ is any kind of a friend, he'll wheel you down to the pub on a Thursday night."

"But . . . but Maeve! I love you!"

"You don't. Not really," she said kindly.

"How do you know how I feel?" He was getting angry now.

She calmly loaded three suitcases into the boot of the car. The children would be coming with her. "I'll be staying with Jacinta until I find somewhere to rent."

"Jacinta! Your . . . your *lesbian* friend!" This was the worst insult he could think of. "I saw the way she was watching *Bathtime Buddies!*"

Maeve said, "No, Jacinta's not a lesbian. She thinks she might be bi, though."

Brendan looked at her with a kind of a horrified fascination. "All these years we've been married and I never realized what you were really like!"

"I didn't either until recently," Maeve agreed.

"You're like that Michael Douglas fellow! Obsessed with sex! You should go and get help—if not for yourself, then for the sake of the children!"

She looked at his red, uncomprehending face, and tried to summon some affection, at least. "Oh, Brendan. Surely you don't want to go on living like this? Surely you want more?"

"What, more *sex?*"

She gave up. "Goodbye, Brendan."

Brendan, in his helplessness, grew spiteful now. "I'll tell, you know. I'll tell Harry and everyone about you and your friends watching porn!"

"Tell away."

"Well . . . well, you won't be watching any more of it! Because I'm keeping the TV!"

"You're welcome to it. To be honest, we were all getting a bit tired of porn anyway. It's quite desensitizing. Jacinta says it's much better when you use your imagination," she told him.

"Your *imagination.*" Brendan was nearly apoplectic now. "You're sick! Sick, do you hear me?"

Maeve moved into a lovely little cottage by the river, and took her first lover six months later—the waiter from the bistro—and she began to paint, watercolours mostly, and even began to sell some of her work. She never got around to buying a new TV; instead she cultivated a small patch of ground and she planted sunflowers, and she would look out on them from her kitchen window as she worked, their brilliant yellow petals turned to the sun.

CLARE DOWLING trained as an actress and began writing for theatre in 1992 with *Burns Both Ends,* produced by Glasshouse Productions, of which she was a founder member. She went on to have six plays produced. She has subsequently written for film, television, and radio. She has published children's fiction and drama for teenagers. Most recently she has written three novels: *Fast Forward, Expecting Emily,* and *Amazing Grace,* published by Poolbeg and Headline. She is currently a scriptwriter on RTÉ's *Fair City.* She lives in Dublin with her family.

Façades

Patricia Scanlan

"You're coming home for Christmas. Fantastic! We'll have to get together. You'll have to come over for a meal." Kathy Reynolds injected a note of false gaiety into her voice as she spoke to Mari Clancy, an old schoolfriend who was ringing from Dubai. "Is Brett coming with you?"

"Er . . . no, not this year. Can't get time off. Things are a bit crazy with the Iraqi situation." Mari sounded glum.

"Oh . . . poor Brett," Kathy sympathized, privately relieved that the wealthy consultant wouldn't be around to patronize herself and Bill with his boastful tales of life in the Emirates.

"So look, how about the day after Stephen's Day? You know the way the diary fills up, and Mam will have me doing the rounds like nobody's business," Mari said briskly.

"I'll be looking forward to it," Kathy lied, thinking that a visit from Mari was the last thing she needed.

They talked for another while, swapping gossip and news and Kathy was glad it was Mari who had called. It must be costing a fortune but Mari was loaded and money wasn't an issue for her, unlike herself.

Later, in the kitchen, she found herself humming "My heart is low, my heart is so low, as only a woman's heart can be . . ." To her way of thinking it was one of the greatest songs ever written for and about women. The woman who had written that song knew *exactly* what Kathy was feeling at that moment. Low, disheartened, dispirited, depressed and extremely agitated.

She wiped along the top of her worktops vigorously. When Kathy was agitated she cleaned her worktops over and over again, lifting the bread bin and matching set of coffee, tea and sugar containers, annihilating any unfortunate crumb lurking in the vicinity. Today the worktops were getting a rigorous going-over, as were the fridge-freezer doors and the top of the cooker.

It was funny, how she headed for the kitchen when she was under pressure. Her sister always attacked the bathroom in her moments of stress. Kathy's best friend, Laura, would invariably cut the grass.

She sighed deeply, feeling totally stressed out. Her husband Bill had been out of a job for the last fourteen months and there was no sign of anything on the horizon. Christmas was just ten days away and her three children were up to ninety with excitement at the thoughts of Santa's impending arrival.

The Christmas shopping had to be done. She and Bill had just had a row about it. Now, to crown it all, she'd had the call from Mari to say she would be back in town for Christmas. More expense. Kathy gave a sigh that came from the depths of her being. Normally she loved having visitors and it would have been a pleasure to see her old schoolfriend, but these days, she didn't want to see anyone. She just wanted to shrivel up inside her shell and stay there.

In the last few months all her hope that Bill would have no

problems in finding another job had become harder and harder to sustain. As money got tighter their savings dwindled and their standard of living noticeably diminished. Kathy increasingly felt like burying her head in the sand like the proverbial ostrich.

She didn't want Mari Clancy coming to her house when she had no oil for the central heating. Kathy didn't want her to know that she'd sold her Fiesta and Bill's Volvo was in the garage because they hadn't got the money to tax and insure it. Mari would have to put up with cheap wine and a simple meal. Kathy just didn't have the money for steaks and champagne. It was months since she'd been able to afford luxuries like that.

Kathy rubbed viciously at a particularly stubborn piece of grit that was embedded between the curved edge of her drainer and the muted grey worktop. To think she couldn't even afford to go to an off-licence any more. Who would have ever thought it? Who would have ever thought that their family's affluent, comfortable lifestyle would have been so severely shaken, and disrupted that gut-wrenching evening when Bill had come home from work, grey-faced and shaken, to tell her that the multinational computer company that he worked for was closing its Irish operation in favour of their American outfit, with a loss of five hundred jobs.

"I'm finished, Kathy, I'll never get another job at my age." Bill sat with his head buried in his hands while Kathy tried to take in what her husband had just told her.

"Don't be daft, Bill!" she said firmly. "You're only forty-three. That's young and people are always going to need human resource managers. *Experienced* human resource managers."

"Kathy, you don't know what it's like out there, I'm telling you, it's cut-throat. They can get fellas half my age with better degrees who'll work for half my salary because they're so desperate to get a job. The Celtic Tiger's well and truly vanished." Bill had tears in his eyes and Kathy, horrified at the state her usually cheerful and easy-going husband was in, flung her arms around him and hugged him tightly.

"Stop worrying, Bill, we'll manage fine, you'll get a job, I know you will. You're the best there is, you'll be snapped up in no time," she comforted, absolutely believing every word she spoke. Bill was bloody good at his job. He'd get another job . . . and soon.

Week after week, month after month she'd said the same thing over and over, trying to keep her spirits up as much as his. Unemployment didn't happen to people like her and Bill with their pretty, four-bedroom, semi-detached dormer bungalow in a lovely wooded cul-de-sac in Sandymount.

They had always been able to afford a fortnight abroad every year, trips to London where Kathy's sister lived, music and swimming lessons for the kids. It had all been available and Kathy had never envisaged that it would ever be otherwise.

When she'd thought about unemployment she had a mental image of people whose lifestyles were a million miles from her own. Kathy wasn't a snob or anything like it, she was lucky and she knew it. She'd never thought that unemployment could happen to her family. Bill was a trained professional, for God's sake, with years of work experience. Being a human resource manager for a staff of five hundred employees was an important job. People like him didn't end up on a dole queue. Or so she'd thought.

"Get real, Kathy!" her younger sister, Ella, remonstrated one day several months after Bill had been made redundant, when she had been moaning about their situation. Ella was a community welfare officer and knew a lot about unemployment. "Don't kid yourself that it's all people from so-called deprived areas that are on the dole, it isn't. There's a hell of a lot of people like Bill, in middle management, who are out there suffering behind their lace curtains and going to the St. Vincent de Paul for help with their mortgage repayments. People who enjoyed a lifestyle just like yours."

"St. Vincent de Paul, but that's for poor people!" Kathy exclaimed in horror.

"These people are heading for poor," Ella said gently. "They're living in lovely houses, with no heating and no phones and not enough money to pay the mortgage, in danger of their homes being repossessed. They need help too." Seeing her sister's stricken face she said softly, "Look, I'm not suggesting you're ever going to need to go to the St. Vincent de Paul, but what I'm saying is, start economizing. Use some of Bill's redundancy money to whack a bit off your mortgage. Get rid of one of the cars. I'm not saying that Bill won't ever get a job again, hopefully he will, but just don't think that he's going to waltz into a new position just like that. It doesn't happen that way any more, unfortunately. There's a recession starting out there and it's not going away."

Kathy came away from her chat with her sister more scared than she had ever been in her life. For the first time since it happened, she had lifted her head out of the sand and taken a long, hard look at their situation. Ella's words might have been harsh but they had stiffened Kathy's resolve. It was time to sit down and take stock and face the hard facts. Bill was unemployed and likely to stay that way. The future had to be faced.

That night when the children were in bed, she sat down with her husband and calmly announced that it was time for them to discuss their financial situation so that they could make long-term plans. Bill slumped down at the kitchen table and lit a cigarette. She could see his fingers shaking. "I don't know how we're going to manage," he muttered.

I'd like to kill the bastards that did this to him, Kathy thought viciously as she saw her husband's hopes and dreams fade to ashes. He flicked on his calculator and they began to work on the figures he had in front of him.

Bill said they had to reduce their mortgage by two-thirds, that was vital and at least they'd have the comfort of knowing that their home was safe enough. They'd use his lump sum for that. They'd sell her Fiesta and with the money they'd make from that they'd continue the insurance policies, the most important of which was the policy they had taken out for their children's education. They'd pay the VHI for another year. If Bill didn't get a job after that there'd be no more private health insurance.

They went to bed subdued.

Kathy began to take her calculator to the supermarket. Before, she had never considered the cost of food that much. Whatever she felt like had gone willy-nilly into the trolley. But those days were gone. Now it was coming up to the second Christmas of Bill's unemployment and her money was cut to the bone. Any saving, no matter how small, was welcome. Thank God for big impersonal supermarkets, she thought one day as she stood at the cash desk with her trolley full of Yellow Pack and Thrift. It would be a tad mortifying if the neighbours saw her or the girl at the check-out knew her. That was always a little worry. Silly, she knew, but she couldn't help it.

It wasn't that Kathy normally gave a hoot what people thought of her, it was just these days she seemed to be a bit more vulnerable. Only the other day her seven-year-old son, Matthew, had come in, his little face scarlet with emotion.

"Mammy! Jason Pierce says that Daddy's got no job an' that we're going to be poor an' that you can't afford to take us to Euro Disney. He's a big liar, isn't he? I told him to put his dukes up an' I gave him a puck in the snot an' he went home bawling," her son added with immense satisfaction.

"Say 'and,' Matthew, not 'an,'" Kathy corrected automatically, hoping that Jason Pierce's nose was well and truly bloodied. Little brat! Since the Pierces had moved in next door, six months ago, there had been nothing but fights with the youngsters in the cul-de-sac. It wasn't really Jason's fault; it was that obnoxious father of his, Owen. Owen Pierce was the most big-headed, boastful, superior individual Kathy had ever had the misfortune to encounter.

Owen was a broker, who had begun to make good money. On the way up, he revelled in his yuppie lifestyle. He and his wife, Carol, and their two children Jason and Emma, had moved into the house next door mid-summer, and had proceeded to make themselves utterly unpopular with their neighbours.

At first, the six other families in the cul-de-sac had welcomed them and been friendly and chatty but gradually Owen's thoroughly bumptious ways had begun to grate. It was his hail-fellow-well-met "I'm a broker what do you do for a living?" carry on that got under people's skin. Owen had the biggest satellite dish, the biggest barbecue pit, the most expensive shrubs, the flashiest car. He loved boasting and always made sure that when he was telling Kathy or Bill something, the rest of the neighbours could hear as well.

Kathy normally did not make snap judgements about people, but she knew very soon after she met him that he was someone she couldn't stand.

Late one afternoon she had been sitting out at the front sunbathing and keeping an eye on her two-year-old niece who she was minding for the afternoon. Jessica, her three-year-old, was entertaining her cousin to a tea party with her toy tea set. They were sitting on an old tartan rug having the greatest fun. Kathy, lulled into a drowsy lethargy by the balmy heat and the sun caressing her face with golden rays, had pushed all her problems to the back of her mind and was content to relax in languorous sloth. Eyelids heavy with drowsiness, she lay on her lounger and felt a rare sense of wellbeing and peace. In the distance she could hear Matthew and Rachel, her elder daughter, playing with their friends across the road.

A bee hummed lazily by, a lark opened his throat and sang his little heart out. Bill had gone into Dublin on the Dart to check out the employment agencies and wouldn't be home for ages so these precious few hours were her own. Kathy's limbs twitched as she sank deeper into relaxation and she was just about to drift off into slumber when a monstrous whining drone jerked her to wakefulness.

Owen was out with his petrol-driven lawnmower. It was, of course, a state-of-the-art lawnmower but Kathy wasn't impressed. Her lovely peaceful afternoon was ruined.

"Hello there, catching a few rays? Carol's out the back on the new swing lounger we bought. You should get one, they're great," he said cheerily as he began to zoom up and down his lawn with the mower.

Smart alec, thought Kathy sourly as she gave a polite wave. He knew very well Bill wasn't working and wouldn't have money to splash out on swinging loungers and the like. She watched him covertly beneath her eyelids. Honest to God but you'd think it was the Botanic Gardens he had to mow, with his petrol lawn-mower, instead of a little handkerchief of green that the rest of them managed to mow with electric mowers. The *noise* of it. She felt like gritting her teeth.

"Carol's trying to get up a tan before we head off to Malta next week. She wants to be able to head right out into it, I've told her she'll probably have to have sunbeds, the sun here just isn't strong enough," Owen announced as he took a breather.

"Hmm," Kathy murmured non-committally. Bullshitter, she fumed. She closed her eyes again, hoping he would take the hint.

Five minutes later, he was zooming around her front lawn, which adjoined his in the open-plan design of the houses.

"Might as well do yours while I have the machine out," he declared briskly, coming up right beside her lounger.

"It's OK, Bill will take care of it," she said hastily, pulling up her boob tube which she had slipped down low over her breasts.

"It's no bother," Owen leered, "besides, it will save you a bit on your electricity." Kathy's face flamed. The cheek of him, the utter unmitigated *cheek* of him. Who the hell did he think he was going on about her electricity? They weren't paupers.

It was as bad as the day Carol had invited her in for a cup of coffee. Carol, with her heavily made-up face and her perfectly manicured nails, who made sure to let Kathy know that she had a woman who came in to clean twice a week and who had timed the coffee invite with the arrival of the woman who did her ironing. Carol's daughter, Emma, was the same age as Jessica and as they sat drinking their freshly ground coffee, the other woman paused in their conversation and said meditatively, "I wonder if I have anything I could give you for Jessica. She and Emma are the same age and Emma has *so* many clothes. She gets so many presents, I've lots of stuff she's never worn." Kathy was flabbergasted. She'd only met the woman twice, for heaven's sake, and here she was offering her clothes for Jessica. Did she think the Reynoldses were on their uppers just because Bill was unemployed?

Kathy had assured her new next-door neighbour that Jessica had *plenty* of clothes and hastily finished her coffee and made her escape. Even if Jessica had to go around in rags, she wouldn't accept such impertinent charity from the superior Pierces.

"If you just move your lounger and the girls' rug I'll be finished in a jiffy," Owen ordered.

"Thank you, Owen, but if you don't mind leaving it, Bill

will finish it off. The girls are happy playing and I'm trying to relax here," Kathy said politely. She had had just about enough of the boastful, intrusive Owen Pierce for one afternoon.

"Well, if you're sure." Owen was clearly taken aback that she wasn't falling all over him with gratitude.

"I'm sure. Thank you," Kathy said curtly.

"Fine, enjoy yourself," he said stiffly, moving off with injured dignity. Two minutes later, he was mowing the lawn of the neighbour on his other side. Like a bloody dog marking his patch, Kathy thought grimly as she lay back against her cushions.

You weren't very neighbourly, she accused herself silently as she tried to regain her former state of slumberous indolence. Was she being so prickly because her pride was hurting and she didn't want to seem like the poor man at his better's table? If Bill had been working and she'd been free of all her financial worries would she have handled Owen and Carol differently and felt differently towards them? Was she, in fact, just indulging in a fit of extremely large sour grapes?

"Definitely not. Most definitely not, Kathy!" Irene, her other next-door neighbour, retorted emphatically when Kathy, shame-faced, put this scenario to her after telling the other girl of her encounter with Owen earlier that afternoon.

"The pushy shagger!" the other girl exclaimed irritably. "The nerve of him going on about you saving electricity. If he comes near my garden with his lawnmower I'll give him his answer. Who does he think he is? The Lord of the Cul-de-Sac? Those Pierces are as thick as two short planks. It's obvious they're not used to money. Did you ever hear your wan trying to put on the posh accent? I'm telling you, they're the greatest pair of blowholes going and if I didn't dislike them so much I'd feel sorry for them. They haven't a clue!"

Kathy giggled. Irene in full rant was always entertaining. "For God's sake, will you just listen to Superdad." Her neighbour was fit to blow a gasket. She nodded at Owen who was now out in the middle of the street with a gaggle of kids from the cul-de-sac. He was organizing races.

"Now, Emma, you stand there just a bit ahead of Jessica and Catriona and Laura and you, Jason, a bit behind, and then Matthew and Rachel and Patrick . . . On your marks . . ."

"Did you ever see the huge odds he gives to his own pair?" Irene murmured. "Come on, kids, beat those two little horrors," she muttered as the race began.

"It's not really their fault." Kathy grinned as she watched Emma and Jason trying to burst a gut to win the race. "I mean he keeps telling them how wonderful they are and of course, naturally, they believe it and our lot just love to bring them down a peg or two."

"I know. It just brings out the pettiness in me watching the carry-on of your man. Last weekend, Jason, God love him, came to the door all togged out in his rugby gear and asked John to come out and play a game of rugby with himself and Big Daddy. 'Aw naw,' says John. 'I'm a soccer man myself.' He's not a bit impressed with any of their carry on. Oh, to be an eight-year-old again." Irene grinned as Owen roared at his son and daughter urging them on to win the race.

"Brilliant race, Jace and Emms," they heard him brag moments later.

"Pleeeze, just pass me the sick bucket." Irene scowled and Kathy didn't feel so bad knowing that it wasn't her straitened circumstances and envy of her neighbours that had put her off Owen, Carol and their offspring.

"Mammy, can we go to Euro Disney sometime?" Matthew's big blue eyes stared up into hers, wide and innocent, as blue as two cornflowers. "Are you listening to me, Mammy?" Kathy came to with a start.

"Of course I'm listening to you, pet, and some day, please God, we'll get to Euro Disney. We'll just have to say a prayer that Daddy gets a job soon and never mind what Jason Pierce says, we're not poor, we're very very lucky to have a lovely house like this and a very special family."

She smiled down at her son who had gone trotting off saying, "Dear Holy God, please let my daddy get a job soon so he can take us to Euro Disney before scummy Jason Pierce goes."

That had been a few days ago and Matthew hadn't mentioned it again, but as Kathy gave her worktops one last wipe, she thought ruefully that it wasn't a prayer that was needed to get them to Euro Disney . . . it was a miracle.

Sighing deeply she walked into the sitting room and gave a little shiver. The house was cold. She felt so resentful and frustrated that she could no longer just flick a switch and have instant heat. Even though they had tried to conserve oil by turning on the heat later in the evenings, because winter had come early, they had run out of that precious dark liquid a week ago. Since then, Kathy had been lighting the fire and, because they were economizing on fuel, the back boiler was never hot enough to give off more than a lukewarm heat to the radiators. Because of Christmas and all its expenses, they wouldn't be able to afford oil until well into the New Year. If even then.

I'm sick of this, Kathy thought bitterly as she walked over to the floor-to-ceiling window and stared out at the lowering sky that threatened snow. Snow! That was all they needed to make life even more miserable. Come the New Year she was actively going looking for a job. She'd been a clerical officer when she had married Bill. Maybe she should have stayed working instead of taking her lump sum. Then they wouldn't be so hard hit now. If she got a job it would affect Bill's means-tested dole money so the salary would have to be pretty good. Who was going to employ an ex-clerical officer with rusty secretarial skills who wasn't very computer literate, Kathy thought glumly as she straightened the folds in her lace curtains. She had washed them yesterday and they were pristine. Most of the other houses in the cul-de-sac had roller blinds, net curtains being rather old-fashioned, but Kathy had always liked "proper curtains" as her grandmother called them. She hated the idea of people being able to see through her front window. Her home was her haven, not a showpiece for the neighbours to view every time they walked by.

Owen, whose latest foible was practising his putting shots on the front lawn, was always trying to gawk in the window and it gave Kathy no small satisfaction to know that he couldn't see in. Her curtains were her protection from his prying eyes.

He was out now strimming the edges of the grass and she grinned as the catgut broke and flew across the lawn. She knew she was being petty but she didn't care. He just got on her nerves. She had got so fed up of him strolling in front of her windows and playing rugby with Jason on the front lawn that she had asked her brother, a horticulturist, what she could put down to separate the gardens and keep her unwanted neighbour out. A nice thorny orange-berried pyracantha trained along a white wooden picket fence now formed a border between numbers 7 and 8 Maple Wood Drive curtailing Owen's and Jason's sporting activities somewhat.

Jason was driving poor old Matthew around the twist about the new computer he was getting for Christmas. It was going to be "the best computer in the world" with better games than that old Dell one that Matthew had, according to Jason. Every mother in the cul-de-sac could cheerfully have wrung Jason Pierce's neck as their own envious offspring demanded "a best computer" as well.

That's what Bill and Kathy had been arguing about this morning—what to buy the children for Christmas. Bill, as sick of penny-pinching as she was, wanted to borrow a couple of hundred euro from the credit union to splash out on Christmas and to hell with it. Kathy had argued that they needed oil. The house insurance was coming up and all of the children needed new shoes. If there was one thing Kathy was very particular about, it was getting good shoes for her children and nowadays a pair of decent shoes for a three-year-old could cost the guts of fifty Euro. Paying out fifty euro each for the three of them would leave her fairly skint.

"We can't afford it and that's that," Kathy asserted. Bill's face darkened with impotent fury.

"Don't rub it in, for Christ's sake! I know we can't. I just want to give the kids a decent Christmas. Is that too much to want?" he snarled.

A red mist descended in front of Kathy's eyes. It wasn't *her* fault that they had no money. She was only trying to keep them out of debt. "Listen, mister, you can do what you damn well like. I was only trying to help. Do you think *I* don't want to give them a good Christmas? I'm trying to do my best for all of us and it's not easy. So don't you take it out on me, Bill. It's not my fault you're unemployed. It's not me who can't get a job." Kathy was so angry her voice was shaking as months of suppressed rage, fear and frustration fuelled her outburst.

"God, you really know how to put the boot in, don't you?" Bill raged. "You should have married someone like bloody Superdad over there, not a loser like me." With that he'd picked up his anorak and strode out of the front door, slamming it hard behind him. Sick at heart, Kathy sat down at the kitchen table, put her head in her hands and bawled her eyes out. She had never felt so sorry for herself in her life. What had she done to deserve this?

She sniffled. After a good twenty minutes of alternate cursing and sobbing she felt somewhat better. A good cry was just the thing sometimes, it helped to get it all out of your system. Fortunately the children had spent the previous night on a sleep-over with their cousins so they hadn't witnessed the row. She didn't want them being upset as well.

It was almost 3 p.m., Kathy noted, and still no sign of Bill. She wondered what he was doing. It had got even darker outside, the clouds so low they seemed almost to touch the rooftops. The frost, which hadn't thawed all day, cast a silvery sheen to the lawns, the flaming orange of the pyracantha berries a startling contrast. The stark silhouettes of leafless trees encircled the cul-de-sac protectively; a robin nestled in the shelter of an evergreen shrub. Normally Kathy would have enjoyed the picturesque, wintry scene outside her big window but today it just seemed bleak and cold and again she shivered.

"To hell with it," she muttered crossly and with a determined set to her jaw she walked over to the fire and struck a match, watching with pleasure as the flames caught the firelighters and roared up the chimney, the kindling catching fire, spitting and sparking and scenting the room with the freshness of pine. The glow of the orange-yellow flames casting their shadows on the walls soothed Kathy. She sat cross-legged on the rug in front of the fire and pulled two large carrier bags, overflowing with presents, in front of her. This was the ideal time to sort out the Christmas present situation. It was something she had been putting off all day, but she might as well do it while Bill and the kids were out of the house. If she were quick and organized, she'd have her task complete before he was home. Then her husband wouldn't have the added indignity of seeing the presents they had received last year being wrapped to be given to their relatives this year. If only she could remember who had given her what. It would be a disaster to return a gift to someone who had given it to them in the first place.

Kathy gave a wry smile as she unloaded the bags onto the floor. The only other time in her life when she had had to recycle presents was that first year she had moved into a flat with her two best friends and they had all been practically penniless. It had been fun then, though, not like this.

She eyed the assorted collection surrounding her. Tablemats, they could go to Aunt Sadie. A basket of Body Shop soaps and shampoos. Now who had given her them? She cast her mind back, was it Clare? No, it was Rita, her sister-in-law. Well, Clare could have the Body Shop basket and Rita could have the lovely red angora scarf that her godmother had given her. Kathy fingered the scarf, enjoying the feel of the soft luxurious wool between her fingers. It would have been nice to have been able to wear it herself, she thought regretfully, but needs must and Rita would like it.

She wanted to give her sister-in-law a nice present. Rita was very good to them, as indeed were all of their families. That was why Kathy wanted to give them presents at Christmas. And she wanted to show that she and Bill were not completely on their uppers. This year, she decided, she would keep a list of who gave what, so that next Christmas, if Bill were still unemployed, it would be easier for her to match up presents. If people saw her this minute, no doubt they would think she was dreadfully mean, but it was the best she could do under the circumstances.

She spent a peaceful hour sitting in the fire's glow sorting out the presents and wrapping them. She had just stood up and was trying to get rid of the pins and needles in her feet when she saw Bill marching into the cul-de-sac. He was lugging the biggest, bushiest Christmas tree she had ever seen. A broad grin creased her face. Bill was a sucker for Christmas trees. The bigger and bushier the better.

She flung open the front door as her husband struggled up the path with his load. Panting, he stood looking at her. "I'm sorry, love. I didn't mean it." Their eyes met and a flicker of happiness ignited briefly. "You're the best wife a man could have and I know I'm dead lucky."

"Oh Bill, it's all right, I didn't mean what I said either." Kathy, happy that their little tiff was over, flung her arms around him, ignoring the prickly tree, and was rewarded with a one-armed bear hug. "It's brilliant, where did you get it?" She eyed the tree admiringly.

"Down in Ringsend from a fella on a lorry. Look at the width of it and look at the fullness up top and the symmetry is almost perfect." Bill, who was a connoisseur of Christmas trees, enthused about his find. "It's the best ever."

"You say that every year." Kathy laughed. "Come on in, I have the fire lighting. It was cold so I lit it early so the place will be warm when the kids get home," she added a little defensively.

"You did right, Kathy, it's bloody freezing out today," Bill declared stoutly and they smiled at each other. "Hey, what do you think if I rang Rita and asked her to keep the kids for another hour or two and we decorated the tree for them as a surprise?"

"Oh yeah, just imagine their faces." Kathy felt her previous despondency lift as a rare light-heartedness enveloped her. "Do you think Rita would mind?"

"Naw." Bill shook his head. "Sure we'll take her gang if she wants to go shopping or anything."

"Right," Kathy said briskly, "you ring her and I'll put the kettle on and we'll have a cup of coffee then get going." Unemployment be damned, they were going to have the best Christmas tree ever.

Rita obligingly agreed to keep the children for longer and gratefully agreed to Kathy's offer to take her own children the following afternoon so she could do some Sunday shopping in peace and quiet. For the next two hours Kathy and Bill thoroughly enjoyed themselves as they transformed the six-foot tree into a magical delight adorned with twinkling lights and glittering ornaments and frothy tinsel.

They laced the ceiling with festive garlands and Kathy prepared the crib, decorating it with scrumpled black paper to give the impression of mountains and twining ivy across the top and down the sides. She arranged a little light in at the back and laid the straw that she kept year after year on the floor of the crib. Bill hung up a sheriff's star from an old cowboy set that he had had as a child and it glittered in the fire light as bright as any star of Bethlehem. They would have a little ceremony when the children were home. Jessica, being the youngest, would solemnly place Baby Jesus in the crib.

They stood back to admire their handiwork. "It's lovely," Bill declared, as Kathy fussed at a piece of ivy, wanting to have it just so.

"So is the tree." Kathy smiled. "Definitely the best ever."

"It's a biggie all right." Bill grinned.

"Bigger than Superdad's," Kathy murmured wickedly. Bill caught her knowing eye and laughed.

"And real as well. Poor Jason has to make do with an artificial yoke, even if it is the biggest and most expensive one there is. It's just not the same, sure it isn't?" His eyes twinkled.

Owen and Carol had put their tree up over a week ago. They had been the first in the cul-de-sac to put one up. Great wreaths of holly hung on their doors and windows and Jason and Emma were bursting with pride. Each day, Matthew enquired anxiously if they were going to put their tree up and Kathy reassured her young son that indeed they would. She was dying to see his face when he saw the six-foot giant that now reposed all alight in their front window.

Ravenous after their exertions they decided they deserved a rare treat and ordered a Chinese. They ate it sitting in front of the fire, thoroughly enjoying their spare ribs in barbecue sauce, their crispy duck and their prawn crackers. The twinkling lights of the Christmas tree and the amber luminescence of the fire enveloped them in a cocoon of golden warmth as rain and sleet lashed against the windows and the wind howled like a banshee as it swirled and eddied around the cul-de-sac. Kathy and Bill enjoyed their fireside meal, all their troubles put behind them for the precious few hours they had to themselves. Later they made slow, tender love in the firelight. It was the nicest time they'd had in ages and Kathy, renewed in spirit, felt she could face anything.

That evening, the dishes tidied, the lights of the tree switched off and the sitting room in darkness, they heard Rita's car in the drive. The children, tumbling out of the car, ran to greet their parents and shelter from the sleety rain. "I won't come in," Rita yelled, sticking her head out of the window. "I'll see you tomorrow around two with my gang."

"Fine, Rita, thanks a million," Kathy called back as Bill helped the trio divest themselves of coats and hats. Waving at her sister-in-law as she reversed down the drive, Kathy was glad to close the door and shut out the wintry night.

"We have a surprise for you now. You've got to close your eyes and no peeping," Bill warned as he led Rachel, Matthew and Jessica to the sitting-room door.

"What is it? What is it?" Matthew was hopping from one leg to the other with impatience.

"Matthew, they're not going to tell you 'cos it won't be a surprise then," Rachel said sagely, doing her big-sister act, but Kathy could see her eyes sparkling with anticipation.

"Huwwy on." Jessica had her fingers up to her eyes and was peering anxiously through them. Watching the capers of the three of them Kathy experienced a rare moment of happiness and knew that whatever happened in the future no one could ever take these precious moments away from her.

"Keep those eyes shut," Bill warned as Kathy took Jessica by the hand and led them into the darkened sitting room illuminated only by the firelight and the little red lamp in the crib. "Open up!" Bill ordered as he plugged in the lights. He hugged Kathy as the children squealed with delight and excitement.

"Oh Daddy, it's **MEGA!**" Matthew was beside himself.

"Oh Mammy, isn't it *beeeautiful?*" Rachel breathed. Jessica stood speechless, her big blue eyes getting rounder by the minute. Hesitantly she stretched out a chubby little hand and touched one of the ornaments.

"Tanta Plause," she exclaimed triumphantly, stroking the little fat Santa, her eyes as bright as the Christmas tree lights.

"Oh look at the crib, Mammy. Can we put the Baby Jesus in?" Rachel beseeched.

"Daddy and I were waiting until you came home so we could say a little prayer to welcome Baby Jesus into our family." Kathy smiled and hugged her elder daughter. She wanted her children to appreciate the special spirituality of Christmas and the crib ceremony was one of their most important family events.

With great solemnity, Rachel placed the infant Jesus in his manger in her younger sister's hands and guided the toddler to the correct spot in the centre of the straw, between Mary and Joseph.

"Welcome, Baby Jesus," they all chorused reverently.

"And we hope you'll be very comfortable in your manger,"

Rachel added as she patted the straw down. Jessica planted a big wet kiss on the newly installed infant.

"I bet he *will* be comfortable, our crib is *much* nicer than Jason Pierce's an' they don't have a light or straw either," Matthew declared with satisfaction as he took a bit of straw and placed it in front of the two little sheep on the mountainside. "In case they're hungry," he explained to his parents who were having a very hard time keeping their faces straight.

The following Monday morning Bill arrived upstairs with a cup of early morning tea for his wife. "What kind of a day is it?" Kathy murmured sleepily. She and Bill were going shopping for the Santa toys. They had decided on a compromise and planned to borrow one hundred and fifty euro from the credit union and use a hundred euro out of the two hundred and fifty that Kathy had managed to put by for expenses. Through a chink in the curtains she could see a sliver of daylight. The wind of the previous two days had died down.

Bill drew back the curtains and peered out. "I don't believe it," she heard him say. "Kathy, come here, you've just got to see this!"

"What?" she asked intrigued, wrapping the duvet around her as protection from the early morning chill. She followed her husband's pointing finger. And burst out laughing. "What a prat! What a prize prat," she chortled as she viewed an outsized noble fir decorated with multi-coloured lights, standing in a tub in the centre of the Pierces' front lawn.

All in all it hadn't been a bad Christmas, Kathy decided as she put the finishing touches to the creamy homemade vegetable soup she was serving as a starter for lunch with Mari. It was made with the stock of the turkey bones and there was eating and drinking in it. There'd be plenty for tomorrow she thought with satisfaction.

It was the day after Stephen's Day and Bill had taken the children on the Dart into Dublin to go to the pictures, so Kathy and her friend could have a bit of peace. Kathy had lit the fire early and had piled on the coal and briquettes so that the back boiler was boiling and the radiators were fine and hot. They were going through coal at an awful rate. Once the children were back at school it would be back to lighting a fire in the evening. Still at least the house was warm for her guest today.

It had been two years since Mari had last been home. Kathy had known her since they were in their teens. They'd gone to secondary school together and worked in the civil service before Mari had fallen in love with a young doctor. They had married and gone to live in Dubai ten years ago. Kathy and she kept in touch by email and the occasional phone call. Mari had come back home several times over the years and Kathy had marvelled at how glamorous and sophisticated her friend had become.

She had by all accounts a glittering lifestyle out in the Emirates. A life full of parties and shopping and exotic travel. Her husband, Brett, had become a very successful consultant and now they were very affluent. Brett and Owen would get on well, Kathy reflected, grinning. In fact it would be hilarious to listen to the pair of them trying to outdo each other.

She lifted the lid of the saucepan beside the soup and added the chopped chives to the flaked salmon in cream and wine sauce that was simmering gently. Her mother had made a Christmas pudding and trifle for her and her mother-in-law had baked a Christmas cake so at least she had dessert and afternoon tea taken care of. She also had a decent Chardonnay chilling. Someone had given it to her ages ago and she had put it aside for a special occasion. This was just such an occasion.

It was just as well Mari had picked the day after Stephen's Day because there was precious little left in the kitty and what was in the fridge was going to have to do them for the rest of the week. Still, Rachel and Matthew had been thrilled with their new bikes and Jessica was playing her ABC computer morning, noon and night. It had been a good idea putting those few euro from the children's allowance aside over the year. It had gone a long way towards paying for their Santa gifts.

Kathy turned down the salmon even lower and went to give a last look over the house. She had hoovered and dusted thoroughly that morning and the house was fragrant with polish and pot pourri. A thought struck her and she ran upstairs to her bedroom and slid open her sliderobes. On the bottom shelf of her make-up area there was a three-quarters-full roll of soft green toilet paper. Kathy took it and went into the main bathroom to replace the cheap, rough, off-white thrift roll that was in the toilet-roll holder. Maybe she was being daft but she badly wanted to keep up appearances. She always kept the expensive roll for when there were visitors. There was no need for Mari to know anything about Bill being unemployed. She couldn't explain exactly why she didn't want her friend to know of their plight. Mari wouldn't look down her nose at them in the least, she wasn't a bit like that for all her wealth. She'd be very sympathetic if anything. It was just her silly pride, Kathy decided. But Bill's being unemployed seemed almost tantamount to failure in the light of Brett's success. It was a horrible thing to think, she scolded herself shame-faced, but even so . . .

Just for good measure, she produced a box of matching tissues that she was also keeping for "good wear" out of her wardrobe, and placed them on the shelf under the mirror. They gave a nice coordinated touch and, satisfied, Kathy went back downstairs to await her guest.

She paused in front of the mirror to check her appearance. She'd got her hair cut and blow dried on Christmas Eve and it still looked good, and a bit of make-up did wonders. The last year had added a few grey hairs to her chestnut curls, she thought ruefully, and the fine lines around her wide hazel eyes had deepened perceptibly. Still, she didn't look too bad considering and the cream pants and amber blouse looked very well on her. A ring on the doorbell made her jump and she glanced hastily at her watch. Mari was early.

"Happy Christmas," came the cheerful greeting as Kathy opened the door and was hugged warmly by her friend who was certainly dressed for the weather in a magnificent, expensive sable coat.

"Come in, come in." Now that she was here Kathy was delighted to see her.

"God above, I'm freezing." Mari grimaced as she shut the door behind her.

"I've a blazing fire lighting, come in and sit down beside it," Kathy urged, leading the way into the sitting room.

"I've been cold since I came home," Mari explained. "The heat thins your blood and I know the animal lovers won't approve of the coat but it really stops me from freezing to death." She looked tired, Kathy thought, despite the fact that her make-up was perfectly applied and her blonde, high-lighted hair in its classical chignon was the height of chic.

"Well how are you, Kathy? How are the gang?" Mari smiled as she moved towards the big armchair in front of the fire and held out her hands to the blaze.

"I'm fine, we're all fine," Kathy said cheerfully. "Sit down there and relax, and what will you have to drink?"

"I have the car, Kathy, so I'll just have one glass of wine," Mari replied and Kathy gave a mental sigh of relief. The good wine would last through lunch and she wouldn't have to open that awful bottle of plonk she'd bought on special offer. She should have remembered, Mari always hired a car when she was home. She took her friend's coat and hung it on the hallstand and went to the kitchen to pour the wine, which she had chilling in the fridge. "There's a lovely smell." Mari followed her in. "What's for lunch?"

"Salmon and pasta," Kathy answered as she did the business with the corkscrew.

"Oh yum, you always made great pasta dishes, Kathy." Mari lifted the lid of the saucepan and sniffed appreciatively. "I've really been looking forward to seeing you and catching up on all the craic and the gossip. Where're Bill and the children?"

Kathy handed her a glass of wine. "He took them into Dublin on the Dart, for a treat. They've gone to the pictures." Mari's face fell.

"I will get to see them, won't I?"

"Oh indeed you will," laughed Kathy.

"Oh good, I've brought them a few presents and I've a bottle of brandy for yourself and Bill."

"Mari, you shouldn't have," Kathy exclaimed. Her friend was terribly good like that and, knowing that she wouldn't come empty-handed, Kathy had wrapped up a hardback copy of bestselling author Miranda Carr's brand new novel, which her Aunt Patti had given her. She'd been dying to read it herself but she knew that Mari, who was an avid reader, would thoroughly enjoy it and it was a decent present to give her old friend.

"I suppose I won't recognize the children." Mari sipped her wine appreciatively. "Jessica was only a baby the last time I was home."

"Well, she's well and truly a little girl now, marauding all over the place and up to all kinds of mischief," Kathy grinned. Mari had no children but she always took an interest in Rachel,

Matthew and Jessica and always brought them something on her trips home from Dubai.

"Will I serve up our lunch now?" Kathy cocked an eyebrow at the other woman.

"Why not, if it's OK with you. I haven't eaten all morning and I feel a bit peckish," Mari agreed.

"Go on into the dining room and sit down and I'll bring in the soup," Kathy instructed. She had the dining table set with the good silverware and crystal and her best linen tablecloth and napkins. And she had a lovely centrepiece on the table made up of holly and ivy that she and Bill had picked in the woods. She lit the candles, served the soup and garlic bread and the pair of them sat down to a good natter.

Although Mari had said she was peckish she didn't do justice to the meal and Kathy was terribly perturbed that perhaps she hadn't liked the dish. Her friend always ate like a horse and never put on an ounce, unlike Kathy who only had to look at a cream cake to put on weight.

"Was it OK, maybe it was a bit rich?" Kathy said apologetically.

"No, no! It was fine. Really!" Mari assured her. "I just wasn't as hungry as I thought."

They had their coffee by the fire, chatting about inconsequential things and somehow Kathy, listening to tales of the glamorous life in the Emirates, just couldn't bring herself to tell Mari that Bill was unemployed.

He and the children arrived home around six and they were full of their trip on the Dart and their visit to the cinema and McDonalds.

"It's lovely and warm in here," Matthew said appreciatively, and Kathy, being extra sensitive on this day, prayed that her son would keep his mouth shut and say nothing else. She didn't want her affluent friend thinking that the house wasn't always this warm.

When Mari produced their presents there was as much excitement as when Santa's arrival had been discovered on Christmas morning. Mari was in her element as they all vied for hugs and kisses before Bill took the three of them out to the kitchen to get some hot nourishing soup into them.

Rachel, en route to the kitchen, sighed and said wistfully, "I wish it was Christmas every day of the year so we could always have this gorgeous food." Kathy nearly died. Her face actually flamed as she stood waiting for her child to say something like she was sick of beans and mince and fish fingers, but she said nothing else and carried on after her sister and brother.

"Turkey and ham and Christmas pud always seem so exotic when you're a child, don't they?" Mari remarked innocently, quite unaware of her friend's angst.

"Hmm," agreed Kathy distractedly. God only knew what the children were going to come out with next to land her in. She should have been honest with Mari at the beginning and told her about Bill being unemployed. There was no shame in it. It could happen to anyone, but it would look a bit odd to go suddenly blurting it out now, especially when she had led Mari to believe that everything was normal in the Reynolds' household. She was going to be on tenterhooks for the rest of the evening. She must excuse herself for a minute and grab Bill and tell him to say nothing about being unemployed. She'd tell him she'd explain later. He'd probably be annoyed with her and feel that she was ashamed of him. By trying to keep up a façade she'd made a right mess of things, she thought miserably.

"They're just gorgeous, Kathy. You're so lucky," Mari said enviously, interrupting her friend's musings.

"I know that," Kathy agreed, carefully folding up the expensive wrapping paper and mentally reflecting that it would come in handy next year.

"Mammy, I did wee wee all by myself." Jessica appeared at the door with her dress caught up in her little panties.

"You're a great girl!" her mother exclaimed. "Come here until I tuck in your vest." Jessica cuddled in against her as Kathy adjusted her clothing.

"There's lobely soft toilet woll in the bathwoom, it's nice and soft on my bum bum," Jessica announced, staring at Mari.

Jesus, Mary and Joseph, Kathy thought in mortification. Next she'll be saying we're poor people or something. Heart-scalded, flustered, she told her daughter to go back out to the kitchen to finish her soup. Jessica wrapped her little arms around her neck. "I lobe you, Mammy. The next time will you come to the pictures?"

"Of course I will, lovey." Kathy hugged the little girl to her before she went trotting out to the kitchen.

"She's so beautiful," Mari said and her voice sounded terribly sad. Kathy caught her friend's gaze and to her dismay saw that Mari's eyes were bright with tears.

"God! What's wrong, Mari," Kathy exclaimed, closing the door and rushing over to her side. "What is it? Tell me what's wrong." Kathy was horrified, putting her arms around the distraught woman.

"Me and Brett, we're finished. He's been having an affair with this American bimbo half his age and now she's pregnant and he wants a divorce. He wouldn't let me come off the pill, he kept saying to wait another year and then another and now this tart's pregnant and it's fine by him. I hate him, the bastard." Mari sobbed. "I didn't want to tell you, I was just too ashamed."

Kathy couldn't believe her ears. What a shit. She knew Mari had always wanted children.

"You've nothing to be ashamed about," she said, outraged. "He's the skunk. He's not worthy of you."

Mari lifted her head from Kathy's neck. "I don't know why *I* feel ashamed, I did nothing to be ashamed about. It's just . . . Oh you know what I mean, Kathy, my poor mother will be mortified. The first divorce in the family, what will the relations say?" She hiccuped.

"Don't mind the relations or anyone. It's your life and your business." Kathy snorted.

"And then when I see how happy you are with Bill and those beautiful children . . . I just couldn't tell you. Can you understand?" Mari managed a wry smile.

"I understand exactly," Kathy said slowly. "Actually, Mari, I've been keeping something from you as well." She met her friend's tear-stained gaze. "Bill's been out of work for over fourteen months and it's a bit of a struggle. Like you, I just couldn't bring myself to say it out straight. I wanted to keep up appearances. I'm sorry, it was just silly pride."

"Oh Lord, I know." Mari gave a shaky grin. "But that's awful for you and Bill. He'll get another job and at least the pair of you are as crazy about each other as ever. You can spot that a mile off. God, I was so gutted when I found out about Brett and that . . . that pea-brained, simpering idiot who's got her claws into him. The thing that hurt most of all is that she's pregnant. Every time I suggested trying for a baby he said to wait another year. He didn't want his cushy lifestyle disrupted by crying babies. I'll probably never have a child of my own now." Her voice wobbled and she burst into tears again.

"Of course you will, you'll meet someone, you're still a relatively young woman," Kathy soothed, shocked by what she had just heard. Her own circumstances might not be the best but they were a hell of a lot better than Mari's. No wonder the poor girl couldn't eat her lunch. No wonder she'd seemed so on edge for the afternoon.

"I haven't told the family yet. Ma will have a fit."

"She'll get over it."

"It's such a relief to tell someone, Kathy," Mari confessed, wiping her eyes with the back of her hand. "It's been so hard being at home and everyone thinking everything's normal. I told them Brett couldn't come home because of the situation in Iraq . . . A bit feeble, I know, but no one's questioned it. It's bloody hard trying to keep up the façade."

"Of course it's been hard, Mari, but you've got to tell them. You can't go around keeping that to yourself. You'd crack up. And I know your family, they'll be very supportive, it's amazing how kind people are when the chips are down. I know," she added ruefully.

"Oh Kathy, what idiots we've been, trying to put on brave faces. If we can't tell each other our problems then who can we tell?" Mari said.

"Exactly!" Kathy agreed. "Now look, why don't you phone home and tell them you're staying the night and we'll open the brandy you brought and have a really good natter about things."

"Oh Kathy, that would be lovely," Mari sighed, beginning to feel better already.

"I'll just run up and put the heat on in the spare bedroom, and fish out some towels and a clean nightdress." Kathy patted her on the shoulder.

"Now don't go to any trouble," Mari remonstrated.

"It's no trouble for an old pal," Kathy said firmly.

She switched on the radiator and laid a clean, long-sleeved nightdress on Mari's bed. That would keep her snug, she thought, and she'd put the electric blanket on later. To hell with the electricity bill for once. Mari was undergoing a bad enough trauma without spending the night shivering in bed.

Kathy stood at the bedroom window staring out into the night. A sliver of new moon hid behind a wisp of cloud. The lights of the Christmas trees illuminated the cul-de-sac. Below, Owen's noble fir stood proudly on his front lawn. Owen had got a new Saab for Christmas and had spent a lot of time sitting in it making calls on his car phone. Kathy smiled. He was pathetically childish really. Maybe there was some reason for his childish behaviour. Maybe he'd had a terribly deprived childhood. Who knew? Who knew what went on in people's lives? Who knew what went on behind the façades? Look at poor Mari. Who would have believed it?

No matter what, she and Bill were lucky, they had each other and they had the children. She could hear them laughing and chattering in the kitchen. Gently pulling the curtains, Kathy straightened the folds, switched off the light and went downstairs to her friend.

Born in Dublin, where she still lives, **PATRICIA SCANLAN** is the author of many bestselling novels, including *Two for Joy; Francesca's Party; Mirror, Mirror; City Woman; Promises, Promises; City Girl; City Lives;* and *Finishing Touches.*

The Irish Girls Are Back in Town

Suzanne Higgins

*T*illy was in a thunderous mood. This was downright unnatural! Surely she was the only twenty-five-year-old in the country up before 10 a.m. on a Sunday morning? She knew all her friends were still asleep—most of them wouldn't even surface before twelve noon. That was how it should be. "Only old people and babies wake up early," she fumed aloud as she crunched her gears with considerably more force than was necessary.

Her conscience was quick to remind her, however, that she had an agreement to honour. James Adams, Tilly's father, had made her an amazing offer two years earlier and she had instantly accepted his deal. All she had heard was the phrase "your own apartment," and she was in. Bloody hell, how many girls her age in Dublin had their own apartments?

"Still," she sighed as she began to stab at her stereo, the memory of Charlie lying in bed back in her Sandymount apartment almost made her cry. They only had the weekend together and then he would be gone again for at least another week. On the radio, Britney Spears was singing "I Was Born To Make You Happy" and Tilly began to sing along. She was born to make Charlie happy, not bloody Granny Matilda! How long would she be gone this morning? An hour, maybe two? It depended on what form dear ol' Gran was in. If she was really lucky, she reckoned she could be in and out in thirty minutes. She could be back to Sandymount with the papers and the bacon and eggs before Charlie even woke. Then she could take up where they had left off last night . . .

Tilly thought longingly about her boyfriend. He was quite a bit taller than her, with dark brown hair like her own. He wore it cut very short which suited his long, thin face. Our babies would probably have dark brown hair, she thought to herself. "God, he's a fine thing," she sighed contentedly.

She turned into the car park of the Sunnyside Retirement Village. Not surprisingly, she found a parking spot easily. It wasn't exactly jam-packed at eleven o'clock on a Sunday morning.

"Hi," one of the nurses at the reception desk said, smiling brightly.

Tilly pulled a smile out of somewhere. "Hi, Jenny. How are you this morning?"

"Oh, fine, thanks. You?"

"Great. A little tired but I'm fine."

The nurse looked at Tilly. She was wearing a pair of light blue jeans and sand-coloured boots. The baggy cream jumper masked her petite frame but with her hands plunged firmly into her jeans pockets, it was clear to see that Tilly was of slight build. Her dark brown hair was cut in a bob that just reached her shoulders. "You do look a little worn out," Jenny said, smiling knowingly. "Late night, last night? You're a wonderful granddaughter to visit Matilda so often, you know that? We don't see many as loyal as you, Tilly Adams!"

The young girl smiled a little awkwardly from under her dark fringe. Although she knew the nurses in Sunnyside fairly well, thanks to her regular visits every second Sunday, she would never admit to them that her loyalty was in fact the product of bribery, thanks to the deal she had made with her dad.

"Your father arrived with loads of Easter eggs last week," Jenny added. "He's a very nice man, your dad!"

"Isn't he?" Tilly agreed but she wasn't really interested because her mind was on an even nicer man who was at home in her Sandymount bed.

"Tell him I said thanks a million!"

"I'll pass it on." Another forced smile. "Where's Gran this morning?"

"Oh, she's enjoying the sun in the conservatory."

"How is she this week?" Tilly asked, as she usually did. This time, however, the nurse's mood altered slightly and Tilly spotted it. "Jenny? Everything's OK, isn't it?"

The nurse came out from behind the reception counter and gestured to the two large armchairs nearby. "Actually, perhaps I should have a word with you before you go down to see her this morning."

"Ohmigod, she's not ill, is she?" Tilly pleaded, all thoughts of Charlie well and truly vanished.

Jenny took the young girl's hand and gently guided her to sit down.

"Her physical health is fine, Tilly. It's her mind." Jenny paused to let this sink in. "You do know she's been slowly slipping away from us?"

Tilly nodded anxiously.

"Well, it appears that she has had a little setback."

"What does that mean?"

"She seems to be out of touch a little more than she used to be."

"You mean she's beginning to lose it even more?"

"Yes."

"But she'll improve over the next few weeks again, won't she?"

"It's not likely, Tilly. Your grandmother is a grand old age now. She's well into her eighties. God knows, she's one of the leading lights here at Sunnyside and has been for the last five years. Everybody knows and loves Matilda but it does appear that she's becoming frailer. And she really gets quite confused now." Again Jenny paused to see how Tilly was taking this. "Unfortunately, when a woman of your gran's age slips further into dementia, she doesn't return."

Tilly covered her mouth with her hands.

"Look, try not to let it upset you too much. I'm sure she'll recognize you today but if she gets a little confused, don't be too surprised and don't take it personally."

"What should I say if she starts talking rubbish?" asked Tilly, dark brown eyes wide.

"Well, that's up to you. If you feel you can, you could try to put her straight, but if she seems very addled, perhaps you should just go along with it. You make that call as you see fit."

"Does Dad know about this?"

"Yes. Now, remember that nothing significant has changed. Your grandmother is just ageing like the rest of us. You did know that she had dementia?"

"Yes, I just hate calling it that. I like to call her forgetful."

"Well, let's stick to that then," Jenny agreed. "Put simply, Matilda has become a little more forgetful." She smiled at the pretty young girl who suddenly looked a lot younger and less sophisticated than she usually did.

Tilly nodded shakily. "I can deal with that. Gran is a little more forgetful than usual. Right?"

"Right," the nurse agreed.

"OK. You said she was in the conservatory?" Tilly got to her feet.

Jenny nodded up at her. "Come and have a talk with me if you're upset after your visit."

"Thanks."

Tilly walked down the bright corridors of the Sunnyside Retirement Village. In the first room she passed through there were old folks playing cards, backgammon or chess. A little further on there were some people watching Mass on the television. The room was quiet but for the TV which was ridiculously loud. It had taken her a few visits to Sunnyside before she realized that the TV was loud because most of Sunnyside's residents were half deaf!

She passed into another room. It was considerably more active and also louder. Here, families sat with their older relatives and made conversation. Small children rushed around the floor squealing and laughing. Tilly knew her way around the home well. She headed into another corridor which also had large reception areas off it. You could see into the rooms because the walls were made of glass. She wasn't sure whether that was to let the maximum amount of light in or whether it was to keep a watchful eye on the residents. Probably a bit of both.

Next, she passed a smoking room, no less. It was kind of funny that you couldn't really smoke anywhere in public now and yet it was still allowed in here. Her grandmother had once explained to her that there were some residents who had been smoking forty a day for practically eighty years and they weren't going to bloody well stop now! So it was more sensible to give them somewhere to smoke rather than have them sneaking fags under the bedclothes at night. She had a point. The next room Tilly passed was an adults-only room. Naturally, some of the residents were a little intolerant of the younger visitors and so this was their refuge.

Finally she arrived in the conservatory. While the entire home was bright and airy, this room was definitely the warmest and the sunniest. It was the one Matilda usually sat in and it was also Tilly's favourite. Matilda Dempsey might be getting more forgetful but she wasn't stupid!

"Hello, Gran." Tilly bent down to kiss Matilda. She forced herself to be cheerful. "How are you this fine morning?"

"Hello, pet. I'm very well, thank you. How are you today?"

Phew, Tilly sighed to herself as she pulled up a chair. Gran was the same as usual.

"Oh, I'm grand," she answered. "It's a lovely sunny spring morning and all the daffodils are out. I see you're enjoying the view from here."

Matilda seemed to notice for the first time that she was next to a large expanse of glass. "What? Oh yes, it is lovely, isn't it? The rhododendrons are about to come into full bloom and as for the forsythia! Isn't it wonderful?"

"Wonderful," Tilly agreed with relief.

"Tell me now, how's your husband? What's his name again?"

Tilly froze. "Sorry?"

"Your husband, Sheila. My, my, I can't believe I've forgotten his name! How silly! Sheila, how's your husband?"

Tilly's heart sank. She took Matilda's two hands in hers and whispered gently but sufficiently loudly for the hearing-aid to pick it up. "Gran, it's me, Tilly—Sheila's daughter. Do you remember that Mum—Sheila—died in a road accident fifteen years ago? I'm Tilly. I'm not married. Sheila—your daughter—was married to James Adams, my dad."

Matilda's eyes brightened. "James! That's the name I was searching for! Now, what are you saying? James is your father?

Gosh, I am getting confused." Her face began to look distressed as uncertainty flooded in. Her lower lip began to quiver. "Heavens," she muttered, "Sheila is dead and you're Tilly."

"Now you have it," the young girl encouraged. "I'm called after you! Tilly is short for Matilda. Remember?"

This seemed to cheer the older woman up. "You're called after me? Well, isn't that nice?" She smoothed out the non-existent creases in her skirt. "Tell me now, how's your husband?"

Tilly thought she might cry. It was quite obvious that her grandmother had left reality behind. Then she had an idea—change the conversation.

"Gran, can I tell you a secret?"

Matilda's eyes widened. "I love secrets," she chuckled.

"Well," Tilly leaned closer to her grandmother so she could whisper, albeit loudly, "I think I'm in love!"

The old woman clapped her hands in glee. "You lucky, lucky thing," she enthused. "What's his name? Where is he from? And most importantly, does he love you?"

"His name is Charlie Magill. He's from Wimbledon, so he's English. He lives over there but I met him here in Dublin when he was over for a stag. He comes over here most weekends now. I haven't been over to visit him yet." Then she paused and thought about her grandmother's last question. "Regarding the love bit, to be brutally honest, I don't really know if he loves me."

"Oh, angel, you must be very careful, so. You have to play the game, you realize."

"What game?"

"You mustn't let him know that you love him. Not until he has fallen deeply in love with you."

"I see."

"Trust me, I know. The only relationships that really work are the ones where the man is more in love than the woman is."

"Well, you loved Grandad and he loved you!"

"Yes, that's true and our marriage was fine—but it wasn't the greatest romance of my life."

"*What?*"

"Oh, no," Matilda chuckled again. "I once met a lovely man who told me that he loved me." She looked out of the window but her gaze rested on something that was a thousand miles away. It was in a different place and a different time, somewhere far in her past. "He told me he loved me and he begged me to leave my husband."

"You were married at the time?" Tilly was aghast.

Matilda snapped back to the moment in hand. She looked around the conservatory nervously. "Shhh, do you want the whole place to know?"

"Sorry," Tilly whispered, "but did you say you were married to Grandad at the time?"

The old lady seemed to have slipped comfortably back into her memories.

"His name was Charlie."

It was then Tilly realized, with profound sadness, that her grandmother was dreaming again.

Matilda continued, "Charlie Cranwell. I will never forget him for as long as I live. In fact I'm thinking of looking him up again, now that Frank is gone to his great reward."

At a loss as to what to do, Tilly decided that it was easier to let her gran enjoy her fantasy world. She was obviously very settled there and, after all, at her age, what was the point of trying to force her to live in the real one?

"Gran, tell me about Charlie Cranwell."

Matilda gazed back out of the window at the ocean of daffodils. They swayed back and forth in the light spring breeze. A starling flew down onto the grass just outside the window. His dark brown feathers glistened in the sunshine.

"He was a pilot in the war." Matilda watched the bird. "Frank—that's my husband—and I, we lived in England when war broke out in 1939. I was nineteen years old and married only a few months but then, of course, we all got married much younger in those days. Anyway, Frank said it was only right and proper that he should go to war and so he did. Suddenly I was left alone in that great big city in the middle of a war."

"Why didn't you come home to Ireland? It would have been safer."

"That was the plan. That's what I agreed with Frank. As soon as he was dispatched off, I was to catch the boat home. But Maura—that's my friend—she said that she was going down to Surrey to help with the wounded as they came back from the war." Matilda looked at Tilly. "Well, what would you have done? If your husband had just gone off? And it was a terrible war, love. Men were being shipped home wounded as fast as they were being shipped out, it seemed. Everybody was pitching in. How could I leave at a time like that?"

"And of course you were a nurse."

"They needed nurses and I was one. The decision was simple for me."

"So you went to Surrey?"

"That's right. Me and Maura. Father Matt, our local priest, sorted us out. He got us a lovely post in a convalescent home for the wounded. It was in a pretty town called Epsom."

"I know Epsom. Isn't that where they have the races?"

"That's the place. The town is a little way from the racetrack but you should go there sometime, love. From the top of the racecourse you'd think you were on top of the world! On a clear day you can see right across the countryside, the whole way into London. In fact, I'm thinking I might go back there soon, just for a visit, like." Then she gave a soft melancholic sigh as if somewhere deep within a voice was telling her that that wouldn't be happening. "Anyway, for the entire war Maura and I worked there, nursing the sick, sore and wounded."

"You must have seen some pretty horrendous sights."

"That we did, but for the most part Maura and I were there for the moral support and a little bit of geeing them up."

"Geeing them up?"

"You know what I mean. Giving them a bit of a lift. If you only saw the sorry state of some of them! They had lost limbs and eyes but, worst of all, some of them had lost their spirit."

"That must have been hard." Tilly had never heard her gran talk about the war before. She hadn't even known that her grandparents lived in England for a time. She felt a stab of guilt for begrudging her grandmother a few hours' chat every second Sunday.

Matilda continued, "They all went off to war, determined to show that madman, Hitler, what he was up against but I'm afraid Hitler got the better of some of them. A few of the worst cases just sat quietly in a corner and shook all the time."

A bit like this place, Tilly thought to herself, but stayed quiet. "Well, where does Charlie fit into all of this?"

"He arrived in the January of 1945. We had just celebrated Christmas as best we could. There were no presents, of course, but we sang carols and made decorations out of old cloth. We tried to have a good time. After the celebrations of Christmas, modest though they were, January was so bleak and depressing." Matilda looked morose for a moment but then quickly lifted her head and smiled. "Then one particularly cold wet Wednesday I arrived at the home. I was freezing and soaked through. I was also a little down because I hadn't heard from Frank in weeks."

A thought struck Tilly. "Gran, do you mean to say you spent the first five years of your marriage parted from your husband?" she asked incredulously, still surprised at how little she knew about her grandparents' life.

"Not at all—he was often let home on leave. He wasn't on active service. Frank worked in printing."

"Printing? What did printing have to do with the war effort?"

"I'll have you know it was a significant part of the war!" Matilda said proudly. "Millions of leaflets were dropped all over Europe. Don't forget there was no television, never mind your computers. God, to have a radio was a big deal! Most people got their information about the war through the leaflets that were dropped in by the planes. So, luckily, Frank wasn't in any particular danger. Well, no more than the rest of us. You know, we saw aerial combat in Surrey."

"Never!"

"Oh yes—you young people have no idea what it's like to live through a war!"

"Gran?"

"Yes?"

"Charlie?"

"Oh, yes. Charlie. Now *there* was a man. I walked into the parlour soaked through to the skin and feeling utterly fed up. Maura was with me, and she was in an equally foul mood. Then, there sitting by the fire, large as life—smoking and playing cards as if he was on a holiday—was the finest-looking man I had ever seen in my life." She clapped her hands gleefully and rocked in her chair.

Her eyes were bright and happy, more so than Tilly had seen in a long time. Surely this entire story wasn't simply her imagination?

"What did he look like, Gran?" she encouraged as it was obviously giving the older woman such pleasure.

"Well, it was really the way he carried himself. He was always in a good mood. I suppose that was it mainly. He had a grin on his face all the time that would make you think he was up to no good and his eyes were the brightest blue I ever saw"—Matilda was on a roll—"and he had this shock of blond hair . . . I had never seen such a colour in my life!" She stroked her own soft white hair.

It had become very fine, Tilly noticed painfully. She could see Matilda's scalp quite clearly if she looked closely.

"Surely women were bleaching their hair in the 1940s, Gran?"

"Of course they were, but not to the colour and sheen of his. No, his blond hair was really something to behold. But it was really that he was always laughing and joking and he made the people around him happy—that was what made him especially attractive. But his eyes, Tilly! Lord, how those eyes danced with mischief!"

"Well, he certainly got your attention, didn't he?"

Matilda didn't answer in words. She just smiled at her granddaughter's flippant remark but her eyes had a look of jaded resignation. She nodded ever so slightly and then turned to look back out of the window. Tilly didn't breathe. She thought she had somehow broken the spell with her remark and maybe her grandmother wouldn't want to continue with her story. A minute dragged by in silence, then another. Tilly bit her lip to stop herself from talking but then the old lady started up again.

"'Look what's just walked in,' he laughed, looking at myself and Maura. 'Two poor drowned rats!' Well, I looked at him indignantly and threw my head back proudly. 'We're quite all right, thank you very much, sir. A little bit of water will hardly get the better of us!' Oh, if you saw how fine he was as he tilted his forehead towards me and laughed. 'I see,' he said. 'Two highly self-sufficient drowned rats if I'm not mistaken! And do I detect a slight Irish accent there?'

"'You do indeed,' I said, 'and proud of it I am, too.' It was only at that point, when he put his cards on the table and struggled to his feet with the aid of two crutches that I saw he was missing a leg. He hobbled away from the fire. 'Come in and dry yourselves, ladies,' he said. Then he addressed the other men in the parlour with a laugh. 'We're all safe now, chaps. The Irish girls are in town!' I'm not sure what I was more embarrassed about—being the centre of attention, realizing that he was so badly wounded or being called a bloomin' rat—but I ran out of that parlour and down to the kitchen faster than light and poor Maura right behind me!"

"I don't blame you," Tilly agreed. "It's awful being put on the spot like that. But how had he lost his leg?"

"Well, I found out later that he was shot right out of the sky. A real hero was my Charlie."

"'My Charlie'?" Tilly couldn't believe her ears. This was a heck of a story even if it was just a fabrication.

"He was a Wing Commander, you know."

"That sounds important."

"Oh, it is. You start out as a flight lieutenant and only the best make it to Wing Commander!"

"I'm impressed. So you obviously made up again pretty soon?"

"Soon?" the old lady laughed. "He hobbled down on his one leg and two crutches straight after me! I was next to the Aga drying myself off and blowing my nose when he caught up with me. 'Now, now,' he said, 'pretty Irish girls shouldn't cry just because of some silly fool like me.' 'I'm not crying because of you. I sim-

ply have a cold,' I explained, 'but I'm sorry for running off on
you like that. It's just that—well, I've never been called a rat
before.' 'Good Lord, I am sorry! It's just an expression I picked
up somewhere. I assure you I wasn't being literal.' He was so
attentive and sincere, Tilly, he took my breath away. 'I don't even
know your name,' I said to him. 'Wing Commander Cranwell at
your service!' He saluted me and then stretched his hand out to
shake mine. I have to admit I was very taken with his manner
and charm. 'Look,' he said. 'I really am most dreadfully sorry for
embarrassing you in front of the chaps like that. Can I make it up
to you? Perhaps we could have lunch together?' "

Matilda stopped talking again and looked at Tilly.

"And so it began," she said simply.

"*What* began? Your affair?" the younger girl asked, barely
above a whisper.

Matilda shrugged. "What is an affair? Does it happen in the
head or in the heart?"

I thought it usually happened in the bed, Tilly mused to herself but didn't dare say. It was as if her grandmother had read her
mind however.

"It was World War Two, child. I was a good Catholic girl and
a married one at that. If I had been single I dare say things would
have been different but I was married and that was an undeniable
fact so the answer to your question is no, I did not have that sort
of a relationship with Wing Commander Charlie Cranwell."

"I didn't ask you any such thing!"

"No, but you were wondering!" Matilda winked at Tilly.
"Don't think my blood didn't burn just as hot as yours does
now." For a brief moment, Matilda's eyes bored into Tilly's with
absolute clarity. Then she seemed to drift off back to Epsom in
Surrey. "The spring of 1945 was one I will never forget. Charlie
and I became inseparable. I read to him in the mornings and, in

the afternoons, if he wasn't too tired he would take a walk about the gardens with me. Sometimes we played cards together and he even taught me how to smoke! Now that was something Frank would not have approved of!"

"I doubt Frank would have approved of any of this!" Tilly murmured.

"Once we went on an outing."

"You and Charlie?"

"Yes, and a few others. One of the doctors thought it would give the men a bit of a lift. We went to visit the bluebell woods."

"The bluebell woods? That sounds like a lovely place, Gran."

"Oh it is, child, it's a magical place—the carpet of purple around your feet is a joy to behold but the rich perfume that hits your nose would knock you into the middle of next week!"

Again Matilda's face was bright with the vivid and fragrant memory. You'd never think there was anything wrong with her mind at this moment, Tilly thought.

"Anyway," the old lady continued, "the terrain was a little uneven and so the able-bodied men were a little faster than Charlie. 'You chaps, go ahead. We'll catch up with you,' he told them. Well, he was really only doing the decent thing. It would have been unfair to keep everybody at his slow pace, wouldn't it?"

"Quite," Tilly agreed, laughing to herself. Oh pulease, that kind of thing is one of the oldest tricks in the book, she thought privately as her grandmother continued on her glorious trip down memory lane and into the bluebell woods.

"Soon the others were totally out of sight and earshot. That's when it happened."

"What?"

"He stumbled and fell. I'm not really sure how he tripped— he was usually so good with the crutches—but however it tran- spired, he ended up on the flat of his back and me with him."

"Never!" Tilly squealed.

"Charlie held me in a way that Frank never had. In a bed of bluebells he cradled me in his arms and told me that he loved me."

Tilly had to bite her knuckles to stop herself from laughing with delight. It was a wonderful story—she wanted them to get it together.

Matilda continued, "He stroked my cheek so softly and begged me to leave my husband. He cried then and so did I. I had to explain that I never could and I never would leave Frank. Then he kissed me and I let him. I thought I would burst with pleasure. I didn't want him to stop. It was the nicest feeling I have ever felt in my life and I am in no doubt that I loved him with every bit of me—mind, body and soul. But"—Matilda blinked and suddenly she was back in Sunnyside—"it was quite impossible."

"Oh, Gran, if you loved him that much I'm not sure that it would have been such a bad thing!"

Matilda looked at Tilly straight in the face. "That, my child, is the big difference between your generation and mine." Then quite unexpectedly the old woman, with enormous effort, rose to her feet.

Tilly jumped up. "Are you OK? Do you want to go somewhere?"

"Yes, girl, why else would I be on my feet?" She began to shuffle forward. "Believe me, at my age you don't get up unless you absolutely have to!"

"Where do you want to go?"

"Please take me to my room. I have completely forgotten which way to go. My, my, I must be getting old!"

Tilly stopped asking why. She just took her grandmother by the arm and gently guided her to the bedroom. Thankfully, as it was a custom-built retirement village, the entire building was on one level and so getting her grandmother to her room was no great ordeal. That said, it dismayed Tilly to see how much it took out of the old woman.

Exhausted after the exertion, Matilda sat on her bed. "Fetch me the brown leather box in my bedside locker, child."

Tilly did as she was requested. Matilda took the little box in her tiny hands. The younger woman noted with deep sadness that her grandmother was becoming much slower and weaker. Her bones were now quite visible under her incredibly thin and translucent skin. With great determination, however, she unclipped the brown leather box and opened it. Inside was a fine gold chain with a tiny flower pendant.

"What's this?" Tilly asked.

"This was his goodbye present to me." Her eyes became glassy. "It was the thirtieth of April—I'll never forget that day— when the doctors told him he was well enough to leave the convalescent home. He didn't want to go, he didn't want to leave me but I told him he had to go—I told him that Frank would be home soon. Everybody knew that the war was nearly over. Then I told him the biggest lie I have ever told anyone in my life."

"What did you say?"

"I told him I didn't love him."

"But you did."

"With all my heart."

Tilly thought she might cry. "Would you like me to put your necklace on now?" she asked gently.

"No, thank you, love. I have never ever put it on and I don't think I could do it now. I am quite sure it would break my heart." Then she looked at Tilly and handed the necklace to her with the little leather box. "You take it now. It's for you and your Charlie."

"Oh, Gran!" Tilly took the thin gold chain in her hands. It was then that she realized that the tiny flower was in fact a golden bluebell. The piece was light and doubtless of little fiscal value but Tilly buckled under the enormous weight of its emotional worth. "I can't take this. It's too precious."

"Now, now, before you get all sentimental on me, let me give you a word of caution. Charlie Cranwell was the finest-looking man I have ever seen. Everybody loved him and most looked up to him despite the fact that he had only one leg. I am convinced that the reason he loved me so much was because I was out of his reach, unavailable so to speak. Remember that, if you want to keep Charlie Magill for life."

Tilly was startled to hear her grandmother call her boyfriend by his full name. How could she remember his second name and not remember her son-in-law's name? She didn't dare mention it.

"I know what you're saying, Gran. Play hard to get."

"That's it, exactly! Clever girl."

"Look, why don't you keep this necklace for a few more years. I don't want to take such a precious memory from you."

"Don't worry about that now. Nobody will ever take my memories from me."

Then Tilly asked gently, "Who knew about you and Charlie?"

The old lady smiled. "You're the first person I've ever told."

"You mean you've kept this a secret all your life?" Tilly was aghast.

But Matilda simply nodded. "You'll find, my love, that the older you get, the easier it is to keep secrets. And, anyway, who would want to know about my little life?"

"I dare say Grandad may have had a thing or two to say!"

"Sure, it would have destroyed the poor man! Neither does my daughter know. God, it would kill her to discover that her father was not the real love of my life! You won't tell her, will you?" The old lady looked worried.

Tilly's heart sank. Hadn't she just reminded Matilda that Sheila was dead? She sighed softly. How could she have been so naive as to believe her grandmother's story? It was probably total fantasy. Her grandmother was simply away with the fairies most of the time now, as Jenny had warned her. Tilly cursed herself for her own stupidity. Matilda had just made up the story when Tilly mentioned that she had a boyfriend from England called Charlie. Tilly refused to let herself cry. She decided not to remind her grandmother again of the painful truth.

"Don't worry, I won't tell her," she finally managed to say. She noticed that her gran looked really worn out. "Would you like to lie down for a while?"

"Yes, I think that's a good idea. I can rest now."

"Would you like me to leave you?"

"Not yet. I would like to ask you a favour, child."

"Sure, what is it?"

"Would you tell Charlie that I'm ready for our rendezvous?"

"Sorry?"

"Go to Charlie. Tell him I'm ready when he is. The whole reason I've told you my story is so you can help me now."

"I don't understand."

Matilda lay perfectly still on her bed. She closed her eyes gently and explained. "On the day he was to leave, he came to me and gave me that necklace. Then he made a suggestion. He said, if I wouldn't spend this life with him, would I at least meet up with him in the next? And I told him I would."

"Oh, Gran!"

"It's quite all right, pet. I'm tired of this world now and I miss my Charlie."

"What about Grandad? Maybe he's in heaven waiting for you right now."

"No, the arrangement I had with your grandfather was *till death us do part*. Eternity, I'm saving for Charlie." She opened her eyes and turned her head so she looked at Tilly. "Will you tell him I'll be waiting for him?"

The young girl began to sob at her grandmother's bedside. "I don't want you to go. Stay here. I'll visit more often! I'll get Dad to come more often too. Please, Gran, don't go!"

Nurse Jenny popped her head around Matilda's bedroom door. "So this is where you two have got to! Matilda, how are you this morning? I see your lovely granddaughter has come to visit you again. Aren't you the lucky woman!" Then she saw Tilly's tears. "What's all this?" she asked, coming across the room to put an arm around the girl's shoulders. "Tilly, why the tears?"

Seeing that Matilda was becoming drowsy, Jenny quietly led the girl out of the bedroom.

After Tilly recounted the conversation, the nurse made her a coffee and reminded her that her grandmother was not altogether in touch with reality. She told her that she was not to worry about Matilda's imminent death.

"There are residents in Sunnyside who have been threatening to depart this planet for decades!" she joked.

"What about the necklace?"

"Probably a gift from her husband," Jenny answered with conviction.

Tilly cheered up enough to go in and kiss her grandmother on the forehead while she slept.

"I love you and yes, I promise I'll tell Charlie," she said, keeping up the fantasy. Then she left.

◆   ◆   ◆

When Tilly's father phoned her on Monday to tell her that Matilda had passed away peacefully on Sunday evening, a large part of her was not surprised.

"You seem remarkably calm at the news," James Adams said anxiously. "I would have preferred to tell you in person, only I'm in the States right now. I'm flying home tonight but the funeral is on Wednesday and I thought you would want to know as soon as possible. I'm so sorry I'm not with you, honey." ·

"I'm OK, Dad. I had half an idea that this was coming. It's going to be a small funeral, isn't it? You and me and a priest. Is there anything I have to do?"

"No, Sunnyside will do everything. They have a funeral home there and of course the chapel is there too. There'll be a brief service on Tuesday night and a full funeral Mass on Wednesday morning. Thankfully we just have to turn up. Why don't you take a friend along for moral support? Although I will be there for you, of course."

Tilly smiled. Her father did his best, but affectionate he was not. Since her mother died, James Adams had buried himself in work. To the best of Tilly's knowledge he hadn't even dated another woman in the last fifteen years. Then she thought of the story of Matilda and Wing Commander Charlie Cranwell. Her father should take a leaf out of her grandmother's book, fact or fantasy!

"I'll be fine, Dad. I might ask a friend to come if he can make it."

As she hung up the phone she thought about her boyfriend, Charlie Magill, and the pilot, Charlie Cranwell. Would her grandmother have even told the story if she had been dating a John or a Simon? Did it matter? The story was probably pure fantasy anyway.

Tilly's Charlie arrived back in Ireland on Tuesday afternoon in plenty of time for the services. That's when she told him her grandmother's story of love, the bluebell woods and the necklace which she now wore.

"We have to find him!" her boyfriend insisted.

"The nurse on duty was sure that Gran was just hallucinating!" Tilly explained.

"Was this the same nurse who said that your grandmother was in fine health and was not going to die?"

"You have a point."

"Leave the tracking down of this guy to me. As soon as I establish that he's still alive, I'll fly you over to London and take you down to Epsom."

"He's not there any more. That was where the convalescent home was."

"Trust me, if he's alive I'll track him down."

The evening service and the funeral Mass were considerably harder on Tilly than she thought they would be. For the last number of years, she had seen Matilda as a bloody inconvenience, somebody she had to visit every second Sunday while James visited her the other Sundays. When she began to complain about this arrangement, her father had bribed her with her own apartment if she would continue to visit her grandmother. What kind of spoilt cow did that make her? Matilda was a kind old woman who was loyal and strong-willed enough to leave the man of her dreams, the love of her life, to stay with her husband, a man she barely knew. If Matilda had not been so strong, she would never have had Sheila and that would have meant no Tilly! God, the least she could have done was visit her every second Sunday! Now there would be no more Sunday visits, no more chances to talk about Charlie or Frank or whatever other realities or fantasies her grandmother chose to throw at her.

✦   ✦   ✦

As the weeks passed, Charlie made no more reference to tracking down Charlie Cranwell. Then one day in May he told her.

"He's alive."

"Who?"

"Your pilot."

"What?"

"I've found a man called Charlie Cranwell who was a Wing Commander in the Second World War. He lives in a lovely little town called Cobham."

"Where's that?"

"It's in Surrey, not far from Wimbledon—or Epsom, for that matter. Do you want me to take you there?"

"Oh, God, I don't know," Tilly replied.

"Look, at least you know he exists. He wasn't a figment of your grandmother's imagination."

"But what if the affair was?"

"OK, that could be the case, but there's only one way to find out." He hugged his girlfriend tenderly and continued gently, "But there is also that small matter of the promise you made her."

"I know, I know," Tilly conceded. "Perhaps I should write first."

"Perhaps."

Tilly was quite terrified at how quickly Charlie Cranwell replied. His writing was spidery and difficult to read but the message was quite clear: *"Come as soon as you can."*

She flew over to meet him the following weekend.

Tilly's Charlie was a rock of support. He drove her over to Cobham on the Saturday morning. But even with him by her side, Tilly was scared. What was she doing there? What if her grandmother had totally lost it and this guy was in fact married, or a priest, or God knew what?

Charlie rang the doorbell.

Presently a tall slender woman opened the door. "Yes?" she enquired, somewhat condescendingly.

"Hello, my name is Charlie Magill and this is Tilly Adams. She has an appointment to meet with Mr. Cranwell," Charlie explained confidently.

"Oh," the lady at the door seemed to know nothing of any such arrangement but her tone did soften. "In that case you had better come in." She guided Tilly and Charlie into the drawing room and gestured for them to sit down. "Can you wait here for a moment, please?"

"Sure." Charlie was a good deal more at ease than Tilly was.

Within a matter of minutes the lady came back. "Daddy says he was expecting you. Come this way." She turned on her heel and they followed.

Tilly looked desperately at her beau. "Daddy?" she mouthed at him manically.

"It's OK, don't lose it now," he said. "We've come this far." He squeezed her hand.

They followed the lady into a bright room at the back of the house and there, sitting in a large cane chair, was a little old man. He had a blanket wrapped around his legs (or was that leg?) and his back was hunched over slightly. His snow-white hair was swept back from his face in proud defiance of his receding hairline. As he looked at his visitors his eyes were bright, clear and spectacularly blue. He took his time to study Tilly and then he nodded sagely.

"At last," he sighed. "The Irish girls are back in town!"

In that moment she knew that every word her poor confused grandmother had told her was true. Every minute detail was accurate and honest. Here sat the great love of Matilda Dempsey's life. It was Tilly's proud and painful duty to inform Charlie Cranwell that Matilda was ready for their rendezvous.

"Forgive me if I don't get up," he excused himself and pointed to the wheelchair parked nearby. "I'm afraid I'm not strong enough for the crutches any more."

"I hope you don't mind us barging in like this," said Tilly hesitantly.

"Barging? Who's barging? I think it was very civil of you to write before visiting. Now tell me, what news of my beautiful Matilda?"

Tilly looked anxiously at the daughter she hadn't even been introduced to.

"Oh, don't worry about me," the woman laughed. "All our lives we've heard about Matilda Dempsey, Daddy's first love. Perhaps I should give you three some space." And she graciously withdrew.

Tilly took the necklace from around her neck and placed it in Charlie Cranwell's right hand. He closed his fingers around the little gold bluebell and with the other hand wiped away the tears that had begun to flow.

"If you have this in your possession, it can mean only one thing," he whispered. "She's ready for our rendezvous, isn't she?"

For the next two hours Tilly filled the Wing Commander in on her grandmother's life and he in turn told her about that wonderful spring in 1945. Tilly even mustered sufficient courage to tell him that her grandmother had been dishonest with him. She had loved *him* more than anything or anyone else in the world. Tilly explained that Matilda had lied to make him go. To her surprise and relief, the old man got a good laugh out of that. He said that he had always known that to be so.

"She made this big drama out of telling me that she didn't love me, but I knew she was fibbing," he chuckled and Tilly watched his eyes dance just as her grandmother had described. "Why else would she have agreed to meet up with me in heaven?" he added simply. "To say she didn't love me was a lot easier than to say she did."

He explained that his wife and his family had known about and accepted that he had once been truly and deeply in love with another woman—an Irish girl—who wouldn't have him. They joked about it in the family. They were, in fact, relieved, because if Matilda had taken up with him they would never have been born and so it was a good thing that she had such strong resolve and high moral values! Charlie Cranwell had three children and seven grandchildren. His youngest daughter was called Matilda.

When they were leaving Tilly promised that they would stay in touch but, in his honesty, Charlie smiled at her and said, "Of course, I won't be at this address for much longer—not now that Matilda is ready for me."

Tilly was weak as they walked back to her boyfriend's car. She felt utterly drained from all the tears and memories they had exchanged.

"Have I just sentenced a man to death?" she asked through her tears.

"On the contrary, I think you've just liberated him," Charlie replied. "Now come on, you've kept your promise to your gran. You've wiped the slate clean. Cheer up." He opened the car door for her but she made no effort to get in. She was still distracted.

"Cheer up? How can I cheer up after a meeting like that? Where will we go? What will we do?"

"I know exactly where we're going and I even have an idea of what we can do there." He looked at his girlfriend. "In truth, Tilly, there's something I want to tell you, but I think I should do it in a very specific place."

She looked up into her boyfriend's eyes. "Charlie, what are you talking about?" she asked, but she knew from his tone that it was going to be "something" nice. "Where are you taking me?" She snaked her arms in under his jacket and around his waist.

He smiled mischievously at her. "It's a lovely little place not far from here."

"What is it you want to tell me?"

He wrapped his arms around her shoulders and studied her face for a moment. Then he smiled and shook his head, "No, not here. I'm not saying it until we get there."

"Where?"

Charlie kissed her on the forehead and then on her earlobe. Then he whispered into her ear, "Let's go to the bluebell woods, Tilly."

Her face lit up at the suggestion.

Then he kissed her properly on the lips and smiled. "After all, the Irish girls are back in town!"

SUZANNE HIGGINS was a radio and TV presenter in Ireland for over a decade but she stopped to spend more time with her family. She lives with her husband and three daughters in south County Dublin. She is the author of two bestselling romantic novels: *The Power of a Woman* and *The Woman He Loves.*

How Emily Got Promoted

Sarah Webb

$\mathscr{E}$ mily tapped her nails against the wheel impatiently and scowled at the learner driver in the ancient dark blue Volkswagen Golf in front of her who was crawling along at just over 20 miles per hour.

"You're not even supposed to be driving on the motorway," she said out loud, feeling foolish as soon as the words had left her mouth since there was no one but her in the car. Hardly a motorway, she thought. The M55 was being dug up (again) for some hair-brained reason to do with drainage, leaving only one lane of traffic on either side of the road, framed by hundreds of orange traffic cones, a host of luminous-yellow-vested, bum-scratching workmen, JCBs and yet-to-be-laid steaming piles of crumbly, hot black tarmac.

The Golf stalled, stopping the traffic dead, and the cars and lorries snaking behind Emily began to beep their horns—short parps with some semblance of restraint at first, gradually getting longer and longer, until the young man behind her, a sales rep she had no doubt, decided to rest his hand on his air-enhanced horn (which played the theme tune from *The Simpsons*) for several seconds, blasting Emily out of it.

"Men!" She sighed in exasperation and indicated left. She'd had enough, she was damned if she was going to sit in this heinous traffic for a moment longer. There was a garage just ahead of her, she'd turn the car around and use the back roads to Kinbarr Village, the chi-chi County Wicklow village where Baroque Shoe Emporium and several exclusive clothes shops were located, and where her friend Cathy lived with her husband and two children. It might be almost twice the distance but at least the roads would be quieter and less stressful.

As she drove along the leafy back roads, her mobile rang. She grabbed it from the passenger seat, clicked it on and held it to her ear.

"Hello? Yes?" she demanded.

"Are you all right?" the voice on the other end asked. It was Anita, one of her oldest friends, an ex-journalist who now ran her own fashion PR company. "You sound a little stressed."

"Oh, sorry, Anita. I've just had one of those mornings. I was supposed to get shoes I borrowed for a shoot back to Baroque before twelve. And then I have to go to Cathy's house for some charity lunch thing."

"Emily, it's ten past one."

"Tell me about it. Listen, I need your help, do you have a second?"

"Sure, fire ahead. But should you be talking and driving simultaneously?" Anita asked with concern.

"Of course not," Emily tried not to snap. She didn't have time for this. "But I'm running so late . . ." She sighed deeply, hoping her friend would take pity on her and drop the subject. Anita was a stickler for the rules and talking on your mobile while driving had recently been made an offence in Ireland.

"What happened to that hands-free kit I bought you?" Anita continued unabashed.

Emily ignored her. It was still sitting in its packaging on her desk, buried somewhere under the magazines, newspaper clippings and general work detritus. "Anita, I promised Kitty three thousand words by the day after tomorrow for the July edition." Kitty was the editor of *Ruby* magazine, a strong, ambitious woman who, although three years younger than Emily, had clawed her way to the journalistic top and intended to stay there.

"On what?" asked Anita.

"That's the problem. I haven't a clue. She wants something glitzy and 'now,' maybe an interview with a designer, something about shoes, sex . . . oh, I don't know. I'm all out of ideas. That's why I need your help. Have you got anything for me?"

Anita thought for a moment. "How about an interview with Steve Bailey, he's over from London at the moment and his new collection is creating quite a stir."

"Did him in January."

"A feature on Bez Goggin's shoes? Barney's in New York have just started stocking them and—"

"Kitty interviewed her in March. And I did her for the *Irish Times* magazine a few weeks ago."

"Oh, yes, I'd forgotten about that. Um, the Fuchsia Pink Fashion Ball?"

"May."

"The new velour tracksuits from the Bebop range?"

"Nope. Done to death. And anyway I couldn't do a whole three thousand words on tracksuits. What is there to say?"

"Thongs?"

Emily wrinkled her nose. "Or on thongs."

"What about that glam celebrity chef—Hannah Wixton—

isn't she over this week promoting her new book?" Anita suggested, refusing to admit defeat. She wasn't in PR for nothing. "Lou Lou Brady represents the publishers; I could give you her number. She might be able to set something up. She owes me one—I helped her organize the Red Letter Ball for Crumlin Children's Hospital last autumn."

"Anita, you're a genius! Hannah would be perfect—give me Lou Lou's number and I'll ring her right now. Hang on, I need to pull in and grab a pen."

"You could key it straight into your mobile," Anita pointed out.

"I could, if I was mobile literate, but I'm not," Emily reminded her. "I haven't worked out how to do that yet without cutting you off. And anyway, I'm driving, remember?"

"I'll explain anyway," Anita began, "it's a useful skill to have. It's easy, you just—"

"Another time. Right now I have things to do and Lou Lous to ring."

Anita smiled as she clicked off her mobile. She hoped to goodness that Emily got the staff job at *Ruby.* It might make her friend a little less manic. Emily had been freelancing for three years now, ever since *Dublin Today,* the newspaper where she had been fashion editor, had gone belly-up. And freelancing was exhausting—no security—you were only as good as your last piece and you had to spend your life licking up to editors, in the hope that they would throw some decent work your way. She should know—she'd done it herself for long enough. Then again, maybe Emily would always be manic. In all the years they'd known each other, she'd barely even paused for breath. Emily's long-term boyfriend, Harry, was the most easy-going and patient man in the world and they made the perfect couple—his relaxed nature grounded Emily and gave her the stability she didn't have in her working life, and she gave him the spark and vitality that at times, to be frank, he lacked. They were a great couple—oddly well matched but it seemed to work. It was the type of relationship Anita herself aspired to—in a few years—no mad hurry. She had a PR empire to build up after all. She was currently enjoying a rather fun flirtation with a much younger male model called Freddy. In fact, she was meeting him this weekend for a drink (she'd asked him!) and who knows where that might lead.

Anita sat further back in her generously sized orange swivel chair, put her pen in her mouth and clicked it against her teeth. She supposed she should really do some work but she desperately needed some new knee-high boots to go with her leather skirt, so she could wear it on her date with Freddy. She'd worn her old boots so much that they were shot. She smiled—that was the joy of working for yourself—you could go shopping whenever it was quiet and catch up with work in the evening. She stood up and grabbed her brown suede handbag from the top of the desk. Brown Thomas, here I come. She skipped out of the office, swinging her bag and sweeping her sunglasses from the top of her head where they had been perched, onto her eyes.

"Lou Lou, it's Emily O'Brien, Anita's friend."

"Hi, Emily, how can I help you?" Lou Lou came straight to the point. Like Emily, she was a busy woman.

"I'd like to interview Hannah Wixton for the July issue of *Ruby.* Any slots free?"

"Plenty. But I should tell you, *Joy* are doing a feature on her for their July issue. Is that a problem?"

Shit, shit, shit, Emily thought. I should have got in there earlier. *Joy* was another Irish women's magazine, *Ruby*'s main rival. "Has Hannah already done the interview?" she asked Lou Lou.

"Yes, on Monday. With Valerie Powell. They're doing a three-page spread and they might use a photograph of her on the cover."

Emily held back her expletives. "That's a pity. But I'm afraid I can't do anything then. Anyone else around?"

Lou Lou thought for a second. "I probably shouldn't tell you this, but Rex O'Hara's new film is opening tomorrow tonight in the Savoy—"

"Is he in Dublin?" Emily asked excitedly. Rex was one of Ireland's biggest stars, a local boy made good in Hollywood and the darling of the media. He was polite, well mannered, a fantastic, classically trained actor and devastatingly good looking, a killer combination.

"Yes. I can't promise anything, his schedule is packed, but leave it with me. I'll get back to you within the hour, OK?"

"I really appreciate this, Lou Lou," Emily said. "Thanks."

"No problem. Talk to you later."

Emily clicked off her phone and breathed a sigh of relief. Rex O'Hara. If she could just pull this one off then the staff job would be in the bag. What Anita didn't know was that Harry had suggested buying a house together in the autumn, and Emily knew that banks didn't look too kindly on freelancers. Hence her interest in the staff job. Emily loved Harry to bits and living with him would make everything just perfect. At the moment he spent most nights in her apartment in Donnybrook, but it wasn't the same. What she really craved was a little house near the sea, in Shankhill or Bray maybe. She'd had enough of town living, it was time to go suburban. She wanted to spend more time with him, in a place they both owned. Harry, a primary school teacher, wanted to buy an old place and do it up—he was a dab hand with a power drill and was itching to get stuck into a project. She had no interest in DIY but was looking forward to putting her eclectic stamp on the interior—mixing functional new pieces from Ikea and Arnotts with some inherited antiques. And she couldn't wait to hit the stately home auctions—she'd covered one for a travel magazine recently and it had proved to be a fascinating day out. She'd even bought an old oil painting—for the ornate gold frame—and had had it transformed into a stunning mirror. All she needed now was the fireplace to put it over.

She checked in her rear-view mirror and moved away from the side of the road. She was *so* late for Cathy's lunch thing. But she'd promised to make an appearance so she'd better get moving. Luckily she was only ten minutes away from Kinbarr Woods, the housing estate where Cathy lived. She'd drop the shoes into Baroque in Kinbarr Village and be at Cathy's a few minutes later. Perfect.

It was always a struggle keeping in contact with Cathy as she lived such a different lifestyle to her own. Cathy had got married at twenty-five to Arthur Ryan, a highly respected fine art auctioneer twelve years her senior—the wedding had been a sumptuous affair in a marquee in the in-laws' huge back garden, with all the trimmings. Cathy had completed a year at beauty college before taking a typing course and landing a good, steady job as a receptionist at an auction house, where she'd met Arthur. She'd left her last and final job (as Arthur's PA) as soon as she was married and dutifully produced children in quick succession—two blond-haired dotes called Arthur (after his father, of course, although Emily found it rather confusing) and Annabelle. It didn't help that Anita and Cathy just didn't get on—Anita found Cathy exasperatingly smug and Cathy couldn't understand Anita's reluctance to find a husband and settle down. The three women did occasionally meet for lunch but Emily always ended up keeping the peace, which she found exhausting.

Emily dropped the shoe boxes into Baroque without a hitch, finding a parking slot just outside the shop, and pulled up out-

side Cathy's house at bang on twenty past one. The road outside
the house was littered with four-wheel drives and large people
carriers, all with the obligatory car seats fitted and the bright
pink and light blue "baby on board" stickers. Emily always wondered what exactly these stickers meant—beware, driver likely to
swerve at any moment? Or maybe, beware, driver likely to ask
you extremely personal questions like (a) when are you getting
married, (b) when are you thinking of starting a family or (c) isn't
it a shame you're still single and would you like to meet Cousin
Fred, he has a bit of a BO problem, but sure, isn't he available
and beggars can't be choosers? Emily parked behind a spanking
new black Range Rover jeep, with not a speck of mud on it,
grabbed the bottle of wine from the floor on the passenger side,
where it had been rolling around, but luckily hadn't broken, and
locked her car. As she walked towards Cathy's house she heard
shrieks from the front garden and watched as Arthur junior
soaked two larger boys with the garden hose. She smiled. Good
old Arthur, always in trouble. The boys were dressed in white
linen shorts and carefully pressed matching light blue shirts, and
Emily just knew that their mother wouldn't be too amused at her
little darlings' soaked apparel. Arthur, as usual, was butt naked.
At four, he was a little old to be constantly naked, and Cathy
hated it, she spent her days running after him, cajoling him to at
least put some shorts on. But Arthur was a stubborn little fellow
and always ripped his clothes off at every opportunity. Only in
his father's presence was he ever fully clothed.

"Hi, Arthur." Emily grinned. "How are things?"

Arthur looked at Emily, at the hose and then back at Emily.

"Don't even think about it," Emily threatened. "I have something for you in my bag but don't tell your mum, OK?"

Arthur nodded eagerly, dropped the hose at his feet and ran
towards her, his blond hair splattering water all over the path.

"Hi, Emily," he said, giving her a wide, toothy grin. He immediately stared at her bag.

Emily laughed. "Expecting something to eat?" she asked.

He nodded again. Emily, his godmother, always brought him a treat when she visited. Cathy always gave out to her for it— Arthur was only allowed sweets on Saturdays, and even then he had to wash his teeth carefully afterwards, taking most of the fun out of the consumption.

Emily dug her hand into her red leather bag and pulled out a packet of Starburst, Arthur's favourite. "Here you go." She handed them over and smiled at his obvious delight.

"Thanks, Emily." He threw his arms around her thighs and gave her an almighty hug.

"You're welcome, pet." She extracted her legs and looked towards the front door. There on the front doorstep was Cathy, her arms folded in front of her chest, with a serious expression on her face.

"Uh-oh," Emily murmured. "Caught in the act. I'll see you later, young man." She ruffled Arthur's damp hair and patted him gently on the bottom. "Off you go."

He toddled off happily towards the paddling pool, his mouth jammed full of fruity flavour.

"Hi, Cathy," Emily said a little too brightly. She leaned over and kissed her friend on the cheek, then thrust the bottle of wine into her hands. Cathy looked tired—there were faint purple shadows under her eyes and her skin was pale, but Emily thought it better not to say anything.

"Thanks," Cathy murmured. "But I've asked you before not to give Arthur sweets. It ruins his routine."

"Sorry," Emily said, not in the least bit contrite. "I'll try to remember next time. Now where's the food, I'm starving?"

Cathy stood back and allowed her friend to walk inside. As

soon as Emily entered the hall she was hit with the dulcet screams of a baby coming from the living room.

"Who's strangling the cat?" she asked.

Cathy glared at her. "Simon O'Kelly's teething. It's hardly his fault, poor lamb."

"I suppose not," Emily said. Cathy seemed to be in a right old mood—it was better to humour her. "The hall looks lovely, I like the cream. Very classy."

"The painter left only yesterday," said Cathy. "Do you really like it? I'm not sure. It's very plain, isn't it?"

"I really do," Emily reassured her. "It just needs a couple of pictures to brighten it up, then it'll be perfect."

Cathy smiled at her gratefully. "You're right. That's just what it needs."

Just then two toddlers dashed past them, arms akimbo. Emily curved her body backwards to avoid their flailing limbs. "More kids." She laughed. "Oops, forgot to bring mine."

Cathy went quiet for a moment. She had a peculiar expression on her face. Emily couldn't quite read it.

"Cathy?" she asked. "Are you OK?"

"I forgot to tell you."

"Tell me what?"

"It's a Tiny Tots lunch."

"A what?" Emily asked in confusion.

"You know—the mothers and babies club I'm in."

Emily stared at her. "You mean everyone here has a baby with them?"

Cathy nodded. "Or a toddler."

"What were you thinking?" Emily demanded. "You practically begged me to come along."

"I know, but I really want to talk to you about something and you're always so busy at the weekends." She began to play nervously with the ends of her hair. "We have such different lives these days and it's so hard with two kids and everything and . . ."

Emily put her arm around Cathy's shoulders. Her friend was obviously upset about something. "Not to worry, Cathy," she said soothingly. "I'll stay for a little bit and we can talk."

Cathy smiled at her gratefully again. "Thanks, I really appreciate it. Maybe you'll even enjoy it."

"Maybe." Emily attempted a smile. She'd met some of Cathy's Tiny Tots friends before and they weren't exactly overawed by her childless state. In fact some of them had been positively hostile towards her when she'd explained that her career came first at the moment and that she had no intention of breeding quite yet, thanks very much. She was not yet thirty after all, there was no rush.

"Come into the kitchen and get something to eat," said Cathy.

Emily didn't have to be asked twice.

Once in the kitchen, Cathy handed her a large dark blue pottery plate.

"These are nice," Emily said, tapping the plate with her finger, making a hollow ping. "New?"

Cathy nodded. "Yes, they're from the Avoca shop. Do you really like them?"

"Sure. They're a great colour."

"Do you honestly like them or are you just being kind?"

Emily looked at her friend. "Cathy, they're just plates."

Cathy blushed. "Sorry, yes, I know. Help yourself to salads and bread." She pointed at the table which was groaning with plates and bowls full of delicious-looking food. "And there's homemade pizza slices and quiche over there on the sideboard. And pavlova for dessert."

Emily whistled. "You've gone to a lot of trouble." She

began to heap some potato salad onto her plate. Maybe this lunch wasn't going to be so bad after all—at least she'd get well fed.

"Hello, Emily." A tall woman dressed in a white linen top and matching skirt glided towards them. Her long black hair was heaped elegantly onto the top of her head, a few choice wispy tendrils escaping to frame her perfectly oval pale face.

"Hi, Lavinia," Emily said evenly. Of all Cathy's friends she found Lavinia the most painful. The three women had been in the same class in school, but Cathy and Lavinia had only become pally since they'd met again in Tiny Tots.

"How's work?" Lavinia wrinkled her nose as she said work, as if the word alone was distasteful.

"Fine, thanks," Emily replied. "And how are the twins?"

"Very well, thank you. Milo's just started Suzuki violin and Eliza is taking ballet and Greek dancing. Good to expand their cultural sides, don't you think?"

"Quite." As the twins were only just four Emily thought Lavinia was clearly throwing her money away, but who was she to judge? After all, Lavinia had married rich—to Cormac O'Hare, a property developer twenty years her senior.

Emily wasn't exactly sure what to say next, so she said nothing. Lavinia immediately filled the conversational vacuum.

"And what are you working on at the moment? Still freelancing in the fashion world? Or have you managed to move on yet?" Lavinia gave Emily a sickly smile. "Must be annoying being stuck in a rut like that."

"Still in fashion," Emily said, refusing to be goaded. "I spent all morning shooting flat packs of shoes. Nothing terribly glamorous. All the latest ranges for autumn from Italy, France, the US . . . boring really."

Lavinia raised her eyebrows. Profound snob she might be, but she did have rather a well-developed shoe fetish. "Really?" she asked, her interest piqued.

"But you wouldn't be interested in something as rutty as shoes, now would you, Lavinia? The Emma Hopes and Bez Goggins of this world are so frightfully boring, darling." With that Emily turned towards Cathy who was listening to the two women's conversation open-mouthed. "Now, Cathy, you had something to ask me?" Emily asked pointedly.

Cathy thought for a moment. "Um, yes, um it was about a dinner I have to attend. I wanted some advice on what to wear."

"I'll see you later, Cathy." Lavinia swept out of the patio doors into the garden.

"Did you have to wind up Lavinia like that?" Cathy asked Emily.

"Lavinia!" Emily snorted. "She was plain old Lucy when we were all in St. John's together. And what right does she have to question my career? Stupid cow."

"Don't let it get to you. She's just jealous. She'd love your job, you know. I think she's a little bored to tell the truth."

"It can't be easy with a nanny *and* an au pair *and* a housekeeper," Emily said scathingly.

"Don't be so sarcastic, it doesn't suit you," Cathy scolded.

"Sorry, I'm just tired. It's been one hell of a week."

"And why were you putting furniture together?" Cathy asked.

"Sorry?"

"Flat packs."

Emily laughed. "Not those kind of flat packs. It's what we call photos of shoes or clothes taken against a white background."

"Oh, I see. But how—"

"Cathy, have you got a cloth? Joe has had a little accident, I'm afraid." A large, pink-faced woman stood in front of Cathy, interrupting their conversation.

"That's OK, Jen," Cathy assured her. "It's nothing to worry about. Boys are like that."

"Potty training," the woman mouthed to Emily, who really didn't want to know.

A few minutes later Emily's mobile rang and she excused herself and moved into the hall to answer it.

"Emily, bad news I'm afraid," Lou Lou said on the other end of the phone.

"Oh?" Emily asked.

"Rex is completely booked up for the whole day and night. And he's not doing any interviews tomorrow as he's spending the day with his family. Sorry. I gave it my best shot."

"Not to worry, thanks for trying."

"Not at all. Talk to you soon. Must dash. *Ciao.*"

Emily clicked off her mobile. What the hell am I going to do now? she thought.

Emily ran her spoon around the bowl, picking up the remnants of her pavlova.

"Hi, I'm Polly," the dark-haired woman sitting beside her on the sofa volunteered. "And that's Molly." She gestured at the blonde-haired girl who was playing with a Barbie on the floor in front of them. "She's nearly four."

Polly and Molly? Emily looked at the woman's face for any trace of irony, but found none.

"Hi, I'm Emily. I'm a friend of Cathy's."

"And which is yours?" Polly asked.

"Excuse me?"

"Child? Which one is yours?"

"I don't actually have any children," Emily said evenly.

"Really?" Polly said, raising her eyebrows. So what are you doing here? her expression read.

"I just came to see Cathy," Emily explained. "I'm not in Tiny Tots, of course . . ." she tailed off, not knowing quite what to say.

Molly stood up, ran over to her mother and climbed onto her knee. "I'm hungry, Mummy," she said.

Polly smiled and stroked her head. The child nuzzled into her chest and Polly lifted her sweatshirt and put her onto her left breast.

"Doesn't she have teeth?" Emily asked before she could stop herself.

Polly smiled at her indulgently. "Yes, but she doesn't bite. She puts her lips over them, see?"

Emily didn't really want to look, but thought it rude not to. "Ah, yes. Well, I'll leave you to it." She jumped up and made her way back into the kitchen.

"Are you all right?" Cathy asked her. "You look a little flustered."

"There's a woman in the living room breastfeeding a four-year-old."

Cathy shrugged her shoulders. "Some mothers continue that long all right."

"That can't be right," Emily stated.

"Shush, keep your voice down," Cathy warned her, looking around.

"I shouldn't have stayed," Emily said. "I'm sick of being asked where my children are. I haven't had a normal conversation yet."

"What's normal?" Cathy asked with a smile. "It's just different, that's all. Not what you're used to."

"Maybe."

"Anyway, you can't go yet; I haven't had a chance to talk to you properly. Please stay."

Emily glanced at her watch. "OK. I'll stay for half an hour. But that's it."

"Great. I'll introduce you to Pamela. You'll like her. She's very normal. She's keeping an eye on Annabelle for me."

Pamela was sitting outside with some of the other mothers, including the dreaded Lavinia, who looked up, caught Emily's eye and immediately looked away again.

"Pamela, this is Emily. We're old friends."

"Hey, less of the old," Emily laughed.

"Nice to meet you, Emily." Pamela smiled up at her, shielding her eyes from the hazy sun. She was dandling a very contented Annabelle on her knee. "And you know little Annabelle."

"Of course. And which are your children?"

Pamela waved her hand at the back of the garden where several youngsters were playing on the wooden climbing frame and slide. "Dan and Sally are over there somewhere, but let's not talk about them. Emily's told me about your job, it sounds fascinating. Sit down and tell me all about it. I'm so deprived of adult conversation these days. I used to be a journalist for one of the dailies and I really miss it."

Emily was only too delighted to do so and began to tell Pamela about *Ruby* magazine and some of the recent fashion pieces she'd written or styled.

"I'll be back in a moment," Cathy said, delighted that the two of them seemed to be hitting it off.

"Two journalists in one garden," Lavinia called over from the garden chair where she was sitting. "That must be a first for Tiny Tots."

"What would you call a group of journalists?" the small, fine-boned woman beside her asked. It was Lavinia's "bestest friend," Millie, also a St. John's old girl. They'd been painful in school, and if you asked Emily they were still painful.

"A gaggle?" Lavinia suggested.

"I'll think you'll find that's geese," Pamela said mildly.

"How about a gossip of journalists?" Emily suggested.

"Oh, very clever, Emily." Lavinia smiled, the smile stopping at her lips and never reaching her eyes. "How about a scum of journalists?"

Pamela looked at Emily and back at Lavinia. "And what about us mums? A comfort of mums?"

"Oh, but we're not all mothers here, are we?" Lavinia pointed out.

"Do you have a problem with that?" Emily asked sharply.

Pamela put her hand on Emily's. "I think you're very lucky, personally. I'd love to have some of my own time back. And a job. I never thought I'd say it, but I miss working."

"I certainly don't," Millie sniffed. "Highly overrated, work."

"Surely not," Pamela said. "And besides, looking after children is work. It's much harder than my job ever was."

Lavinia and Millie said nothing. Both had more staff than was strictly necessary.

"How's Daisy's lovely boyfriend, Millie?" Pamela asked, anxious to diffuse the situation. "He's doing really well for himself these days. I loved *Bright Water,* he was brilliant in it."

"Rex is fine," Millie replied smugly. "Very busy, of course, with the new film. The premiere is tomorrow night and he's up to ninety with interviews and photo calls. We haven't seen much of him or Daisy this trip."

"You know Rex O'Hara?" Emily asked in amazement.

"Yes," Millie smiled condescendingly at her. "Didn't you know? He's going out with my sister, Daisy."

"No. I had no idea."

"They've been together for three years now but they keep their personal lives to themselves. The whole Hollywood thing can be unbearably tedious otherwise—everyone knowing your business."

"I suppose so. Where did she meet him? Have they been together long?"

Millie sighed. "But let's not talk about him, *très* boring, don't you think?"

"Not at all," Emily insisted. "In fact I was hoping to interview him for *Ruby.* Maybe you could ask him for me. It wouldn't take long—just some questions and a quick photo. I'd be really grateful. I asked his publicist but I left it too late."

Millie stared at her. "Let's just forget you said that, shall we, dear?"

"So crass," Lavinia added. "Really, Emily. Have you no manners?"

"I don't really see what the problem is," Emily said. "I just asked—"

"Let's just drop it," Lavinia interjected. "Better that way. So Pamela, how's the pregnancy coming along? Any morning sickness?"

Emily was mortified. Maybe she shouldn't have asked for Millie's help, but this was Dublin for goodness sake, not Hollywood, people helped each other over here. And it was the media that had made Rex O'Hara the superstar that he was today.

Emily tried not to think about Lavinia's put-down and studied Pamela's stomach. It was certainly gently rounded but she honestly hadn't noticed.

"No, thank goodness," Pamela replied. "I'm feeling great."

"How pregnant are you?" Emily asked. She thought she should try to show some interest.

"Nearly six months."

"Wow, you look great, so slim."

"That's not always a good thing, Emily," Lavinia said thoughtlessly. "It can mean that the baby isn't developing properly."

"But in this case, it's fine, Lavinia," Pamela said pointedly. "The baby is very healthy, thank you very much."

"I didn't for a moment mean to suggest—"

"I'm sure you didn't," Pamela interrupted. "You'd never do anything like that, would you, Lavinia?"

"Um, what's Rex's new film about, Millie?" Emily gabbled, clutching at straws. Cathy would be upset if she came out to find them all bickering. "Have you seen it yet? Is it good?"

"Is this on the record?"

"Of course not, I was just wondering."

"I don't think I can divulge anything about *Land's End*," Millie said sniffily. "Just in case. You'll have to see it at the cinema like everyone else."

"Right," Emily said, tight-lipped. She'd had enough of trying to keep the peace and being "nice." Lavinia and Millie deserved to be horsewhipped. "Um, so Pamela, did I tell you about my new Bez Goggin boots? I interviewed her last week. Lovely woman, not a bit pretentious. She gave me a pair of fab red boots to say thank you for the plugs I've been giving her in the press." She knew it was petty but she didn't care.

"So how are you all getting on?" Cathy asked as she walked back into the garden.

"Oh, just swimmingly," Emily lied. "Aren't we, girls?"

An hour later, Emily was sitting on the bed in Cathy's room. She'd tried to leave the lunch party several times already but Cathy was having none of it until they'd managed to speak.

"So, what's up?" Emily asked. "What's this dinner you're going to?"

Cathy sighed deeply. "That was just to shut Lavinia up. There's no dinner." She looked down at her hands which were clasped on her lap. "Emily, I'm bored out of my tree," she admitted finally. "I love Arthur and Annabelle to bits but I'm going nuts. I spend my time looking for things to do and I'm sick to the teeth of shopping and bloody Tiny Tots. I feel like I'm losing my personality. I need your help."

"Right." Emily was taken aback. She hadn't expected this.

"I want to retrain as a baby masseuse. Do you think I'm crazy?"

"Is there such a thing?"

Cathy nodded eagerly. "I loved massage in beauty college; I was pretty good at it too. I used to practise on you, remember?"

Emily had a vague recollection of having her back rolled and pummelled by an over-eager Cathy many years ago. "Yes, I think so."

"There's a course in Rathmines, three evenings a week for six months, and then you can start your own classes. There's a huge demand for baby massage, apparently. I've talked to three different health nurses and my GP and they are all really positive about the effects on a crying baby and . . ." Cathy bubbled on about the benefits of baby massage while Emily tried to look interested. Cathy hadn't been this animated about anything for a long time, not since the first charity ball she'd organized in the RDS.

"Sounds fascinating," Emily interrupted her. "But what does Arthur think?"

"He loves being massaged and he thinks Mummy should . . ."

"Arthur senior, your husband," Emily said.

Cathy blushed. "I haven't actually told him yet. But he might not be too keen on the whole idea. He wants to have another baby."

"Does he now?" Emily raised her eyebrows. "That would certainly be a miracle of modern science."

"You know what I mean." Cathy sighed. "I just want to do

something for myself, Emily. Earn my own money. Spend some time on my own again. I might like to have another baby sometime in the future, but not right now. At the moment I feel like I'm just Arthur's wife and the kids' mother. I want to be me."

"Toyah Wilcox," Emily said, "remember her?"

"With the orange hair?"

"Correct." Emily sang a few bars of the song.

Cathy winced. "Never could sing, could you?"

Emily elbowed her. "Thanks. So what are you going to do about the baby massage? Are you going to take the course?"

Cathy shrugged. "I'm not sure. What do you think?"

"Talk to Arthur. Explain how you feel. He's a reasonable man and he adores you. He might surprise you."

"When exactly?" Cathy asked. "He's always working. I'm in bed before he comes in most evenings and the weekends are spent doing boring house things."

"Why don't you go away for a weekend together without the kids?"

"I wish." Cathy sighed again. "Who'd mind them? Mum can't cope with them for more than a few hours and Arthur's parents are up north."

Emily thought for a moment. "I'll do it," she suggested. "I'll move into the house for the weekend and look after them. How about next weekend? No time like the present and all that."

"I can't ask you to do that," Cathy protested. "You have things to do. And what about Harry?"

"If it's OK by you, he could stay here too. He gets on great with the kids and we'd both enjoy a weekend in the country."

"Hardly the country," Cathy snorted.

"It is to us." Emily smiled. "Compared to Donnybrook, it's the sticks."

"Are you serious about next weekend?" Cathy asked. "Because I could book somewhere and surprise Arthur. He's not as busy as usual at the moment and if I found somewhere with a spa and a good restaurant I know he'd be delighted. He's not usually a man for surprises, but a weekend in a hotel without the kids"—Cathy grinned—"now that would be the best surprise he's had in a long time."

"Go ahead and book," Emily said. "I'll check with Harry, but I'm sure he won't mind one little bit."

Cathy threw her arms around Emily and gave her an almighty hug. "I can't thank you enough."

"It's only one weekend." Emily smiled. She was delighted to be able to help and in a funny way she was quite looking forward to it.

After Cathy had gone back downstairs, Emily was waiting in the upstairs hall to use the toilet when she heard light footsteps coming up the stairs. It was Lavinia's little girl, Eliza.

"Are you all right, Eliza?" Emily asked kindly. "Looking for your mummy?"

Eliza looked up at her with her cornflower-blue eyes. She was a startlingly attractive child. "She's in there with Millie," Eliza said, pointing at the door of Annabelle's bedroom. "She said not to go in." Eliza was jigging up and down and clutching her white muslin dress in front of her stomach.

"Do you need to use the toilet?"

Eliza nodded.

Just then the toilet door opened. Pamela bustled out. "Sorry, guys. It's all yours."

"Thanks. Eliza, do you need any help?" Eliza ran past them and closed the door behind her with a slam.

"Obviously not," Pamela laughed. "See you downstairs. And

don't let Millie and Lavinia get to you. They can be terribly catty at times, just ignore them."

"I will. Thanks."

As Pamela walked down the stairs, Emily wondered what Millie and Lavinia were doing in Annabelle's bedroom. It was a little strange. Curiosity got the better of her and she tiptoed towards the door, put her ear against it and strained to listen. Nothing. If they weren't talking what were they doing? Maybe Eliza had got it wrong and they were actually downstairs or in the garden.

Eliza opened the bathroom door and stared at Emily, who had jumped back from the door where she'd been eavesdropping. "Can I go in there?" Eliza asked. "I'm bored. There's no nice toys in this house, only baby toys. I want my Barbies. And the food is yuck."

"I don't see why not," Emily said and smiled encouragingly at the rude little girl. "Go ahead."

Eliza pulled on the door handle and pushed the door wide open.

Emily couldn't believe her eyes. Lavinia and Millie were entwined in a passionate embrace, lips locked together.

"Mummy," Eliza said, running towards her.

Millie and Lavinia jumped apart, Millie's pale face blushing furiously and Lavinia looking equally flustered.

"Um, what are you doing in here, Eliza?" Lavinia demanded. "I told you to stay downstairs. Mummy's busy."

"Why were you kissing Millie, Mummy?" Eliza asked nonplussed.

"I was just making her better," Lavinia said quickly. "Now go back downstairs and I'll be down in a minute, OK?"

"Can I have some crisps?" Eliza asked shrewdly. "There are crisps on the grown-ups' table. And biscuits."

"Have whatever you like," Lavinia said. "Just go downstairs."

Eliza ran off happily.

Emily stood looking at the two women, a smile playing on her lips. "Well, well," she said finally. "Who would have thought?"

"You won't tell anyone?" Millie asked anxiously. "It was only a silly little experiment. Nothing serious."

Lavinia glared at Millie.

"Well, it was, wasn't it?" Millie asked. Lavinia stormed past them both and down the stairs.

"Looks like you've upset your girlfriend," Emily said, trying to suppress a gleeful giggle.

"Don't call her that," Millie insisted. "Please don't say anything to anyone, Emily. Please?"

Emily thought for a moment. "I might, then again I might not. It depends."

"Please," Millie begged again. "I'll do anything. Please . . ."

"Anita, you'll never guess what happened at Cathy's lunch," Emily said that evening. She sat back in the sofa and wound the telephone wire around her fingers.

"What? Did her brand new Designer's Guild curtains fall down? Or did one of her Louise Kennedy glasses break?"

"Anita!"

"Sorry, I shouldn't be so catty. She's just so perfect, it makes me spit."

"Actually, Cathy's about to start a baby massage course. She's bored at home, she wants to do something for herself. She's going to take a course in town and then set up her own class for mothers in the Wicklow area. To be honest, I think she needs to get some of her old self-confidence back. I think she feels a little faceless at the moment."

"Really? She always seemed very happy with her lot to me."

"Appearances can be deceptive," Emily said. "Money isn't everything, you know."

"I suppose not. Listen, tell Cathy I hope her course goes well and if she needs any help later on with publicizing her class . . ."

"Do you really mean that?"

"Sure. Why not? She's your friend, after all, so she can't be all bad. I didn't realize she was unhappy. It just goes to show—you never know what goes on behind closed doors."

"You have a good heart, Anita." Emily smiled. She was lucky to have them both as friends. And maybe Cathy and Anita would finally start to get along. Stranger things had happened and it would certainly make her life a whole lot easier. "Speaking of closed doors," Emily said, "wait till I tell you. But you have to promise to keep it a secret, OK?"

"Sounds interesting."

"Interesting is an understatement, Anita. It's dynamite!"

Kitty looked up at Emily over her trendy red half-moon glasses. "Emily, we'd like to offer you the staff job at *Ruby* if you're interested. You have a good solid CV and you're not afraid to go after the big stories. We were most impressed with the Rex O'Hara interview," she added. "Most impressed. How did you wangle that? He gave only one other interview to the Irish press and that was to *The Irish Times.*"

"Contacts," Emily said smiling, not giving anything away. She said nothing about the spoilt little girl called Eliza.

_____

SARAH WEBB is the bestselling author of *Always the Bridesmaid, Something to Talk About, Three Times a Lady,* and *Some Kind of Wonderful.* She also works as a children's book consultant, appears regularly on Irish television's *The Den,* and has written four children's books. She has recently completed her fifth adult novel, *It Had to Be You.*

Sarah lives in south County Dublin with her partner and young family.

The Wake

Una Brankin

Pearl Lovett gave me seventy-nine, let's say, interestin, years on earth. She fed me sometimes. Indulged me, even. But most of the time, I went hungry. She never realized it. They rarely do, that old Irish breed, even those who will gather soon, to pray for my happy repose.

I will stay with her 'til she's safely in the clay. For the time bein, it's pretty in here. I like the candlelight, and the hush, and the lanky white lilies they've arranged on the walnut dresser. That sweet zingy aroma makes a pleasin change from Pearl's John Players, and the soft flickerin light fairly takes the macabre look off that waxy face of hers. If truth be told, Pearl looks a hell of a lot better dead than she did dyin, and that's in spite of the ghastly Frosted Pink on her clamped-up mouth, and that peculiar fever-spot rouge on her hollow cheeks. Winnie did her best to fix the ludicrous bouffant the undertaker'd fashioned out of Pearl's sparse nicotine-tipped waves, but in the end she just couldn't bring herself to touch her sister's dead face. She'd never laid an affectionate hand on her in her whole life, you see, bein of that old buttoned-up generation who reserve their lovin for infants and dogs.

Pearl was the same, Batty too. He's the only brother, and a right starchy one. He and Winnie have yet to shed a tear between them. Winnie always said she'd only ever cry if she meant it, on account of the immoderate yappin done by their mother on the last day of every month, when the rent had to be paid. She'd have the money all right; she just wept at the partin of it, and as children Pearl and Winnie would look up at her on rent day and cry too, without really knowin why, the result bein a lifelong pecuniary anxiety of the most pointless kind. Mark my words, girls, there's nothing worse for the complexion.

No doubt Pearl would've seen those shop-bought lilies as an extravagance when there's an explosion of tea roses and hydrangeas in her garden, and I can picture her wincin at the sight of Winnie pullin out the new towels and best linens she'd been hoardin for years on the top shelf of the hot press. Pearl was always one for keepin things good, like she was constantly preparin for life instead of livin it, and she'd never, ever, throw anythin out. "Just in case," she'd say. There are blouses hangin in that woman's wardrobe since 1978, and three slices of tongue and two lamb chops moulderin in the fridge this past fortnight. Well, there were 'til Winnie crammed in two dozen butterfly buns and fairy cakes, and hunks of ham and roast meat for the sandwiches. She was in a notion of liftin that faded Persian runner from the hall a while ago but the thought of the incipient traffic on the carpet decided her against. She insisted, however, on changin the wintry drapes in here and replacin them with lengths of sheer white muslin that jiggle in the warm breeze all day long and diffuse the brilliance of that glorious high-summer sunshine Pearl's missin.

As I recall, she came into the world on a day just like this, back in '25. Accordin to Pearl, though, life didn't really begin until World War Two. Up until then she was a sickly little scrap, always wheezin and runnin low on blood. Poor thing had to lie in bed when the rest of them were out jumpin ditches and playin conkers, her small buttermilky face stuck in an adventure story or a dirty-rat crime thriller from the council library van. She graduated in her teens onto those coy hate-turns-to-passion romances, and never, ever, to my eternal consternation, did she tire of that creaky formula. Man, but I loathed those pussyfootin yarns, yet I do recall the odd glimmer of literary hope for Pearl, such as the week of her eighteenth birthday, when the postman delivered a first edition of *The Great Gatsby* air mail direct from Boston, Massachusetts, if you don't mind.

This fellow has a bit of Irish in him, on his mother's side, Aunt Cissy wrote patriotically of the author on her noisy blue American pull-out envelope. *He wrote this story the year you were born and now they're saying it's the Great American novel. Watch out for him, Pearl. He'll be famous over there some day too.*

Young Pearl devoured the book in three nights and waited for the rest of the world to catch on to Cissy's great Irish hope. When nobody did at first, she put it down to the story's misleadin title, and its rather shallow connotations. Giddy flappers and exceedin'ly long cigarette holders—that sort of thing.

By the time Gatsby made it to the Guild Hall library, Pearl had become the talk of the county for keepin a light on during the Black Out, Edith Piaf had the world at her tiny feet and the Jews had found their homeland.

But back to the war, for just a second. You see, international hostilities left Pearl with a guilt complex and a minor weight problem. Her mother never did forgive her for the ignominy of being publicly fined for that left-on light, never mind for puttin the country in peril for the sake of findin out what happened to Lady Chatterley's lover. Pearl never dreamed that the Luftwaffe could've spotted the faint halo of light from her pink-tassled bed-side lamp as she read hungrily into the night. Well, *they* didn't, but conscientious Mrs. McCoobrey from the house across the meadows did.

As for getting fat at thirty, Pearl blamed the war. "It was the rationing: I never wanted to feel that hungry ever again," she would chime to anyone who would listen, as she slapped a wedge of butter and a splat of jam onto a whole soda farl. This would be after a dinner of meat and vegetables and half a dozen decent-sized potatoes, by the way. At least half a dozen. Hard to believe she'd ever had an extra pick on her, to look at her now, wasted away in that frilly box Batty said cost the price of a second-hand car. He had to order a deep-fill one because bone erosion has made an arc of poor Pearl's back.

Like his older sister, Batty is fine featured and frugally minded; I can tell you now that in one week's time he will pay only for the fresh new insertion on the family headstone to announce Pearl's entombment therein. He will leave faded and forgotten the names of his long-departed father and mother, along with the detailin of their births and deaths, above Pearl's glitterin gold letterin, and his survivin sister will stand and seethe by the two-tone absurdity at the month's mind.

Mind you, Pearl might have approved of the economizin. The only thing she never skimped on in her fat days was her feedin. I could have told her that the emptiness she was tryin to fill wasn't in her stomach, if she ever got herself onto my wave-length, that is. But to tune in to my frequency requires silence and solitude, and those were the radio days, and Glenn Miller was at the top of the hit parade, and suddenly the wireless was at the very epicentre of Pearl's universe.

Sometimes she'd listen to jazz and blues on that old two-band. What a lightenin for my load it was when Ella or Billie or Baisie or Nat King Cole came over the airwaves. Pearl would close her goosey blue eyes and those tender black voices would utterly subsume her and she'd clean forget she worked in a cannin factory for minimum wage and barely two weeks holiday a year.

Truth is, deep down the real Pearl was a free spirit with an enquirin mind, but that spirit never got to fly. Like the rest of you, she had that basic human need to fit in, and that meant bowin to your man-made conventions and keepin me at arm's length. The closest we ever got was in those unselfconscious moments when she closed her eyes to the world and sang along to the blues in her sweet high voice, shrill though it may have sounded to your ear. Or when she flew along the empty back roads on her bicycle with the wind in her hair, or when she dabbled in watercolourin and lost herself for hours in her amateur seascapes, or when she put wild mushrooms from down the meadow into a lamb casserole and sat up all night hallucinatin.

But, at the end of the day, a closed mind will brook no bendin. Save for those near misses, I was always kept on the outer edges, and she'd lose me completely in those long deadenin hours on the factory floor. I suppose the girl just switched off. Couldn't blame her for that. There were no other jobs for those of her persuasion and scant schoolin back in those days, brains or no brains. As for all those endless nights in front of the goggle box, now that's an entirely different matter. All that viewin was mighty hard to take. I damn near faded away, not that Miss Pearl would have noticed. Enchanted, she was, from the moment Batty brought the second-hand 20-inch deluxe model into the house. Those patronizin promotions with their nerve rattlin jingles have to be the worst assault on the senses I've ever witnessed in my time on earth. And the variety shows? Excrement, I think the word is.

It was different when she went to the picture house. Oh, I had to sit through some baloney there too, but every now and again there'd be a treat, usually starrin that Laurence Olivier— *Wuthering Heights* or *Hamlet* or *Rebecca,* with their restless roamin spirits and guilty hearts. But when the chips were down Pearl would always succumb to *Steptoe and Son* and *Peyton Place.* You see, Pearl took to nights with the television set because she'd begun to feel like a wallflower at the dance halls. She'd had all these whimsies about marrying an American GI, but the opportunity never did present itself. It's not that she wasn't pretty. She had the loveliest baby-blonde hair and peachy skin, a well-turned ankle and the most charmin smile in the whole county. Truth is, when a girl got into her thirties in those days, the boys could always find metal more attractive, with far less mileage on the clock.

Suppose it hasn't changed so much. There's Pearl's uncomfortable niece now, doin the dishes and makin tea all day long out of sheer desperation to make herself useful—she'd near swipe the saucer from under your cup to get it into the sink. Thirty-six if she's a day and still no takers. Polly doesn't know it yet but she will meet a divorcee in three years' time. His children will drive her mad with jealousy but she'll marry him anyway out of loneliness and grit her teeth for the rest of her life.

She used to go to see Pearl near the end, and do her ironin. Always hurryin, Polly was. Pearl couldn't understand her rush, or anybody else's for that matter. It was one of the things we would've agreed on. Life passes you by when you're in too much of a hurry, Pearl used to say.

Anyway, she had just about resigned herself to spinsterhood when she got a little elevation in her life. She'd gone and taught

herself how to type and to condense words into squiggles, and
what with all that readin she'd done, didn't she land a job doin
the accounts for a modest insurance firm in town. Now, I was
almost as estranged from this accountin carry on as I was from
the cannin, but Pearl at long last was able to use her brainpower
and her latent initiative. She grew a little self-respect and got a
smile back on her face, and she became a much more pleasant
bein to be around.

Then she got herself a suitor.

In the ripeness of her thirty-eighth year, Pearl married Donie
Hellenback, a mild-eyed insurance man with a Hitler haircut and
a smidge too much padding on his hips for a man, but good
shoulders on him all the same. Donie introduced Pearl to the Sun
Session recordins of Mister Elvis Presley, and *man,* did I up and
soar at that surge of pure, honest-to-God energy. Pearl liked the
way Elvis moved, and he was a regular contributor to some of her
most intimate secret fantasies, healthy imaginins that would've
surprised—who knows, *delighted*—his plainer stand-in.

Blissfully unaware, Donie got Pearl pregnant on their honeymoon in Kerry. If the baby had been a boy, the Hellenbacks were
all set to name him Aaron. It turned out to be a girl, dark like her
father, and they named her Millie, after that squeaky little daisy
who sang "My Boy Lollipop." A little while later, Pearl was
singing to Millie in her cot when the news came that John F.
Kennedy was shot. She hugged her so tight, the child almost
passed out. Then the huggin stopped.

Pearl got angry and all political. She took to marchin for one
man one vote and got herself arrested for sittin down on a road.
Problem was that Pearl didn't quite connect with the peace and
love stuff, not deep down inside of herself, where there was a little of that Irish self-loathin simmerin with her shiftin hormones.
This emotional stewin would lead to broodin silences and petty

fightin in the Hellenback household, particularly at the full moon, if my memory serves me right. It eased a little after Pearl hit fifty and quit marchin, but she couldn't find anywhere else to put her intelligence, and eventually she stopped shavin her legs and Donie started pickin his nose out in the open and teenage Millie stopped listenin to Abba and started dyin her hair magenta. Now, I wasn't averse to the Sex Pistols; they had that undiluted energy thing goin on, but Pearl could not abide punk rock and its unusual fashions. Mother and daughter stopped speakin the day Mrs. Thatcher turned the Sermon on the Mount into an emetic. They've never exchanged a soft word since, not even when a rogue wave knocked Donie off a rock on the Donegal coast and swept him out to sea, never to be seen again.

Yet on her deathbed, the night before last, Pearl held out as long as she could, waitin for Millie to come. She'd gone through the waitin for Winnie to get home from Toronto, and for her spoiled godson Nigel (who I'm afraid hasn't inherited the Lovetts' good looks) to get back from his holidays in France. Then she'd scared the wits out of the lot of them when she came out of one of her turns, sat straight up in the bed and declared, "What's Mary-Agnes doin here?"

I've never seen a row of faces blanch as fast. Nobody had had the heart to tell Pearl they'd burned Cousin Mary-Agnes a week ago in an English crematorium. Pearl had been in for her last round of tests at the hospital at the time and they'd agreed it wouldn't have been right to tell her. After all, Batty'd reasoned, Mary-Agnes hadn't been back home in years.

Of them all, then, he was the most dumbfounded at Pearl's sudden outburst. Naturally, they couldn't see what Pearl and I could in the sunbeam on that radiant day. Their long-lost grandmother was lurkin there too, as a matter of fact, but Pearl kept that to herself. The fully evolved return in their temporal likenesses near the end, so they can be recognized by the soon-to-be departed. The veil between the worlds is at its thinnest then. I'm sure that conceited marmalade cat saw somethin too, just before Pearl passed out.

The Mary-Agnes incident proved, however, to be of some comfort to Winnie and Concepta Best, next-door neighbour and lifelong friend, as both of them know, in their own private universes, that they are not long for this world. "You used to be tall," dotty Winnie told rusty Concepta when they met in the hall. That was the precursor for the beginnin of the battle of wills in the organizin of Pearl's dyin. How you crowd struggle to bring order to that which you cannot control! Only the Easterners have come close to getting it right, but try tellin the likes of Pearl that the half-naked little roly-poly with the big smile and the heavy eyelids just could be the font of all wisdom. Her liberalizin never did get that far.

Meanwhile back at the bedside, Batty thought he had it all in hand. When she'd come round again that day, Pearl'd begun to fidget like an ant in the bed, complainin that she couldn't get herself comfortable, and cursin the bumpy mattress. *Oh Pearl.* Those bumps on her mattress were really lumps on her crumblin spine, you see, so Batty came up with the inspired idea of slidin a towel under Pearl's shrunken little body and movin her from side to side by tuggin on this towel.

"That was my idea, that was," he announced, just like a child, when the portly nurse came by. She gave him an understandin smile and leaned down and told Pearl she'd be more comfortable back in the hospital. "NO!" Pearl howled, clear as day. They all tittered. The home-bird knew her own mind, spots on her brain or not.

The thickenin started in her left breast twenty-odd years ago, not long before Donie drowned. I'll tell you how it started, if you like. You see, not being in tune with me when Millie decided to cop out of the mainstream and quit college, Pearl had acted from the Ego, and the Ego was mad as hell from the accumulation of life's disappointments. On more than one occasion, I have to admit, Pearl went and lost the stillness at her centre and lifted her hand and struck young Millie hard as she could. Created her own hell right under her own roof, she did. Eventually Millie fought back, then ran away to London to be a model, and over the years, the guilt grew inside Pearl like a bush of rag-weeds 'til the only way she could deal with it was to stamp on it and try to pretend it wasn't there. And, well, you guessed it. Pearl went and made that great big blockage inside her bosom herself. (The aluminium tracin under her arms didn't help matters, I should warn you girls.)

The upshot was that Millie never did show up at the sickbed, and as the day waned, Pearl began to give up hope. It was a mercy, in a way. Along with the hope, she began to let go of the resistance to the inevitable. At teatime Concepta tried to get her to eat a little ice cream but she refused point blank, and none too politely. Then, in one of her more eloquent moments, she sighed and whispered "I'm done" into Winnie's pre-grievin ear.

After that she finally began to relax a little. They were all mighty relieved after all the wrigglin she'd been doin, tryin to get her skinny ulcerated legs out of the bed. Much to Winnie's disapproval, though, Pearl seemed determined right until the end to smoke as many cigarettes as her spongy lungs could inhale. Seventeen, she smoked that day, out of a pack of twenty. Concepta reckoned she was tryin to get them all finished before dyin. Even when her voice was fadin, she managed to muster up the where-with-all to ask for a faig, as she called them, usually before the one between her fingers was smoked. And even after the big injection, when she finally began the slow process of takin her leave, she'd be tappin away on an imaginary butt.

Pearl took up smokin late in life, after she'd got her gold watch for thirty-three years' loyal service at Mandolin Insurance. Millie was gone, Donie was gone, and there was little else to do but smoke and read. She'd make jam in the summer and bake bread in the winter, and all year long she'd read. Pearl read books to know she wasn't alone in this world; same reason an author writes, I suppose.

Then she took to ridin Millie's old bicycle into town when she became eligible for her pension. That didn't last long. One day a speedin truck sent her careerin head-first into a ditch, crushin vertebrae and crackin bones. The driver never stopped and Pearl was never the same again. Arthritis set in and Pearl took to her armchair, propped sideways at the top of the kitchen table, where she could look out of the window and see her Banty hens struttin round the yard, and watch Concepta's sheep— daubed electric blue like they were in some sheep gang—munch their way through Batty's one and only field.

Pearl grew increasin'ly immobile as she sat day after day by that handsome honey-pine table but she exerted complete unwaverin control over all that she surveyed, includin the endless callers to her door. They'd come in and tell her all the news and all their troubles, and Pearl would sit up and enjoy bein attended on. It's funny peculiar how the ones who don't hear the voice of truth within themselves turn out to be the best listeners and the most profound counsellors. Pearl was a tonic, better than a shrink, to anyone who sought her advice, but deaf as a post to my whisperins.

Take Winnie, fussin about the place there with a never-endin tray of sandwiches in her hand, the image of Pearl in her better days. Winnie phoned Pearl once a week for her wisdom, confidin family intimacies she'd never dream of sharin with an outsider like her husband. Well, I can see right now, if only by that costive pallor, that Winnie's large intestine has gone on strike in protest at the loss of her confidante, and that an enema will be required before the month's out.

Concepta's the complete opposite. Her plumbin started to gurgle the minute she caught sight of the morphine needle. She's been runnin ever since. Cepta, as Pearl called her, quit tryin to control events from that moment on, and simply let go of everythin, includin her bowels. Pearl really started to slide then. There was no more fidgetin and mumblin; just the odd half whisper and tappin of invisible ash.

At eight o'clock Batty went to get chips; everyone was sick of the sight of Winnie's sandwiches. Concepta went home to make dinner. Winnie went for a lie down. Polly mopped the kitchen floor and the bathroom floor and vacuumed the lounge. Nigel the unlovely nephew lay up on the couch and read the paper. Pearl and I were alone for the first time in two days, and as she began to descend into free fall, my colours began to bleach out, royal blue fading to cerulean, indigo to lilac, sapphire to azure.

By the time Batty came back with the chips, I was almost entirely back to my original hue, and Pearl, I'm afraid, would have scared the livin daylights out of you. I'm sorry, but I've never seen such a spectral head on this earth, all long and toothy and lipless, with huge unseein filmy pupils and skin like whey. Pearl would have been rightly insulted to see what Grim was doin to her face. By ten o'clock, he'd taken up residence and lodged for the duration in those once delicate features, and as the Irish say, he wasn't goin to go away empty.

The decline was swift and mesmerizin to behold, if you are that way inclined. It is a most fascinatin transfiguration. Claude Monet was so intrigued by the transient colours of his dead wife's face that he got his paints out and recorded those wildly protean images for posterity.

But nobody wanted to remember Pearl at her worst. On her return, Concepta took one look and scurried back to the bathroom. Winnie braved it, but sat at Pearl's side so she wouldn't have to look into the face. Polly draped a piece of lacy finery over the dressin table mirror at the end of the bed, just in case Pearl happened to wake up and get frightened to death, and Batty began to talk incessantly. Nigel got the whisky out, and together the five of us began the long wait.

It wasn't dissimilar to her birth—any birth, come to that. The same breathin patterns and cycles of spasm, and plenty of waitin. Pearl arrived prematurely but, fragile or not, she grew into a bossy toddler and never lost that infantile impulse to control, right until the bitter end.

By midnight, the throat snorin had begun and the life force was dwindlin from Pearl's limbs like an agein oak. It takes the oak tree three hundred years to die, so you don't exactly know which parts are livin when you encounter one. I'd say Pearl's feet were long gone before the rest of her, and in the final hours, all that was Pearl was reduced to the barely perceptible shallow breaths from her concave chest. The ghastly apparition that was her face persisted in its supernatural lengthenin, as the puckered mouth gaped and the redundant dentures fell loose.

As the night wore on, Winnie and Polly forgot themselves and began to talk across the bed as if Pearl wasn't there. Concepta, standin with a duster in the doorway, was suitably horrified.

"She can hear you!" she mouthed at the stricken Polly, tears standin in her big brown eyes. She was right, too. Pearl hadn't missed a thing, and when Polly turned towards her and asked her idiotically if she wanted to take a little nap, Pearl answered, "Ub," or somethin to that effect. It was the very last time her jaw or anythin else moved. By two o'clock in the mornin, the snorin had segued into a full-on death rattle. Polly summoned Batty and

Nigel from the kitchen, Winnie led the rosary and Concepta started cryin. For some reason, they all knew instinctively to stand up around the bed, like a guard of honour preparin to take her to her rest. She would've felt like a queen.

They weren't on their feet for too long. Concepta knew it was all over when Pearl's tear glands broke and a lone drop slid down into her gapin mouth. The breathin faltered then and the spaces between the rattles began to get longer, until they all realized, in the middle of the third sorrowful mystery, that Pearl was gone.

Action Stations!

No, he didn't actually say that, but he may as well have. No sooner had they closed Pearl's empty eyes, than Batty was out of the door and on the phone to the undertakers. Oh, and the doctor, just to confirm everythin. And while Concepta stood and sobbed, and Nigel stood and stared, and Polly put the kettle on, Batty and Winnie stood and argued over whether to phone the priest.

"No," Batty said, "you'll get the man out of bed and he was here this morning and did the last rites."

"But," Winnie said, "Pearl would want him here."

"No," Batty said, "we'll only need him again in the morning when the coffin comes in."

And so it continued, back and forth, 'til Winnie finally conceded. Now that the eldest was gone, Little Brother, Only Boy, was finally the boss—and man, did he get a kick out of that. Now the fussin kicked in big time, tidyin away the drugs, hidin the commode, openin windows, stoppin clocks, talkin non-stop. And in the middle of it all, an all-out scramblin search for Millie's phone number.

In the end, all Batty got was an answerin service with an Englishman's clipped vowels. He delivered the news to the machine, promptin much rollin of eyes, but you know, the man wasn't

thinkin straight. Then he forgot Pearl's number and had to holler
down the hall for it in the most unbecomin manner for a wake
house. They knew they'd be lucky to see Millie after that, but the
palaver went on. It's a natural knee-jerk reaction, to try to create
order in the face of the ultimate absurdity. You've just had to con-
front the one thing in life you have absolutely no control over,
nada. So, sure, you're gonna flap and fluster and try to organize
the hell outta all the little details that need doin in the aftermath.
But do ya hafta make so much Goddamn noise?

Forgive me. I tend to slip into one of the old tongues at
times, and you must understand that Batty's constant nervous
twitter can be mighty hard to take. It's now fifty-nine hours,
thirty-five minutes and eight seconds since Pearl bowed out, and
he's *still* yakkin, lips flappin like a sheet on a washin line.

He means well, of course. Look at him there, showin people
in, and choosin the readins for the funeral, and decidin who's
gonna read what, and what hymns the choir's gonna sing, and
who's gonna play the organ, and how much the priest's gonna get
paid, and he's already phoned the death notice into the paper and
rung the whole parish with the news.

Winnie was relegated to less important Women's Jobs, like
pickin out Pearl's coffin outfit. This wasn't as straightforward as it
sounds, for Pearl had managed to burn holes in all belongin to
her—blouses, vests, sheets, nightdresses, even towels. Winnie
tore through rows of hangers, givin way to the vituperation of the
reformed smoker. In the end, Batty had to stick his well-sculpted
nose in there too, and veto the red dress Winnie had chosen as far
too Christmassy. He had a point here.

Anyway, they settled on a demure high-collared teal blouse
and a sensible navy skirt, thick matchin pantyhose and good
leather walkin shoes, and had them all pressed and folded, well
before Pearl grew cold. In the middle of all this, the wan young

GP, dragged needlessly from his warm bed, dutifully recorded old age and osteoporosis for the death certificate, knowin full well from his dealins with the Lovetts that the C word is not spoken. One look at the lifeless face, of course, told different; simple old age cannot wreak such a radical demolition. It was the hangin mouth that caused Winnie the most annoyance.

"Would you, for God's sake, go and get something to hold her chin up," she implored Polly, as she tried to arrange the rapidly stiffenin Pearl against the pillows. "I don't want her looking like that for people coming in."

Poor Polly had no idea what to do. Fleetin'ly she considered a headscarf, knotted on the head like Stan Laurel when he had the mumps, but decided it would look kinda disrespectful. I must admit it was with some amusement that I watched her standin there under Winnie's glare, lookin around her wildly, rackin her brains for somethin.

"Hurry up, Polly, before she gets any stiffer."

Desperation can yield some less travelled paths, but Polly's solution to the death-gape was amongst the most unusual I've ever seen. For years Pearl had kept a slim rectangular box of miniature Paris Parfums on her dresser. No sooner had Polly's frantically searchin eye fallen on them than they were lodged under Pearl's slack jaw, keepin her chin up and her dignity intact, for the time bein at least. Of course I knew what was to come as regards the unmentionables, so when Mr. Corbiere the undertaker arrived, I opted to stay behind.

Now this guy had obviously trained himself to speak in a reverential tone just nudgin above a whisper, and his manner had a calmin effect on the house and all within its uneven old walls. This serene presence was a welcome respite after all the squawkin and commotion, and when he silently shooed them all into the kitchen for the removal, in his own elegant way, they went quietly, like chastened children. He was, of course, sparin the family the upset of seein him and his youthful assistant zippin Pearl into a big black bag and carryin her out to the hearse, and despositin her into the secret slot under where the coffins normally sit. But the minute they left, Winnie cried hard anyway at the thought of Pearl lyin in an oul shed all night, as she imagined it. I don't have that knowledge because I didn't care to look. I preferred to take a little while to myself in the domicile, quiet at last, after Batty and Concepta went home. Winnie had retired exhausted to the guest room and Nigel had bedded down on the couch, not that he could sleep much, what with the pressure in his sinuses. I could see the fizzin pollen drifting into his airways as he dozed but there wasn't much I could do. Irritants like that are notoriously hard to get hold of.

So I left him snifflin and moved from room to room for the last time, past stacks of dog-eared romances with their yellowed pages reekin of cigarettes, past little heaps of change and keys and Post-its, past framed black and white family photos, past the kitsch religious statuettes on the window sills. Pearl might have become a gallopin racist in her advancin years but her favourite effigy was that of St. Martin, whom she believed to be alive and well and helpin his brothers score goals for Manchester United.

At dawn I returned to the bedside, and by noon Pearl was back, plugged and painted. Only I noticed the inferior and stained base of the coffin under all that polished oak and fake brass as they lowered it on the bed, but soon Winnie will see it too, when they carry Pearl aloft into the chapel, and she will bristle and silently curse her penny-pinchin brother up and down.

Right now, she's in full flight, forcin the last of the callers to view the remains, even the reluctant ones who protest that they'd rather remember Pearl as she was. Winnie and Batty are beginnin to panic, you see, because time's runnin out. Millie still hasn't phoned and Father Black has said the final rosary in advance of the removal to the chapel for the funeral, and the siblings are usin the latecomers as an excuse to delay nailin down the coffin lid. It's obvious for all to see, and they appear a little pathetic in their childish temporizin. Father Black's lookin at his watch and Mr. Corbiere's silently drummin his long tapered fingers on the upright lid, Polly's goin red and Concepta's shufflin her feet and compressin her lips.

In the end it is Nigel who takes it upon himself to step forward and give Mr. Corbiere the nod, and with that simple gesture, the boy grows into a man.

They all know Millie's not comin now. Winnie lets out a yelp as Pearl's face disappears under her gleamin nameplate and a nerve between Batty's high cheekbone and his sharp jaw starts to pummel under his close-shaven skin. It's the only bit of emotion his face will betray, until he's shoulderin the coffin out of the chapel and the choir are singin "I'll Take You Home Again, Kathleen," on account of that bein Pearl's favourite song of all time, and the only tune she ever could carry.

Nigel won't cry but the spicy incense at the graveside will make the water run out of his stingin eyes just like hot tears. Polly and Concepta will hold up well, until the diggers balance Pearl on their ropes and jerk her down into the earth.

I will take my leave then, and make my way to the appointed maternity ward. It's back across the Atlantic, I'm told, and a lot more sophisticated than the casualty floor where Pearl came into the world seventy-nine years ago, far too early for her own good. I had only seconds to fight my way through the mortuary traffic and wrap myself around that little blue body before it gave up at the first hurdle.

Truth is, Pearl had an old soul.

Me.

Such a pity we never met.

Journalist and media consultant **UNA BRANKIN** is the author of the highly acclaimed novel *Half Moon Lake*. She lives in Sandymount, Dublin, with her husband, musician Declan Murphy. Una is currently working on her second novel.

The Calling

Cecelia Ahern

"Seven and eight, seventy-eight."

Her age.

Mags threw her eyes up to heaven and grumbled under her breath, in her raspy voice.

"WHAT'S THAT, LOVE?" Agatha shouted, moving her ear closer to Mags's head. "YOU'RE GOING TO HAVE TO SPEAK UP, LOVE, IT'S ME DEAF EAR YOU'RE SITTIN' BESIDE."

Mags wrinkled her nose up in disgust as she watched the black wiry hairs clinging to Agatha's chin bounce up and down as her mouth opened and shut. Her teeth became loose from her palette and were quickly clamped back into place as Agatha's bloodshot tired grey eyes darted around the table to see if anyone had noticed.

Mags threw her eyes up again and mumbled questioningly to the Good Lord.

"WHA'?" Agatha's blue rinse brushed off Mags's forehead as

she leaned in to hear. Mags shook her head and swatted Agatha's head away as though it were a fly. She concentrated on what was going on ahead of her again.

"Two and two, twenty-two."

The year she was born.

She gritted her teeth and exhaled loudly. She leaned slightly to the left in her chair to sneak a glance at how her neighbour was progressing. The woman slowly raised her hand and covered her card. Mags raised her eyes slowly from the wrinkled hand blotched with brown patches, and came face to face with a tight smile.

Mags cleared her throat awkwardly, sat upright in her seat and tried to look insulted as she covered her own card with her hand as if to accuse her neighbour of cheating. The woman grunted and pulled her chair away from Mags. The steel chair legs which had long lost their rubber grips screeched along the tired oak wood floor. Faces winced and looked up. Her neighbour's face reddened and became buried in her hand as pained expressions stared at the cause of all the noise. Mags "hmmphed" loudly as though she had been victorious in that particular round.

"WHAT'S EVERYONE LOOKIN' SO MOANY FOR, MAGS?" Agatha shouted, while looking around confused. "DID SOMEBODY FART?" She sniffed the air and moved her head around animatedly, not wanting to be left out of the group's obvious discomfort. "I CAN'T SMELL IT, MAGS," she shouted again. "IS IT AWFUL? IT MUST BE AWFUL." She sniffed the air one last time then shook her head looking defeated. "CAN'T GET IT OVER HERE AT ALL."

Mags elbowed Agatha in the ribs a little harder than she had meant to, to silence her friend. It had the opposite effect.

"AAGH! JAYSUS, I'M DEAF NOT NUMB, MAGS.

WHAT'S WRONG WIT' YA?" She looked at her friend with a horrified expression whilst rubbing her sore side.

"Would you ever shut your trap, Aggie O'Brien," she hissed.

"WHA'?" Agatha yelled, moving her head closer to Mags.

Mags stared at the blue rinse mound of curls that had been shoved in her face and tutted at the patches of pink skin that were visible through the thin wispy hair.

After not hearing a reply, Aggie turned to face Mags in order to read her lips. The two thin red lines were pursed together, the deep cracks in her skin gathering around her mouth as though being pulled by a drawstring. A crooked finger stood perpendicular to her lips with a bright red nail ordering her to Stop!

"Ssshh!" was all Aggie could just about make out. Then she realized what her friend meant.

"OH JAYSUS, SORRY, MAGS," she yelled a little less loudly but not so much that the surrounding tables couldn't hear. "I DIDN'T REA-*LIZE* IT WAS YOU THAT DONE IT. SURE I CAN'T EVEN SMELL IT MESELF AND I'M RIGHT BESIDE YOU."

Mags's cheeks pinked as they always did when she was embarrassed; they looked as though she had dabbed two balls of baby pink blusher onto her cheekbones. Her father used to say she was as pretty as the pink carnations that grew in her mother's flower garden of their country home. A circus clown, her mother had always used to rant angrily as though the very vision of them offended her. Her mother would cover her face in clouds of white powder before Mags would head out to the local dance on a Friday night. No daughter of hers would find a man with awful pink cheeks on her face, especially not her *only* daughter. The bristles of the powder brush used to scrape away at Mags's cheeks, causing her eyes to water and her irritated skin to redden even more. Faster and faster her mother would brush, nearly scraping the layer of skin away so it would reveal pure whiteness. The angrier and angrier she would get, the redder and more sore-looking her daughter's face would become.

Twice a week Mags would have to endure this. Once on a Friday before the local dance and again on the Sunday morning before they walked along the pot-holed road to eight o'clock Mass. Mags would have to sit for an hour for her mother while she tied up her hair and powdered her face. Mags wondered why she couldn't just dip her face into the bowl of flour her mother left sitting on the kitchen counter in preparation for the Sunday homemade apple tart. At least that way not a pink blotch would be in sight.

She would be ordered to sit still, afraid to move a muscle in case she felt the sharp sting of the back of the brush against her flesh, which inevitably caused her cheeks to turn rosy. It was a vicious circle. So she sat tight, hands on lap, back straight ("A man wouldn't want a wife with bad posture now, would he, Margaret?") while her five brothers could remain in bed for the extra hour. Mags often felt like questioning her mother on why it was that men didn't need to make the same effort for women. Mags certainly had no desire for a man who smelt of cow manure, sweat thick with the stench of stale black coffee, muddy big black boots with faded trousers, dried muck in their creases, tucked into thick black socks (no doubt darned by their mothers and sisters) all held up by a pair of braces. Mags was convinced that the only reason for these was so the men would have a place to rest their thumbs while they stuck their chests out and strolled the town like they hadn't a care in the world.

Mags had sometimes wished, while sitting for her mother, that she had been born a man. There were few or no rules, less expectation and what appeared to be no pressures apart from watching the weather and worrying about the amount of milk they could get from the cow that morning. But she wouldn't dare share these thoughts with her mother especially not while she had the spiky brush in one hand and a lock of her black silky hair firmly grasped in the other. Mags had no doubt her mother would have no problem scalping her in an instant, however the only thing that held her back was the knowledge that a bald patch on a girl is not easy on the watchful eye of a hot-red-blooded young male. No, the hair remained untouched—it was pulled at and twisted, knotted and pinched, but remained unscalped.

Once ready, her mother would call the boys. Mags would hear them mumbling and grumbling and moaning about having to get up at such an early hour. Mags would stare desperately in the mirror at her reflection, her powdery white face appearing ghost-like against the whitewashed walls of her bedroom in the background. While her mother banged around the boys' bedroom pulling open curtains and laying out clothes, laughing and pretending to be angered by their protests but secretly loving the attention, Mags sucked in her cheeks, widened her eyes and pretended to float around as the ghost she felt like. It was as though her mother *wanted* her to be invisible and it wasn't only the make-up that made Mags feel it.

Her father, when he wasn't at the pub or working the farm, doted on her. Her mother despised her for it. But he wasn't one to argue with the woman he married and sure didn't she know best how to treat a growing young woman when she herself was one? One thing Mags loved him disagreeing with was all the make-up she wore going to see the Lord in His House. "Our Lord doesn't need nor require young Margaret to wear a mask in his home, Grainne," he said one Sunday.

"Ah yes, but our Lord does want young Margaret to find a suitor so she doesn't grow old a shamed woman. And unless the Lord requires her to be a nun there is no need for her to be without a man. The world isn't designed for a woman without a man and as far as we know she hasn't received the Calling."

Her parents and five brothers all stopped walking at that point to stand still and stare at Mags. Her cheeks flushed instantly and her mother let out an exasperated sigh as though Mags was deliberately acting out against her mother's hard work.

Mags gulped and stared back at her family wide-eyed. "What is it?" she stammered.

Her mother shook her head sadly at the lack of grace of her daughter.

"Have you received the Calling?" Jackie, her twenty-year-old brother, asked her with a smirk on his face.

"Margaret! Margaret!" her younger brother called her name playfully in the background.

To Mags's surprise her mother started laughing and then immediately smacked her son over the head with her handbag for joking about the Lord. Only Mags's father watched her face curiously.

"Em, no, I haven't," Mags whispered in embarrassment. He simply nodded his head once as he absorbed this information and then continued walking. The rest of the family trudged on after him, overtaking Margaret whose feet remained firmly fixed to the spot with pure terror and shame. She knew what they were all thinking, if she hadn't received a Calling like Kathleen from down the road and she hadn't courted a man at the age of twenty then maybe she was one of those 'funny ones' that cut their hair short and moved to the city.

"Hurry along, Margaret," her mother spat angrily, even more disappointed. "The Lord waits for no one, especially not twenty-year-old girls who dilly-dally."

Margaret's heartbeat quickened at her mother's tone and she ran to catch up with her family.

"Sorry," she whispered to their backs as they walked ahead of her. And she meant it. Sorry she wasn't more like them. Sorry she lacked the social graces of her mother, the personality of her father, the popularity of her brothers, the beauty of all the other girls in the town.

They arrived at the church at seven-thirty in the morning as they did every week and gathered with the rest of the congregation for the next half hour. Mags hated the way the women gossiped about that week's scandal, hated how her mother pretended not to be interested even though Mags knew she looked forward to those chats all week more than the Mass itself. The men would talk about the weather and how it was affecting the crop. Mags loved when the weather was good because her father became a whole new man. They would stay up until all hours listening to his stories and listening to his songs. But when the farm wasn't going well, it felt to Mags as though there was a stranger in the house. He became an intruder who conversed in only grunts and monosyllabic words and appeared only at eating time. A man she didn't much like.

Finally the gossip would end when the church bell signalled eight o'clock. They would all pile into the church, which would quickly become packed to the brim with hung-over men, crying children, coughing teenagers, women hiding their yawns out of respect for the Good Lord in case he struck them down for such an act of humanity. Mass for Mags was a real-life cattle-mart. Her mother would herd the family down the aisle, Mags would walk towards the crucifix to hisses in her ear of "Watch your posture, Margaret" or "Look happy for Our Lord, Margaret" until they reached their usual spot in the front row.

Mags knew now it was no more for Our Lord than for the mice in the field, it was for the lines of young single men that lined the outer aisles, backs against the cold white stone walls, thumbs tucked into their braces, wandering eyes staring back at her under floppy fringes. There was one man in particular her mother had her eye on. She tried to convince Mags it was for her of course, but Mags had her suspicions. Her mother became another woman when he was around, laughing at his jokes, being shockingly polite and being *far* too interested in what the young boy had to say for Margaret's liking. Ploughing a field really wasn't that comical in Margaret's opinion and her mother never seemed as enthusiastic to listen when her father talked about it. Seamus O'Reilly was his name, a local who worked on his father's farm and who probably would be doing the same for the next fifty years of his life. He was twenty-five years of age, strong as an ox, great with his hands and a "decent sort of a lad," according to her father.

He reminded Mags of her five brothers with his cheeky smile and over-confident stroll. She could see him demanding food on the table, hot water for his bath and freshly washed clothes every morning, just like the boys. He leaned against the confessional box and watched all the single girls from the village be led in a neat line up the aisle by their mothers. The stone floor beneath his feet was scattered in muddy clumps as the mucky soles of his leather boots dried, cracked and fell to the floor. So Mags felt far from upset when she watched him walk down the aisle with Katie McNamara that year. As all the women had watched the bride and gasped in awe at her dress as she passed, Mags had more interest in watching the soles of Seamus's feet as he walked away out of the church a married man. Her suspicions had been correct. The mud cracked and fell with every step. To Mags, an obvious sign of what future lay ahead for poor Katie Mac-Namara.

Mags wanted to find a man with shiny shoes, a man who didn't sweat for a living. If such a creature existed in Kilcrush.

Her mother had been visibly devastated and had dabbed at her eyes throughout the wedding ceremony, claiming to be *"so happy for Seamus and Katie"* between sniffles. Mags didn't think it was her posture or her smile or her hair or her walk or her conversation or any of the other things her mother claimed it was that drove him away. Mags didn't think Seamus even cared about any of those things. He had explained to Grainne that it was Katie's "healthy glow" that did it for him. Mags had wanted to grab her mother by the hands and dance and twirl her around the room when she heard that. For as much as she hated that brush scraping the powder onto her skin, it removed the healthy glow that could have imprisoned her in Seamus's farmhouse.

But despite her joy at not being chosen by the best boy in the village, it left Mags still as a single woman at twenty and as much as her parents prayed for it, Mags's Calling never came. Not of the sort they wanted anyway.

Agatha's sniffing the air brought Mags's mind back to the present. "I STILL CAN'T GET IT, MAGS, SO DON'T WORRY."

Mags rolled her eyes, "There is no smell, Aggie."

"HA?" Agatha yelled, squinting her eyes in concentration as though doing so would help her hear.

"There is no smell, nobody farted, Aggie, now stop screaming," she raised her voice a little more.

"IT'S ME BAD EAR MAGS, WHA'?" Agatha shouted.

That did it. Mags's blood boiled. She was sick and tired of having to repeat herself, and not only that, her voice was sore at having to shout at Aggie all day every day. If they weren't careful Aggie would be deaf and Mags would be dumb from having to raise her voice. "THERE IS NO SMELL, AGGIE, OK? I. DID. NOT. FART."

Agatha jumped, the announcer on stage was silenced and a few chuckles were heard around the hall. Mags's cheeks went pink again and she thought immediately of how angry her mother would be, just as she had been programmed to.

"Eh . . . four and four, farty-four, I mean forty-four, excuse me," the bingo caller stuttered.

The hall erupted in laughter and Mags snorted. She quickly grabbed her nose to stop it from happening again. Agatha looked around the room confused, and turned to stare at her friend with her hand over her nose. "DON'T TELL ME YOU DID IT AGAIN, MAGS. IN THE NAME OF JAYSUS ARE YOU TRYIN' TO KILL US ALL?" Agatha yelled, sounding exasperated. This time her words weren't heard by quite so many people over the sound of all the laughter.

Mags tried to control herself, not wanting to be seen to be enjoying herself at the weekly bingo. She liked to think that it was now something she had to do for her friend Aggie and refused to accept the notion that she looked forward to the few hours every week she spent in the local school hall. Her life was far too interesting to be excited by bingo because . . . well, that would make her old.

And she wasn't old.

She was seventy-eight.

All the same, she couldn't wait to tell her Connie when she left the bingo hall. How he would have laughed his heart out at this. Oh yes, there was a man in the end. Cornelius Kelly was his name and Mags adored that man with all her heart. Still did. She couldn't wait to tell this story to him.

The bingo caller tried to recover from his embarrassment and when the giggles had died down in the hall he resumed his job. "Four and three, forty-three."

Mags smiled. The year she met her Connie.

She had found a man all right. A real man, not one of those ones her mother kept trying to pair her off with either. She hadn't wanted to marry a dirty local and have to spend the rest of her life tending after his every unnecessary need. She wanted to fall in love, she wanted to work and not the kind of work that involved scrubbing clothes and dishes, sewing socks and buttons and cooking. She wanted to work *outside* of a house.

So she left Kilcrush in the west of Ireland and headed to Dublin City. The big smoke. Her mother and father had been horrified at the very idea when she told them one evening that she was going to join her best friend from school, who had moved up the previous year. Her mother had been convinced she was one of the "funny ones" and no daughter of hers was going to hang around the likes of her in a city full of sin. Dublin City, they said, was not designed for a single woman.

Her parents wouldn't hear of it.

So she didn't tell them.

With the money she had saved from selling eggs from the hen her father had given her for her twenty-first (also selling the hen and a small amount of farm produce) at the local market, she bought a train ticket and disappeared into the night. Standing on the pavement on O'Connell Street she took in the sights, sounds and smells that her new life had to offer. She stared with delight in the great big windows of Clery's department store and had a pain in her neck from standing at the foot of the large granite structure and looking up at Nelson's Pillar, which she had previously only ever seen in photographs. She breathed in the smoke, the noise, the crowds, the buildings, the trams, so much concrete and such little green—she loved it.

She moved in with her friend Agatha O'Reilly from school to a dark, dingy bedsit in the heart of the city. It was dirty and grotty, noisy and smelly and within days it felt like home to Mags. She took to life very quickly in Dublin. She loved the freedom, she loved being able to go to eleven o'clock Mass on a Sunday morning when she could wear her hair any way she liked it, go bare-faced, sit in the back row and yawn to her heart's content without being struck down by the Lord. She worked Monday to Friday as a chambermaid in a city hotel near the bedsit and she tried to save every shilling she made, stashing it in a box under her bed. She planned to create the best life for herself.

One night the sweet, sweet music that filtered up through the floor of their bedsit from the smoky club below made Mags and Aggie sit up in bed and listen. The voice of an angel accompanied by the tinkling sound of a piano flowed like warm silky caramel through their ears. Mags closed her eyes and pictured herself and Fred Astaire dancing around the room. It was music so unlike anything she had heard in real life. This was the stuff she only saw and heard in the movie theatres she went to occasionally with Aggie. It wasn't like the "Fields of Athenry" she was used to hearing being sung in the pubs and at parties at home. There was no screeching fiddle or banging *bodhrān,* there were just silky soothing sounds that made her feel like she was a million miles from home.

Every weekend she was transported to New York City, to a smoke-filled jazz club full of sophisticated, strong, beautiful, confident women with big made-up eyes, rich sparkling jewels and glitzy dresses that revealed more flesh than any man in Mags's home town dared to even dream about due to the fear of having to confess immoral thoughts. The kind of women who inhaled sexily on a cigarette balanced effortlessly between gloved fingers, not a hint of their bright red lipstick left behind on the cigarette tip. They would laugh flirtatiously as they tipped the ash into the tray right on target without even looking, while sipping on a cosmopolitan, being adored by men, envied by other women, not a care in the world.

Every Friday and Saturday night Mags and Aggie would

become those women in the privacy of their own bedsit while they let the music take them away and let the noises from below make them feel like they were in the very room. They would doll themselves up to the nines in their Sunday best, flicking cigarette ash around the room, revealing so much flesh their parents would be saying decades of the rosary. She lived life happily alone in a city not designed for single women.

The voice called out to her louder and louder, week after week, until Mags finally felt confident enough to leave the safety of her bedsit in order to explore downstairs. And when she left the room that night she left the Margaret Divine of Kilcrush behind her. For onstage performing was an angel, the stage spotlight acting as a beam from heaven shining on the man who sang as though he were from another world. His eyes sparkled at her as his magic hands glided gracefully over the keys and he sang with a smile. A smile all for her. He just seemed to *glow* to Mags, she could hardly take her eyes away from him, couldn't stop listening to his voice. There was an air of sophistication about him and at the age of twenty-one Mags knew she had already fallen in love with the voice of an angel and now she had fallen in love with the man. It had been the Calling she had been praying for. His voice calling her to leave her safety net behind and come downstairs.

He was smart *and* friendly *and* funny *and* listened to Mags's stories, laughed at her jokes, seemed interested in her opinions, made her feel loved and intelligent and sexy and this was all new to her.

They became engaged only weeks later and as Mags's parents still refused to visit her in Dublin, she embarked on the train journey to Kilcrush with her love. He made her feel strong, like she could take on the world and perhaps even her mother.

And for a woman who didn't think much of city people and their ways, Mags had never seen her mother so uncomfortable and nervous, so well-dressed, she had never seen the cottage look so clean, it was not even that clean when the local priest visited. It was as though her mother thought royalty was among them. But Connie was a man of the world. He had seen countries, learned of things Grainne could never teach her daughter or preach to her friends. Mags was surprised to find her mother intimidated by this confident young man who looked at her daughter in a way she found uncomfortable.

While Cornelius became acquainted with the men in the living room, it was required of Mags to help prepare tea with her mother in the kitchen. Her first greeting was a slap across the face.

"That's what you get, Margaret Divine," her mother said breathlessly while rubbing her hand in her apron as if to try and rid herself of the guilt of the act. "That's what you get for not obeying me, for running off and becoming a scorned woman who hangs around smoky clubs with men like you were some sort of fancy woman," she hissed. "That's not the life you were reared to know, not the life your father and I worked hard to provide for you. And this is how you repay us?" She busied herself making sandwiches, slicing the tomatoes with neat precision, almost with obsession.

Mags stared at her mother, her eyes glistening from the sting of the slap.

"Well? Margaret, what have you to say for yourself?" She stopped slicing the tomatoes and turned to face Mags, sharp knife in one hand, other hand on hip, trying to appear menacing.

Margaret saw her then for the first time, for what she really was. A woman who knew very little about the real ways of the world. She realized that the woman who scared her all of her life, knew very little at all. Margaret began to laugh, to her own surprise. Quietly at first but then she reached to the very bottom of her soul and found a loud belly-aching laugh that made her eyes run with tears of sadness and relief. This unusual act of disobedience angered her mother even more and Mags received an even harder slap on the other cheek.

This stopped her laughing immediately but her eyes still glistened with bitter amusement.

"What have you to say for yourself, young lady?" her mother said angrily through gritted teeth. Loose grey hairs flailed around wildly as though they celebrated their escape from the tight bun in her head, her face aged in an instant in Mags's eyes, the sharp knife aimed pointedly at Mags's face. "Well?" she pressed, the delight of putting her daughter back in her place causing her shoulders to relax a little.

Margaret glanced at the small mirror over the kitchen basin, at the small wooden stool that she was forced to sit on twice weekly through all of her teenage years and endure the pain of covering her flushed cheeks. She didn't know what to say. Margaret caught her reflection in the mirror and her stinging cheeks slowly broke into a sad smile. "Why, Mother, you seem to have made my cheeks rosy."

Her comment was greeted with an icy stare. But a shocked one, at that. No words came from her mother's mouth. And as the unusual silence hung in the air, Margaret turned her back and walked out of the kitchen, out of the cottage and out of the place where her mother had tried to hold such control over her.

She and Cornelius married a few weeks later in a small church in Dublin. Her mother could not bring herself to attend, but for the last time Mags's father led her down the aisle of the church, with make-up on her face, up to the front row.

"Four and seven, forty-seven."

Mags smiled. The year she and Connie had their first baby.

He had been like an excited child himself when he found out about the pregnancy. He had picked her up and danced her around the living room of their new home, then quickly put her down again with worry, afraid of hurting her and the baby. They had finally managed to gather the money together to buy their first home in a new housing estate of brand-new three-bedroom homes in Cabra, Dublin. They had spent the first few years of their married life working all the hours under the sun to help pay for the house and now they would have an addition. Mags smiled again, she couldn't wait to talk to Connie later about the day they moved in. She loved doing that. Going over the memories of years gone by with him.

They named their first son Michael after Connie's father and over the following years they had three more children. Two more boys, Robert and Jimmy and one girl, Joyce. A daughter Mags allowed to dress, act and speak for herself just as she pleased. They were all married now. Only Joyce lived in Dublin, the rest were living overseas with their families. They tried to get home as much as they could. Their eldest was now fifty-three years old. Not a baby any more.

"Number eight, just a single eight."

The number of her grandchildren.

She couldn't wait to finish up here and talk to Connie, she still loved him with all of her heart and every time she thought of him butterflies fluttered around her tummy. He used to work at the bingo hall until a few years ago when the arthritis in his hands became too bad. He had missed playing the piano so much and Mags missed listening to him as she played her bingo. It was nice to hear his familiar sounds in the background and she liked being able to look up and watch him when he didn't know she was looking. His face furrowed in concentration as he played the tunes he had been playing for over fifty years. They had never been able to find a replacement piano player. But there was no one near as good as Connie anyway . . . her thoughts diminished as she stared down at her card.

"Oh," she said quietly, with surprise.

"WHA'?" Aggie yelled.

Mags smiled at her lifelong friend. "I got bingo, Aggie." She clapped her hands together with glee.

"YOU GOT WHA'?"

"Bingo, Aggie." She rolled her eyes. Here she goes again.

"HA?"

"FOR THE FIFTIETH TIME, I SAID I GOT BINGO!" she yelled, the veins in her forehead throbbing from the volume of her voice.

The room stopped what they were doing and stared at her.

"I'm so so s-s-s-sorry, Mrs. K-k-kelly," the bingo caller stuttered, "I'm afraid I d-d-d-didn't hear you the first t-t-t-time. Would you like t-t-t-to come up and collect your prize. You've won t-t-t-ten euro. Everyb-b-b-body give Mags a round of ap-p-p-plause."

Mags's cheeks blushed as she slowly stood up from her chair and made her way shakily up to the stage. Her hip was at her again. Wait till Connie heard all her good news today, she thought happily accepting the crisp ten-euro note.

Mags said her goodbyes to Aggie, eventually settling on just a wave after Aggie had questioned Mags's "goodbye" over and over again. Glowing from her win she stopped at her local newsagent and bought a small bouquet of flowers, €1.99 for a bunch. She opened the gate and walked up the path to her husband. Seeing him in the distance she started to explain, "Oh Connie, you'll never believe the day I've had. I won ten euro in the bingo and poor old Aggie accused me of farting in front of everyone." Mags laughed at the memory. "Well, these are for you," she said, thrusting the pretty flowers towards him. She placed them on the grass of her husband's grave.

"I miss you, love," she said, her eyes filling with tears. "I miss you so much. This life's not designed for old single women at all."

Twenty-two-year-old **CECELIA AHERN** is the author of the international bestselling novel *PS, I Love You*. A film adaptation is currently in pre-production with Warner Brothers and Wendy Finerman Productions. Cecelia lives in County Dublin.

You, Me and Tallisker

Julie Parsons

*I*t was love at first sight for Amelia Dillon the day she met Tom Hegarty. She had never believed that such a thing could happen to her. After all she was intelligent, rational, careful about the decisions she had made in her life. The senior producer in a television production company, she was a woman with all her wits about her. Or so she thought until she met Tom.

It was last summer, one of those rare days when it was actually hot enough to wear sandals and apply sun block. She was out on a shoot, a gardening series, knee deep in organic vegetables. Tom was the expert. He was explaining how to make the best compost, how it needed to be kept wet, how the addition of comfrey, nettles or yarrow would speed up the decomposition of the organic matter. She was standing behind the cameraman, a notebook in her hand and a biro jammed between her teeth when she suddenly began to feel dizzy. Bright lights flashed in front of her eyes and perspiration broke out on her smooth pale forehead. She stumbled, staggered then felt her legs give way beneath her.

Is this what death is like? she wondered as darkness began to press in on her eyelids. And then she thought no more. When she regained consciousness a few seconds later, Tom was the first person she saw. He was kneeling beside her, one hand on her forehead, the other at the back of her neck. She gazed up into his sunburnt face and felt a strange sense as if she had known him for ever.

"What happened?" she asked, aware that her head was pounding and her stomach was hollow and sick.

"You fainted, that's all. It's the heat. Come on, we'll go and sit down and you can have a large glass of cold water. You'll feel better then." And he began to help her up.

On the way back to the office the camera crew slagged her unmercifully.

"Never would have put you down for a swooner," they joked. "Weak at the knees was it? A sucker for a handsome stranger, eh?"

And they hooted with laughter, already anticipating the stories they'd tell to the rest of the staff, and the response to the sneaky footage they'd taken of the two of them together. She said nothing. She knew that Jackie, the cameraman, liked nothing more than to grab a few extra, unusable shots. Always good for a laugh at the end-of-season wrap party. She rested her head against the cold car window and closed her eyes. She wanted to relish the moment when Tom had leaned down over her. She had been able to smell his sweat. It was a strong, pungent but sweet smell which made her long to be close to him again. She could see his face so clearly still. She loved the way his eyes crinkled when he smiled. The creases had made small white lines in his tanned face and she longed to stroke them and kiss them. He had put his arm around her to help her to her feet and now she felt as if she would never be able to stand alone again.

Idiot, she thought, such an idiot. It was the heat, that was all. You should have had breakfast before going out to work, she chided herself. A cup of coffee just isn't enough when you've a long day ahead.

But it wasn't just the hot day and the lack of breakfast that had made Amelia feel like this. She realized as the days passed that all she wanted was to see Tom Hegarty again. She sat in the edit suite and watched the tapes of the filming from that day. She played them backwards and forwards, listening to the cadences of his speech and watching the nuances of his gestures. And her heart ached with longing.

"He's good, that Hegarty guy," her boss, Janet, said as she watched the finished programme. "I think we should bring him in for a chat. See if he'd be interested in doing the presentation and the voice-overs for the finished series. He's got real presence and the camera loves him."

Not just the camera, Amelia thought as the tape came to a finish.

"Great," she said, standing up and switching off the viewing monitor. "Good thinking, Jan, I'll give him a call tomorrow."

And so it came about. Tom Hegarty was to be the new face of *The Growing Season*, and Amelia, his producer. She had never been so happy or fulfilled before in her working life. Tom was a delight. He took her advice about how to perform in front of the camera. They worked on his scripts together and she took him shopping to buy clothes.

"This is fun," he said, as he emerged from the changing room in one of Dublin's trendiest men's shops. "I've never done this before. It's always been jeans and boots and an old sweater that's seen better days." He did an elaborate twirl, showing off the fine linen shirt and trousers she had suggested. "What do you reckon, will I do?"

She nodded. Her throat was tight. There were so many things she wanted to say to him, so many endearments she wanted to pour out into his ears. But all she could do was nod.

"You know," he said to her that evening after they had finished work, "it's been great getting to spend some time with you. I've really enjoyed it. Here," he put his hand in his pocket and brought out a small box, "this is just a little something, a token, to say thank you."

"Oh," she turned it over in her hands, "oh, you shouldn't have."

"Shh," he said, "open it."

Inside the box, resting on a piece of cream satin, was a small pendant. She held it up. Hanging from a long silver chain was a tiny garden fork.

"How lovely," her smile widened across her face, "how absolutely lovely." She held it out to him. "Put it on for me, will you please? I can never manage to do up catches like that."

He lifted her hair from the nape of her neck as he fiddled with the fastener.

"There," he said, and she felt his body press against hers. "How's that?" he asked and his mouth brushed her skin. "Is that all right?" he said as his lips caressed her earlobe.

She took a deep breath and felt again the weakness in her legs. She leaned back against him.

"Wonderful," she said, and she reached for his hands and brought them together around her waist. "Just wonderful."

It was all wonderful. Within a couple of weeks Amelia had moved into Tom's rambling old farmhouse on the outskirts of the city. It added hours onto her trip to work, but she didn't mind. Waking early in the morning with Tom beside her was compensation enough for the extra commuting time. And there were always the phone calls. Whispered protestations of love to her mobile phone and the beep of the text message to remind her of his presence. Dinner would be waiting for her no matter what time she got home. He would sit with her while she ate, drinking a glass of wine and listening while she told him about her day.

"Should I be jealous?" he often said, when she had been out filming with actors or models or minor celebrities. And she would laugh and shake her head and kiss him in reply. But of course since the showing of *The Growing Season* Tom himself had become something of a celebrity. Suddenly his phone was ringing non-stop. There were invitations to open garden fêtes, horticultural shows, a guest column in a national newspaper, interviews and photographs. Now when they went to the supermarket on Saturdays or to the local pub in the evenings there would be a queue of admirers waiting to congratulate him, ask his advice, invite him over for dinner or a drink.

"I'm sorry," Amelia said to him one Sunday afternoon after they had endured the demands of a very pushy lady who just had to ask him about her problematic dahlias. "If it hadn't been for me you wouldn't have all this terrible aggravation."

But Tom just laughed and ordered another drink and slipped his hand around her waist to give her a comforting squeeze.

"Don't worry, sweetheart," he said, "it's kind of fun and besides it's fantastic for business. Before I met you, sometimes I couldn't even give away my vegetables. Now I can't keep up with the demand. This winter I'm going to put in a couple of poly tunnels and a new heating system. After all," he looked at her over his pint glass, "I've responsibilities now, haven't I?"

The months passed in a haze of bliss. Soon Amelia could hardly remember what life had been like in her one-bedroom apartment on Dublin's quays. The farmhouse, inherited from Tom's parents, needed plenty of work. Tom was happy to leave it up to her.

"I know what I'll do," she said to him. "Why don't I ask one of our designers to come out and have a look? The particular woman I'm thinking of, you'll like her, she has a great eye. We've been friends for years. She did a great job on my apartment. I'm sure she'll have some good suggestions."

"No," Tom groaned, "not a designer, please. A lick of paint here and there and a bit of tiling in the kitchen and bathroom, won't that do?"

But Amelia insisted. This was her home now and she wanted it to be right. Besides, already her thoughts had jumped ahead a few years. She was, after all, thirty-one. She could feel her biological clock ticking. She knew that Tom would make a wonderful father. So she insisted and Tom eventually conceded.

Grainne arrived in time for dinner.

"I'll ask her to stay the night, that way she'll get a true sense of how the house works."

Tom sighed. Amelia persisted.

"You know, Tom, things like where the sun rises and sets, how much light the kitchen gets at breakfast time, all those elements are so important."

Tom sighed again. Amelia cast around for an example.

"You know the way when you're planning your vegetable patch, you need to know where the maximum heat is going to be, don't you?"

Tom nodded grimly.

"She's no oil painting, is she, your friend?" he whispered as she stirred the sauce for the pasta.

"Tom," Amelia shook her finger at him, "handsome is as handsome does, remember that."

But much to Amelia's relief, she could see that Tom and Grainne were hitting it off. The wine flowed freely over dinner and afterwards Tom got out one of his special single-malt whiskeys.

"My father left these to me when he died. There was a big box in the spare room and when I opened it, it was all his favourite drinks. This is a stunner." He held out the bottle.

"Yes, fantastic." Grainne's round face lit up. "I love that one. My father was a great whiskey drinker too. He used to take us all to the Highlands for special whiskey-buying expeditions." She picked up the bottle, pushed her glasses back onto her head and scrutinized the label. "Tallisker, yeah, terrific. Here," she held out her glass, "give us a dram."

Amelia shuddered slightly. No matter how much she loved Tom and wanted to share everything in his life, whiskey was not her choice. Her father was a teetotaller, a Methodist minister whose sermons invariably included a reference to the demon drink. "Wine is a mocker, strong drink is raging; and whosoever is deceived thereby is not wise," he would thunder, his eyes fixed on her, his youngest child. She still remembered the shame when she had got drunk on her twenty-first birthday. Somehow or another Amelia's mother had affected a truce between them. But still whenever Amelia saw or, worse, smelt whiskey she felt the weight of parental disapproval on her shoulders.

But Tom and Grainne were past noticing Amelia's reticence. As she lay in bed upstairs she could hear their voices and their laughter.

"It's good," she comforted herself, "at least now Tom will listen to Grainne's advice about the house."

And he did. When he woke the next morning he lay groaning beside her, hiding his head beneath the quilt.

"Sorry, sweetheart," he muttered. "Your friend is quite a lady. Not often I can meet someone who can finish the bottle." He rolled over and snuggled against her side. "And you know you were right about the house. She's full of great ideas."

It was early summer now, nearly a year since Amelia and Tom first met. A second series of *The Growing Season* had been commissioned, but to Amelia's dismay Janet said that she was no longer to produce it.

"It wouldn't be right," she said firmly, "not good to mix business and pleasure. Here"—she pushed a folder across the desk to her—"here's something for you to get your teeth into. It's a new reality show. A month on an island with a bunch of nutters. You'll love it."

In vain Amelia protested. Janet wouldn't budge.

"So if I'm not going to produce Tom's programme, who will?" Janet stared over her head at a spot on the wall.

"Well, I thought Grainne would be good for it. Yes, I know," Janet held up her hand, "strictly speaking she isn't a producer, but neither were you when you started here. You were a video editor, and a bloody good one too. Grainne's a production designer and a bloody good one too. But in this game we all need to be multi-taskers. There's no room for specialists any more. OK?"

Tom comforted her.

"Don't worry, love. You go off and do your TV show and I'll be here doing my TV thing. I'm sure we'll manage weekends together. And in the autumn let's go away. Somewhere exotic, the Caribbean maybe or even Australia."

The weeks passed. Phone calls and messages flew backwards and forwards. At last Amelia got the chance to come home for a few days. When she arrived the house was deserted. No sign of Tom. She pulled out her phone and punched in his number. She heard the burble of his ring tone. She walked from the sitting room into the kitchen, then upstairs to the bedroom. His phone lay on the bedside table. A text message was displayed on its screen. She smiled. He was just as sentimental as she. Couldn't bear to clear them away. She bent down to pick it up. Her eyes scanned the message.

"Wow," it read, "double wow. You, me and Tallisker. Fantastic."

Again that familiar sensation. Her knees softened and bright lights flashed in front of her eyes. Her chest heaved and she gasped for air. She felt winded, just the same as when she was a little girl and she fell, landing hard on her ribs. She sat down on the bed, the phone in her hand. Her fingers moved across the buttons as she searched for the message inbox. She scrolled down. Message after message, and all from the same person. Grainne. She opened them one after the other. The more she read the sicker she felt. The trajectory of Tom and Grainne's relationship was revealed to her as plainly and brutally as if she had come upon them making love in her bed. Which of course, it quickly became apparent, they had. In her bed, in Grainne's bed. In the beds of the hotels and guest houses in which they had stayed while they were shooting the series. And not just in beds. There were references to uncomfortable car seats, the prickling of nettles, the biting of midges on exposed flesh. And even, Amelia shuddered with disgust, the removal of a tick from an intimate part of Grainne's body.

She lay on the bed and wept. How could he have done this to her? All she had ever wanted was to love him, honour him, trust him. And as for Grainne, her friend and her confidante . . . she pressed her fingers against her eyelids to try to block out the sudden images which crowded in. Grainne with her round red face and glasses, her black hair that stood out like a badly clipped hedge, her overweight ungainly body, her nicotine-stained fingers and loud raucous laugh. How could he? And how could she, her friend, betray her too?

She got up and stood in front of the mirror above the dressing table. Her own pale, heart-shaped face stared back at her. She picked up the hair brush and drew it down through her straight fair hair. And noticed. Caught among the bristles were thick wiry tendrils. She flung it from her with disgust and it struck the bevelled edge of the mirror with a loud clang. Cracks radiated out across its shiny surface and she saw her face now, distorted, twisted, changed for ever.

And then the phone beeped loudly. She picked it up again and opened the message. She read it out loud.

"Is she back? Are you bored? Think of me. Can't wait." She lifted her head to the image in the mirror. And heard the sound of a car on the drive. Door slamming, footsteps in the hall. And Tom's voice.

"Hi, sweetheart, where are you?" Quick footsteps in the kitchen, in the living room, then on the stairs. She flung the phone away. It skidded under the bed and she kicked it out of sight. The door opened and Tom was there.

"Amelia, how wonderful to see you. Darling, I've missed you so much." His arms around her, his familiar smell, the comfort of his embrace. She closed her eyes and rested her head on his chest. For a moment she could forget. But only for a moment. She opened her eyes and met the eyes in the mirror. She could not forget. Not for an instant.

"Hey, what happened here? The mirror?"

She raised her head and looked at him.

"I was hoping you could tell me. It was like that when I came home. Perhaps," she pulled away, "perhaps there's been an intruder, a break in. Ugh." She shuddered. "What a horrible thought. Someone in our bedroom, an outsider. Someone who shouldn't be here."

She watched his face. For a moment he looked guilty, anxious. But then his expression cleared and he was the old Tom again.

"God, I hope not. I'd better have a look and see if anything's missing. Tell you what," he tilted her face up to his and kissed her gently on the forehead, "there's a special bottle of wine in the fridge for you. Go and open it. I'll just tidy this up and I'll be down in a couple of minutes."

It was hard to believe that Tom had betrayed her. She watched him all evening. He cooked dinner. He was charming and sweet and loving. Full of concern for her wellbeing.

"I've missed you so much," he said, as they sat together on the sofa in front of a dying fire. She pulled away from him, just a little bit.

"Tell me," she said, "how are you getting on with Grainne?"

"Well," he said, "where do I begin?"

"Hold on a minute," she stood up, "just need to go to the loo."

It was amazing, really, how sophisticated recording equipment had become. It was all so miniaturized. Her fingers fumbled with the tiny clip on the microphone as she attached it beneath her shirt collar. She slipped the recorder into the pocket of her jeans and switched it on.

"Now," she snuggled up close, "you were going to tell me about you and Grainne."

The rest of the weekend passed slowly. She heard his mobile phone beep at regular intervals. She tried to ignore it. Soon it was time for her to go. There was still another week of filming on the island off the coast. Then she would be back for editing.

"Don't worry, love," Tom said, as he closed her car door and leaned down to kiss her goodbye. "Soon we'll be together again and everything will be back to normal. And do you know something, sweetheart, I just can't wait."

She watched him in the rear-view mirror as she drove slowly down the drive. His phone was in his hand and she could see his fingers moving across the keypad. Tears welled up into her eyes. They spilled down slowly over her cheeks. She thought of her father in the pulpit on Sundays. She heard his voice. Surely he with his love for his Old Testament God would approve of her? Surely he would. She remembered the words he used to quote from The Song of Solomon:

> *For love is strong as death;*
> *Jealousy is cruel as the grave;*
> *The coals thereof are coals of fire*
> *Which hath a most vehement flame.*

The days flew by and before she knew it she was in the edit suite in the production company. On a shelf above her head she could see the neatly labelled rushes from *The Growing Season*. She reached up and pulled down a handful of tapes. The machine clicked and whirred as she fed them into its greedy mouth. Soon she had found the pictures she wanted. Jackie, the cameraman, had been up to his old tricks. There was shot after shot of Grainne, each less flattering than the one before. And quite a few of Tom and Grainne together. They were laughing, their heads tucked in close. Tom's arm resting casually around Grainne's shoulder as they drank coffee first thing in the morning. Grainne handing Tom her powder to dab on his face to cut down the shine on his nose. Grainne and Tom and the rest of the crew having a quick dip in a beautiful private swimming pool. Amelia shuddered as she watched Grainne's massive thighs wobble but she could see how happy Tom looked as they splashed together in the pale blue water.

It was very late by the time she was finished. The whole place was deserted. She opened the door to Janet's office. In the cabinet behind the desk she found the master tapes for the finished series of *The Growing Season.* She selected the first one. Computerized editing was so easy she thought, remembering her early days in film and video. A few clicks of the mouse and the programme was transformed. So simple to replace parts of Tom's voice-over with the words she had secretly recorded. As long as the duration of the programme was the same as the original, no one would ever know its contents were slightly different.

There was to be a party for the transmission of the first of the series. Grainne had insisted that everyone come to her house.

"You too, Amelia," she said to her on the phone. "After all, if it wasn't for you I wouldn't have got the job. Besides, Tom wants you to be there to share in his moment of glory."

It was late by the time Amelia arrived. The editing of the reality show had taken her longer than usual. Tom was already a bit drunk. His face was flushed and his voice was slightly slurred. He was sitting beside Grainne on her large comfortable sofa. When Amelia walked into the room he did not stir. He did not even notice. Her stomach churned, but she smiled calmly, poured herself a large glass of wine and sat down on the floor beside Jackie and the rest of the crew.

"Shh," Grainne hissed loudly. "Ten seconds to go." She turned up the volume on the huge flat screen TV. Amelia sipped her wine. The familiar sig tune began to play and the opening animation flashed across the screen. She settled back to watch. At the commercial break midway through she got up to replenish her drink. Tom was deep in conversation with Grainne. He barely seemed to notice Amelia at all. She could see that everyone else was slightly embarrassed. They grinned sympathetically at her and Jackie put his arm around her as she took her place for the second part of the show. She had to admit, she'd done a great job of the re-edit. The transition was seamless. One minute Tom was waxing lyrical about new varieties of Brussels sprouts; the next he was talking about the size and shape of Grainne's bottom.

"It's bloody huge. I can't imagine what size jeans she must take. Triple XL, I'd say."

Sure enough, Amelia had found a good shot of the offending part of Grainne's anatomy. But Tom wasn't stopping there. Over a selection of shots of sandwiches and pints at lunchtime, giant courgettes and pumpkins growing in a garden in Tipperary and a friendly farmhouse pig, Amelia had constructed from Tom's recordings a paean to Grainne's size, shape and enormous appetite. The room fell into a stunned silence. But there was worse to come. In the middle of an interview with a renowned botanist from the Botanic Gardens, over shots of Grainne yawning loudly, mouth wide open, Tom could be heard to say, "Thick as two planks, drinks far too much, the old Tallisker's taking its toll," before neatly segueing into his closing piece to camera.

As the credits rolled, Grainne stood up and switched off the TV. Amelia, closing the front door behind her, heard the crash of breaking glass.

Multi-tasking, that was what Janet had called it. Amelia had many skills and abilities. She could call upon them all when she went looking for her next job. And her next man? She was in no hurry. Again she heard her father's voice. "When pride cometh, then cometh shame, but with the lowly is wisdom." It was a lesson learned and learned well.

JULIE PARSONS was born in New Zealand but moved to Ireland at an early age. She worked for many years as a radio and television producer with RTÉ, and is the author of four internationally bestselling and critically acclaimed thrillers: *Mary, Mary; The Courtship Gift; Eager to Please;* and *The Guilty Heart.*

Julie Parsons lives outside Dublin, with her family.

Blue Murder

Joan O'Neill

The house at the end of the curving driveway bore signs of serious neglect, the trailing, wind-bitten roses and rampant nasturtiums the only remnants of the once-beautiful gardens, the soft cooing of pigeons the only welcome.

The inside was drab and airless, the furniture shrouded in dust covers. I'd spent my money unwisely paying Ben, my cousin, for a caretaking job he hadn't done. I pulled back the drapes and opened the grimy windows. The sea that I'd craved so much glinted silver in the afternoon sun, lifting my spirits. Boats listed sideways as they sailed along the eastern seaboard. To my right the proud church and adjoining graveyard, where both my parents were buried, dominated the village.

I was home and that was all that mattered. There would be plenty of time to put things right.

That evening as I was in the local supermarket to stock up on groceries, Mary, the friendly cashier, eyed me with surprise. "It's been a while," she said.

"Yes, it has," I agreed.

"Staying long?"

"I haven't decided." I packed up quickly to stop her curiosity taking her questions any further and left.

The following morning the phone rang.

"Hi, Tanya, heard you were back in town." It was my friend Rachael.

News travels fast in Kill.

"I got back yesterday."

"I've been on to the others. We're all dying to see you. What about a get-together, Thursday night suit you?" she rushed on.

"I have a tight schedule. Interview Friday morning," I lied in an effort to wriggle out of it.

"You can leave early," she said, determined to get me there at all costs. "Do come."

"OK."

"Great! It'll be lovely to see you again," she coaxed, giving me her new address.

Nervously I replaced the receiver. We hadn't seen each other for five years. I was sure they would have changed, I knew I had.

Rachael, Kirsten, Lucy and I had been friends since our school days, exchanging advice on hair and contraceptive techniques, and boyfriends. Rachael had always been the organizer of the group. Her "get-togethers" were lively, gossipy affairs, dinner parties really, for which you were expected to dress up and make an effort. I was under no illusion as to the reason why she was having this one. Dad's death five years ago had been sudden and shocking. I'd returned from a well-paid PR job in London to look after him. Overnight I'd become a curiosity, my every move the subject of speculation. Even with the generous offers of help to deal with it from the girls, especially Lucy, to whom I was closest, I couldn't cope. That was when I decided to leave Ireland altogether. I travelled extensively and ended up teaching English as a foreign language in Madrid, a city that throbbed with excitement, but where I had often been homesick.

They had all tried to contact me. Lucy wrote to my home relentlessly begging me to get in touch. Ben re-addressed the letters, the least he could do. Eventually, worn down and missing home, I emailed her. We kept in touch sporadically. Now that I was back I knew they'd want to check me out to see how I was looking, find out what the real story was. I was scared.

Rachael lived on a quiet leafy road in the suburbs. The house, with its extensive lawns, was a magnificent white edifice. I took a deep breath to fortify myself before I knocked on the door. What was it going to be like facing them again? Was I always going to be thought of as a suspect in the murder of my father?

Rachael came to greet me with a frisson of excitement.

"Tanya! You haven't changed a bit. You look terrific! Elegant as ever!" She hugged me.

"I can return the compliment," I said.

Striking in a vibrant red dress, her copper hair shining, her blue eyes gleaming, she looked not a day older than when I'd last seen her, though she was in her late twenties now.

"Come on in, the others are here," she said, leading me down the hall.

The interior of her house was expensively furnished, with stripped pine floors. Rachael's husband, James, a top criminal barrister, spent long periods at the Bar, leaving her to earn a fortune with her successful graphic design business.

A bright star in the scholarly firmament, she had achieved her goals. I had to admire her.

Kirsten and Lucy turned as we entered the sitting room.

"Hi," I said with as brave a smile as I could muster.

"Tanya!" Lucy was up first. "Great to see you!" she said, pleasure and curiosity in her eyes, her scent of Giorgio, her choice of perfume, a reminder of earlier, happier days.

Kirsten was more restrained in her greeting.

"Congratulations, I heard you had a baby," I said to her.

"Emma's six months old now." Her face glowed with pride and fulfilment.

"Still on vodka and Diet Coke?" Rachael asked, anxious to get a drink down me as fast as possible to put me at my ease.

"Just the one, please, I'm driving."

In the awkward silence I tried to make myself comfortable on my allocated chair. We were all like strangers.

Lucy asked, "Did you enjoy Madrid?"

"Yes, I loved it. It was a mad lifestyle, always something to do," I said.

Always the judgemental one, Kirsten scrutinized me. "And you like to have something on the go, don't you?" she said.

"Or someone!" Lucy probed, her eyes dripping with curiosity.

My heart lurched as I thought of the dark jostling restaurant where I'd met Havier, the gorgeous Spanish waiter I'd fallen for and told her about.

"That was just a fling," I said, smiling. "He went off to seek his fortune in the States," I added, feeling compelled to make conversation as three pairs of eyes bored into mine but not wanting to admit that he'd dumped me en route.

Kirsten asked, "What have you been up to since you got back?"

"Job hunting. It's not as easy as it seems."

"Don't we know," Lucy said. "Things have changed in the last year."

"Will you be staying this time?" Kirsten asked.

"I haven't made up my mind yet."

"I do hope so," Lucy said. "We can pick up where we left off."

In the awkward silence Rachael and Kirsten swapped censorious glances. I knew from their closed expressions that the circumstances of my departure were uppermost in their minds.

"Don't you miss working?" I asked Kirsten.

A career girl, she'd run her own department in a local, very successful corporate law firm.

"I miss having my own money. Ken's a bit tight with the cash, but having Emma more than compensates."

"It's your cash too," Rachael reminded her.

"Give me a career any day. I couldn't bear to be stuck at home," Lucy said.

"Nor me," said Rachael.

"Doesn't James want children?" Kirsten asked her.

"Not yet. He doesn't want the hassle," she said.

"But surely it would settle him down, stop all those long working hours."

"That's what she's afraid of," Kirsten laughed.

"How are you coping in that sprawling house all on your own?" Lucy asked me, genuine concern in her voice.

"I'm fine."

"Don't you get nervous at night?" Rachael asked.

"I have a good alarm system," I assured her.

My eyes flicked back to Lucy.

Always full of change and contradictions, she'd switched from one job to another. Gone was the bubbly, curvaceous blonde. She was thin and anxious and I wondered what had brought about this change.

"Anyone special on the scene?" I asked her.

"No, single and enjoying it!" Her smile indicated that she was making the best of the situation.

We chatted on, the conversation stilted, until Rachael announced that it was time to eat.

In the dining room there was a magnificent spread of salmon en croute, Mediterranean salads, and chicken Provençal all laid out in dark blue Denby ware amid the silver and plain crystal.

"Wow! This won't do my figure any good," Kirsten said, patting her stomach.

"Forget your special dietary requirements for once," Lucy suggested. "I'm going to."

"You look as if you could do with a good feed, you're positively anorexic," Rachael scolded her with a mischievous smile.

"You say the nicest things," Lucy scowled.

"Delicious," Kirsten pronounced through a mouthful of prawns in aspic. "I don't know how you do it."

"Caterers," Rachael informed her without a flinch. "You'll never guess what I found the other day," she said.

"What?" the others chorused.

I held my breath.

"The topless photographs we took on the beach the summer we did the Leaving Cert," Rachael said.

"You showed mine to the boys in sixth form," Kirsten admonished her.

"That was a horrible thing to do," said Lucy with disgust.

"I know! It put Ken right off me. We'd just started dating and I fancied him rotten. I had a hell of a job persuading him that I wasn't giving it away," Kirsten laughed good-naturedly.

"Well, you got him in the end," Rachael consoled her.

"You've got the one with the looks," Kirsten said, her eyes on Rachael and James's wedding photograph on the sideboard.

"Yes, you made sure of that." Lucy smiled but her eyes were oozing jealousy.

I shot Lucy a look of sympathy, remembering that James had been her boyfriend before Rachael had swiped him from her.

"Remember Roper, the physics teacher?" Rachael said, changing the subject fast. "He stalked you, Tanya," she reminded me—as if I needed to be reminded.

"Made your life miserable," Lucy said, wrinkling her nose in disdain.

"Dirty lecher," Kirsten said.

"Whatever happened to him?" Rachael asked.

"I heard that he died in mysterious circumstances," Lucy confided.

"Maybe he was bumped off," Kirsten said with her eyes on me, the unasked question in them stopping the conversation abruptly as Dad's death came to the fore.

The sense of fear and panic that I had come to accept was suddenly a living nightmare. The things I tried to forget and put behind me had returned to haunt me. BODY FOUND IN WOODS the headlines had screamed at the time. He'd been gone for several days before his body was found in the woods behind our house, with his neck broken. Murder was suspected. There had been an inquest. With no witnesses and lack of evidence it wasn't proven. The case had been the talk of the town, a horrific time for me.

I'd moved back to Wexford after a stroke had left him partially crippled. Things hadn't been good between us. I found it difficult to live in the same house as my cantankerous parent who'd never had much time for me and resented his dependence on me.

We survived a year of rows and arguments, but the following winter took its toll of my patience. More and more I'd felt like a prisoner with his asking me where I'd been every time I stepped through the door. He took to drinking heavily, though the doctor had advised against it. He would limp to the pub and home again, taking the short cut along the woodland path at the back of the house. There were the inevitable battles with him using obscene language, the likes of which I'd never heard him use before. Once he'd come after me wielding a knife like a raving lunatic. Had he been stronger he might have killed me . . .

When I looked up they were all watching me.

Lucy caught my eye. "You had such a hard time," she said with sympathy.

"Yes, awful," Rachael agreed. "I felt so sorry for you."

Lucy said, "It was dreadful what they put you through. All of that questioning and cops swarming all over the place."

"The injustice!" said Rachael indignantly.

"The law must be upheld," Kirsten said with cool authority, flicking her eyes towards me.

"Yes, they had to do their job," I agreed in an effort to get off the subject.

Rachael amused us with anecdotes about some of her wackier clients. Kirsten talked about breastfeeding Emma. She had become sickeningly smug, and happy.

At ten-thirty I made my escape, promising faithfully to keep in touch with them all. James drove in as I was leaving. He got out of his car and came over to me.

"Good to see you again, Tanya," he said with a friendly smile.

"You too," I said.

"Enjoyed yourself?"

"Yes, thanks," I said. "It was nice to see everyone again."

"Keep in touch now that you're back."

"I will."

He walked me to my car. "I've been taking a keen interest in your father's case again. I'm always hoping they'll turn up new evidence."

"But it's dead and buried," I said, surprised.

He looked me straight in the eye. "That's where you're wrong. There are many questions left unanswered and I'm determined to get to the bottom of it."

The self-righteous look he gave me made me shiver. "You got away with blue murder, Tanya, and you know it." There was no doubt in his mind that I'd killed my father.

Shaking, I unlocked my car, and got in.

Through his farewell smile he scrutinized me. "I just hope his death was instant and that he didn't suffer."

I slammed the door shut and sped off.

I heard the report of James's death on the lunchtime news the next day.

"James Masterson, top criminal barrister, killed in head-on collision this morning on his way to work," the newscaster said.

I stood glued to the floor.

The phone rang. It was Lucy.

"Have you heard about James's accident?" She broke down, sobbing, beside herself with grief.

"Yes, awful, shocking," I said.

"Oh, Tanya, I don't know what I'm going to do. I was having an affair with him," she blurted out. "He was going to leave Rachael. We were—" She sobbed hysterically.

"Lucy, calm down. Take a deep breath," I advised.

"And now he's gone," she said, distraught.

No matter what I said she wouldn't be consoled.

Kirsten phoned soon afterwards. "The Guards suspect foul play," she said. "The brakes of his car had been severed."

"But why would anyone want to kill him?"

"There could be a few motives. Maybe he was on to something or someone."

"Or maybe someone was on to him; rejection, love turned to bitterness," I suggested.

"You know about his affair with Lucy, then."

"Yes, she told me."

"The Guards will be interviewing us all. They'll want proper answers this time, Tanya."

"They got proper answers the last time, and technically I know nothing about car engines," I assured her.

"Then you've nothing to worry about." She clicked off.

Later on, the doorbell rang. The silver-haired detective with the weather-beaten face and sharp eyes I recognized from the past was on the doorstep. My heart somersaulted with fear. The nightmare of endless questions, strange looks, and disbelief was starting all over again.

"Detective Inspector Grey," he said, flashing his identity card at me, not bothering to introduce his sidekick, a young Garda who stood respectfully behind him.

"Miss Fox! You spent the evening at the Mastersons' home, I believe."

"Yes, I did," I said, trying to control my shaking.

"What time did you leave?"

"Half past ten."

"Was James Masterson there?"

"He arrived as I was leaving."

"Did you speak to him?"

"Briefly."

"What time did you get home?"

"About a quarter to eleven."

"Can anyone vouch for that."

"No."

"Seen much of the Mastersons recently?"

"No, I've been abroad."

He looked me in the eye. "This is a murder enquiry, Miss Fox. We're investigating everything, questioning everybody who was in the vicinity of the Masterson home between the hours of ten-thirty and eight o'clock this morning. We're looking for any fragment of evidence, any scrap of information. The brakes of Mr. Masterson's car were severed intentionally."

I met his shrewd gaze. "So I heard."

"We can only speculate, as we have no proof yet, but we know that Mr. Masterson made enemies in the course of his work. We thought you might be able to help us with our enquiries." He raised a curious eyebrow.

I shook my head. "I'm sorry. I know nothing about it."

After they left I leaned against the door, trembling uncontrollably. In the kitchen I poured myself a glass of wine, took huge gulps and tried to calm down. I had a shower, studied my reflection in the bathroom mirror. I was beginning to look the way Dad looked before something snapped in him and he went on a self-destructive path. It was in my eyes, that same look of abandonment, and the shocking loneliness that accompanied it.

All I had to do was stay calm, ride the storm like I had done the last time. Soon I'd be off again to a new job; new friends in a new location, and it would all blow over. Though I'd never be able to forget what I'd done, I certainly could appear to do so. I had plenty of practice.

JOAN O'NEILL began her writing career in 1987 with short stories and serials. Her first novel, *Daisy Chain War,* published in 1990, won the Reading Association of Ireland Special Merit

Award and was shortlisted for the Bisto Award. It is regarded as one of the foremost Irish novels for teenagers. Since then, she has also become a bestselling novelist for adults with *Leaving Home; Turn of the Tide; A Home Full of Women; Something Borrowed, Something Blue; Perfectly Impossible;* and, most recently, *Concerning Kate.*

Flesh and Blood

Marita Conlon-McKenna

*I*t always rained in Dublin. Pissing wet grey dirty rain. Nothing's changed, thought Christine as she tipped the surly-looking taxi driver who had spent the past twenty minutes in heavy traffic discussing the merits of the Kerry football team despite her obvious disinterest. The rather ancient silver Mercedes pulled up across from St. Stephen's Green and the porter and bell-hop immediately helped her with her luggage as she checked into the Shelbourne Hotel. The travel agent had done his best to persuade her of the merits of staying in one of Dublin's newer flash designer hotels but tradition and the childhood memory of feeding the ducks and swinging on the swings in the city's public park had won out and she had insisted on a room overlooking the Green for old times' sake.

The room was somewhat chintzy but was in classic good taste and certainly not in need of the services of some fussy hip interior designer. It smelt faintly of stale smoke and Christine raised the window to let some air in. Standing looking out at the rain, she felt a shiver of anticipation, a rare tingle of joy at being home. She grabbed her purse and pulled out her address book, she was jet-lagged and exhausted but there were phone calls to be made, meetings to be set up and visits to be organized, then she could collapse and sleep in the enormous king-size bed.

The hot water had sluiced her awake as she lavished her favourite Sonoma shower gel on her naked skin, wrapping herself in the plush white bath towels as she dried her short highlighted strawberry blonde hair. Not bad for going on thirty-eight, she thought as she considered herself in the mirror, good skin, no amount of money could buy you that and she thanked God for genes that gave her a flawless pale complexion. She moueed her lips, kissable in the extreme, a little bit of collagen discreetly done, along with her tinted lashes and ten thousand dollars worth of dental work. She was in good shape, no one could dispute that! Worth every penny, that's what Larry would say. She dared herself not to cry, knowing that if her husband had accompanied her on the trip this hotel suite would be full of fresh flowers, champagne chilling in a bucket and the staff would be dancing attendance on them. He was that kind of man. The kind of man who in his own fashion, commanded respect and notice the minute he stepped into a room. She gathered herself together, there was no point getting maudlin just because she was alone, back home, back in the city she'd grown up in. Dear old Dublin, there hadn't been much dear about it when she'd left nineteen years ago with her tail between her legs.

She carefully put on her make-up before taking the expensive cream suit from the wardrobe. Size eight. It gave her inestimable pleasure to read that label hand sewn on the back of the jacket. Achieved by dedication and daily Pilates and a personal trainer once a week. She stretched automatically as she slipped it on over her vanilla-coloured silk top.

Now a bit of glitz. She took her silk jewellery pouch from the bedroom safe and spilled the contents out on the bed. Pearls. Larry had bought them for her the last time they were in Nassau, discreet, expensive. She fingered her diamond choker and bracelet from Cartier, certainly not discreet, slightly bling-bling as the Americans would say. She fastened the sparkling stones around her neck. The bracelet! Perhaps too many diamonds! No, tonight she wanted to create an impression and pushing thoughts of good taste and elegance aside, she fastened the sapphire and diamond-encrusted band to her left wrist. She fingered the large Tiffany diamond set in white gold on her finger. These stones and jewels were all she'd left of Larry and the memories of their time together, she'd flaunt them, she thought, as she consigned the pearls back to the safe.

Downstairs Christine sipped her dry martini as she waited in the plush residents' lounge for her sister, Mary, and brothers, Brendan and Liam, to appear. She had checked with the head waiter and the table for twelve was all set up in the dining room. She glanced at her watch hoping they weren't going to be late. She hated tardiness.

Outside in the lobby there was a hullabaloo and instinctively she guessed it was created by the arrival of her siblings and their spouses and children, and stood up to meet them.

"Chrissy!" called her sister, rushing forward and wrapping her in huge plump arms stretched taut in a navy velour top and matching skirt. "You look wonderful, beautiful! Doesn't she, boys!"

Christine smiled back. She couldn't believe that the plump motherly figure was her older sister. Only three years separated them, but they seemed a generation apart. "You look wonderful too," she said politely as she tried to take them all in. Bren had put on weight too, a large beer belly protruding from his pristine white shirt, and was already going grey but was otherwise as handsome as ever, and Liam was still wiry, his tightly curled red hair cut close to his head. She tried to push all critical thoughts from her mind as she embraced them, remembering that after all they were her flesh and blood.

"God, you look gorgeous!" teased Brendan, her older brother.

"And do you still break the ladies' hearts?" she teased back.

"Not since I met Sheila," he grinned, introducing the thin mousy-looking woman beside him.

Her hair was a state, thought Christine, botched by some local hairdresser no doubt, but she had good bone structure, and great eyes.

"Nice to meet you," smiled her brother's wife, "I've heard so much about you."

She raised her eyebrows.

"What I meant is Bren is always talking about when you were kids and growing up on Meath Street."

"Those were the days!" chorused her brother.

"I'm not sure I'd agree with you," she interrupted, thinking of the small two-up two-down terrace house with a tiny concrete yard where they had been raised, as her sister-in-law introduced her niece and nephew.

"Say hello to your auntie."

Karen at fourteen had a wide face with perfect features and long skinny legs that seemed to go on for ever and disappear under the shortest of denim mini-skirts, while her brother Jamie had a great look of his grandfather. Christine was taken aback by the resemblance.

"Nice to meet you," they said politely.

"We left Lisa and Brendan junior at home," apologized her sister-in-law. "They hate fancy food. It would be a waste of money dragging them along here. Sure you'll meet them when you come to the house."

Liam gave her a smacker of a kiss and his wife, Mairead, greeted her warmly. Her younger brother had fallen in love with Mairead Collins when he was fifteen years old and by the look of it they were still cracked about each other.

Christine, delighted, hugged her and complimented her, noticing the perfectly cut blonde hair that touched her shoulders.

"We're delighted you're home, but you could have stayed with us. We'd have loved to have you."

"Thanks, but I've always liked this hotel and I didn't want to put anyone out."

Their son, Colm, was the spit of Liam, and she could tell he was blessed with the same bright enquiring mind as his father as he took in everything around him. His younger brother had been left in the care of a babysitter.

Her brothers were getting into an argument about paying the drinks bill as the waitress tried to keep track of the order.

"Charge it to my room, number 231," insisted Christine, relieved to sit down with Mary on the massive red couch as the numbers of beers and glasses of wine got sorted.

"It's so lovely to see you again," smiled Mary, squeezing her hand. "We've all really missed you."

She knew by her sister's voice that she meant it. That was one of the things she liked about Mary, she was not a bullshitter! Tony, her husband, stood with a pint of Guinness in his hand, the total opposite of her sister, he was the greatest bullshitter she'd ever come across. She didn't know how Mary stuck him.

Christine gave a silent sigh of relief that neither of her sister's children bore the slightest resemblance to their father. Orla was a smaller sexier version of her mother with huge dark eyes and a pert little nose and an engaging laugh, while Eoin still possessed the round face and big eyes and dimple of the Kavanagh side of the family.

"I'm studying business in DIT," he said proudly.

"And I'm nursing in St. Vincent's."

Christine stifled a pang of envy as she chatted to her sister's children. Two genuine nice kids. Mary was lucky! Larry had been emphatic about not having more children. He'd raised two families and had no intention of starting a third. No amount of cajoling and pleading would get him to change his mind and Christine had grudgingly come to accept their child-lessness and enjoy the lifestyle that wealth and prestige pro-vided.

She was trying to be pleasant to Bren's wife who seemed devoid of personality or wit and sipped on her glass of white wine as if her life depended on it.

Another round of drinks was ordered, Tony asking for a whiskey to go with his pint.

"We were sorry to hear about Larry, he seemed such a good man. You must miss him terribly!" Mary's plump face filled with concern. "I don't know what I'd do if anything were to happen to Tony. I couldn't survive without him."

Christine tried to control herself. She didn't want to break down and cry here with everyone looking at her. She took a deep slow breath that reached right down beyond her solar plexus, mentally saying the word relax.

"Being on my own, it has been hard," she admitted slowly as her sister squeezed her hand and she discreetly tried to protect her nails.

Tony had finished off a second pint of Guinness and was about to order a third when Christine stood up and insisted it was time for dinner. She wasn't having that bowsie getting drunk and disgracing her.

"I'm starving," murmured young Jamie as they all trooped towards the dining room.

The dining room was busy and the head waiter showed them to their table; the young people were down one end, Mary and Liam on either side of her as they all studied the menu.

"Janey, look at the prices," shouted Karen.

"Your auntie Christine is treating us," beamed Bren, obviously determined to go the full hog as he eyed pheasant and venison and lobster on the menu.

"Have what you want, please!" insisted Christine as she perused the wine list. "This is my treat."

They did have what they wanted and the waiter's face was nonplussed as the teenagers asked for tomato sauce and some chips along with their roast duckling main course.

"How long are you staying?" Liam asked.

"A few days, maybe a little longer. I have business to attend to in the States when I get back."

They all looked up at her inquisitively.

"Papers to sign, legal documents," she said with a toss of her manicured hand.

"God, it must be awful," sympathized Bren. "Larry was a good man, but with all his businesses and the like there must be lots of stuff to sort out."

"I am fortunate to have very good legal advice," she said softly.

"That's good, that's what I'm saying. You need the best, the very best. Larry's likely left you millions with all his stocks and bonds and shares."

Christine flushed. She had absolutely no intention of discussing her financial affairs with her family.

Mary Leonard shifted uncomfortably. Why did Bren have to bring the whole money thing up? Their little sister, home for the first time in a long time. She wished her brother would keep his big trap shut and not be so overawed by her marriage to a multi-millionaire like Larry.

Down the far end of the table the boys were squabbling over the merits of hot fudge or chocolate sauce poured lavishly over their chosen dessert, Christine secretly wondering if they would have been better off in McDonalds!

Over tea and coffee they chatted.

"Are you going to see Daddy?"

"I don't know, Mary. I'm not sure. He probably wouldn't want to see me."

"Of course you should see him. That way you'll have no regrets."

"I know but I keep remembering back, thinking of the things he said to me, the way he treated me. I'm not sure I actually want to see him again."

"He's weak, Chrissy. He's not going to live for ever. You should try to forgive him."

"I'm not sure I can."

"He's an old man. The staff in Bellaire are good to him but a lot of the time he's lost in some world of his own. Some days he doesn't even know Tony and myself or the kids. It's very sad really."

Christine didn't know if she could ever forgive him for the way he'd treated her, for driving her away from home.

"I'm going over tomorrow. I could pick you up. We needn't stay that long, honest. You should just come and see him."

"I'll think about it," she promised.

As more tea and coffee and glasses of Baileys were served the talk turned to their childhood and Christine joined in the fun and laughter, wondering how her sister and brothers had managed to whitewash their childhood in such a way that they only remembered the good bits, the funny bits, the bad days banished from their shared memory. It was weird! Looking around the dining room she could see the ageing couples, the business partners, the corporate table, all throwing an envious glance at the large family dinner she had assembled. Christine realized that somehow she had let them all become strangers and deliberately turned her back on the past. She caught the waiter's eye and blinked barely an eyelash when she saw the massive food and drinks bill her clan had managed to run up in only a few hours. She ran her eye over the figures, trying to disguise her dismay before signing the bill with a flourish.

"Thank you, Christine," murmured Mairead appreciatively. "It must have cost a fortune!"

"That was a great feed," added her brother, belching appreciatively. "Thanks a lot, Chrissy."

Afterwards she walked them all out to the hotel door, basking in their gratitude and thanks for the meal as, relieved, she watched them disappear into the traffic and the night.

"Promise me you'll think about coming to see Daddy tomorrow," insisted her sister.

"I'll see," she said, non-committal.

Back in her hotel bedroom she flopped into bed exhausted, drained from the evening's efforts, barely brushing her teeth and wiping her face with the wet cloth before falling into a heavy tormented sleep. She hated sleeping alone. She still missed Larry's snoring and warm breath.

◆   ◆   ◆

Mid morning, Mary was waiting for her in the foyer in a pair of stretch denim jeans and a sweatshirt. Christine was embarrassed as her sister hugged her against her massive breasts. She still wasn't sure this was a good idea despite her sister convincing her to change her mind. She felt drained and hung-over and would have welcomed two hours in the hotel's leisure centre with the attentions of a good masseuse. Still, she sighed, it had been one of the things on her list.

"I'm parked just across the road. Hopefully I haven't been bloody clamped."

Christine sat in the front seat of the Toyota, trying to nonchalantly brush the dog hairs and evidence of crushed Tayto crisps from under her. This was a nightmare, she thought, as her sister swerved out in front of a white van, giving the driver the fingers cheerfully as he honked at her.

The nursing home was about four miles out of the city, situated in a converted old Edwardian house, and Christine said little as Mary drove, letting her sister ramble on about Tony and the kids and her life as she tried to collect herself at the thought of the visit.

She hardly recognized him He was an old man. Wizened, hunched and grey in a special support chair near his bed and locker in the ward of eight beds.

"Hello, Daddy," she said softly.

His eyes stared back at her, blank, innocent, without a glimmer or trace of recognition. She couldn't believe it. The miserable bastard didn't know her. Didn't remember her or the things he'd done to her. She wanted to haul him out of that fucking chair and shake him like the doll he'd become.

"Daddy, it's Christine. You remember Christine. I was talking to you about her a few days ago," pleaded Mary. "She went to America."

Nothing. No response.

"He's like this sometimes. I tried to warn you," apologized her sister as she bent down and kissed his cheek and said, "Hello, Daddy!"

Christine stood, looking at him, waiting for some flash of recognition. For God's sake, he was her father! He couldn't just sit there pretending he didn't remember. She wouldn't let him. His eyes stared blankly at her. He was wearing grey carpet slippers and thick navy wool socks that clung to his skinny ankles, and was nothing like the man she remembered. The man who shouted and screamed and bullied and for most of their childhood years made their life a hell. Her mother had spent thirty years of her life trying to keep the peace, to create a normal family life, doing her best to be like their neighbours, the McEvoys and the Dalys. But nothing could disguise the raised voices and the shouting as Tom Kavanagh tried to reign control over his daughters and sons. The minute they heard his key in the lock everything changed. He shouted and complained constantly, the carpet was dirty, there were leaves on the doorstep, the windows needed polishing, there were dog hairs everywhere, the food was cold, the gravy was lumpy, the meat was gristly. She closed her eyes remembering the small kitchen and her mother silently signalling to eat the dinner quickly and disappear to do their homework. They learned how to close their ears as he constantly harangued and belittled their mother, treating her like a skivvy in her own home. Usually it was just words, but sometimes there was more! Christine could feel bile rise in her throat at the memory of it. Bren had challenged him. At sixteen he'd stood up to him, pulled the belt from his hands and told him he'd fucking choke him if he touched him again. Tom Kavanagh had never laid a finger on his eldest son after that. Liam on the other hand, to avoid confrontation, had stayed out, played football till it was dark, hung around town, keeping away from home. He'd been made to feel welcome by Mairead's family and, once they were able, had married her. Mary had also tried to escape. She'd jumped into the arms of Tony Leonard, a northside Romeo with greasy black hair who had promised her the sun, the moon and the stars when she'd let him go the whole way with her, her sister oblivious to the fact that Tony, a warehouse man, was going nowhere and fast. After a hastily arranged wedding Mary and Tony had lived in a flat in Kilmainham for the first few years, then a small three-bedroomed terrace house in Ringsend. Poor Mary.

She stared at her father. She was the one left at home, stuck with him. Studying for her Leaving Certificate, doing a secretarial course, trying to get a job in the banks or the civil service. She wanted wings! She wanted to fly.

Then Aidan Flynn had come into her life. She danced with him in Zhivago's Night Club. He was everything she wanted and, besotted, she'd thrown caution to the wind. Finding out she was pregnant, Aidan had taken the news of impending fatherhood badly. There was no trip to McDowell's "The Happy Ring House." Instead he had given her money. Paid her off. Talked about studying, learning the business and not being ready yet to settle down.

Her mother had held her hand and promised to stand by her when, hysterical, she confided in her, telling her to delay saying anything to her father for as long as possible and to keep out of his way. She had. She'd crept around the house like a mouse, wearing baggy jumpers and leggings until at six and a half months he'd finally found out.

"Filthy slut! Tramp!"

Despite her mother's protests he'd flung her out.

An elderly couple in Crumlin had taken her in. Three days after her baby was born in the Coombe, she had signed the papers giving her up. A fresh start, that's what she needed. With Aidan's money, she had wings and she could fly!

"He's not usually this bad! Grumpy, off-form," apologized Mary. "Maybe he had a bad night."

Christine tensed. Was he doing it deliberately to wind her up?

"Would you like a cup of tea or coffee? There's a coffee shop down the hall."

She shrugged. The coffee in Ireland tasted shite.

"Listen, you sit with him. Anyway, you should have some time with him on your own and I'll go and get two coffees."

She watched the heavy bulk of her sister disappear through the door.

She pulled the metal chair closer to the old man. He smelt faintly of urine and that strange scent of age. His fingers were thin, fidgeting with the material of his cardigan.

"Don't pretend you don't know me, Daddy. You know well who the fuck I am!"

The old man looked up at her, the rising note of her voice grabbing his attention.

"You gave us hell growing up and not one of us will forget you for it. Never. I'll never forgive you for what you did to Mammy and Bren and Mary and Liam, never! If you live to be a hundred, wizened away in that chair of yours, I won't forgive you."

His hands were shaking as, agitated, he pulled at the button, his face now turned to hers, listening.

"I'm Christine, your daughter. You remember! When I told you I was going to have a child, you threw me out. Told me to get out of your sight and that you never wanted to see me again! Do you remember, Daddy? 'Cause I do. I remember what a shite father you were, who wouldn't even stand by his own flesh and blood."

She could see the pupils in his eyes alter. He was listening.

"You told me I was worth nothing! I went away to America. I worked damn hard in restaurants and bars. Made a new life for myself and in time met a good man and learned to enjoy life. You hate to hear that! Hate to hear that someone in our family had a good life. I have a swimming pool and a tennis court and a maid and a gardener and a house with twelve bedrooms. I married a millionaire and I've more money than someone like you can ever imagine."

A nurse walked by, darting a concerned look in their direction. Christine smiled and nodded and patted her father's hand.

She could see the slight glimmer of recognition in his eye.

"Chrrr—" he started to say. She could sense he was afraid of her.

"Sorry, they only had plastic cups," interrupted her sister passing her the coffee and a chocolate KitKat. "How have you and Daddy been getting on? It'll do him good to see you. He doesn't get half enough visitors. Tony hates this place and you know what Bren's like! He can't stand being around sick people."

Christine cradled the hot cup in her hands.

"You're glad to see Christine, aren't you, Daddy?" chorused her sister, treating their father like he was a four-year-old.

"I think we should get going soon, I've a lot on with only being here for a few days."

"Of course, I usually spend hours with him but we'll finish our coffee and get going then, OK."

Mary kept up a patter of chatter that reminded Christine of dealing with a kid in kindergarten.

"Daddy, we've got to go," her sister explained eventually as she kissed him and brushed his hair.

Polite, Christine lightly grazed the top of his head with her lips, relieved to leave. They were at the door of the ward when she excused herself to Mary.

"I mightn't ever see him again," she explained as she ran back towards the bed and bent down as if she was going to embrace him.

"Daddy I've something to say. All the prayers and communions and rosaries in the world won't save you. You are a miserable old bastard and Mammy was a saint to put up with you. She's up in heaven now but you, you can go to hell as far as I care!"

She turned on her heel and left.

"Ah Tommy, don't cry 'cause your daughters are gone," consoled Nurse Regan half an hour later as she attended to him and slowly spooned the minced meat and mashed potato mixture into his mouth.

Mary insisted they go for lunch and have a chat but Christine was anxious to get back to the hotel as the music blared in the busy pub in Glasthule and she ate thick mushroom soup and chomped her way through chunks of rubbery cheese and crusty bread, served with a side salad.

"I bet you feel the better for seeing him," smiled her sister, "for putting the past behind you. Anger never did anyone any good!"

"You're right, I do feel better."

Still jet-lagged, back in the Shelbourne she napped for a while, then got food sent to her room before ordering a taxi. She directed the driver through a warren of back streets that led towards Flynn's pub, noticing the fancy new apartment blocks and smart offices that littered the way. She had phoned, looking for the owner, a bargirl telling her he would be back by seven. The houses were the same, the bookies, the grocery store was now a red and green Spar that looked spick and span instead of the dirt-encrusted and mouse-infested store of the past. There was a dry cleaner's and a florist. Who in God's name would buy flowers in a place like this! The pub stood right at the end of the block and had been painted a yellow creamy buttermilk colour, the window and door frames picked out in black, the huge Guinness sign still hanging on the side, loopy signwriting declaring the name Flynn's Fine Establishment. Nervous, she pushed open the door. Over in the corner a large screen TV flickered, Sky news.

A few seats were taken up at the bar and a group of men were huddled around a table arguing figures. If she sat down she would be pretty inconspicuous, she thought, choosing a small table at the far end. A young girl in a black mini-skirt and a white blouse came over to serve her, unsure when she ordered a dry Martini.

"Forget it. I'll have a gin and tonic instead."

The girl immediately looked relieved.

The upholstery was new as were the light fittings and wooden tables and floors. Gone was the richly patterned red carpet, replaced with stained and polished floorboards.

"Is Mr. Flynn here?" she enquired as she paid for her drink.

"He was due in but he must have got delayed in traffic. He'll be here shortly."

"Tell me, does Mr. Flynn have any other pubs or businesses?"

The girl hesitated.

"No, it's just that a friend recommended me to be sure to go to Flynn's when I was over in Dublin and I wasn't sure if this was the only one or not."

"No, this is the only one."

"That's fine then," she smiled, placing a ten-euro note on the girl's tray.

She was finishing her second gin and tonic when he came in the bar. A small stocky figure with a receding hairline. His eyes were still good. She'd always loved brown eyes but that moustache! He looked like Burt Reynolds on a bad day, a very bad day. She watched as he checked the till and gave orders to the young one to collect the empty glasses and ashtrays off the tables. She used to be mad about him, besotted. She'd begged him to stay going out with her, bawled her eyes out when he'd dumped her. That little piece of shit, look at him now. He had a gold band on his finger, married obviously.

"Would you like another order?"

She considered, twisting the lemon around the end of her drink.

"Sure. But would you be a good girl and ask Mr. Flynn to bring it over himself."

She stifled a laugh at his puzzled expression as he put in the measure of spirit and filled the glass with ice before carrying it over.

"That'll be four euros, please."

"Aidan, do you not recognize me?" she teased.

The middle-aged publican seemed stumped.

"Nineteen eighty-four."

"Jaysus, it's Christine, isn't it! I haven't seen you in years."

He looked dead embarrassed.

"Nearly twenty years."

"That long ago," he tried to laugh. "God, you look as young as ever."

"Not since I told you about the baby."

He was frozen to the spot.

"Jaysus, Christine! Give me a break. We were just kids then.

The old lad would have had my guts for garters. You know what he was like!"

She smiled as she sipped her drink.

"I used your money. I went away."

"Well, there you go then."

She could see him running his eye over her appreciatively, noticing her long tanned legs and low neckline.

"There you go!" she laughed. "I'm only in town for a few days, and I said I'd look up some of the old haunts. Didn't expect to find you still here, behind the bar."

"The old fellah made it over to me before he died. Looking after this place is a full-time job," he defended, "got to keep the customers happy and keep the trade."

She raised one eyebrow slightly, as she scanned the half empty bar.

"So I see."

"What about yourself?"

"Well, when I went away first I did a bit of this and that, bar work, restaurants mostly. That's how I met Larry."

"Larry?"

"My husband."

"Ah, so you got married, like myself."

"Yeah, I married an American. Big into pet food."

"Pet food!"

"Dog food, cat food, bird seed, dog biscuits, bones treats. Americans do love their pets, and Buddies, Larry's company, has twenty per cent of the market. Do you know how many dog and cat lovers there are in America?"

"I haven't a clue."

"Millions."

She could see the envy in his eyes as he took in her expensive jewellery and suede jacket and immaculately cut fawn trousers.

"So you did all right," he said.

"Will you join me for a drink?"

"We're a bit busy right now," he began to say.

She raised her eyebrow again, taking in the vacant tables beside her.

"Well, I suppose I'd have time for a quick pint before the rush starts."

Minutes later he was sitting beside her, like an old married couple, she thought, cringing. He was telling her about his wife and the help she was to him in his business and about the long hours and hard work he put in. Unfortunately, they hadn't been blessed with children.

She stifled a yawn. She hadn't remembered him being boring.

They talked about the old days and she waited for him to ask her.

Another pint later the question came.

"What did you do that time, Christine?"

For a fraction of a second she was tempted to tell him the truth but, seeing his plump weak face and thinking of herself at nineteen, she lied.

"I did what you told me to do, Aidan. You wanted me to get rid of it, so I did."

He drank deeply from the dark black Guinness.

"It was a little girl. They told me after."

"Jesus," he said, holding his head in his hands.

"Aidan, you gave me the money. It's what you wanted."

The silence between them was drowned out by the television and an argument between an elderly pair at the counter, the girl behind the bar glaring over at him.

"I'd better sort it out." He stood up. "Excuse me, Christine."

"I have to go anyway. I'm meeting someone back at the Shelbourne."

"It was nice to see you again."

She watched him try to placate the old fellah in the knitted jumper, who looked like he'd had far too much whiskey already, as she pulled on her jacket. Her last glimpse of him was washing some glasses and pulling a pint of beer, a shudder of relief going through her at the lucky escape. The cab driver was back outside, waiting for her across the street, in the place they had agreed.

"God, get me out of here," she ordered as she sank into the back seat.

She looked at the list. Crossing out things accomplished. Now only one big thing left to do. For the first time she felt nervous, unsure. She rifled through her wardrobe. She didn't want to look austere or glitzy, or even too fashionable. That was not the impression she wanted to make. Nor was she going to dress young. She wanted to look attractive but her age. At least, thank heaven, it was dry, the Dublin sun splashing through the tall windows. She settled on a cream cashmere sweater worn under a tan jacket and soft wool trousers. She fixed her make-up, going easy on the eyes, and sprayed herself with scent. The address was written out. It was on the south side of Dublin, in an expensive area. The nuns had been unhelpful to say the least and had refused her repeated requests for information. Detective Ray Maguire and his Irish contacts had been thorough and she had a two-page dossier with all the relevant details and a photograph. At this stage she nearly knew it verbatim. Knowing didn't make it any easier and she wished that she had confided in Mary. No, this was something she had to do alone.

She was silent as they drove through the leafy suburbs, unwilling to engage in the usual Dublin taxi-driver banter. The houses were neat and tidy with large front lawns and cherry and maple and chestnut trees. They passed Foxrock golf club and a tennis club and a classy cluster of shops which included a bistro, a gallery and a designer boutique alongside an expensive-looking wine shop and restaurant. She tried to compose herself as they passed women in expensive leisurewear and golfing outfits.

The place was not what she imagined and she could feel herself tense as the car drew up in front of a large red-bricked home, a cherry tree in the front garden in full bloom.

Neat and tidy, red and yellow tulips danced gaily from the large clay pots up near the front door.

"Would you mind waiting? I just want to be sure someone is home."

"Work away," he joked as she passed him a twenty-euro note.

She could feel her mouth dry, her heart pounding as she walked up the driveway and rang the bell. A small dog yapped in the hall, racing madly to the front door.

God, maybe she should just turn around. There were footsteps, and a voice, young, mock-teasing the dog as the door was opened.

"Hello."

The girl looked at her with curiosity. Pale faced, long dark hair with a fringe and those big fancy fashionable hooped earrings.

She had rehearsed it over and over again in her mind.

"Is Catherine here?"

"I'm sorry?"

"Catherine Donahue. We were friends a long time back. I've been away in the States. I said I'd try to look her up."

"I'm really sorry, but my mother's not here. She's in Galway. She won't be back until next Sunday night. My granny's sick and she's gone to stay with her."

The taxi driver was looking impatient.

"A wasted journey, then. I was hoping to catch up on old times with her. I'll just take the taxi back on into town."

"Why don't you come in? I'll give you her number."

"Are you sure?"

"Have a cup of tea. I'm just about to take a study break. It'd be nice to have a bit of company, especially if you are a friend of Mum's."

She signalled to the driver to wait for a while and said a silent prayer for the thoroughness of Ray Maguire's research and information as she stepped inside.

The hall was painted a warm ochre red, the carpet a pale gold, a collection of Irish art hung on the walls. The dog yapped at her and ran around her feet.

"Tilly, be good or there'll be no walk later!" warned her young mistress.

The kitchen was fitted with a range of cream-painted units and looked out over a beautiful lawn and immaculate flowerbeds.

"I see your mother likes the garden," she mused, suddenly feeling envious.

"I'm Rachel," the girl said, introducing herself as she put on the kettle. "I'm in second-year Medicine."

"Following in your father's footsteps."

"Sort of, I suppose, but I've no interest in dermatology."

She was prettier than she had imagined. The last photo she had seen had been taken when she was fourteen, a shy girl blinking in the sun, captured by a stranger with a camera.

Christine felt awkward as she watched her make two mugs of tea and produce a packet of biscuits.

"No thanks," she demurred, pushing the tempting chocolate away. "This is a lovely room."

"Yeah. Mummy says the kitchen is the heart of a house."

"You and your mum must be close."

"Yeah, I suppose. How do you know her? Were you at school together? In college? Or was it through work?" Rachel asked, studying her over the blue rim of the mug.

"No! Not school. With Catherine and I the connection goes a long way back. Through mutual friends mostly."

"Mum will be mad to have missed you," she sighed. "Granny's had pneumonia. That's why she's up in Barna."

Christine needed to steer the conversation away from relatives she had no clue about.

"Tell me about college," she prodded.

The girl's eyes lit up. She was not only attractive but also intelligent and bright, thought Christine proudly, as she animatedly told her about second year and the drama soc and the hockey club she had just joined.

For a few minutes Christine let herself be lulled into the pleasant feeling of two generations chatting in the sunshine. The rapid beat of her pulse had at least eased but could feel her stomach clenched with nerves as she searched for the courage to tell Rachel who she really was.

There were photos around the kitchen. On the walls, on the counter, Rachel as a baby held by a proud young mother, Rachel in a pink ballet tutu, with her mother and father making a snowman, riding a pony, the family together on a beach, tanned and grinning. Photos of her daughter, smiling, happy, something perhaps she had not expected.

Christine stared at them intently. She had to tell her. The beautiful young woman sitting across the table from her was entitled to know who she really was, who her real mother was!

Once it was out in the open it would be all right, she tried to tell herself. She had her opportunity now. She remembered the day nineteen years ago when the social worker had come and sat by the bedside and asked her to sign the papers, agreeing to give

up her daughter for adoption. She was exhausted, sick. It had
been like a bad dream as she watched the nun walk down the corridor with her baby. She had packed up and left the hospital the
next day. But today, this was different. They were on their own,
relaxed, comfortable. It was perfect. She had her opportunity to
explain it, how young and stupid and crazy she'd been! About her
family, her father, Aidan! How they had all let her down.

"Would you like another cup of tea?"

She hesitated.

"Rachel, I need to talk to you, please sit down."

Concern filled the young girl's face. Her brown eyes widened.
Christine noticed she had long lashes.

"Yes?"

The silence hung.

The gallery of photos around the wall, a lifetime, shifted into
focus, witness to a lifetime of love, of her daughter being part of
a family, of belonging.

She swallowed hard. She thought of all the times she had
rehearsed this scene in her head, the words she would use, the
emotion, the love, the grand reunion she had imagined over and
over again as mother and daughter were re-united. Always she
had replayed it from her point of view, never from that of the
brown-eyed girl across the table from her.

Rachel looked puzzled, alarmed.

She couldn't do it. Sweat soaked her body. It was like there
was a lump in her throat, and it felt like it was going to choke
her. She stood up.

"I have to go. My taxi is waiting."

She needed fresh air.

"Stay!"

She shook her head. Politely she thanked Rachel for the tea
and stood up and made for the front door.

"Mummy—"

She stopped for a second, unsure, frozen by the word.

"Mummy'll be in touch with you. If you leave your phone number or email address."

She watched as her daughter scribbled a number on a pad in the hall.

"It was nice to meet you," she grinned.

"Same here."

Out of impulse she hugged her goodbye, feeling her arms around her, breathing in the smell of her hair, the softness of her skin.

Relief and self-contempt washed over her as she walked back down the driveway and sat in the taxi turned back towards the village. She had waited nineteen years to be re-united with her daughter, thought of little else, and now when she had the perfect opportunity, she had let it slip away. Perhaps she should turn back to the house, try to explain. She thought of Rachel's life and its simple perfection. She longed to escape Foxrock, the cosy smug suburb and the foreign landscape of motherhood where she did not belong.

She was overwhelmed with need for her sister. Mary would hold her and soothe her in her plump arms. Mary would listen when she told her about her daughter, and about Larry, who had not died like she insinuated but had just run off with a twenty-eight-year-old tramp, a PA who was five months pregnant. Larry had got his lawyers to instigate divorce proceedings so he could re-marry as soon as possible, the terms of the pre-nuptial contract suddenly coming into play. Christine sighed. The generous amounts that were normally lodged in her Visa and bank accounts were already a thing of the past and Larry was fighting over every piece of property and was quickly showing himself to be a mealy-mouthed miser. The driver was listening to the radio.

It was drizzling rain as they drove back towards town. There was really nothing to go back for except to haggle with lawyers and try to sort out legal details. She could either fly straight back to San Francisco or stay in Dublin, make a clean breast of it, tell Mary and Bren and Liam the truth. The black wipers on the taxi were going back and forth, back and forth, as Christine closed her eyes.

Ireland's bestselling children's novelist **MARITA CONLON-McKENNA**'s debut novel for adults, *The Magdalen,* was a No.1 bestseller in Ireland in 1999. This was followed by two further bestselling novels, *Promised Land* and *Miracle Woman.*

Marita Conlon-McKenna lives in Dublin with her husband and four children.

Insight

Annie Sparrow

25 September

There's nothing like death to focus the mind. The trouble is, it's too damn permanent. Knowing of one's imminent demise is like showering in a waterfall of clarity; everything you should, would, and could have done is infuriatingly obvious. But by then it's too late. *Why is it that we only appreciate something when it's about to be taken from us?*

I am thirty-nine years old, in less than a month I'll be forty, and I am dying. *Dying!* I think it deserves to be in italics.

It seems absurd. I am incredulous. I'm not quite sure I believe those doctors. Dr. Cunningham's nose was running as he told me that I had an inoperable brain tumour, Glioblastoma something or other. I was surprised he didn't wipe it. A man of his position should be aware that appearances are important. Even his office was surprisingly dusty and situated in a shabby outbuilding behind St. James's main hospital.

I am a distrusting, cynical control freak so of course I got a second opinion. It seems old runny nose was right. Due to the location and size of the tumour, even radiation treatment would be futile.

I have no fear—not yet. I have only anger; an all-consuming, burning rage, an internal fury that is probably incinerating the mutant growth inside me anyhow. Dying young was not part of the plan.

I think of all the money I put into my pension scheme. What a waste! I should have had a boob job instead, become a glamour model and dated overpaid and over-sexed Premiership footballers, then sold my story to the highest bidder. I could have made a fortune that way. Instead, I took the sensible and respectable path. I wrote the book on being sensible.

Damn the Careers Office for giving me such logical and tedious advice at school. Damn the Church for installing a conscience in me more vast than a black hole. And damn my mother for furnishing me with the guilt complex that follows me around every second of every day, like a truculent Siamese twin. At least when I die my twin will die too.

What has my virtuous life achieved? How dare I not reap the rewards of my virtuous life.

I wonder how to spend these next few months?

First, I shall get very drunk; even more drunk than I am right now. *Who needs a healthy liver!*

Then I shall do whatever I want. The normal rules no longer apply to me. I shall rid myself of all the programming I have undergone as a citizen of this crazy world.

Every second I shall experience something new. Something delightful. Something very wrong!

26 September

I told my pig of a boss, Paul, to stick his job. It was quite wonderful really. All the team were sitting in a sales meeting listening to him harping on about higher targets and the need for more profit. I almost burst out laughing. It seems so ridiculous now. Poor George hasn't hit his target for the last three months. He looked nervous, stressed and ill. Ironic really, I'm dying and I look damn healthy today.

"Christine, what's your month looking like?" he abruptly asks.

Everyone else has listed off their potential deals, whereas I merely say, "Well, Paul, that depends on how you look at it."

Everyone is edgy; Paul doesn't like blasé comments like that.

"Explain," he demands with his menacing eyes.

I smile. I have to keep from laughing as I've already drunk half a bottle of champagne. I was keeping it for when I brought in the Unilever account, but that's not going to happen now. *It's funny how we always put things off until a time in the future.*

"I'm going to really enjoy the next two months," I say with a beaming smile.

He smiles too. He obviously thinks I'm happy because I'm bringing in a lot of new business.

"You see," I add, "I'm going to do all the things that I wanted to do but was too scared to do, too shy to do, too embarrassed to do. But now I'm dying, an inoperable brain tumour, so I thought, *what the hell.*" I laugh but notice that everyone is staring at me as if I am mad. I suppose I'd better get used to that look. I sit silently waiting for Paul's reply but he momentarily looks speechless. I make a note to remember his facial expression to enjoy later, when I'm in hospital or some hospice, bored and with nothing to do.

"I'm having a shit day, Christine," he snaps. "Don't piss me off even more."

It was then that I really launched into my little performance. I can't remember it word for word but I called him something like an egotistical, thick, sexist little Hitler who walked around as if he had the Leaning Tower of Pisa in between his legs.

"Stick the job up your hairy arse," I said as I stood up. All twelve people looked stunned, mouths open, amused, confused and again looking at me as if I was totally mad. For good measure I jumped up onto the oval table and did a quick rendition of the Charleston, kicking my legs high into the air. It was one of the most enjoyable experiences of my life.

I am dying, but I am also free.

27 September

My answering machine is full of messages. Word has spread of my little performance yesterday and I am a hero to all the other oppressed workers. Most of my colleagues assume I just have another job. Paul is livid and is threatening to give me a bad reference—*as if I need one where I'm going.* Sally the receptionist is telling everyone that I must have won the lottery. Only Tina, another sales rep, was concerned.

"I'm worried," she stated uneasily. "If that was a joke about you dying it's *not* funny. Call me. Tell me what's going on."

I deleted all nine messages and made a mental note to telephone Tina another time. Right now there's too many other things to do.

I picked up the phone and dialled my mother's number. It rang twice but I quickly hung up. I decide not to tell her yet that her daughter is dying. It's not that I'm trying to protect her—I am feeling far too selfish to even consider another person's feelings right now. I don't tell her because she will become fanatical. She will gather the whole family, loony aunts and crazy cousins; I'm sure my family was inbred some generations ago. The relatives from Sligo look and act very strange. Plus she'll bring belligerent priests and militant nuns—how they all love a bit of drama. They will feed off my sickness and impending death and I will end up spending what little time I have in banal conversation with people who have already had too much of my time in life. They will not steal what time I have left in death.

You see, I am the person who has lived as one was told to live; I obeyed the rules, I paid every single penny of tax, I didn't park on yellow lines. I have spent my life worrying about the world, poverty, crime and the environment. I gave money to charity. I put other people first. I didn't drink too much, never did drugs and I've refrained from casual sex. In fact I haven't had much sex full stop! How galling.

I am sick to my stomach; angry sick as well as terminally sick.

"I am angry with you, God," I shout out in my kitchen. My Siamese twin is glaring at me. *How dare I speak such words.* But I am too angry to retract them. "I am angry with God," I shout again. "I have a right to be angry." It feels like my twin is pressing down on all my internal organs, cutting off my oxygen supply. I jump up and down brushing myself off. If I could punch her I would. *Guilt will have no hold over me any more.*

Where the hell is my happiness: the loving husband, the happy children, and the house in the country? For this is the sum—I will never live my dream. It was merely a mirage, shimmering in the distance, a game of happy ever afters. Did I truly want it?

Why do people hide behind their dreams? It's all an imaginary security blanket so as to view the uncertain future with a little more ease.

I am dying but I will no longer lie to myself.

28 September

I went over to my boyfriend's. Yes, I do have a boyfriend, or rather I did—Mark Thompson. I finished with him tonight after four years together. In truth, he was never what I wanted. He was a lazy sod who worshipped the television; his choice of a drug. *I now see that the majority of people are addicted to something.*

It was sheer folly of me to think that I could change him, but I tried none the less.

Why do people expend so much energy trying to change another instead of changing themselves?

Everything is so clear to me now. I should have ended it ages ago but I was too scared. Loss terrifies me. I can't cope with it or at least I'm scared that I can't cope. So I stayed with what I knew, trying to keep everything exactly in place, doing anything to avoid my perceived downward spiral of hurt and despair. If guilt is my Siamese twin then fear is my shadow and I have allowed both to choose my path.

Mark and I sat on his couch while he watched football. I had learned not to talk while football was on. I had learned a lot of rules while going out with Mark. He had tried to change me as much as I had him. At least our disappointment in each other was mutual.

"I need to tell you something," I say.

"Can't it wait until half-time?"

I turn sideways and gaze right through him. There is no substance to his character. I see only frustration and anger in him. He wanted to be a rock star instead of an accountant in an insurance company. He still talks about writing an album one day, but that's all he does, talk!

"No, it can't wait." I pick up the remote and switch the TV off.

Sacrilege! He looks mortified! *Hmm, how our priorities get muddled.*

"What's so important?" he growls.

In a calm and matter-of-fact manner I reply, "I'm dying."

He frowns heavily, yet another person who thinks it's a joke. They're all going to feel pretty stupid at my funeral—that's if they're allowed to come. It will be a select affair, by invitation only.

"Is this about ignoring you again?" he asks. "Look, I'll give you some attention after the match." He reaches for the remote but I throw it to the floor.

"Chris . . . tine . . . !"

"I have an inoperable tumour on my brain. The hospital appointments, remember?"

His frown fades and he stares at me with circumspect eyes. "Don't be stupid," he says in a less certain voice.

I was about to launch into an explanation of the tests I've had and results, but I stop. I can't be bothered. Strange, I genuinely can't be bothered. I laugh; a loud, vibrant, belly laugh. Inappropriate laughing is becoming a habit.

He scowls then picks up the remote, switching the TV back on. There's been a foul and a penalty awarded. Just as it is about to be taken I say, "Our relationship is over Mark. We don't love each other. We're just too scared to live without each other."

He jumps up and punches the air in delight; Manchester United has scored. He comes to hug me but I stand up.

"Goodbye, Mark."

"Christine. Don't be silly. It's nearly half-time. I'll make you a cup of tea."

I smiled, turned and left.

I sat on my bed at home waiting for the tears but they never arrived. Instead, I have a wonderful sense of relief. I feel lighter, as if I have rid myself of a burden. Nothing is more powerful than the word "goodbye."

I am dying but I will no longer accept second best.

29 September

Secrets. Every family has secrets. Things that are hidden at all costs, shoved under the carpet, turned a blind eye to. Why? Too uncomfortable to deal with. We all take secrets to our grave. I'll just be taking mine earlier than I thought. My secret's too big to even write in a diary. No one will ever know. Shameful. Keep it inside, bottled up since childhood. Too damn shameful.

2 October

I caught the Dart to Dublin city centre today.

Dublin is beautiful in October. The leaves on the trees in St. Stephen's Green are vibrant shades of red, yellow and chestnut brown. They fell all around me. It is autumn, in every respect.

My headaches are getting worse. I have tablets but I don't take them as they make me drowsy and I don't want to be drowsy. I want to be totally alert, taking everything in.

I had plans of running up a huge bill on my credit card, but when I got there I felt no desire to shop. *There is nothing I want apart from time.* I considered having a top stylist cut my hair but in truth I don't care how I look. I now realize that appearance is grossly overrated. So much time wasted on pointless things, like waxing legs, plucking eyebrows and shaving under the arms, slaves to the stereotypical view of the smooth-skinned feminine woman. Enough! When they put me in my coffin I'll be as hairy as a koala bear and proud of it. Prehistoric woman makes a comeback.

I walked aimlessly down Grafton Street then headed into the Westbury Hotel and ordered a large roast beef dinner, extra rare. A strange choice as I'm vegetarian. However, labels and restrictions aren't something I'm concerned with right now. I want to smash down the walls that I have defined myself by. Brick by brick they will tumble.

I sat alone in the busy restaurant eating my beef and drinking a whole bottle of vintage champagne, grinning broadly. The other diners kept glancing at me so I blew kisses over to them. Again I spot the *"she's mad"* expression on their faces. And they're right. I am mad and loving every bit of it.

I retired to a corner in the hotel bar and almost immediately a man approached me, Brad—an American businessman in his late forties, who travels Europe, selling laboratory equipment. He is handsome and bursting with confidence, overly so. What makes a person like that and others, like myself, flawed with so many insecurities? Neurosis is the plague of the spoilt and wealthy West. We obviously have too much time in which to beat ourselves up.

Brad is married with three children. He loves his wife and family. Brad would like to sleep with me. He hasn't said it yet but it's obvious. He flirted with such expert charm, well versed in saying the right thing at the right time. Normally, I'd find an excuse to leave, hotels are filled with lonely gentlemen wanting female company and he was typical—full of insincere compliments and false enthusiasm for my conversation, which is hardly enthralling. I have never been enthralling. But I am dying. I promised myself to experience everything!

Another bottle of champagne later he invited me up to his

room for . . . a drink! I stared directly into his eager eyes.

"I've never had sex with a stranger," I said in a matter-of-fact manner.

He looked taken aback with my bluntness. Cryptic innuendoes are the required language for casual encounters. Before he could respond I stood up. "OK, let's go up."

He smiled, smugly really. It wasn't attractive. In fact, the more I had spoken with him the less attractive he had become. It's funny how that happens. Nevertheless, I took the lift up to his room.

Once inside he took my hand and led me to his bed. He removed his jacket and went over to the minibar where he took out a bottle of white wine and poured two glasses, which he left on the side table. *Half-time refreshments, I suppose.* He looked down at me with the oddest expression.

It was then that things became like a film. It was as if I was watching two other people on a big screen. After all, I didn't do things like this. This was not me.

He kissed *her.* He tasted of garlic and some strange meat. He undressed himself and then her. She felt odd being naked with a total stranger but what did that matter now. She wanted to delight in his touch, lose herself in wild abandon, rid herself of all the moral and emotional shackles, be crazy, be free, be downright dirty! She wanted to roll around like other film stars, strangers in the night, dizzy with multiple orgasms, head banging off the headboard. BUT? Something wasn't right. She didn't feel any of that. The rush of erotic ecstasy hadn't materialized. Instead it felt clumsy and awkward.

This was no film. *I* am the woman naked on the bed. I looked down at his so-called manhood and admitted to myself that that part of a man was pretty ugly, no wonder pornographic magazines of men never really caught on.

Brad was touching my breasts. It felt mechanical and self-ish, his intent purely to enjoy himself. *I* was irrelevant. *I* didn't exist. I had spent my life not existing, why should I spend my death that way too. I realized that I didn't like him and I wasn't enjoying one moment of this. *It occurred to me that being free doesn't mean we should do everything, it means we have the choice not to.*

Tears filled my eyes, the first tears since being diagnosed. I didn't want to cry, I wanted to remain angry, angry with every-one; strength comes from anger. But the tears descended.

The stranger was about to enter me so I pushed him aside and jumped up. "I can't do this," I said. I was scared he would grab me, but he didn't. Yet his anger was obvious. He glared at me with eyes that told me to get out fast.

"I'm sorry. This isn't me," I shouted, dressing in the quickest time ever.

"A strange fucking time to realize it," he spat.

I ran from the room and down the stairs, leaving my jacket behind. Once outside I ran through the street and into a nearby alleyway behind some shops, where the tears overwhelmed me. I could hardly breathe and fell into a huddle on the ground.

I am dying and I am petrified.

10 October

I didn't want to be alone so I relented. For the last week I have surrounded myself with my family. My poor mother came up from the country and has been going to Church every day to pray for me. I pray too, for patience. *She's driving me mad!*

The first two days were lovely, we talked and cried, then talked and cried some more. However, since day four we've annoyed the hell out of each other. I wish it wasn't the case. I wish I was a better person. I do love her but the fact is—*she'll have to go.*

She tidies to the point where nothing can be found and, like a master sculptor, she chips away at me with subtle criticisms of who I am and how I've lived my life. She cannot believe I never married, which of course is my fault. What man would put up with me? Too opinionated, apparently. I have even had to censor the television programmes I watch for fear of offending her and embarrassing me; swearing and even the merest hint of sex are definitely taboo.

I'm dying and I can't even watch *Sex and the City*!

11 October

God forgive me but I asked my mother to leave. I told her she could come back nearer *"the time."* She looked hurt and cried as I put her on the bus for Sligo. I am now alone in my apartment apart from my Siamese twin, who is back in full force. She sits proudly in place beside me with a huge smug grin on her face. *As if I could have got rid of her that easily.*

I spent the day watching trash TV and then at four o'clock my doorbell rang. I opened the front door and saw the most gorgeous man standing before me. I wonder if I have already died and an angel, a mixture of George Clooney and Johnny Depp, has been sent to greet me. He was around forty, tall, slim with thick dark hair and deep hazel eyes that had a mysterious glint in them.

"Hello. Are you Christine?" he asked.

I nodded, several over-excited times. And then the bombshell. "Your mother asked me to call in on you."

"My mother?" An instant frown.

"Yes. I'm from St. John's."

A priest? But he was wearing plain clothes.

"I'm Martin. I was wondering if this was a good time to come in and talk with you?" He beamed a huge smile at me, both sexy and sincere. I wanted to tell him to go away but he was just too gorgeous so I stepped aside and Martin came in.

"How are you feeling?" he asked, sitting down on my sofa with a mug of coffee in his hand.

"Fine." *I'm such a bloody liar.*

He looked at me. I mean really looked, as if he knew me and all my bullshit! I glanced away.

"How are you *really* feeling?" he asked again.

"My mother told you, yes?"

He nodded.

I scowled. "She's told everyone, milkman, postman, old school teachers. The world and his uncle all know that Christine Murphy is dying."

"Death is a difficult time for everyone. Personally, I'm fascinated with the subject."

Surprised, I asked, "And what exactly fascinates you?"

"People's reactions to it. How they cope and of course their regrets. So many regrets. People have intelligence but they're so stupid." He smiled. "I'm fascinated by people's regrets."

How odd, I thought, he was more self-indulgent than compassionate.

"So," he said. "What's yours?"

I eyed him dubiously but for some reason went along with it. "Where do you want to begin? That I wanted to be a ballerina?"

He frowned. "Boring. Get to the exciting stuff."

I thought harder. "I've worked for fifteen years in direct marketing. It's well paid, I'm good at it, but I can't stand it. It's false and superficial and gives me no sense of fulfilment."

He looked unmoved.

"I've gone out with some real jerks. Wasted years trying to please men who couldn't be pleased."

He shrugged, still dissatisfied.

"Fear and guilt have controlled me."

He rolled his eyes.

"I'm not honest enough. I pretend to like things when I don't."

He sighed loudly.

"Well what else am I supposed to regret?" I asked angrily. "My life hasn't been all bad."

Martin sat forward on his chair and glared at me. "There must be something else, a biggy. Everyone always has one big regret."

I hesitated, then glanced away. "I suppose there is something. If I had more time I'd go back to college and do a degree in social science, become a social worker. I've thought about it for years and nearly did it ten years ago, but . . ." I sighed. "Four years back at college without a salary. I'm not getting any younger and it seemed too much of a risk. Would I get a job at the end?" My head lowered and I thought I would cry. I wish I had done it. If only I'd had the guts to change my life instead of playing it safe.

I eventually looked up and saw that Martin was now smiling broadly. He was obviously satisfied with this regret, which infuriated me.

"How the hell can you smile?"

"I told you, I'm fascinated by people's regrets."

"That's awful. It's like you're gloating."

"Not at all. I am merely providing a service."

"You can't be a priest," I snarled.

"No."

"If you're some sort of counsellor for the dying, take it from me, you're crap."

He laughed. "No, I'm not that either."

"Then who the hell are you?" I was becoming anxious. "What are you doing here?"

He crossed his legs, then cleared his throat. "I run a company, a very profitable company. In a sense we're like actors with a missionary zeal. We change peoples lives, give them *insight*. Believe me, our clients are never the same again. You don't need to know who hired us, that's confidential." With that he stood up to leave. "In a few months, when your anger and confusion die down, I guarantee you'll be grateful for this experience."

"A few months? I don't have a few months. I don't understand."

Martin winked at me. "Thanks for the coffee." He put down the mug, then calm as can be walked out to the front door with me chasing after him.

"What are you talking about? Who are you? How did you meet my mum?"

"I didn't," he said as he opened the front door and walked down the path to a waiting car. I froze, dumbfounded. Dr. Cunningham was driving it. I then spotted Dr. Bentley, the specialist who I got the second opinion from, sitting in the back. *He smiled and waved.* The car then disappeared around the corner but I remained in the exact same spot, stunned and dazed-looking.

18 October

It has been a week since I've written in my diary.

I may have lost my mind, that's what Dr. O'Connor thinks.

That afternoon after the car drove away, I rushed over to St.

James's Hospital. It turns out that they had never heard of a Dr. Cunningham or a Dr. Bentley. The outpatient building around the back was now a storage facility. I demanded, hysterically, to see a senior manager and was taken to a Mr. Cahill, a friendly and helpful young man. He listened to my tale in astonishment, then set about checking the hospital records more fully.

"We have a record of your Catscan last month, but that came back all clear," he said.

"So I'm not dying."

"Absolutely not."

It didn't really sink in.

"Mr. McGuire, who you saw, diagnosed stress as a possible cause of your acute headaches. A letter went to your GP and one to you."

"I never received any letter," I insisted. "I got a phone call referring me to Dr. Cunningham."

"Who saw you in our storeroom?

"They made it look like an office."

He stared at me with both eyebrows raised. "We made no such call."

"Well, someone did," I yelled.

Mr. Cahill spent over an hour with me and at the end he scratched his head, totally baffled.

"I need to make a phone call," he said as he left the room. I assumed he was calling the police but ten minutes later he reappeared with a stern looking man in his late fifties—Dr. O'Connor, a psychiatrist.

Of course I protested. "I'm not mad," I screamed several times at the top of my voice—not unlike a mad woman! Eventually I was persuaded to *"just have a conversation."* If at the end I still wanted to involve the police, they would contact them.

I reluctantly retold the whole story.

"And then they all drove off in a car. Dr. Cunningham driving. Dr. Bentley even waved," I said.

Dr. O'Connor looked at me like I was an interesting case. I cried, knowing how ridiculous it sounded. I might just as well have been telling him that aliens had abducted me.

"Has anything like this ever happened to you before?"

"Of course not," I snapped.

He asked a string of strange questions like why I felt the need to do the Charleston on the table.

"I thought I was dying."

"But why that particular dance?"

"I don't know," I cried, exasperated. *He seemed madder than me.* When he started asking about my childhood, alarm bells went off. I knew I'd better watch myself.

"Is there any history of mental illness in your family?"

"None." *I won't mention the relatives in Sligo. Anyhow, they're odd crazy, not insane crazy.*

"I understand you've been quite stressed recently. It's amazing how stress can affect the mind."

"I suppose so," I said, just wanting to get out without being sectioned.

20 October

My fortieth birthday!

Tonight there's a party for me in my local pub. Friends and family have organized it as a joint celebration of my birthday and my recovery from my brain tumour. I've told no one about Martin and the bogus doctors and have decided against police involvement; they wouldn't believe me anyhow. Instead I've told everyone that the tumour is shrinking naturally; I read on the Internet that in some cases that can happen.

"Praise be, it's a miracle!" my mother screamed aloud when she heard. Apparently every church in Sligo is celebrating as they were all praying for me. Maybe it is a miracle, after all I'm not dying. I have been granted more time and I can hardly believe it.

I am so confused and unsure as to what's actually gone on. It can't have been some manic delusional episode as Dr. O'Connor thinks, although occasionally I wonder. At times I'm furious; I've been put through hell. Why me? Who hired them? So many questions and emotions.

I do know one thing, like the mysterious Martin said, I am changed, for ever.

My twin, guilt, and my shadow, fear, still lurk somewhere in the background, but the more I ignore them, the fainter they get. They may never disappear totally but they will never control me again. I'm in charge now.

At ten o'clock the postman came and he handed me numerous envelopes plus I had to sign for a large box. I sat down at my kitchen table and opened it to find a smaller blue box inside. I felt excited wondering what it could be but when I lifted off the lid it was empty apart from a small white card, which I picked up. The hairs on the back of my neck stood up. I wasn't sure whether to laugh, cry or scream. In fact I did all those things. Typed across the card was *"Happy Fortieth Birthday, Christine. The present you have received is Insight. What you do with it is down to you."* It was signed *"A friend."*

I must have sat there gazing at the card for nearly an hour. At least I'm not mad! It was late afternoon before I felt ready to open the rest of my post. There were several birthday cards and a brochure on Venice. I've decided to take my mother away for a long weekend; I considered a week, but hey I'm no saint. There were also three application forms for universities—degrees in social work.

I am living and I intend to make the most of it.

ANNIE SPARROW is the author of two bestselling novels, *Said and Done* and *Matchstick Love*. She is currently working on her third.

A Life of Two Halves

Deirdre Purcell

Based on an interview with the celebrated Irish
artist Pauline Bewick.

They come and they go, these journalists and writers, delving (subtly, they think), mining, flattering, each hoping to find something more, something new, a titbit none of the others has managed to extract. Their techniques vary. Like cannibalistic fish, some eat me, or parts of me, regurgitating "insights" into my life and waiting to see how I will react; some, the analytical type, tell me what I must be feeling. Some throw out a little empathy to see if I can be opened up in comradeship; some, for sure, know formally more than I do about fine art and lecture me about what they see in mine.

There really is no need for them to try so hard. I answer all questions honestly, or in the light of truth at that moment; like Harry, I believe in everything being upfront and open and I don't really care any more what they write. My life, you see, is for all to view in my pictures. I am Pauline Bewick, the painting diarist.

It is a symbiotic relationship between me and the media in any case. They need me to fill their newspapers, magazines and programmes, but like all visual artists, writers, actors, comedians, stars and starlets of all disciplines (even footballers angling for that vital contract or transfer), I need them too. It is swarming and raucous now in the world out there and buyers have to know when I have a new exhibition coming up. I am a businesswoman too, my paintings are for sale.

That being said, there is a philosophical point to be made here. Although my art exists for its own sake and is its own justification, although I dream these paintings and dolly them up in nice frames so they can put their best faces forward, really, I think, I work out my life in them, try to make sense of it. But as the tune played by a violinist in an attic is ephemeral because only he hears it, a picture achieves full life only when a third party sees it, reacts to it, and, all going well, buys it. (Of course no one ever "owns" my pictures. The use of them can pass from hand to hand but even after my death they will forever be mine.)

This latest interviewer—for a book in aid of the St. Vincent de Paul Society and Barnardo's, I believe—has just left. So she shouldn't labour under any illusions, I have told her there is something she should know: while I am with her, I am right there, mucking in with her, that we are remembering things together about me and Harry, because that seems to be the aspect of my life she wants to take. But after she has left, she has completely left and my life will flow on as if she has never been here. This trait too, I share somewhat with Harry. *Move, move,* facing always forward, like a fish darting through a coral reef.

The writer taped everything—most of them do nowadays—and when we had finished I was very tired. It is exhausting, you know, trying to recall exactly what you felt more than sixty years ago, like on that day when Harry fought so fatally with my sister, Hazel.

It would have been rude, of course, to send this woman on her way immediately and anyway, I had invited her to stay for lunch. She had travelled far to see me, now had to travel back and although I had put her up in the big, floral bed in our spare room the previous night, she had to be tired too, mentally and physically. For her, our house in Tréanmanagh is a long way from home, plus, to spend a couple of hours concentrating on the spirals of Harry's story, even with a tape turning, has to be quite demanding. So to soothe both of us and to settle the silt we had stirred up together, I took her for a walk on Dooks Strand. I lent her a coat, because hers was white and new. I wore my pale suede boots, soft as butter, and, under my hooded, vellum-coloured raincoat, my yellow dress, deep yellow, like the yolk of a good egg.

We had Dooks to ourselves. The tide that day was low, exposing long, fat sandbanks like the backs of whales. The seabirds were resting, riding on water as calm and shiny as gunmetal while all around, the mountains were gently shaded with violet. The writer and I were certainly glad of our coats: although it was mild, the air was full of soft Kerry drizzle. We had brought along my dogs, Púca and Star, and while we humans paced quietly, they raced each other, raising whirligigs of sand, trying to get us into the game by making Maypoles of us and bumping into our ankles.

After a few minutes, I peeled off and headed for the dunes because I had to pee. She carried on, being polite, not looking, so the poor dogs didn't know which of us to follow and dithered this way and that, then celebrated when I caught up with her again. We talked little now, she and I, our business was done. But both of us, I was sure, thought mostly about Harry.

You know, Harry never spent a night in the lovely little roundhouse I built for her beside our own. I had heard that she had been telling everyone back in Wicklow: "Pauline is building me a lovely little house. But I won't move there yet. Not yet." She never said that to me.

The interviewer had said—and I know she meant it—that we, my husband, Pat and I, live in Brigadoon. And I suppose we do now, with our daughter, Poppy, beside us in her house with her two little boys and her husband. In search of a site, almost thirty years ago, we and our friend, the artist Maria Simmonds Gooding, drove all over these mountains and were about to give up, when, cresting one last peak, below us we saw the spread of our valley. The colours! The greens, the greys, the purples and browns, the pale tans and ochres, with the startling, deep blue topaz of Caragh Lake at the glowing base.

Back in the house after our walk on Dooks, I gave this writer lunch: smoked salmon, Betty's lovely salads, fruit to follow. She seemed to like the beetroot so I gave her lots. I haven't mentioned Betty yet, we could not live without her; she cooks and irons and keeps order for us all. Order, as you will see, is terribly important to me now.

We were having coffee and the writer was making noises about getting on the road when a van pulled up in the yard outside. A courier's van.

Great excitement. My tapestry, the big one, with the vivid reds and the little fox, had arrived from Aubusson and we all, even the writer, played our parts in ripping it from its wrappings and then unrolling it. It was so big that Poppy had to stand on a table to hold it up for full-length viewing. Then I had to hold it up so Poppy could see it properly.

Have I told you yet that both my daughters are artists too? Holly lives with her family in her own Italian Brigadoon, a farmhouse in Tuscany. Holly did not paint but her blood is obviously strong.

The writer liked my tapestry. At least I think she did. Her opinion, while welcome, did not matter all that much at that point. She was about to leave and getting ready for my exhibition as I was, I had to think of other work in my studio. Like *Woman Flying Through Magnolias,* still on the easel, like *Woman Flying Over Nesting Hens,* just framed.

Faithful to Harry, I was already moving forward, leaving the writer behind as I had warned her I would.

Harry is my mother—let me draw you a picture of her. Unlike me, who is strong and bony, she is petite and sprightly, with straight hair cut short and close to her head like a Juliet cap. Her lipstick is Tahiti pink, she shaves off her eyebrows and then pencils them on again. From being out of doors so much, her skin is fiercely tanned and she is a magnet for the young: she genuinely emanates a sort of force field which attracts them.

Strangely, I find I never use the past tense when talking about her, even though I am in my seventieth year—a serious aberration I find almost impossible to understand. To say it aloud, *my seventieth year,* feels like a small accident happening in my heart.

Please do not misunderstand me, I truly do not mind the prospect of getting older or even of dying: in fact right now we, Pat and I, are busily deciding what to do with all my personal paintings, stacked in my studio on the other side of the yard at Tréanmanagh. Should I give them to Poppy and Holly now, before I die? What should we do with everything else? This is what we are deliberately and calmly discussing and planning these days.

You will find it hard to believe, I am sure, but it does not bother me what happens to everything. My massive worktable, my studio, my storeroom, my easel, my lovely red *chaise longue* covered with the fringed shawl, my precious colourful crockery and vases and huge comforting kitchen, I would not care if they all went up in smoke. It is this decision Pat and I are making now that is important. Once I have it all cut and dried and organized it will already be gone from me and I will not miss anything— not deeply. So for sure it is not attachment to the world, or fear of age or death or even of letting go that startles me when I realize how old I am. It's that, as I said, I simply don't know why I am nearly seventy.

Speaking of letting go—I have a lifelong recurring dream where, high in a cloudy sky, I hang by my fingers on a very thin wire for a very long time. There is nothing beneath me so I cannot uncurl my fingers. Then, I decide, oh well, I will let go. But instead of shooting downwards, I float, slowly, slowly, until I come gently to earth, curled up on a prickly grey army blanket.

This dream, I now know, because Harry told me, is based on a real incident from one of the real-life "progressive" schools in England that Harry and I attended, Harry as the resident vegetarian cook, I as a very young pupil. On coming back from a walk, she found me, naked, hanging from one of a set of goalposts and surrounded by a semi-circle of studious small boys. Someone had mentioned to the small boys that babies had a great grip and, counting out how long it would take for me to fall, they were testing the theory.

The sensuous part of my dream, I am sure, comes of seeing Harry galloping to the rescue, letting go of the goalpost and feeling my naked skin coming to rest on the prickly surface of the green tweed coat she wore. (In another of these schools—it may indeed have been the same one—she found me sitting naked in a bath filled with snakes and surrounded by a posse of similarly intent small boys. Apparently I was having a wonderful time, pat-patting the creatures, lifting them up and gleefully revelling in their squirminess, while the small boys closely observed.)

Sometimes I have no idea whether these things happened yesterday or six and a half decades ago. Certainly, when dreaming, or painting or remembering, while talking to an interviewer, my life with Harry foams forth in a great torrent of undifferentiated past, present and future. Does it happen to everyone, this blending of time? When the past is the present and the future might be the past if you could only catch it, although it remains just out of your reach like a butterfly climbing a butterfly bush?

There cannot be many people left in Ireland who do not know what a wonderful, what an extraordinary childhood I had with Harry.

Her name was not Harry, you know. It was Alice. Alice Graham. But she had always hated the name "Alice" and one day, when she had been clumsy, someone said to her: "Oh, you're just like Harry, the gardener, and so we shall have to call you 'Harry.' " My mother seized on it and Harry she became.

The youngest of seven, she was born into a conventional, middle-class family in the north of England; her father, my grandfather, was an engineer. Her mother died when she was quite young and her father made a fatal mistake. He got married again, to a woman the same age as Harry's oldest sister. From then on, Harry was nobody's and although terribly young, she kept company with the local coal miners, a definite no-no in middle-class Newcastle circles—and would not be disciplined. But then Corbett Bewick, tall, red-haired with a long face in the shape of an egg, and—most importantly in her family's view—from her own class, came calling. To everyone's relief Harry abandoned the coal miners and allowed Corbett to court her.

He did, however, make one awful mistake. Although they were not officially betrothed, Corbett had thought they had at least reached an "understanding." So when one evening his beloved went out to dinner with another man, thinking himself clever, he sent a bouquet of red roses to the table in the restaurant where she and the new man were dining.

The gesture backfired in spectacular fashion and although not immediately fatal because they eventually married, she never forgave Corbett this intolerable intrusion into her privacy and independence. She rarely talked about him at all, as a matter of fact, but the red roses story was one that caused her always to spit. "How *dare* he send red roses! I'd once gone out with some-body else and he had the nerve to send red roses—how *dare* he!"

Corbett Bewick. Who may, or may not, be my father. Anoth-er mystery which will not now be solved because my mother did not want him to be my father.

Her firstborn, my sister, Hazel, was tall, red-haired, slightly buck-toothed and with a lovely fresh look about her. Definitely Corbett's.

But then, five years later, Harry was walking across the stub-ble of a cut cornfield when she saw a young man coming towards her. He stopped her: "Is there a house around here for sale? I heard there was."

"Oh yes," Harry became most helpful, "there's one opposite my house: come to my house and I'll show it to you."

As far as I can gather, they did not even get as far as her house. They lay down there and then in the cornfield and, according to my mother, conceived me. She was thirty, he was nineteen.

I have made feeble efforts over the years to verify any or all of this, who my father is, or was, but it was never an obsession and it no longer matters now. Hazel could not tell me—although she did remember seeing the young man about the house, so the affair was not simply one episode in a cut cornfield—nor could

Minnie, Harry's sister: "Harry was always a story teller around herself and although that young man existed, I believe you are actually Corbett's daughter."

"Nonsense," Harry scoffed when I put this version to her. "Corbett was an alcoholic. I didn't let him into my bed. So how could you be his?"

She carried this denial to the end. She, who saw the artist in me from early childhood, who beggared herself so I could have a good sable brush or a new tube of paint, who kept every scribble and drawing of mine from the time I could hold a pencil (roughly at the age of two and a half) never revealed that through Corbett I would have been related to the very famous north of England naturalist and supreme wood engraver, Thomas Bewick. This Thomas Bewick, a close friend and colleague of Audubon, is also the person after whom the species Bewick's Swan was named.

It was as though my mother wanted to erase every possible avenue of enquiry I might make into my Bewick connections. She even decided on my behalf that I should not sign my paintings "Pauline Bewick." "Your second name is Gale. That's a nice name. Call yourself Pauline Gale"—so until my teens, I signed all my work "Pauline G."

I once found a portrait of this possible ancestral relative of mine. He had very much the same kind of eyebrows as I have, brown eyes, high cheekbones and a big lower lip—although his was tucked in whereas mine sticks out.

More exciting, however, is that there are similarities in the way he worked his wood and I my paint. Small details. We share little technical things, such as a liking for pictures-within-pictures: a pastoral scene within the crook of a human being's elbow, for instance, or a flying bird framed by the branch of a tree, all sorts of things going on in corners. So if Thomas

Bewick's great-nephew was not my father, why do I instinctively use the same small techniques? Where did I get these looks? However, Bewick or not, I am simply delighted I am here.

Perhaps Harry did not want me to know about Thomas Bewick because of her conviction that Corbett was not my father, or, more likely, I think now, because of her desire that he should not be; in her mind, if she thought it, said it often enough, it would become the truth. Perhaps, however, it was because she believed so absolutely in the concept of living in the present and not bringing along any garbage from the past. For whatever reason, she raised me totally uncluttered and with no history whatsoever.

In any event, Corbett was shed early on.

We literally ran away from him. I was only two, Hazel was six or seven and Corbett's mother sent a taxi after us and grabbed Hazel back. Although the Bewicks seemed content to leave me in my mother's arms, for a time there was all this tugging over Hazel, a dreadful tussle. Such drama! But Harry finally won this contest and we, the three of us, ran again and found ourselves staying, fatefully, in a hotel in Letchworth. The owner was an Irishwoman who quickly became friendly with us: "You really should go over to Ireland," she said to Harry early in their friendship, "I've got a farm there and two children who need fostering." The parents of these two orphans had died of TB and they were being looked after by their uncle who was struggling with their rearing because he was a postman and could not be at home all that much.

Harry, who knew not a thing about Ireland, jumped at once: "I'll do it. I'll go!"

So we packed our bags and went in a boat and a train and then a car until we landed in a mountainy farm outside Kenmare. I was not yet three, remember, and now I cannot tell whether I truly recall our arrival, or whether it is a very strong picture planted in my mind by much repetition. But this strong picture shows us coming into the farmyard with the mountains all around, and there were Lucy and Michael peeping around the jamb of the farmhouse door, two little reindeer, tiny, timid little children. Lucy was Hazel's age, and Michael was a year younger.

For seven years, we had a lovely life on that farm with the donkeys, Peata and Mara, and Lassie the dog and Shamrock the horse, and the hens who wouldn't sleep in the henhouse but who scuttled away each night to roost under the trees, driving us all mad because we had to search everywhere for their eggs. We helped lift the bull onto a low wall to service our cow because he was so small and she was so big (and laughed hysterically when he fell off on his chin); we four children were bathed in a big butter barrel in front of the kitchen fire and, every day, watched Harry hunker down outside to pull up huge bunches of onion tops and masses of the herbs she grew, then jam handfuls of them between two slices of bread to make enormous herb sandwiches.

We slept outside, at least that was the intention. All her life, Harry has slept in the open, outside whatever caravan or boat or glasshouse was her fleeting home. Here in Kenmare, under the nut and holly trees and beside a stream, she made a big raised sleeping platform from corrugated iron; each night, especially in summer—but sometimes in winter too—we would all roll up our mattresses and bring them out to sleep with the cra-ak-cra-ak of the corncrakes and the stream's trickle-trickle, and the wheeling of the stars. (It is perhaps because of this cat's-eye view of the world, grasses, rushes, flowers, insects and so forth, that my paintings are frequently from this perspective.) She had built the platform with a gap beneath so if it rained we could take our mattresses and, using it as a roof, crawl under it, but that never worked and frequently we had to roll up again in the middle of the night and trail back inside. (In later life, when she lived in her glasshouse in the Wicklow field, a proper, if small, propagating greenhouse, Harry never let the weather drive her inside. Once I found her, snug on her bed of Boland's bread trays but, at the height of a snowstorm, only half-visible under a ton of whiteness. I forced her inside but she went only reluctantly, grumbling and grousing that she had been perfectly comfortable and that I had ruined a perfectly good night's sleep by waking her up and causing an avalanche of snow to invade her sleeping bag.)

And it was in Kenmare that I went to school for the first time. How lucky I was! Long before it was popularly known how widespread (and disabling) is the condition of dyslexia, even before people knew the name, my teacher in Kenmare National School recognized that I was in difficulty. Her solution was magical, for me at any rate. "We know you can't spell, Pauline, but you can draw. So you draw, all right?" And she would hold up my early efforts at flowers, birds, our classroom, our farm, for the approbation of my classmates. When added to Harry's ecstatic adulation of my earliest scribblings ("You're a *genius,* Pauline, you don't have to wash up, you just sit there and you *draw!"*), Miss Murphy's affirmation underpinned my confidence to such a degree that not being able to read or write properly never subsequently bothered me as child or adult. Together, Harry and Miss Murphy convinced me that my vocation in life was to be a world-class artist, to the extent that my lack of academic achievement at any of the many schools I went to after Kenmare was immaterial.

For example, I survived the regime at the conventional establishment to which I crossed by a jumpy bridge from the Thames houseboat where we lived at that point, by being able to copy the other pupils' exam work if I could scan it upside down.

I did like living on a houseboat; I was very popular with my fellow pupils across the bridge who adored the novelty of visiting Harry and me, tied precariously to a tree! Yet one always wants what one does not have and all through my peripatetic youth, exciting and life-affirming though it was, I coveted other pupils' High Tea on tables with white tablecloths, the smell of their mother's meat cooking, the neatness and order of their homes, their routines.

My interviewer spotted how, at Tréanmanagh, I have reversed Harry's way of living, not only because our house here is tidiness itself, but because while we were recording, I at one point click-clacked my jars of paint to the proper, *left-hand* side of the wood-en compartments of their tray, then squared off the tray so its rectangular edges were parallel to the edges of my big studio table. (I had noticed, you see, out of the corner of my eye, that some of the jars had drifted a little out of line, and as we spoke, their small disorder was irritating me.)

When she commented, I showed her then how the purple ingrained in my palette was driving me mad because *that palette should be virgin clean.* Then, a little time later, while searching for something in one of my studio filing cabinets, I noticed *her* noticing the apple-pie order and labelling of my myriads of files. We were conspiratorially alert. I suppose this is why these meet-ings between two people are referred to as *inter*viewing.

The idyllic Kenmare years came to a dreadful end when Lucy, our non-related sister, died of galloping meningitis. This was tragic enough, but the ripple effect on our lives was calamitous.

The aunt, the hotel keeper from Letchworth who had sent us to Kenmare in the first place, took Michael, who was about four-teen now, and sent him off to Switzerland for the sake of his health—and also to learn the hotel business. I was not affected as much as Hazel was, possibly because I was so much younger, but for my sister, on top of the trauma of Lucy's sudden death, to have her beloved Michael taken away was catastrophic. As a result, she overnight became a rebellious teenager, and I remember enormous rows between herself and Harry and her telling Harry to f-off, straight to her face! In this day and age when every street corner, even every sitting room, it seems, harbours a foul tongue, it is hard for me to describe how shocked I was by this *language!* This *insubordination.* Living as I did, curled up in my mother's heart, I remember closing my ears and vowing never, ever, as long as I lived, to talk to *my mother* like *that!* The rows and fights continued from then on and the upshot of it all was that what had been heavenly was now full of strife and grief.

To add to the confusion, Harry quickly decided that we could not stay on in the farmhouse since the reason for being there—to look after Lucy and Michael—no longer existed. So although she was an animal lover, our mother again set about detaching. She sent the cattle and Shamrock to market, but then, because no one, she said, could possibly take on our tree-dwelling hens, using some kind of dope she killed them all, a great massacre of hens. She killed Lassie too. It was awful, we were leaving Kenmare and everything had to die.

The three of us now took off for Belfast. It was as if once she had decided to go, Harry had to get as far away from Kenmare as possible.

We had some money. Having inherited Corbett's house after his early death, Harry rented it for a while and then sold it to Lever Brothers, the soap people, for a good sum. Characteristically, she also rid herself completely of its riches: antiques, art, rare books, a first edition of *Alice in Wonderland.*

So we bought a caravan and placed it behind an advertising hoarding, across the road from the Belfast city dump.

For me, the consolation was that I made a friend there, a little girl whose legless father made a living by making chalk pavement pictures and who lived nearby, not in a conventional van like ours, but in one with a barrel top. She and I would visit one another and play with what we could find in the treasury of the dump. The best was "weddings." We found a great cache of cemetery wreaths and having carefully extracted the lovely porcelain flowers from under the beat-up plastic of the protective domes, we attached them to our hair, steepled our fingers like proper brides and were very holy. This, extraordinarily, has remained one of the strongest images of my life.

But soon I had to say goodbye to this playmate too because we and our caravan were on the move again, this time to a clifftop in Portrush where there was a lovely wind and soft, scutchy grass and where I learned consciously how it felt to fly.

One very dark and stormy night, the caravan began to rock dangerously in a gale and Harry, fearing it might go over, pulled me out of it and instructed me to crawl with her on our bellies away from the cliff towards a couple of cottages nearby. Wearing only our nightdresses, we bellied as far as a wall surrounding these cottages. I climbed it, but in jumping down on the other side, the wind got under my nightdress, which, in my memory, served as a parachute and lowered me gently to the ground. It certainly *felt* like flying and this, taken with my early goalpost experience and that recurring dream I told you about, might explain the airiness in my paintings and why my current preoccupation is about women flying and with trying to recreate these marvellous, free sensations with paint and canvas.

At this point, Hazel was no longer in our lives, she had run back to the Bewick grandparents in England after one final, appalling blow-up with Harry and no one, not the Bewicks nor us, nor even Hazel herself, made any effort to keep contact after that. I know it is hard to believe, but she simply vanished for ever. If you remember, I said this was a trait somewhat passed on from Harry to me. She must have passed it on to Hazel, who never reconciled with us. When it is over, it is over for the Bewicks.

Shortly after that storm, Harry decided again to move. "I think we'd better get you to a school."

She had read about A. S. Neill and his progressive theories on education at Summerhill School but we did not go there right away. Instead, we went first to a school in Monmouthshire, a great big Georgian house where Harry got a job as a vegetarian cook and the headmaster took us for trips in his truck, instructing us to cling on to the outside of the frame, like poor train travellers in India or Bangladesh; where the teachers were Children of the Sixties long before that era, bearded, barefoot types we called by their first names and who all had lovers and sweethearts and all lived together in a big tangle of love.

We had lovely theatre times in that school, in a big shiny room with shiny floors and floor-to-ceiling windows where we pupils would act. Anything. Anything we felt like acting, while our teachers, sitting around in their big heavy knitted things, applauded everything and told us all we were brilliant.

I remember one of those teachers in particular for the socks—no shoes—he wore to class. He was the only one who did not have a sweetheart and therefore no one to darn for him, so he used to hide the holes by tying the edges together in little bunches. He would stomp in to class with these great big mushroomy things blooming all over his feet and he would teach us how to build boats. Now I have to say that a lot of us in the class did not have much interest in boats so while (in landlocked Monmouthshire!) he was drawing keels and ribs and all sorts of things all over the blackboard, I, among others, was given plasticine to do with what we liked. So I could not say how many kids from that school became boat builders!

This same teacher rebelled against my mother's vegetarian cooking, and during a blizzard announced that he was going out to catch rabbits. He did not come back, leading to a small consternation.

Where's he gone?

He went that way to kill rabbits . . .

So we put out a search party and had to dig him out of a snow drift.

But quite soon, Harry and I were on the move again, this time to a school in Bristol, where she once more became the vegetarian cook and where, for hours and hours on one warm summer evening, I continued my academic career by dancing naked, alone save for my partners, the warm wind and a long floaty scarf *à la* Isadora Duncan, to no one's alarm, or even surprise.

That school, however, turned out to be a mere blip in the graph of my educational progress because, in Harry's view, the teachers there were not quite as open and liberal as they had at first appeared.

The gardener, you see, was a conscientious objector to the war and for some reason his stance disturbed the rest of the staff and he was asked to leave.

"Burn your own spinach!" In support, Harry, who had become friendly with him, snatched me up and we left too.

Somewhere in here—as I have told you, time is no longer parcelled out in neat chronological lots for me—were the schools, or school, where I floated to Harry's prickly coat from the goalpost and bathed in the living snakes—plus the famous Summerhill establishment. Although much has been written about him, it might be worth giving you a flavour of A. S. Neill's educational style as observed close-up.

One of the boys in the school had a habit of stealing chickens from the local farmers, much to their loud and repeated annoyance. Neill decided to do something about this and went individually to each farmer: "Bear with me," he said, "I'm going to be stealing your chickens quite often until this boy is cured."

For some (unfathomable) reason, they all cooperated. So he took the boy aside: "Listen, there's no point in stealing these chickens on your own. It's not very efficient. Two can do it better than one. So I'll steal them with you and that way we'll do a really good job. Meet me in my office at midnight, so we can sneak in and get them when they're asleep and dopey and they won't make noise . . ." It took two or three raids, but the boy quickly got bored with officially sanctioned chicken-rustling.

Similarly, when a girl ran away to London, Neill jumped into his car and chased the train, boarded it at a halt, found her and told her she was crazy to go without money. "Here, take this!"— handing her fistfuls of the stuff—"You have no idea what you face down there. And you have no idea how expensive London is, you'll have to get a well-paying job right away!" She burst into tears and said she wanted to come "home."

Harry and I meandered happily into my twenties and landed back in Dublin, where there were parties and Trinity students, including the man who would become my husband, and a house bought, somehow, on the books of the Building Society, and lodgers taken to pay the mortgage.

And then I was accepted at art school.

I asked Harry to make me a dress: "like the lovely, checked, pink and blue and white one you made for me before. That's getting a little old now and I'd love a new one."

No. The answer to that was no. Flat no. No more dresses made. I was perturbed. I was her darling genius, so cosseted, so loved, and she had said "no" to me? Being young, though, I shrugged it off and went blithely off to art school.

She approved of Pat, from Trinity, who was studying to be a

psychiatrist. "Of all the boys that come around here," she said, "Pat is the easiest to get along with." Pat and I got married and started our lives and family together and I continued to paint.

Then, in the late seventies or early eighties, I was due to hold an exhibition at the Guinness Hop Store, a very big show of more than a thousand pictures, many of which were from the early hoard Harry had so carefully preserved. "I'm not going to go to your exhibition," she announced out of the blue. "I'm through with art. And to think I was the cause of all this rubbish. How could you! Fiddling while Rome burns, in your studio there, it's like masturbating . . ."

The shock. The hurt. No warning, no hint—unless you count her sudden refusal to make me any more dresses when I went off to art school.

And then when I was in my thirties, with Poppy and Holly safe in our house in Tréanmanagh, I went to the postbox and found a letter there from my mother. A most horrific letter, full of hate and condemnation, about my art, about our upbringing of our daughters. About me.

It was the first such letter but far from the last. Each day, when I went to pick up the mail, I would shake and feel sick if there was something there from Harry, because they continued to arrive, these carefully phrased letters of bile and dislike, of rejection of everything I stood for, of everything we had dreamed of together.

Over the years, Pat and I have made sporadic attempts to puzzle out why she went off me so suddenly and thoroughly. Pat, being a psychiatrist, is very wise, but neither of us has got to the bottom of it really. This writer, this interviewer, having heard the story of Harry and me and jolted by this unexpected and bizarre twist, made her own attempt to join up the dots (she falls into the analytical school) and her theory could be as good as any:

that Harry, who presented herself as such a free child of nature, was underneath it all a deeply controlling person. I was *her* genius. *She* would tell me how brilliant I was. And as soon as her voice was no longer the only voice, I was toast.

Perhaps. And this avenue led me to another memory: we were in Dublin, Harry was in a caravan—preceding the glasshouse— in Wicklow and Poppy was small. Harry came to visit us and afterwards I found her carrying Poppy while getting into her taxi to go back. I ran after her: "Hey! What are you doing?"

"I'm taking Pauline to Wicklow." (For many years she referred to Poppy as "Pauline" although the name Poppy had been her suggestion.)

"What do you mean?"

"It's selfish of you to keep her in the city where the air is dirty. She has fresh young lungs, she would love it down there."

"But you can't just take her—"

"—you're so *selfish* wanting to keep her."

And then one ordinary evening, the telephone rang in Tréan-managh. "Hello?"

"Is that Pauline Bewick?"

"Yes?"

"This is the Gárda station in Bray, County Wicklow. And I am afraid I have bad news . . ."

As she did once a week, Harry had taken the bus to Bray from her glasshouse to buy her groceries and the herbs she could not grow in her field. She was killed by a car as she left the bus to cross the road.

Apart from ourselves and our own friends, her funeral was attended largely by her sad young pals in their teens and early twenties. From Bray and the Wicklow countryside, they had responded to that undiminished force field by gathering around Harry's glasshouse to adore her. My own mourning for my mother was complex and private. I did cry, I think, yes, I know I cried.

Her rejection split my life almost exactly in two, giving me a life of halves: *Pauline is a genius. Pauline is rubbish.* For years after the original *volte-face,* my mother was a voice in my ear as I painted: *Here you are, doing little decorations; so what about Ethiopia?* I have forgiven her. At least I think I have. Over the years I have made excuses. She was perhaps motivated by kindness? She turned against me to wean me from her? So I would not love her so much and therefore would not suffer too much grief when she left me for good?

In my seventieth year, however, I have matured, and along with the hateful one, I can again access that other voice of hers, that early, hallelujah paean on viewing each picture: *Wonderful! Marvellous! You are so talented, you are my lovely, unique genius!* And after that extraordinary start she gave me, nothing or no one, not even Harry herself, could completely destroy a great relationship overall.

For very complicated reasons, I have kept those hate-filled letters. Maybe, I thought, I think, I will find a clue if I read them often enough. Or (while Harry was still alive) if she somehow found out I was keeping such a malign totem in my house she might rescind it and take again to worshipping me as her star.

I still have the letters but the mystery is not yet solved. Deep in those parts of my soul that even I do not access, I know instinctively that if I do not keep them, the shock of Harry's turning is going to fade. I do not want it to fade because without the physical presence of that neatly filed mail in my neat, ordered filing cabinet in my neat, ordered house in our mystical valley, I might think I imagined it all.

Born and brought up in Dublin, **DEIRDRE PURCELL** is one of Ireland's best-loved writers. Shortlisted for the Orange Prize in 1998, her bestselling novels include *Love Like Hate Adore, Falling for a Dancer, Entertaining Ambrose, Marble Gardens,* and most recently, *Last Summer in Arcadia.*

First Love

Mary Ryan

"H e's a bit of all right," Carmel said, "but I wouldn't get over excited. Hot Pants Helen has set her sights on him . . ."

Eilie groaned. "She's like fly paper."

"Do I detect a greenish glitter?"

"You certainly do! She'll nab him at your party!"

"If you want François, fight for him!" Carmel advised. "Don't let that one get away with it! You could lighten the hair . . . lose weight . . ."

Eilie bought some Blonder than Blonde in Roches Stores and went home. The stuff had a smell like lion pee, but it was all in the cause of beauty. She followed the directions carefully. When the work had been completed she had become a blonde, a dry and patchy one, but a blonde nonetheless.

"What on earth did you do that to yourself for?" her mother wailed when she returned from her work at the hospital.

"I'm tired of being a mouse! I have decided to become a vamp!"

"What's that?"

Eilie looked at her parent in disbelief.

"Isn't that what they called them in your day?"

"How old do you think I am, child?"

But Eilie was thinking of the next step: the battle of the bulge! Alone in her room, she stripped and looked at herself with as much objectivity as she could. It wasn't that she carried much extra weight, it was just that she was strongly built, and that she possessed unusual muscular power, something she suspected she inherited from her father who used to boast he was the strongest man in Athlone. She could lift the fridge with ease, or the telly, or the table, or pick up her brother, Mark, who was nineteen. Mark didn't like that much, but she always thought it was funny until she realized the benefits to be gained by being a helpless female. Now, as she gazed into the mirror a wonderful svelte being appeared, a Claudia Schiffer body with an Eilie face, who danced a slow number in romantic François's arms. Eilie drew in her breath ecstatically. He had been so sweet to her at that disco, so funny with his French accent, so different to Irish boys who seemed to think they were doing you a favour if they asked you to dance. François had squeezed her hand, and his brown eyes had laughed into hers as though she fascinated him. He was at the same boarding school as Carmel's brother, Timmy—taking a year out from his lycée in Paris—so it wasn't as though she wouldn't see him again, seeing as Carmel lived down the road and her birthday party was coming up during the hols and François would be staying in her house. Eilie was sure he fancied her, that he really liked her, but if Hot Pants Helen was in the race she was doomed.

✦   ✦   ✦

During the days that followed Eilie thought only of François, and how she would wow him at Carmel's party. She got out some of her savings and invested in Suddenly Slender, a low-calorie meal replacement. You were to replace two meals with it, and have a proper meal in the evening. I'll replace all three, she told herself. I can't get thin quickly enough. The liquid meals tasted nice, raspberry, vanilla, or chocolate. She hid them from her mother, and made a pretence of eating her dinners, but as her mother often worked late it was easy to fool her. Suddenly Slender suppressed her appetite and she began to lose weight. The waist of her school uniform loosened dramatically.

"Eilie O'Hare!" Miss Walsh exclaimed in class. "You're daydreaming, and your Mocks are only three weeks away!"

"Sorry, Miss Walsh."

Her teacher took her aside afterwards.

"You're looking pale. Are you all right?"

"I'm fine, thank you, Miss Walsh!"

"Experimenting with the hair, I see!"

Eilie shrugged.

"I hope that's not all you're experimenting with! You seem to be losing a lot of weight!"

Eilie was suddenly terrified. What if Miss Walsh contacted her mother and said she was concerned about her weight loss and her pallor? Her mother would immediately climb the wall and wail that she was on drugs. The aunts would arrive with the two grannies and she would be told yet again what she must do to live up to her father's memory, and then she remembered with a pang how he had often said his Eilie was made of good stuff.

Dear old Dad, she thought. He wouldn't have approved of the hair.

✦   ✦   ✦

Hot Pants Helen was talking to Carmel in the corridor when Eilie escaped from the classroom.

"Hi, Eilie!" Helen said and eyed her. "I like your hair. It took a bit of nerve." She twirled her own lustrous dark locks between thumb and forefinger and looked at her from dark brown eyes.

She looked as good in navy blue as in that fabulous cream silk top her mother had bought her in Brown Thomas. She had come by her nickname because she had drunk too much punch at a party last Christmas and one of the boys had snogged her for ages in the corner.

"Yeah, blonde really suits you . . ." Carmel said. "Very glamorous . . . but you missed bits at the back of your head!"

"They're not too bad!" Hot Pants Helen said. "You have to *really* look—d'ya know what I mean? You could pin it up for Carmel's party . . . no one would notice."

Eilie made an excuse and headed for the cloakroom. Carmel followed her.

"Did you see the way that one condescended? With her reputation?"

"You're the one who mentioned the bits I missed at the back!" Eilie said, now on the verge of tears. "Are they dreadful?"

She twisted her head until she thought it would screw off, pulled at her hair in an effort to see where the bleach had failed her. Right enough, there were one or two funny bits, but you wouldn't get off the bus to look at them.

"You could always put some more on it!"

"Bleach on bleach? Wouldn't that be a bit much, Carmel!"

"If you really want him . . . you'll do whatever it takes . . ."

"How do you resist François? He'll be staying in your house after all."

Carmel laughed, showing even white teeth. She did not look Eilie in the eye.

"Don't be an eejit! François is my brother's friend and we're like brother and sister! Besides, after my French exchange last year . . . !"

Eilie eyed her doubtfully. Carmel had become very sophisticated after her summer spent on the Côte d'Azur where the beach Lotharios had apparently followed her around.

"I'm on Suddenly Slender, you know!" Eilie said after a moment. "Do you think I've lost weight?"

"You have an' all. You'll look great for the party!"

The weekend was coming up so Eilie thought she would try to catch up on her work. But after her Suddenly Slender breakfast on Saturday Carmel phoned her, just as she was about to settle down to Biology.

"Do you want to come into town? There's a sale on in Only For Babes!"

"Funny time of year for a sale, isn't it?"

"They're closing down. We might find something nice for the party!"

"All right."

Only For Babes specialized in clothing for the young and sartorially adventurous. Carmel pulled a red satin two-piece from the rack. The trousers were harem pants, slit at the sides and the top was very low.

"Try that on!"

"It's a bit sudden, isn't it?"

"Don't be such a wimp! Go on."

The trousers were tight. The top was tighter still, and cut low. Eilie's breasts, squeezed together like hairless tennis balls, looked back at her reproachfully. Her bare belly button eyed her with some embarrassment.

"I don't think it's me!" she said. "Anyway my mother would have a fit!"

"Your mum doesn't have to see it! Look, you could put a ring in your navel an' all!" Carmel added authoritatively.

"You think that would look good?"

"Knock him for six. Guaranteed! All the rage in France!"

"Well, if you're sure . . ."

As Eilie was paying for her purchase a stack of boxes full of merchandise near the cash desk began to wobble ominously. The cashier shrieked and Eilie dodged behind the counter and took the brunt of their weight, holding them until they could be righted.

"You're as strong as an ox!" Carmel said in awed disbelief when they had left the shop.

"I know. It's awful!"

"It's bound to come in handy some day!" Carmel said. "You'll be able to get a job as a furniture remover."

"Very funny!"

Eilie did not shine in her Mocks. She dreaded the results, but she still had six weeks to go before the Junior Cert. so she reckoned she could make good where she had slipped up.

"Mum will kill me when she gets my results!"

Carmel was sympathetic. "Never mind, there's my party next week! François has been asking about you. He said he would have written to you only he was afraid your mother would read his letter!"

Eilie brightened. "When did he tell you all this?"

"When we went to visit Tim at school. Mum and Dad took François out too. He talked about you all the time. He said he wanted to ask you to his parents' place in the south of France in the summer, but wondered if your mother would let you go! It's a fabulous villa—pool, sea, palm trees . . ."

"Of course she'll let me go!" Eilie said, wild with joy. "Your parents know his, after all. Will you be going as well?"

"He hasn't asked me—at least not yet! Are you going to get your belly button pierced?" Carmel added in a curious non sequitur. "Looks smashing in a bikini . . ."

"Not unless you really think—"

"I do! I really do! You'll have to stop being such a mouse . . ."

The night before the party Eilie tried on her red outfit. The harem pants were still a tad tight. The top, or rather the absence of top, was certainly eye catching. The ring in her navel accentuated its little protuberance and she wondered if it had been a mistake. For a moment she wanted to change into jeans, but thought of Carmel's scorn and the pointlessness of cowardice. She put more Blonder than Blonde in her hair, and spent ages conditioning it afterwards. It was very pale indeed and it took ages to improve its new-found texture of fresh straw.

"I'm going to Carmel's party tonight!" she informed her mother at breakfast. "So I'll be out when you get back."

"Oh, is it tonight? Home by midnight! Sharp!"

"Yes, Mummy."

"Have you put more of that stuff in your hair?" her mother demanded with sudden laughter. "You look like a tarted baby version of Marilyn Monroe!"

"Who's she?" Eilie said, bridling.

Her mother sighed.

"Mum, if a French family invited me to stay during the summer would you let me go?"

"Depends on the family. Who are you talking about?"

"The Despardieus. François's family. You know the guy who's at school with Timmy Kelly?"

"Is Carmel going?"

"I think so!"

"And Tim?"

"Yeah."

"I'll ask their mother what she thinks!"

Eilie spent a long time dressing for the evening ahead. When she was fully assembled she twirled before her mirror trying to see herself through the eyes of a romantic Frenchman. The mirror reflected back a nervous pale-gold blonde in a tight crimson outfit with a low neckline, bare midriff and pierced belly button. Irresistible! No one would dream I was the strongest girl in the school, she thought with relish as she applied her lipstick. She went downstairs, but halfway down had to clutch at the banister with sudden faintness. I'd better have that damn meal replacement, she told herself. I can't be fainting all over my darling François!

She went to the kitchen, reached into the fridge for some milk to mix her draught, but her eyes rested on the chicken tandoori and the chocolate cake her mother had left for her. Even as she struggled with herself, something in her rebelled. A fierce will, one very much stronger than her own, dictated that she take that chicken dish out of that fridge and the chocolate cake too, and that she put them on the table and eat the lot. It was no use telling this hog brain that she was off to a party where there would be food anyway. She was too busy groaning in ecstasy. But a strange thing happened as soon as she had eaten. The fluttering in her tummy ceased. Her faintness vanished; energy and optimism surged through her veins. This euphoria, however, was quickly replaced by horror when she stood up and felt her harem pants strain against her lower stomach. She rushed to the loo and did something she had only ever read about; she stuck two fingers down her throat and was sick. No giving in at the first hurdle, Eilie, she told herself.

When she got to the Kellys, Carmel answered the door. Carmel was wearing her black dress and the gold chain her parents had given her for Christmas. Her long hair was burnished darkness on her shoulders. With just a smidgeon of eye make-up, a touch of lipstick, she looked like class on legs.

"So you wore it?" she whispered as she took Eilie's coat. "The tarty two-piece! God, I have to admire your nerve!"

"You were the one who made me buy it! Is Hot Pants here?"

"Yeah. But she's brought her new boyfriend, Hughie O'Hanlon. A real stud! God, Eilie, I'd do anything to lift him!"

"Would you?" Eilie intoned, struggling with a sudden dose of acid mistrust. "How would you do that?"

Carmel shrugged.

Footsteps could be heard descending the stairs. Eilie turned to find François just ten feet away from her, looking divine in a pair of Levis and a casual pale cream sweater. Carmel said indulgently, "François, you remember Eilie . . ."

Years would pass before Eilie would forget that frown of surprised consternation and then the languid French voice saying, "You haf changed, Eilie . . . What haf you done to yourself?"

"Our Eilie always likes to knock the boys for six!" Carmel explained with a little laugh for which Eilie wanted to gut her. "Don't you, Eilie?"

François's eyes moved over her, but they were no longer the gentle interested eyes so full of humour that had once looked

into hers. They possessed a glint of excited calculation that hard-
ened his face. Carmel put a familiar hand on his arm.

"Come and meet the rest of the gang," she said and drew him
towards the sitting room, leaving Eilie behind in the hall.

Eilie stood indecisively before the mirror. The red outfit now
seemed appalling. She wiped off her lipstick and tried to pull her
top over her cleavage. But the designer of that particular outfit
had economized on fabric and she was stuck with her charms on
opulent display. For a moment she wanted to go home, and then
she remembered she was made of good stuff. Somehow she had
to redeem the situation. She took a deep breath and sailed into
the sitting room.

When Eilie came into the sitting room every eye in the room
fixed itself on her. The boys straightened like people who had
been shot in the spine; the girls suppressed giggles, but when they
saw the general direction of every male gaze in the room, their
covert hilarity changed to covert fury.

"Wow!" Hot Pants Helen said from her corner where she was
snuggling up to Hunky Hughie (who really was gorgeous), seem-
ingly completely uninterested in François. "Where did you get
that outfit, Eilie?"

"Only For Babes!" Eilie replied. "Carmel thought it would do
as fancy dress for her party. Didn't you, Carmel?"

"But it isn't fancy dress!" Hot Pants said in some consternation.

Carmel grinned uneasily and said she had to nip upstairs and
would be back in a minute. Eilie saw François watching her out
of the corner of her eye. When she turned in his direction she
detected that his gaze was fixed upon her chest. His dark eyes
were molten. He was now surrounded by male company, all of

whom were also staring at her with vacant half grins tacked onto their faces.

Timmy Kelly came forward asking what she would like to drink and she said orange juice.

"With a bit of something in it?" he asked, a sententious edge to his voice as he looked down her cleavage. Eilie realized at once that he was playing to his male peers.

"Timmy, this is me!" she hissed.

"You've got a gorgeous body, Eilie. I never realized . . ."

She felt his eyes travel from her breasts to her belly button and wished she was in Australia.

"Well you can stop realizing! It was a silly mistake!"

Timmy excused himself and went to the kitchen, saying he would bring in some more canapés. François, being a house guest, followed to help. Eilie decided she would follow too. She wanted to bump off Carmel.

It was a relief to leave the sitting room, to find herself alone in the hall. As she approached the kitchen she heard the muted voices.

"What did you think of our little Eilie?"

It was Timmy's voice. "In her little next to nothings?"

"She reminds me of a strawberry lollipop," came the French accent. "*Très bon,* if you just want a lick but not the sort of sweet-ie you would bring home to your mother!"

In the midst of the ensuing male laughter Carmel came downstairs and found her friend standing outside the kitchen door, tears coursing down her cheeks.

"Oh Eilie, I'm so sorry," she whispered. "It was supposed to be a joke. Come on and I'll get you a blouse or something!"

"You just wanted him for yourself! That's why you made me wear this awful tarty gear!"

Carmel looked uncomfortable. "Well, I did like him, but as

soon as I saw Hunky Hughie I knew he was meant for me! I don't
know how I can get him out of Hot Pants's clutches!"

"Get her to dye her hair and deck herself out like a tart!" Eilie
hissed. "And there's one thing you can also do if I am ever to
speak to you again! Do you remember that party game we used
to play when we were kids . . ."

Just before supper was served Carmel announced there would be
a garden game to stoke up appetites—a tug of war—girls versus
boys. Everyone had to draw lots for partners. The rope was waiting in the garden and Carmel administered the lots. Hot Pants
Helen drew Timmy and squealed as she was allowed initial lati-
tude, then gently pulled a few paces across the grass. Breathless
with laughter she let go of the rope. Carmel drew the gorgeous
Hughie and suffered a similiar fate, subsiding gracefully on the
grass near the feet of her new idol. Lorraine DeLacy drew
Andrew O'Leary and although she dug her heels in well—her
mother had been a well-known feminist in the seventies—she
too was dragged a few paces across the garden. It was all very
good humoured. The girls, in the main, did not mind showing
how feminine they were and the boys were delighted at their
masculine prowess. The last girl to draw lots was Eilie. She stared
hard at Carmel as the latter held out the straws and took the one
nudged towards her.

"You're matched with me!" said François, coming forward
and gallantly offering to concede victory in return for a kiss. Eilie
said that she only gave her kisses to men who could defeat her in
open combat. This occasioned some tittering, but she took up
one end of the rope and François took the other.

"Are you ready?" she asked François. "I don't like to take
unfair advantage!"

"Petite," he said, "I am so looking forward to . . ."

"Licking your lollipop?" Eilie asked innocently. She braced herself, then with a sudden wrench she flicked François into the hydrangeas.

The silence was only temporary. It was followed by shrieks and howls of laughter. François was sprawled among the hydrangeas, whose woody parts were interfering with his less woody parts. The girls tried to stifle their mirth, but in vain. The boys made hurtful remarks like "Ah, for God's sake . . ." and "Jesus, give us a break!"

François, now very red in the face, extricated himself with suppressed yelps. Eilie sidled into the house, picked up her coat and made for the door. She was almost at the gate when she heard a male voice behind her.

"Eilie . . ."

It was Hughie Gorgeous O'Hanlon, Hot Pants's latest.

"You're the funniest and prettiest girl here . . ." he whispered, with a glance over his shoulder in case Hot Pants came in pursuit. "Can I have your phone number!"

"I have to go home," Eilie said. "I am beginning to get a headache."

"I just wanted to ask you if you would come to my Debs?"

"I'll have to check my appointments book, but I think I have a vacant slot!" Eilie said and smiled very sweetly at Carmel who had materialized on the doorstep.

MARY RYAN is the bestselling author of ten novels, including *Hope, Glenallen, Whispers in the Wind, The Promise,* and *The Song of the Tide.*

She is based in Dublin.

Carrot for Breakfast

Rosaleen Linehan

The phone was ringing. It was the middle of the night. Sarah shook herself awake. Oh God, had something happened—somebody died? The clock on the bedside table said eleven o'clock—but it was Sunday morning and they had been at a good party the night before and had got to bed at five. She answered, her voice thick with wine and cigarettes.

"Hello, could I speak to Sarah Collins, please?"

"I think that's me, but I'm not totally sure—"

"Sarah, wondergirl. Jonathan Davis here."

A rush of blood to the head. She was wide awake.

"Jonathan! What a gorgeous surprise. Where are you?"

"Dublin. Can I see you? Any chance of breakfast tomorrow morning? I'm here giving a seminar in Trinity all day. Fly back tomorrow afternoon. I couldn't leave without saying hello and I want to know how your life is going."

"Well, I . . ."

Sarah tried to Velcro her brain together.

"I have to be at work at 9:30. Would half past seven be too early?"

"Perfect. I'm an early riser. I'm staying at the Clarion, where breakfast starts at dawn. Let's meet in the lobby at 7:30 and we can catch up with everything. Are you still as lovely as ever, Sarah?"

"Well, I haven't changed that much in twelve months—I think."

"Good, I can't wait. See you then."

Sarah stared at the receiver, then kissed it a long, long kiss and cradled it lovingly before replacing it. She sat motionless for a time, smiling. Then she let out a long Valkyrie scream that wakened her two flatmates.

"What's up, Sarah? Are you OK?"

"No, no, I'm not OK. I'm KO. I'm delirious, I'm insane, I'm ecstatic. I am burning, I'm going mad . . ."

"Cut the drama, Sarah, please. What the hell is going on?"

"Guess, just guess who that was on the phone."

"Who?"

"Jonathan . . . Jonathan Davis."

All three then screamed the long scream—"Jesus! What? How? Why?"

"I'm meeting him tomorrow for an early breakfast in the Clarion."

Breakfast. Early. The Clarion. Another scream.

"Man the fireboats, grab the face packs, the eye pads. Melt the leg-wax . . . What'll I wear?"

"Morna, you can bring my work clothes into the office, it's on your way and I'll go into town and buy something in BT's this afternoon. Oh my God, I can't believe this. Oh, oh, God is good. Maybe I should go to Mass in thanksgiving."

"Oh come on, Sarah, calm down," Morna yawned. "He's only a carrot." And Morna and Jane slipped back to bed.

"A carrot. No. Not *only* a carrot. *The* carrot. The carrot of my life."

She looked at her nails. That would be the number one rehab. Where would she get a manicure on a Sunday? If shove came to push, Morna could do it. She would buy the Chanel nail polish she had balked at buying for twenty-four euro last week. "Unspoken" it was called. That should fit the bill. She made some extra-strong coffee. The aroma was adding to her pleasure barometer, then with gritted teeth she threw it down the sink. She'd had enough toxins last night and early morning puffy eyes were the last thing she needed tomorrow. She made herself a cup of camomile tea, which she hated with a passion, and sipped it, remembering the last time she'd seen him.

Oxford in May. Sarah had been granted a post-graduate scholarship in the Anglo-Irish department in Hertford College. Sarah was clever, very clever. Sarah was pretty, very pretty. Her father, proud as punch, would say that if ever Sarah would only settle herself she could have a chair in Trinity before she was thirty. Her mother, proud as punch, would say that if Sarah wasn't such a feminist and paid a little more attention to grooming she could be a Rose of Tralee.

It was the end of term tutorial and Jonathan had taken them out to the rose garden for their last class. They had brought chilled wine and strawberries to celebrate and they all sat round his feet in the May sunshine. Jonathan Davis, senior visiting lecturer, had his students in the palm of his hand. His lectures were stimulating and witty. His good looks and charm ensured frequent appearances on Arts programmes and critics' panels on the BBC. His wife, a stunning, elegant blonde, worked for Saatchi and Saatchi in London, where they lived in Kensington with their two children. Sarah knew she was his pet in the class of ten. She liked that, just as she liked her classmates teasing her that it was unfair to have the brains and the looks, *and* come out top of the class.

Look at her now. She was working, after all the achievements and scholarships—working hard as a receptionist in a company that imported toilet paper, sanitary protection, incontinence pads and the device they used to keep the smells down in the monkey house in the zoo.

Yes, Sarah was unfortunate enough to have come home to Ireland for the funeral of the Celtic Tiger, and she wasn't going to hang around till the real job turned up, which she was quite sure it would, and soon. She would tell Jonathan she was a copywriter in an advertising agency and it was really challenging.

That last day in Oxford—they had sat on the grass around the tree. The sun was shining, the roses were showing off and the wine had made them giggly and full of what they all knew was a suspended happiness they would always remember. Their snapshot of idyllic student life. Jonathan was leaning against the tree, one hand behind his head. He had the longest legs Sarah had ever seen, always in his uniform of beige cords and brown oxfords. His right foot, which usually moved up and down incessantly, was quiet today. He was reading from an anthology of love poems, when he suddenly put down the book and looked straight into her eyes. She had looked back and he began Yeats's great love poem to Maud Gonne . . . "When you are old and grey and full of sleep, and nodding by the fire . . ." His gaze was so intense that in an unusual burst of shyness she had closed her eyes and leaned back on her elbows on the grass, while the sun and the wine and the words conspired to elevate the moment into pure joy.

At the end they all stood up and, quite formally, to break the spell, said their goodbyes, wished each other good luck in life, and vowed to keep in touch, knowing they wouldn't. Jonathan, too, had left the moment behind. He congratulated them all on being one of the best groups he'd had for years, and what a pleasure it had been to share what he could with them. Then he shook hands formally with everyone and asked if they would leave forwarding addresses and phone numbers with the office in case of any problems with exam papers. Sarah had sent him a few jokey postcards during the year, but hadn't expected and didn't get any reply.

OK, so she had a gigantic crush on him. All her friends had decided that crushdom was the best of all emotional states. They named the object of the crush "the carrot." The forbidden fruit, well vegetable really, the unattainable, idealized, idolized, out of reach—and all the better for that. It made your eyes sparkle, your skin radiant, you were forever sixteen.

Morna had once slept with her carrot and had fallen into a melancholy pit for about six months afterwards. He was married, with a son older than herself, and when the crunch came, had truly awful underpants. They had a pattern of lobsters on them, but were so washed-out that most of the claws had disappeared and they had wear-and-tear holes in the back. After that, Morna, Jane and Sarah had lain down the ground rules. NEVER SLEEP WITH THE CARROT.

This was the beauty of breakfast, Sarah thought. Early morning, minds and emotions well under control in the luxurious dining room of the Clarion Hotel. It was one of Ireland's monuments to the boom-time nineties, along with the Government buildings, the magnificence of the restoration of Farmleigh, and now the seedy remains of what was once the delightful Bohemian atmosphere of Temple Bar. She decided what she would eat. Though she had always lusted after "The Full Irish Breakfast"—especially to see what spin the Clarion would put on it—she figured that the possibility of a trickle of grease down her chin from the Clonakilty Black Pudding might sully the purity of the occasion. No. Coffee, fruit and maybe she'd chance the yoghurt . . . stop daydreaming, Sarah, there's work to be done.

In Brown Thomas she bought the over-priced nail polish—the assistant had corrected her: "Nail lacquer, modom." Then she went up to the designer department. Who in God's name bought these clothes? One hundred and seventy euro for a T-shirt. Not many, she guessed by the absence of customers and the dejected sales girls, who looked as if they hadn't punched a sales register in weeks. The place was so deserted and the clothes hanging so sadly with their unattainable price tags that Sarah decided it would be bad karma to wear them, much less blow her Visa card out of the window. Dunnes Stores wasn't in England and she could pick up a bit of quickglam for the price of "nail lacquer, modom." In Dunnes she found a sky blue wisp of a dress, which would match her Jimmy Choo shoes. In a moment of overweening pride at her going to Oxford, her mother had bought her a designer watch in Harrod's, which she had exchanged the following day for the strappy shoe statement. She bought a lookalike watch at Next and her mum, whose sight was slipping but who hardly ever wore her glasses, never copped it.

Home to the leg wax, the face pack, the hot henna hair treatment. Morna did her magic on the hands and feet. Then she had a long bath in lavender oil and the silly bar that scattered rose petals, which jammed the plughole. She felt like an Eastern bride being prepared for the harem. She went to bed happy and excited, having ordered a taxi for 7:15, her office clothes in the Dunnes Stores bag, ready to be dropped off. In the morning she showered, blow-dried her hair into a gleaming waterfall, and carefully used subtle shades of make-up. On with the dress, no underwear necessary, slipped into the Jimmy Choos and looked in the mirror. She smiled. No doubt about it, she looked gorgeous. Perfume? No, there was a growing feeling that it was a bit suburban.

The doorbell rang. She checked her cash for the taxi and opened the door to the beautiful May morning.

It was silly, this booming of her heart. But wasn't that the whole essence of a carrot? This morning she was sixteen, not twenty-three. The taxi man was moaning on about how hard it was to make a living, as his meter clocked up twice what it would have cost in a London cab. No, Sarah, no harsh thoughts. No, not this morning. He was probably a nice man and just tired after a night on duty. She checked for a good tip for him. They had arrived at the hotel. She paid him, he smiled and said she was a lovely girl, and she teetered up the granite steps into the lobby.

The uniformed commissionaire opened the door and bowed good morning to her. She had a sudden anxiety that maybe she looked like Julia Roberts in *Pretty Woman*! It passed. There he was, draped, yes, draped, across an enormous cream brocade sofa, reading a book. A beam of sunlight caught his lowered head, high-lighting the streaks of grey in his unruly and ridiculously youthful brown curls. Oh my God, he was even more beautiful than she'd remembered—get a grip on yourself, Sarah. She clicked across the marble floor. He looked up, jumped to his feet and gazed at her for a moment. Then he hugged her—and gazed at her again.

"Well—hi, Irish! Look at you—you're all growed up!"

She beamed her greatest smile, happy that her teeth were just perfection, and simultaneously they both pushed their hair back from their faces and laughed out loud.

"Let's just sit here for a moment, Sarah, till I feast on you."

She sat down warily on the huge feather cushions. The dress mightn't flow as well as if it had been silk, not pretty polyester. She draped herself as best she could. He was still holding her hand and sat back staring at her.

"Well, the big question, Sarah. Before or after breakfast?"

He pulled his room key out of his pocket. Her jaw dropped. She didn't just feel it, she heard it dropping.

"Come on, my lovely Sarah. I've waited a year for this since you lay back on your elbows and opened your glorious jean-clad legs that sunny May day. You wanted it, I wanted it. So, now we can fuck . . . at last. I couldn't go near you then, political correctness, you must have understood . . . but now . . ."

Just then, like a stage direction, the sunbeam disappeared and her distress was palpable.

"Sarah, did I read you wrong? I thought you wanted to fuck me too—badly."

The word was a bullet straight to the heart. Oh God! It's all ruined. He's just a dirty old man, sitting there twiddling his fancy keys. He doesn't even want to pay for my breakfast. She noticed that his teeth, though even, were very yellow, like Edam cheese, and that there were a lot of hairs growing out of his nose. She had to keep control.

"How was the seminar?"

The words sounded hoarse.

"Boring old farts, but it will put a case of good wine in the cellar. Shall we go up now?"

He stroked the inside of her wrist. The quick thinking that had helped her win all those scholarships clicked into place.

"I'm so sorry, Jonathan, but my mother's sister has died and I have to catch the eight-thirty train to Cork."

"I like your funeral outfit," he said, stuffing the keys into his pocket.

She rose, an ungainly rise from the down feather cushions, wobbling on her heels.

"I just didn't want to stand you up, Jonathan," she said formally.

"And I didn't realize you were a prick-tease, Sarah," he echoed the formality.

She stumbled out past the commissionaire and down the steps. Then teetered down the side streets to the greasy spoon café on the corner. She was crying with disappointment, rage and humiliation.

In O'Connor's she ordered a full Irish Breakfast, black and white pudding with beans on toast on the side, plus a double cappuccino. She was gobbling it up when a large piece of black pudding landed on the blue dress. She didn't bother to wipe it off. She sat there traumatized, staring out of the window. Suddenly she remembered that, as a child, she had hated carrots. Her mother used to say, "Eat them up, Sarah, like a good girl. They're good for your eyes." She started to smile, the smile grew into a stifled giggle, which exploded into a huge peal of laughter and the breakfast people lowered their newspapers to look at the pretty girl in the blue dress who was obviously a little astray in the head.

ROSALEEN LINEHAN, one of Ireland's premier actresses and comediennes, has performed in Dublin, the West End, and on Broadway in productions such as Brian Friel's *Dancing at Lughnasa* and *Happy Days*. She has also appeared in several films, including *About Adam* and *Mad About Mambo*. Her most recent roles have been in Molière's *Tartuffe* at the Roundabout Theatre in New York and *The House of Bernarda Alba* at the Abbey Theatre, Dublin.

A recipient of the Lord Mayor of Dublin's special award for outstanding achievements by citizens of the city, Rosaleen Linehan was appointed to the Irish Arts Council in 2003.

Secret Letter Writers

Catherine Foley

I t was out of frustration that they decided to write the letter. They'd gotten to the beach at about three o'clock. They'd spent an hour getting there and climbing down. It was always a bit of an expedition. They'd brought sandwiches, crisps and something to drink. They'd eaten their picnic and had a swim. They'd played a bit in the water and now they lay there in the heat wondering what they could do next.

It was a hot day, the kind of day that made the two of them restless. As they lay on the sand, looking out to sea to the far-off horizon, it all seemed so out of their reach. They felt their lives had yet to begin. Janet, in particular, wanted to know what was beyond her world. She lay in the hazy white heat, hemmed in on all sides with the cliffs behind, the sprawling rocks at either end of the beach and the wide expanse of sea spreading out before her.

Janet was sixteen, and Lucy, her younger sister, was fourteen. The older girl was dark and tanned. She was wearing a navy one-piece swimsuit. Her face was narrow, and it seemed to crack in two when she smiled her wide smile. Her hair was shoulder length and now it hung in rat's-tails around her, stiff with the sand that had dried into it after her dip in the salt water.

Her younger sister had longer hair and she was blonde. Her face was more rounded and soft. She had big blue eyes that seemed to soak up all in her path.

The two of them felt beautiful that day but they felt as if it was all a waste. Janet was at the stage when time seems to stand still. She felt as if nothing was ever going to change. The two of them chatted away about boys and the lack of them, and how they wished they could meet a few.

"Where are they?" asked Janet, looking out towards the horizon. "Where are ye, boys? Are ye listening?" she said. They waited. Nothing happened.

Lucy turned over on her stomach and fixed herself on the towel. Janet lay on her side, facing her, when the idea of writing a letter just popped into her head. "Why don't we write a letter with our address and ages on it and ask boys to apply to us and then throw it into the sea?" said Janet in one desperate rush. Lucy looked at her, her mouth opening slightly in amazement and then she smiled broadly.

"Yeah," she said. "That's a brilliant idea. Have we any paper?"

"Yeah," said Janet. "I have. We can put it in a bottle and throw it into the sea on our way home."

"Great," said Lucy, sitting up and rooting for the glass bottle of orange that she'd finished. She ran down to the water to rinse it out. Janet sat up and got some paper from her sketchbook and took a blue crayon out of the tin box she had them in.

She'd already started writing when Lucy dashed up the beach and, breathless, flopped down beside Janet.

"What have you written?"

Janet cleared her throat and straightened her back before she started to read: "Two tall handsome men needed. Please write to Lucy and Janet Kirby as soon as possible." She looked up at Lucy and then scribbled down something else.

"Go on, what else? Are you going to give them our full address?" said an excited Lucy.

"Yes, we will," she said and resumed her reading. "Our address is White Bay House, Furnace, Co. Waterford," she read. "Please reply as soon as possible. We are anxious to hear from you immediately. That's it," she said. "Should I put anything else in?"

Lucy thought for a while. She took the paper from Janet and studied it for herself.

"What about our ages?" she asked, as she read the note.

"Good idea, I'll put our ages after our names."

"Yep, I think that says it all."

"It's short but sweet. Do you think it's enough? We don't want to scare them off."

"No, you're right," said Lucy taking the paper from her. Janet admired her penmanship over Lucy's shoulder.

"Roll it up like a scroll and put it in the bottle," she said to Lucy.

"OK, I think the bottle's dry."

"Right. We can throw it in from the top of the cliff on our way home," she said to Lucy, who rolled the paper into a nice chubby size. Janet held the green glass bottle upside down. "Yeah, that's dry enough," she said, giving it to Lucy.

"I wonder what will happen. I wonder if anyone will find it. It could go as far as Washington or Canada," said Lucy, trying to think of the places that were at the other side of the Atlantic.

"It's likely it'll go south towards France—Brittany," said the older girl, who liked to think that geography was one of her strong subjects. "The tides will probably take it out to sea and it will wash up—maybe on the coast of Cornwall or Devon, even."

"Yes," said Lucy, putting the paper into the bottle. "I can't wait until we throw it in," she said, screwing the top tight.

Janet took the bottle to check that it was secure and to admire it. Lucy admired it too before putting it out of the sun's glare behind her bag of clothes. She was being extra careful, thinking now that, maybe, the crayon lines would blur in the heat.

The time slipped by. The tide had come in a good bit when they finally decided to leave. It was almost up at their toes. The day was still warm but the sun had begun to dip towards its descent behind the cliffs and shadows were beginning to lengthen along the beach. It was time to go home. It was nearly teatime.

Excited at the thought of throwing the bottle into the sea, Lucy began singing Abba's "Waterloo," her favourite song of the moment. They changed quickly into their shorts and T-shirts. When they were ready, they gathered up their wet towels and their other bits and pieces and headed back along the strand. Joining in as they clambered over the rocks, Janet too began to sing. As they went, they gained momentum and speed until soon both girls were out of breath.

They loved coming to this out-of-the-way place. Not everyone knew about it or was able to get down the cliff. It was out of bounds for older people and for children because of the danger. The steep and dangerous section of cliff that had to be manoeuvred added to the lure and magic of the place. It was like a journey of the mind too, a psychological journey, where they travelled to another place, another time, where everything was new and timeless and where anything was possible.

They raced over the rocks, going quickly over the broken stones and crevices along the scarp. Janet thought of herself as one of the head Sherpas going up the Himalayas heading towards the base camp. The two of them were over the stones in no time and ready to begin the ascent.

Going up, they went like goats. Their legs were used to the wide stretches they had to take between each foothold. In three minutes they were up. At the top, they stopped and looked out again at the great expanse of water. Down the coast they saw the lighthouse clearly visible against the skyline. Underneath them, the sea where the water rushed in around the rocks, was a green turquoise. "We'll do it here," said Janet and Lucy took the bottle out of her bag and rubbed it clean.

The two of them felt the thrill of excitement as they stood at the top looking down. Holding out the bottle Janet wondered what was the best way to throw it in. There was a chance it would break on the rocks so she had to wait for the right moment before she flung it out over the waves.

She felt this was a daring, adventurous act. They'd put their names and addresses on this piece of paper. As she raised her arm, Lucy watched in anticipation. They stood nervously side by side for a few seconds and then Janet threw.

They watched the bottle plop safely into the water below. It bobbed up and down and they were delighted. It was safe from the rocks. "Sacred Heart of Jesus, we place all our trust in thee," Janet said on impulse. Lucy looked at her and repeated the incantation. Then she remembered another little prayer: "Little Jesus, lost and found," she said and the two girls smiled at each other briefly.

They turned home then. It was a twenty-minute walk. When they re-emerged onto the main road that led down to the village, they heard Ned's voice in the distance. The two of them looked at each other nervously and raised their eyebrows in puzzlement when they walked around the corner to their home, because Ned was outside on the front step across from their house. Although the girls had often heard Ned bellow from Bridgie's house, they had never seen him out in the open air like that. It was the best vantage point at the top of the village and he would have had a view of everything.

Surprise mingled with curiosity—would they rush by the house or dawdle to see what he looked like? Sometimes, he roared especially loudly, and they'd often wondered what it would be like to meet him up close.

From the road, Janet, who was looking up at him curiously, noted that he was wearing the Waterford colours—a blue and white tank top under a white bib, and peeping out from under his black trousers, she saw that he had a pair of blue and white socks on with shoes that were black and polished up to a great shine. On his head he wore a yellow knitted cap with a pompom, and it was tilted jauntily to one side. Janet thought he cut an intriguing figure at the top of the path.

"He looks like the king of the village," she said and turning to Lucy, asked, "Will we go up to him?"

She and Lucy saw Ned's twisted body stretch in his wheelchair and they could both see that he was trying to greet the two of them. His head rolled back and his mouth drooled. Janet could see that, though awkward, he was beckoning them towards him with his hand.

The two girls began to edge closer. They were curious but careful too. They were both afraid of him but fascinated by him also. They'd heard about him a lot when they were younger. They knew that he was a severely disabled invalid, who was never seen outside and had spent most of his life in a wheelchair. They knew that he was in his late sixties, and they knew that he had defied all the predictions of the doctors by living to such a great age. Bridgie, his sister, had cared for him for all the years they had known her. Janet and Lucy, in spite of their fear, turned up the path towards him.

"Maybe it's the right kind of day for doing unusual things," said Janet to Lucy, smirking.

"It must be," said Lucy as the two moved up the path, drawn as if by magic to the top where Ned sat in his high-backed wheelchair.

As they stood shyly in front of him, Ned shot out his hand towards Janet in a paroxysm of excitement. Timidly, she put her hand into his and discovered that he had a grip of iron. Once he had caught her hand she could hardly move her fingers and she felt she couldn't pull away even if she had tried. She found she was a little bit afraid of Ned up close but she couldn't stop looking at his chalky white face. She noticed how straight his hair was and how black it was over his ears, and she saw that his two eyebrows were inky black too and that, underneath them, his two eyes were looking directly into hers. She thought they were twinkling and she smiled back at him.

Lucy stood rigidly beside her sister. Even though she wanted to turn away, she stood her ground and watched closely as Ned dribbled and held onto her sister's hand with his long, pointed fingers. Then Ned began to roll his head around to see her better.

Shooting Janet one more look, he released her hand and tried to reach for Lucy. For a second, Lucy wondered if she could run. But Ned, who had his own inventiveness, had managed to reach across and grab her hand for himself. He shook it, smiling his crooked smile all the while.

"Hello, Ned," she said quickly and looked at him shyly, afraid as his contorted body continued to move in the chair. For a few seconds Lucy thought he was humming and she listened and smiled at him. He said something too but she didn't understand and she shook her head. He fixed her with a look and she smiled back at him. She tried not to yelp as he squeezed her hand in a vice-like grasp and pumped her arm until she pulled her hand away.

They didn't delay after that. They turned and went down the path, half terrified and half thrilled by their encounter. The two of them left him on his height. They were still shaking as they walked across the road to their own house. They giggled too as their nervousness subsided, and they went in home.

Ned's sister, Bridgie, who was their next-door neighbour, was inside before them. She'd had them under observation all the time. She was smiling wryly at the two of them when they went in.

"Did he give ye his purse?" she said to them.

"No," said Lucy.

"Does he have a purse?" asked Janet.

"He does," said Bridgie.

"He holds his purse out so visitors can give him money," their mother, who was standing beside Bridgie, explained.

"You can call over to him tomorrow maybe," she said. "You can give him something then, if you like."

"We didn't know he kept a purse," said Janet.

Bridgie was the first person they'd met when they had moved to Furnace many years ago: she'd walked slowly across to their house and stood by, studying them individually, not saying anything. She was a taciturn woman who could have a salty tongue on occasion. She also knew how to keep her own counsel, a quality their mother admired, which was how the two had become friends.

She would often arrive, sit down on the arm of a chair and say nothing for long periods. Occasionally she would make just one comment, but from the first, her caustic remarks had kept the girls at bay. She had the measure of them. Her brown eyes saw plenty and they knew that. They felt fenced in by Bridgie. They felt the strength of the boundary that she had erected around them and even though they weren't frightened by her they were bothered and rebellious with her and constantly struggled to move beyond her watchful presence.

"Come over tomorrow," she said. "When ye come back from the swim."

Their mother told them more about Ned when Bridgie was gone home. "He was reared by Bridgie's mother in a tea chest," she said. "The other children used to mind him and play with him but he used to fall out of the box sometimes. His mother used to worry about him and she prayed about him. And then a day came and because he had grown a bit, he stopped falling out of the box. And then they finally got a proper wheelchair for him. And then," she said, "Bridgie took over and began to take care of him when their mother got too old."

Janet watched Bridgie over at her own house chopping wood out on the step that evening. She was thin and wiry. She came across to them nearly every day. She walked briskly, leaning into the window of their hallway when she arrived to rest her arms and watch the world go by.

She would stay for a while, sometimes saying very little and sometimes she'd chat to their mother and talk about happenings in the parish. Bridgie never said much but she always seemed to be keenly interested in what the girls were up to. She'd ask them questions about where they'd been and who they'd met. She would comment on their escapades and cackle sometimes at them, enjoying their embarrassment. At other times she'd ponder deeply on something and then sum it all up in one bubble of speech, allowing her words to sink in before she said anything else.

✦   ✦   ✦

The next day, the girls went swimming. They didn't go over to see Ned. Their mother, Letty, watched them leave with amusement. They'd told her about the letter that they had written and what they had done with it. They were no good at keeping secrets. They'd told her about it the first chance they got. She nodded at them as she waved them off. They were too busy thinking about the reply they were likely to get to their letter to want to call in to see Ned.

For days they raced down in the morning to the postman to see if he had brought them anything new but there never was anything to get excited about. Their father worked all through the summer, returning in the evening to hear about the day's events. He was also told about the letter in the bottle. The entire family waited to see what would happen. Even Bridgie was told. She frowned at the pair of them and Janet wondered if she was annoyed with them or if she disapproved.

Their mother's friend, Ellen Cassin, who often called for a chat, was also included in the speculation. As she sat in the kitchen, having a cup of tea, she listened to their talk. She was home on holidays from Switzerland. A regular visitor to Furnace, she came every summer. Her husband made occasional appearances but mostly she came on her own.

She had red hair that she wore tied up in a bun. "It's a French pleat," she told them, as she patted the smooth coil at the back of her head. She had a lovely accent and Janet felt that she brought a whiff of the other world she inhabited with her.

She loved to call and hear what Letty's girls were up to. And they loved to talk to her too. She admired Lucy's new platform shoes and she said Janet's new page-boy haircut was up to the minute. They could ask her about boys. Their mother was a good source of information on that score but Mrs. Ellen Cassin brought a bit of excitement to their conversations. She lived abroad, and so seemed almost exotic to the girls.

Even Bridgie, who wandered in and out of their house at will, often came over to sit and listen to Ellen Cassin. She'd stay for a while and then leave, limping steadily across to her own house. Both Bridgie and Mrs. Cassin were welcome guests in the house but the girls were always anxious for Bridgie to go because they couldn't wait to have Mrs. Cassin all to themselves again.

They listened to her stories about her life in Berne with delight. They hung on her words. Her son, Edmond, who was not usually with her, came in that day for a few minutes.

They knew he fished off the rocks nearly every day at a spot about a mile from where they went swimming. They had often noticed his tiny figure off in the distance when they were going swimming. Lucy liked Edmond but he was always fishing. He never turned around to wave. They never for a minute thought that he might fish their bottle out of the water and bring it home to his mother.

He was younger than they were. Janet didn't deem him worthy of her interest really, although he was nice-looking. Coming from their swim if she saw him, she'd just note his presence and then carry on up the steep field towards the boreen. They knew from his mother that he was a quiet young man who didn't say much. He was shy around girls, she said.

It was warm all that summer. The two girls walked and cycled for miles. Janet was full of energy, and wanted to cycle as far as she could and go beyond the places they knew so well. She wanted to travel, to meet new people. She waited for something exciting to happen.

Then one day, nearly two months later, when the two of them had almost forgotten about the letter in the bottle, the postman brought a reply. They tripped over themselves trying to reach the letter on the hall floor. Janet examined it carefully before she opened it. Lucy told her to hurry up.

"It has a French stamp," said Janet. "The writing is very small, very pointy," she said.

"Hurry up," said Lucy, not wanting to hear what Janet had to say.

The letter writer's name was Jacques Merlet. He wrote that he was a seventeen-year-old student who was interested in studying marine biology when he left school in Cherbourg, that he had two sisters and two brothers and that he loved music.

"He says he fished the bottle out of the sea off the coast of Brittany," said Janet. "I will going to visit your coast this summer and I hope to be meeting with you family," she read.

"Come on, will we show it to Mam?" Lucy asked.

"OK," said Janet. "Come on."

The two of them trooped into the kitchen. Letty took the letter and read it through, smiling as the two girls danced around the floor, unable to contain their excitement. She was pleased for them.

Janet was delighted but also a little perturbed by the letter. She couldn't put her finger on what made her unsure about it, but she thought that perhaps she was worried about what this visitor would think of them. To receive a letter like that was just a little bit overwhelming. It was also intriguing, she thought, and she began to wonder if it had really happened at all. She looked at the French stamp and at the writing. She couldn't believe her eyes and then, slowly, she relaxed and began to imagine what the world was like beyond Furnace, the world which stretched all the way to the coastline of Brittany.

"I wonder when he'll arrive," Letty said.

"Isn't it great that the letter was fished out of the sea?" said Lucy, looking at the two of them carefully.

"I wonder what he looks like," said Janet. It was a fine day, the morning was fresh and bright. She could easily imagine how she'd feel if she saw Jacques walking up to their front door. She'd be terrified.

She couldn't wait to tell Mrs. Cassin and show her the letter. Lucy and herself both thought she would never come so that they could tell her about it. She arrived in the afternoon and Lucy raced away to get the letter. While she was gone, Mrs. Cassin smiled at their father who had just arrived. He gave the two women a furtive wink, at which they all stifled a grin. Janet noted the look, and looked immediately at her mother, who had seen them and was frowning at the two of them, as if warning them to behave. Janet wanted to be in on their secret but she said nothing because she knew that they didn't see her yet as an equal or an adult.

Before the two women were ready to drive off in Mrs. Cassin's car to go for a walk, the letter was ceremoniously produced. The girls were delighted with Mrs. Cassin's reaction. Her face lit up as she leaned back to read it without her glasses. Janet could see she was trying to suppress a smile. She put her hand up to her hair to fix it in place and it seemed to Janet that she was really intrigued and impressed. Her lively eyes shone as Janet and Lucy tried to hold in their excitement.

"He's coming here," she said to them in disbelief. "What will you say to him?" she asked them. "Will you fight over him?" she wanted to know. "Perhaps, he'll fall in love with one of you," she said. "Is he going to call to the house? Letty, will you ask him to stay?" she wondered. Letty just laughed. She didn't answer that question.

Mrs. Cassin tried to pack in as much walking and enjoyment

into her holiday as she could. Sometimes Janet wondered if she was as happy in Switzerland as she was in Furnace in the summer, or if they were as fond of her there as they all were. She seemed so happy to be with them in their house.

Then the two women left, stopping to chat to Bridgie before they drove off. The three women seemed to have plenty to discuss. Their heads were together for a while and then they all laughed, Mrs. Cassin falling backwards as if she was hearing a really funny story. Janet looked out at them and wondered what they could be talking about. She saw Mrs. Cassin hug Bridgie's shoulders in an affectionate way. What secret were they sharing, she wondered.

The girls went into the garden to sunbathe and after a few minutes Bridgie wandered into the garden. Janet thought about showing the letter to her but she decided against it. As they lay on a blanket on the grass, Bridgie stood above them, looking out to sea, not saying anything. Janet looked up at her curiously, nervous of her silence. Lucy rolled over on the blanket to see what Bridgie was doing. She was just standing there, not saying anything. Her little grey bun was pinned in tightly at the back of her head. Her hair was not lush or high like Mrs. Cassin's. Her frame was pencil thin. The two women were like chalk and cheese.

Bridgie looked down at the two of them, and pursed her lips as if she wanted to say something to them. Janet wondered if she was going to lecture them about something and she became a bit wary.

"Well," said Bridgie. "Are ye well?"

"Hi, yeah," said Janet.

"Any news?" asked Bridgie.

"No, not really," said Janet. "Em, we're just sunbathing. Just relaxing. How's Ned?"

"He's fine, fine," said Bridgie, who stood with her arms

folded over her stomach as if she was settling in for a long chat. "He's watching his favourite programme—the news with Maurice O'Doherty, talking back to Maurice."

Janet looked directly at Bridgie but as usual, the inscrutable face gave nothing away. She didn't mention the letter and Lucy didn't say anything either. After some minutes, Bridgie unfolded her arms and began to wander slowly back home to Ned. Janet watched her limp awkwardly. She was getting old. She saw how Bridgie held her hands behind her back, one hand holding the other, one slapping the other now and then and her back slightly stooped.

The two girls were excited for days afterwards. In the middle of a television programme they would remind each other of the letter. They enjoyed joking about it. What if we have to fight over him? Lucy wondered. Janet said Jacques would just fall in love with her immediately and that there would be no contest. She wondered if he was good-looking. Her ideas about this French person were vague but she knew that this didn't matter.

They had received a letter.

Janet studied herself in the mirror. She lay in the garden, trying to get a deeper colour. The days slipped by. It was nearly September and time to go back to school. The letter made her examine herself more closely. She combed her hair and tried on dresses. She looked deep into her eyes in the mirror and wondered what Jacques would like about her.

Occasionally she puzzled over the letter's arrival. There was no return address on it and she thought this was annoying and a pity they couldn't write back to him. She was worried too that a stranger would arrive at their door some day soon and ask to see her. What would she say to him?

As the weeks went by she wondered when he would call. She

wondered if he would call at all. "What is delaying him?" Janet wanted to know. "He must have been blown off course," she reasoned for herself. Her mother wasn't able to help her either. For a few minutes, the two of them would put their minds to it and wonder about the marine biologist.

Slowly, imperceptibly, the importance of the letter faded. One day, Janet was getting messages for her mother in the local shop and out of the blue she remembered the letter and she realized she had forgotten all about it. She was too busy getting ready for going back to school. She shrugged. After all, it was only a letter.

In time, the letter's significance in the lives of the girls that summer and the impact of its arrival faded completely. As time went by, they didn't worry about why he didn't call and they forgot all about him.

As the summer holidays drew to a close, Bridgie came over more and more to their house for different things, almost as if she was looking for an excuse. One morning when the car wouldn't start for their father she came down her path and helped them push it down the hill so that it would start. She stayed with them all morning. Later that day, she called over to borrow a spare bottle of milk.

At the weekend, Janet helped her repitch a flat roof. While Bridgie stirred the melting pitch in the cauldron over the outside fire, Janet could see into Bridgie's old-fashioned kitchen with its dresser and oil-skin-covered table. She could hear *Wanderly Wagon* on the television. Ned was probably sitting at the fire but she couldn't see him. Every once in a while she could hear him say something to the television. Janet, looking at the bent figure of Bridgie, as she stirred the pot of black pitch, smiled at the figure she cut.

"Bubble, bubble, toil and trouble," recited Janet, taking the stick from Bridgie, who just looked at her quizzically, never passing a comment. Janet studied her again. She tried with all her might to understand what was going on in Bridgie's head but she couldn't penetrate her stern expression. As Janet looked closely at her in the firelight, she noticed the deep lines etched on her face. She noted how concave her face was in the light. Bridgie's face was like the rocks they climbed to reach their beach. It was lined and cracked. Janet couldn't stop looking at her face and Bridgie didn't seem to notice. She never looked away.

A couple of days later, almost at the end of the summer, Janet saw Bridgie hammer at them from her window. The doctor had to be sent for. He walked up her path with his black bag and let himself in. His presence going through Bridgie's door seemed wrong to Janet. He said Bridgie was very ill and would have to go to hospital. His words meant everything would be different.

While the doctor was inside, Janet watched Bridgie's house from their own front door. Lucy stood beside her looking across with her. They both listened to their mother on the phone telling Mrs. Cassin what was happening. After hanging up, their mother looked at the two girls and shook her head in resignation at what was going to happen next.

Together the three of them looked towards the window where Bridgie lay in her bed. They knew Ned was in his room at the back of the house. The ambulance was on its way. Ned and Bridgie would both have to be taken away. Bridgie was going to hospital and Ned would be taken to the local rest-home.

They waited for Mrs. Cassin to arrive and then they went over to the house. The four of them walked to the gate and up to the house before the ambulance came. They helped prepare Bridgie's bag and wrap her in her heavy black coat. Janet held her hand for a short while to help steady her as she put it on.

Outside, Janet could see neighbours gather beside the gate. They waited to watch Ned being hoisted into the back of the van. Then another stretcher carried Bridgie down from the house along the narrow path, through the gate and up into the back of the ambulance. Some of the neighbours cried to see them being lifted in. Bridgie and Ned looked at each other from their stretchers. Bridgie told Ned not to worry.

"You'll be all right," she told him. "You'll be all right. The girls will visit you," she said. Her voice was weak. Janet saw her hair loose around her for the first time and swallowed a lump in her throat. Lucy stood a little behind her, as if hiding from the unfamiliar spectacle.

Suddenly Janet's mind thought back to the letter. As she looked at Bridgie's stoic, lined face, she began to wonder about all the chances she'd had to mention it to her but never did.

With a final wave before Bridgie was wheeled out of view, Janet saw, as if for the first time, how naive she might have been.

———————

Born and brought up in County Waterford, **CATHERINE FOLEY** works as a staff journalist with *The Irish Times*. She has written a weekly column, *On the Town,* for the paper's Saturday edition for the past six years.

Catherine has had a number of poems and short stories published in both English and Irish. Her first published book, *Sorcha sa Ghailearaí*, an Irish novella, won a 2002 Oireachtas Literary Prize.

Dinner with Annie

Gemma O'Connor

The morning George died, Annie happened to drop by after her morning run, so she was with me when the call came. She was marvellous, I simply don't know how I'd have managed without her. She was everything a friend should be: unobtrusive, thoughtful, kind. She seemed to know instinctively what to do and say, when help was needed, when to make herself scarce. Strange, isn't it? Because, until that morning, I'd always been a bit in awe of her. To be perfectly honest, I was a bit jealous. She's so great-looking, vivacious, clever and dresses like a dream. Annie Colfer is a very accomplished woman, socially and professionally. She owns the three most successful shoe shops in Ireland; one on Grafton Street and two more in Cork and Limerick. Fabulous shoes at fabulous prices. She's also on every cultural committee in Dublin.

She was about the last person on earth I'd have asked for help in an emergency. Temperamentally, we're poles apart. I'm the kind who likes to sit gassing with my women friends, over endless cups of coffee, in the kitchen. Dinner parties were much more Annie's style. Formal but relaxed, with divine food. First Saturday of every month, she invites twelve, old friends mixed with new. And the wine! Her husband, Jeff, is something of a connoisseur and generous with his cellar. He and George were at Trinity, part of a close-knit group who still like to hang out together. George calls—called—them "the home team," I refer to them as "the guys." One or two are usually at Annie's dinner parties, so that over the past few years I've met most of them, yet they always remained George's friends, the circle wasn't widened to include a relative newcomer like myself. They always appear happier with each other than with anyone else. I find them a bit intimidating, and on the couple of occasions when they were all invited—impenetrable. They leave the wives, present and future, to fend for themselves.

George died suddenly and much too soon, just four years after we were married and still passionately in love. The shock was terrible, it was so unexpected. He was about the fittest man I ever met, he really took care of his body. Even now, thinking about him, my knees turn to jelly. Ridiculous, isn't it? But George was so handsome. Everyone said he was amazing. For his age. A qualification that was rarely spoken, but you could sense it behind the eyes. It amused us, we'd exchange a look, his right eyebrow would twitch and the corners of his sexy mouth would curl, imperceptibly, except to me. Our private joke. Because George, despite being twenty-five years older, was way more energetic and athletic than I am. Sixty-seven to forty-two—and a few months. But then he took regular exercise. He registered at the new gym at the Merrion Hotel, even before we moved into our house on Merrion Square. It was just a few minutes' walk away. He worked out three times a week followed by an hour charging up and down the pool. Until I got pregnant that is, then he did so every weekday. Is it any wonder he looked so gorgeous? *"Bien preservé"* as Annie often said. Oh, did I mention she's French? Canadian French, but her accent is French French, even though she's lived in Ireland for years. It's charming, not exaggerated in the least, but it gives her that little bit of added chic. She's pretty *"bien perservée"* herself.

I was George's third wife. His first wife died and he divorced his second for me. We met shortly after they were married, when he already realized it was a big mistake. He has two daughters from the first marriage, both married and living in the States, whom I met only once. It was enough. They were upset when he remarried less than a year after his wife died and furious when he and I shacked up. Their reaction was ludicrous; they thought it was "inappropriate behaviour for a man of his age." They must have had a sheltered upbringing is all I can say. Once, when George tried to calculate how many marriages the "home team" had notched up between the six of them, he gave up after fourteen. Quite a score when you consider that Jeff and Annie have been married just the once—to each other—for nearly thirty years. Thirteen between five is going it some, given how recently divorce was legalized in Ireland. It was my first marriage, though I'd had a few long-term relationships before George, serially monogamous, so to speak. He called me his virgin bride. Another private joke; I was three months gone when we married but I miscarried on our honeymoon. And again the following year. But third time lucky, I was seven months pregnant when he died.

I gave up my job as soon as we married. I worked in hospital administration. Actually that's how we met. One day George came in to have his pace-maker checked, I took his details and somehow we got talking. On his way out he popped his head around my office door and asked if I'd like to have lunch in Patrick Guilbaud's. As if it was something I was used to and would have to think twice about. I didn't want to seem like a pushover so I said, "Sorry, can't today," and asked for a raincheck. It seemed cooler somehow. I felt a bit of a fool when he said, "Of course," and went off about his business. But he rang the very next morning, by which time I'd found out all about him. I fell in love with him right away. He swept me off my feet.

George was rich. Very. He ran a worldwide construction conglomerate. "Well," he used to laugh, "what else would I do with a name like Steelyard? I was pre-programmed." But not just because of his name; it was the family business for four generations, which was why he was so keen on having a son. Our son. Now in line to become one of the wealthiest men in Ireland, if the rest of the Steelyard vultures can be kept at bay. As soon as the sex was confirmed, George set about sorting out the inheritance. His daughters flew home the minute they heard. They virtually accused me of cheating on him, said he was too old to father a child. And when they got him on his own, suggested a DNA test. The cheek! Thank goodness I only heard about that later. George kept it from me and sent the daughters-from-hell packing.

He was so wonderful to me, so overjoyed about the baby. As soon as I got the all-clear on the amniocentesis test, we chose the name. He wanted Luke but I insisted on George. George V has a nice regal sound to it. I allowed myself a glass of champagne to celebrate. George V Finbarr Steelyard. George's family hails from Cork, hence the middle name. After the patron saint. We have a marvellous second home there, on a hill overlooking the city, though we rarely use it.

The shock of George's death brought on the baby, six and a half weeks premature. I really thought I'd lost him, but he's a strong little fellow and he survived, though I almost didn't make it. Jeff and Annie took care of the funeral arrangements while I was at the clinic. I'm afraid none of us thought of sending for his daughters until the last minute. Another black mark to the horrible stepmother. That's what they insist on calling me, which is ridiculous when they are very nearly my age, though I'm a good deal more *bien preservée*—or so Annie told me when she brought me a new pair of shoes for the funeral. The baby was still in hospital but they let me out for the day. Annie said my figure was amazing for someone who'd just given birth, but she was just being kind. I'd lost a lot of weight all right, because I hadn't been able to eat after George died; but I felt and looked terrible. My skin had gone to hell and my hair was falling out in chunks. Annie loaned me one of her less flamboyant hats. That and a neatly tailored grey coat and I passed muster, until halfway through the Mass my breasts began to leak. Fortunately I had a Pashmina with me. I suppose that was the moment when the full impact of my loss hit me. I'd only had the baby because George wanted one so badly and now that he was gone I didn't know how I was going to cope. I'd never loved anyone half as much as I loved George. I had only to think of him and I'd burst into tears. I couldn't stop crying.

If only. It was all I could think of. If only I'd got up early that morning. If only I'd noticed he wasn't looking well. Was he looking unwell? I simply don't know, because he must have slipped out of the house as usual, at eight, when I was fast asleep. At that stage in the pregnancy I was tossing and turning all night, keeping George awake, so I moved into a separate room for the duration. He went to the gym every morning and had breakfast at the hotel before going on to the Steelyard offices in Ely Place, nearby. He usually came home for lunch, especially as I became less mobile. It's no joke having a first baby at forty-two. It was a difficult pregnancy and I became neurotic about not being able to carry it to term. Sex was out. I thought it was because I looked too big and awful, but he said he fancied me rotten. He was afraid it would bring on the baby. George was so sweet and thoughtful, he couldn't do enough for me, but he was inclined to fuss, with the result that I was virtually in purdah for the last month of his life. How I wish we'd carried on as usual; we always had such great times when we went out together; dinners, parties, theatre. George loved life and always wanted everyone, specially me, to have a great time.

When I look back on those last few days of his life, I seemed to be perpetually standing by the upstairs drawing-room window looking out on the square, watching the leaves turn from green to gold, watching them drop from the trees. Waiting. For the first time in my life I envied the fitness-freaks jogging past in the early morning when I would creep downstairs with the flask of tea that George always left by my bedside before he went to the gym. Often it was too cold to drink by the time I awoke, but that morning I must have missed him by only a minute or two because it was piping hot. It was also the first time in months that I sat up without feeling nauseous. I rolled out of bed and lumbered downstairs to face another long, lonely day. I remember being appalled at the size of my protruding belly. I felt like a beached whale.

I must have been looking out of the window for half an hour or so when Annie Colfer jogged into the square. I was mildly surprised because it was later than her usual time. She and Jeff lived not far away, on Leeson Street, and I sometimes caught her running past—maybe once a week or so. If she happened to notice me at the window she waved, did her three laps of the park then continued on her way to her shop on Grafton Street. That morning, hungry for human contact—George had been out at a dinner the previous evening—I very much wanted her to stop by, have a chat, but she didn't look up until her second time around.

She waved and continued a few paces, then stopped, and looked back at me. She must have caught something of my loneliness because when I beckoned, she cupped her hand to her mouth, up and down. Coffee. I nodded vigorously. She pulled her woollen hat off and ran lightly across the road towards the house. She was marking time on our top step when I opened the door. We both said, "Coffee?" in unison and I told her how pleased I was to see her. She took one look at my big belly and said: "Tea might be easier for you, Margaret." We went down to the kitchen and she sat me at the table while she filled the kettle and made a pot of peppermint tea for me and a double espresso for herself. I can't remember what we talked about, but I do recall it being the first time I felt really comfortable with her. She must have seen that I was feeling a bit isolated or maybe I mentioned that George was working too hard, going to far too many meetings, because she seemed in no hurry to leave. She stayed nearly an hour and she was just on the point of going when the phone rang.

It seemed very loud or at least that is what I remember. Brrr, brrr. Brrr, brrr. "Aren't you going to answer it?" Annie asked. I had the curious sense of watching myself as I walked over to the extension on the wall beside the door. I raised the receiver to my ear, and that was the moment my world caved in. I stretched out my hand to Annie as I braced myself against the wall and slid slowly downwards. I heard her scream, then she took the receiver from my hand. We sat side by side on the floor while she gently told me that George appeared to have had a stroke. She said the pool attendant found him lying dead on a chaise just outside the steam room and that the hotel doctor was with him. They asked if I could come at once.

Annie rang Jeff and then helped me upstairs. By the time I'd dressed and she'd showered, Jeff had arrived with some fresh clothes for her. I walked around to the hotel with the two of them holding me upright on either side, but as we went through the hotel entrance, Annie suddenly chickened out. She put her hand to her mouth and began to gag. "Please, Jeff," she said, "I can't do it. Maggie and I will wait here . . ."

I surprised myself then. I said: "No. I'd prefer to do it alone, but I hope you'll both wait for me. Please." I didn't want them to see George. I wanted to protect his dignity. I knew from working so long in hospitals how vulnerable and pathetic the dead can look and I didn't want them to remember my George like that. Jeff put his arm around Annie and led her off into the lounge but he caught me up as I followed the hotel manager downstairs to the gym and insisted on staying with me. They had evacuated the gym and pool area, or at least I think they must have done, because there was no one there other than three or four members of staff who stared at me, and a middle-aged woman who introduced herself as the hotel doctor. She said she thought he'd been dead for less than an hour and asked me if he habitually used the steam room. "Habitually" struck me as an hilarious use of the word. I must have been in shock because I kept thinking it meant "habit," like monk's garb. Apart from the towel, George was stark naked. But I caught the underlying rebuke and perhaps too, the fear of litigation. But on whose side?

"Never." I spoke the truth. George may have been vain but he was not a fool, he'd had mild heart problems and the warning notice outside the steam room was clear enough. I thought one of the gym attendants looked dubious. "Never," I repeated firmly. "My husband told me so himself." By then two ambulance men had arrived carrying a stretcher. The doctor signalled them away and took my hand and walked me over to George, her hand on my wrist, surreptitiously checking my pulse.

He was lying on his side with his left arm over his head, a white towel over his middle. His skin was still pink, mottled in places, his eyes were open, his expression surprised. As I lifted the towel she put her hand out to stop me but not before I'd seen his penis was semi-erect. "It happens, sometimes," she murmured and covered him again. I knew what was expected of me. "That is my husband, George Steelyard," I cried. Immediately, a searing pain ripped through my stomach as my waters broke and gushed hot and voluminously across the marble floor.

I don't remember anything else until I woke up in the hospital. Annie and Jeff were sitting quietly at the end of the bed. When I opened my eyes they came and put their arms around me and told me that George V had arrived safe and well. Annie and I cried while Jeff looked embarrassed and shuffled his feet. They took me home to stay with them for a couple of weeks after I left hospital, and while Baby George was still in his incubator, Annie drove me to and fro to see him each day. I could hardly bear to look at him, he was so puny and ugly. The nurses were rather overbearing about that, insisting that I "bond with baby." Annie gave one of them a good talking to, told them what had happened. After that they were a bit more sympathetic.

Eventually I went back to the house in Merrion Square, hired a full-time, live-in nurse for Baby G and a girl to help the house-keeper. I had no idea what my finances were going to be like but I assumed that George had done as he promised. He had made a huge transfer to my account when I got pregnant and there was still quite a lot left so I used that until it began to get worryingly low. When I went to see the family solicitor I discovered that apart from a rather ungenerous personal annuity, my security was firmly wrapped up in the well-being of the child. He was the heir, and as long as he was a minor his huge wealth would be adminis-tered by the solicitor, to whom I would have to go cap in hand "and beg?" I screamed at him. "But my husband told me he would look after me."

"And so he intended to," I was told. "I had prepared the change of will, he was to come in and sign it the day he died. But unfortunately . . ." He shrugged and spread his hands helplessly. "He wanted everything in order before his son was born," he added ruefully, but laid such emphasis on *his* that I realized the daughters had been on my case. He also somehow implied that as the Steelyard family solicitor, his loyalty was to them. My only importance was as mother of Baby G. Just as well I'd insisted on a DNA test on him and on George too, before we buried him. There was never a truer saying than blood being thicker than water. I casually rifled in my handbag, drew out the documentation and laid it carefully on the desk. "You may need this," I said sweetly.

Someone was going to pay. I was very shocked that George had left me in such a vulnerable situation, having treated me like a china doll all through our marriage. In a way that anger helped me through my grief. I went over the events of that morning obsessively, but it was like playing an old, cracked record—there were so many gaps in my memory. One day I made a formal appointment to consult the only neurologist I knew—Jeff Colfer, who had his consulting rooms on the other side of the square. I hoped he'd help me understand how it was that I had no warning of George's condition, and he did. He also managed to ease my mind and I thought I would be able to put the matter to rest, though there were still oddities niggling away, but so vague that I could not yet articulate what it was that so disturbed me. After the consultation, Jeff walked me home and from then on, he sometimes dropped by for a drink on his way home in the evening. By some mutual, though unspoken, agreement we didn't mention the visits to Annie. It was all perfectly innocent but I didn't want to upset her; I was too dependent on her friendship.

I missed George horribly, that didn't change, and I knew I would never again find anyone remotely like him or love again with the same ecstasy and abandon. He was a wonderful lover, inventive as well as considerate; great in bed, brilliant, and more than anything, that is what I missed. Besides Jeff, one or two of the "home team" came knocking on my door with mumbled offers of consolation, but I just laughed. None of them were a patch on George. Besides, I soon realized that however much I missed sex with George I would miss his wealth even more. The final settlement would cease if I remarried—which I had no intention of doing.

Strangely, my looks improved after Baby G. I'd always been young-looking for my age, five foot ten and statuesque, but after the birth, I slimmed down considerably and looked all the better for it. Out of consideration for George I'd always worn flat heels when we were out together but now, with Annie to guide me, I replaced my old wardrobe then raided her shoe shop. By now we were almost inseparable. She was surprisingly gentle and lovely with the baby, much better than I was, and I came to depend on her in all sorts of ways. Eventually, she asked if I would like to work for her in the Grafton Street shop, but I wasn't ready. I didn't resume any social life for nearly eight months after George's death.

My first outing was to one of Annie's dinner parties, in May, and I don't suppose I'd have gone if it wasn't to celebrate her fifty-fifth birthday. Jeff told me her age when I asked him to suggest an appropriate present. I was surprised, because I thought she was going to be fifty, and that suggested something in gold. In the end, I stayed with the idea and found a delicate chain with a single emerald—her birth stone. It was probably too expensive, but it was gorgeous and I knew she'd love it. Anyway it was a lot less than I owed her. I strolled around to her house with Baby G, and posted it through her letter box, to save any embarrassment and I was really pleased that it went perfectly with the gorgeous dark green sheath dress she wore for her party.

It was a fine evening and so warm that we ate outside. The garden had been specially lit with coloured lights in the trees and the table lit by two huge chandeliers at either end. Instead of the usual mixed gathering there was just the "home team" and their partners. George's place was taken by a neurologist colleague of Jeff I'd never before met, but he didn't arrive until after a touching little ceremony when Jeff charged our glasses with vintage champagne and spoke a moving little remembrance of George. I didn't get all the references, of course, but I certainly got the impression that Good Ole George was a bit of a goer while they were students. A couple of times one or other of "the guys" would finish his sentence to raucous laughter. It was all so very exclusive. When I caught Annie's eye I could see she was a little put out that her birthday party was being hijacked. And others must have noticed, because they started competing for her attention. Annie has that effect on people, men and women alike; they all want to be her best friend. Very soon she was looking relaxed and happy again.

Not so the two newest wives in the party. One of them, Maeve, was obviously bored rigid and the other, more agreeable girl, was trying her best to join in a conversation that was too full of past references and shared experience. As I watched Elizabeth struggle to be included, I startled myself with the thought that it was all something of an illusion, that "the guys" were not exactly recreating some past habitual gathering. True, they all knew each other well, true they had all shared many such occasions. Ate, talked and drank too much. Made silly affectionate jokes, got up to some stupid escapades. But suddenly I saw that they weren't all that comfortable with each other and that somehow or other George had been the one who really held the group together.

And there in the midst of the babble I began to sort one or two things out. Under cover of pouring myself another glass of wine, I carefully looked at each of George's old and dear friends singly, seeking out the youthful counterpart, picturing them in glorious, careless youth. Considering their age, and put together in flattering candlelight, they looked pretty good—if one was careful not to make odious comparison with the younger women. I thought of George and then glanced at Elizabeth and Maeve, both in their thirties, and wondered if the brief triumph of acquiring a younger, trophy wife was worth the concomitant diminution of the husband? For it was clear that *mature* looked *old* when compared to young flesh. The elixir of youth was an illusion which obviously gave way to bored disillusion if the girls' husbands, Rory and Matt, were anything to go on. They looked ill at ease, as if tired of trying to keep pace with younger, more vigorous ambitions—or demands, perhaps? Ah George, I thought, no problems for us in that department.

I found it interesting that both Rory and Matt looked most comfortable when chatting to their old friends, while pretending to ignore the envious, somewhat lascivious glances the other men threw at their partners. The two sat on either side of Annie, vying for her attention. They were animated, flushed with wine and the rather oppressive warmth. Annie caught my eye and grinned, then tapped her glass with her knife and asked the men to move two places to the left. I excused myself and went inside to the bathroom.

It had been newly decorated in sparkling white, with neatly folded, pale blue towels, piled high on wide glass shelves. As I touched up my make-up, my eye kept flicking to the reflected image of the towels which awakened something disturbing. I sat down on the edge of the bath and thought about George, lying dead by the pool, and began to dredge through my muddled memories of the scene. The doctor in a dark trouser suit, steel-rimmed spectacles, little make-up; the pool attendants in white, the hotel manager in a morning suit, Annie? Oh yes, Annie stayed upstairs. It was Jeff who stood beside me, looking anxious. Jeff who explained later that George might have had pre-warning of the stroke. Some odd feeling that might have passed, briefly. Something worrying enough for him to lie down. We decided that it must have happened as he went from the gym to the pool. But if so, I now asked myself, why was he not wearing his trunks? George was never one to parade around in the nude, he was surprisingly prudish that way, given his other propensities. Even going from bathroom to dressing-room or vice versa, George always, always, wrapped a towel around his middle. So, I glanced back at Annie's blue towels and realized that the piles of towels folded neatly on the line of chaises at the poolside, were a darker shade of the same blue. But the towel wrapped around George's waist was white. And, as I happened to know, since I had been asked to collect his property from the Merrion Hotel, George kept a room there, and in that room at least, the towels were white. Though I didn't realize why I was doing so at the time—I was too distressed—I checked out the bathroom. As I saw it, there were two burning questions to be answered: why did he have that room on permanent hold? And more importantly, who or what impelled poor dying George from the hotel room down to the pool?

I had a little weep, patched up my make-up and went back downstairs to the garden.

Light finally dawned as I made my way slowly down the garden. Something about the romantic setting, the heat and the laughter. I saw that the way Annie leaned forward, letting the

candlelight play on her clear, pale skin was contrived, deliberate.
How enviably she carried that slinky green dress with the emerald glinting in the plunging neckline. How serene that secret little smile as if she included the whole table in her pleasure.
Included? Surely included was not quite right? Anyone less char-
itable might have drawn other conclusions, less generous, more
nebulous.

What struck me as I sat down was that at some past dinner
party, watching Annie distribute her infectious charm, I had
wondered. Now I knew I'd hit the bull's-eye. The women, even
myself, her newest and latest best friend, were just a backdrop,
invited to add a little frisson of danger. In fact we were no more
than a passive audience. Oh yes, Annie would charm and smile
and treat you, as if you and only you, mattered to her. Yet I knew
without a shadow of a doubt. Knew in my heart and soul. Knew
as if it had been sworn to me, that every man at the table, *every
single one,* had been, and perhaps still was, Annie's lover. As
George had been. Which was why she insinuated herself into my
house that morning and waited for the phone call announcing
his death. As Annie sat there politely chatting to me, she knew he
was dead or dying.

I looked across at her husband, Jeff. Our eyes met. He knows,
and now he knows I know, I thought. Jeff, still handsome and
tall. Surely the top neurologist in Dublin must be almost as
wealthy as George? I could scarcely keep myself from bursting
out laughing. I looked back down the table. The trio at the head
were deep in conversation. An amused smile played on Annie's
lips and though she appeared quite unaware of my scrutiny, she
slyly tilted her head towards me and drooped one eyelid lazily. It
was both seductive and alarming. One eye wide open and the
other closed in a lascivious wink.

"Maggie, come and entertain these two, while I make coffee," she called, re-establishing intimacy. And domination. I got to my feet at the same moment as the two men rose to help Annie clear the table. Jeff never took his eyes off me as I sat down again. Heavens, he *was* good-looking.

I began to plan Annie's eclipse.

———————

Dublin-born **GEMMA O'CONNOR** is the author of six highly acclaimed suspense novels, most recently, *Following the Wake.* Others include *Walking on Water, Sins of Omission, Falls the Shadow, Farewell to the Flesh,* and *Time to Remember.* She has also written several works for the stage based on literary themes and personalities.

The End
(of Their Affair)

Áine Greaney

lan Power is sitting in a white lounge chair at the swimming pool at the Cala d'Or ApartHotel when he decides to end the affair. He has just woken from his afternoon nap. He sits there sleepy-eyed, squinting into that Spanish sunshine.

It has been like this every afternoon of their family holiday: his wife, Carolyn, and daughter, Sandra, parading down from the room with their wraparounds and flip-flops, magazines and paperbacks. Sun cream and all that friendly quibbling over which angle and how close with the sun umbrella, while Alan settles into the front page of the newspaper—though the resort shop carries only the British dailies. Then, just before noon, the voices and the footsteps and the lapping pool water grow distant and his eyes droop just before Carolyn reaches over and, mother and daughter giggling and whispering, she removes his sunglasses. Red and green pinpoints of sunlight behind his eyelids . . . and then he's asleep. Until footsteps or sudden loud voices wake him.

This afternoon, the chair next to him is empty now, Sandie's *Kiss* magazine abandoned, face down. He follows their screechy voices, the high, tittery laughs to the far end of the pool where his wife and daughter are horse-playing—Carolyn in her turquoise one-piece, Sandie in her scarlet bikini with the ties dangling down her back and hips. The two of them elbowing, laughing, daring each other to dive in first.

Sandie, ever the little actress, skitters around and behind her mother, places both hands on Carolyn's waist, and mimics pushing, shunting her mother along towards the deep end. *Ach, go on, Mum, Mum, Mum, go on.*

Carolyn, laughing, lets herself be pushed along like a trolley, her arms straight out, small, shunting steps.

At least she's not wearing that awful white sun hat, Alan thinks, as he realizes he's not the only one watching: the bald-headed Londoner who, every day at the terrace bar and café, always orders a lunchtime bottle of wine all for himself; the German with the dark, bushy eyebrows; and the Irish bloke with the blonde girlfriend and the country—Cork? Kerry?—accents. *Daily Mails* and paperbacks lowered and three strange men watching Alan's wife and daughter. The voices get louder: *Ach Mum, Mu—uum, ach, you're no fun. Go on, Mum.*

Alan sees his wife and daughter as those men see them: Sandie, belly-button ring glinting in her bronzed, seventeen-year-old's body, long legs and full breasts (he has always been secretly pleased that Sandie took after his side, the Power side of the family). And Carolyn, lathered as always in her factor 35, casting that white reflective glow around her, the pin-cushions of fat under the swimsuit elastic—arms and thighs and even the opening down the back.

At last they are lined up, toes to the edge, and Sandie, still in her theatrics, in an Olympic pose of hands high and pointing above her head. She nudges Carolyn to do the same. *This time, Mum. OK, one, two . . .*

And then they dive, Sandie first, the young body arching through the blue afternoon.

And that's when he decides it. When we go back home, suitcases unpacked and settled back into our normal, Dublin lives, I will end my five-year affair with Moira Walsh.

Alan Power and Moira Walsh sleep together on the third Thursday of every second month at the Shannonside Executive Hotel in a town in the middle of the country. Afterwards, on his Friday sales calls or driving back to Dublin, he sometimes thinks how the term "sleep together" doesn't even fit, is a little cozy-sweet for him and Moira. Because the truth is they just have quick, and really quite vicious sex, and always in the morning. And, though he has never told her this, Moira often leaves him feeling a bit . . . well, feeling as if, rather than making love to him, she has swooped and taken bites out of him, like a greedy little dog with his chew-toy. And never any post-coital bliss or murmuring, just her thumping across her hotel room, creaking that ironing board open and plugging in the hotel iron for that day's blouse.

Every second month, they arrive at the Shannonside—he from Dublin; she from Galway—and check into their company-paid rooms; each selecting the express-checkout option so that, next morning, they can depart for their respective work, their respective business in country towns within a twenty-odd-mile radius of the hotel. *Bye then. Until next time. Same time, same place. Toodle-oo.*

In his fifteen years with his sportswear company, Alan has held his spot among their top three salesmen, a source of great personal satisfaction. Especially nowadays, the way those younger fellas carry on with their emailed catalogues and quick phone calls to sports shops and menswear boutiques. But Alan is stubborn in his insistence on face-to-face sales calls, the chat and the laugh, his Ford Focus station wagon with his samples of Adidas, Reebok, Nike, O'Neill, highways and byways and town to town.

Five years ago, Moira Walsh, a trained social worker, went to night college to specialize as a sex therapist for secondary school teachers and principals. She has a monthly roster of schools where she delivers teachers' workshops, ice-breakers and discussion groups on how to talk to their teenage students, how to manage and advise when it comes to dating and safe sex. Or at least, that's how he, Alan, understands it, this gig of hers.

The Powers have come to Spain, a fortnight's holiday with the half-board option, because Sandie will start college next month. She's been accepted to her first choice—media and communications—in the National University in Galway, of all places.

In fact, the letters arrived at their house in Dublin on the same day: their holiday tickets from the travel agent and Sandie's acceptance letter. Carolyn went whooping and screeching through the house, saying over and over that it was a miracle, a pure bloody miracle and, certainly, this would be one in the eye for her sister Florrie—Florrie of the posh husband and the so-called genius kids.

Afterwards, Alan thought how it was indeed quite possible that his girlfriend (could you even call Moira that? No, no, definitely not) and his daughter might meet, sit in some smoky café or pub with a smell of minestrone soup and the sound of a cappuccino machine. And someone—a friend of a friend or a lecturer who once knew a classmate of Moira's—would inadvertently introduce them: *This is a student in one of my tutorials, Sandie Power . . .*

But now, sitting at the Cala d'Or pool, it's not that fear of daughter and mistress meeting that makes up his mind to end the affair. No, it's the prospect of Sandie leaving, of a semi-detached house without her, without the constant friends clomping through, the twitter of CD-player headphones, Sandie's mobile phone constantly ringing.

Oh, yes, long before now, even on their charter flight to Malaga, he couldn't get it out of his mind, the vision of himself and Carolyn in the house now, like the last two guests at a party, wondering what the dickens they were supposed to say to each other.

But the solution hadn't occurred to him until today, watching his wife and daughter play-acting around the Cala d'Or pool. But there it is. Eureka. They'd do better, him and Carolyn, they could do or say more without the shadow or anticipation of Moira Walsh.

The afternoon sun has slipped behind the apartment block, the balconies, palm trees, pathways cast in shadow. The pool area has settled into a sleepy silence. Up and down the lounge chairs, he sees that the three men—the baldie Londoner, the eyebrow German and the young Corkman—have each gone back to their naps or their paperbacks or their girlfriends. The Corkman, as if sensing Alan watching him, reaches to trail a finger down his girlfriend's back, the pale stripe of flesh where her bikini top used to be.

Carolyn and Sandie are standing apart in the pool, all their screeching and messing about over. Carolyn, waist-deep with her back to him, her pale arms jutting behind her, elbows leaning against the pool's edge. Sandie, still in the deep end, wet hair plastered and her pretty face risen to the sky.

Alan calculates. He and Moira were last together . . . yeah, back in July, so the next date at the Shannonside would be the third Thursday in September. Almost exactly a month from now.

Right, Alan thinks. That's that sorted. Moira's a gonner.

Then, reaching over the side of his lounge chair—first left for his sunglasses, then right for his folded-over *Daily Mirror*—he turns his attention to the *Mirror*'s front headline, "Missing Wembley Girl's Family Still Hopeful."

Moira Walsh is sitting at a round, white-cloth lunch table at the annual Galway Seafood Festival when she decides to end her affair.

As usual, the marquee tent is loud and echoey with voices and laughter. The men are in their summer suits or linen blazers, the women in gauzy pastels or Caribbean reds and yellows. Outside, the rain drip-drip-drips from the tent doorways and awnings, the cars have left deep, squelchy tire tracks in the field-turned-car park.

The lunch buffet, with its restaurant chefs in their high hats and white jackets, is actually almost finished, just those usual stragglers arriving in from the festival bar. There are four others at Moira's table—the Mulligans, Marie and Terrence, and the Brennans, Tommy and Dolores. The fold-out chair next to her is empty, of course, waiting for Moira's husband, Frank, who is among those latecomers, detained by handshakes and back-slapping in the bar. Frank Walsh is the assistant bank manager of the bank that, every year, is the festival's corporate sponsor.

Marie Mulligan, who has chatted valiantly throughout their luncheon, announces that what the hell, she *was* going to just have coffee and be good, but God, that Pavolva up there really looks *gorgeous*. Moira and Dolores Brennan urge her to go for it, gosh, Marie, if we had your figure, we wouldn't give it a second thought. "And anyways," says Dolores, laughing, "sure what's

Pavolva but a few egg whites? I mean, we might as well go and live in Lough Derg or some other monastery place if you can't have *that*."

Moira is already weary of the Brennans and the Mulligans, all that small talk across the table, yelping to be heard above the other voices and tables.

Marie Mulligan gets up and makes her way back up to the coffee and dessert buffet.

Moira pours cream, stirs, then takes a sip of her coffee. Already cold. She scans the heads, the crowd, to catch Marie's eye, ask her if she wouldn't mind bringing her back a fresh cup. Ah, there's Frank at last, talking to some woman. They are standing in that grassy space between the buffet and the aisles and the tables, so that others, the men and women headed to the seafood buffet with their glasses of wine and half-finished pints of stout, have to weave and divide around them.

Moira recognizes the woman. It's Fran Tierney, a corporate loan officer at the bank's city centre branch. She has changed her hair from frosted highlights to a full, strawberry blonde.

A man in a white shirt and a tie with yellow stripes is coming from the buffet with a full plate of food. He hesitates, scans the tables for an empty spot or for someone to claim him, beckon him over. Then he sees Frank, and, plate aloft, doubles back towards the bar with the florid, switched-on congeniality. Jesus-Frank-Walsh-is-that-you? Moira imagines him saying.

Moira tells herself not to, and yet she must, and she does: rises from her chair to see better, to study Frank's face as he glances up from his conversation. A flicker of annoyance at being interrupted, trespassed upon. Then Frank's face crinkles into a practised grin, handshakes and gusty greetings, the two men nodding proprietorially around, probably agreeing that, yes, it's a brilliant turnout this year. And in Fran Tierney's face, that same annoyance, and . . . yes, the sheepish, edgy look of someone who might have been discovered. Caught in the act.

Frank is sleeping with her, Moira thinks—knows.

When the yellow-tie man leaves, Frank, a hand fluttering towards her elbow, but then he thinks better of it, whispers to Fran, and she laughs at whatever he said. Then Frank nods them towards the buffet where the chefs are beginning to pack things away.

Fran and Frank, Frank and Fran. Incorporated. And with that same, chill certainty, Moira knows that she will now, finally, end her marriage. And her affair with Alan Power. The shock and the after-shock.

Their lunch plates full with Connemara smoked salmon and smoked mussels in white wine, Frank and Fran are standing together, she at his left shoulder and slightly behind, each scanning the tables for their respective places and partners.

Moira commands herself: Look down. Drink your cold coffee. Stuff yourself with bloody Pavolva.

Instead she stands up fully now, drawn to her full, five-foot-nine height, her face taut under her short brown hair, her body suddenly freezing inside her aqua-green dress. The Mulligans and the Brennans nudge, frown at each other, then busy themselves with coffees and dishes of dessert. Moira stands there, statuesque above the nodding, chatting heads. She doesn't wave or call out, "Yoo-hoo, Frank, over here." But waits for him to meet her gaze.

When he does, he sees that she knows, knows what she has seen.

Three months later, on the Friday before Halloween, Moira Walsh will suddenly leave her armchair in her psychotherapist's office, a room with a creaky floor and tasseled rugs, three floors up over Galway's Shop Street. She will cross to the double-sash windows to gaze down onto the pedestrian street. Even from up there, she will still feel that Friday-afternoon buzz from the strolling university students in their long scarves, cloche hats, oversized shoulder bags. A girl in zebra-patterned tights and Doc Marten boots is laughing. The face, the movements in silent animation. Bent over at the waist and laughing. And Moira will wonder, idly, if it might be Alan Power's daughter, the Dublin girl turned Galway student. And then she will brush the thought away, wonder why it even occurred to her.

Across the room, the counsellor, a befuddled expression and, quite honestly, already fed up with this new client of hers, sits looking at her client's back at the window, blocking the last of the afternoon daylight.

They're always the toughest, people *in the biz,* clients with social work or counselling degrees themselves. Know too much or must prove they do. To Moira's back the woman will repeat the question, what she asked before Moira's petulant (and really quite rude) departure for the window. "Didn't you suspect anything?" the woman asks again, knowing that it's not really relevant, not actually part of her client's healing, but . . . well . . . she wants to know.

Still watching the zebra-tights girl and her friends, the pictures will march through Moira's mind, black and white like those weird, impressionistic movies. Bank Christmas parties. Summer barbecues at people's houses. Dinner parties. The clubhouse and the corporate box seats at the Galway races; afterwards, a packed, city centre restaurant full of punters and winners and losers. Fran the corporate loan officer in all of them, that lipstick smile, those acrylic French manicures, that chameleon personality—shop talk and bank-insiders' jokes with the men; woman-to-woman small talk with the wives. *Wow, that colour is only fabulous on you, Moira.*

Turning from the window, Moira will creak back across the floor. But instead of sitting, she will stand with two hands on the chair back, then demand in a rather pedantic voice: "Is there anyone? Anyone in this city, this country, who has *actually* figured out where denial stops and knowing begins? Which is actually which? Or can we predict when one becomes the other? When, for example, you might sit sipping crap coffee at a stupid seafood festival and you just happen to catch a look between your husband and his little . . . (girlfriend? No. That wouldn't do. Floozy? Yes, that was good, but this psychotherapist has already pegged Moira as the middle-aged shrew).

Later that seafood-festival afternoon, the air under the tent grows acrid, a jungle smell of rain and trodden grass and mud. A brass quartet is playing, toot-toot, parp-parp, trumpet and clarinet rising over the tipsy voices. A couple is dancing, a slithery parody of a 1920s Charleston-style thing, hands flapping and the woman's yellow chiffon scarf twirling. Just, in fact, in the spot where, three hours earlier, Frank stood with Fran.

Earlier, just after the luncheon, a woman she used to work with beckoned her over. Loretta . . . Something. Moira remembered the first name in the nick of time. They caught up on news and their respective new jobs, then Loretta introduced her to the gang she was with. And Moira stayed with them because they were suitably raucous and oblivious so that she could let the conversations billow around her, answer when spoken to, laugh when one of the men cracked a joke.

Just after five o'clock, Moira mumbles that she must go, must root out her husband and drive home. Loretta says again that they *really* must get together some day—lunch in town?

Just at the tent opening, making her way across to the bar tent (Frank, of course, scurried in there after lunch), Moira turns to wave a last goodbye, and Loretta mimics a telephone receiver held to the ear. They must ring, keep in touch. Moira knows they will not.

They are sitting at a traffic light on the Dublin Road, a filling station on their left, a primary school on their right. The rain has lightened so that the wipers squeak. As usual, they have argued over who would drive home—he protesting that he has only had the three drinks all day, plenty of water in between. But this evening, he caves in faster than usual, senses some steadfast viciousness.

"How long?" she asks at last.

He shoots her a wounded look. He sits hunched down in the passenger's seat, the naughty little boy being yanked home early from a party.

She knows that he hates this pouncing, interrogatory way of hers, this social worker's belief that honesty is best.

His words drift out on the sigh. "Does—it—matter?"

Her voice taut, airless. "To me. *Yes,* it matters."

"Nearly four years."

A silly stab of victory. One year shorter, then, than her own affair at the Shannonside Hotel with Alan Power.

They drive in silence. Stop, start and stop again. Brake lights blurry, glistening in the rain. The wipers still squeaking.

They pass a glassy, roadside hotel. A small supermarket on a corner.

They are stopped at a roundabout. To their right, behind a huge housing estate, the dishwater-grey sea. To their left, the gates and a driveway to a hospital.

"So what will you do?" she asks, the voice brittle.

"Do?"

Six years ago, when Frank agreed to accompany her to marriage counselling, this was one of his accusations, how she just came out with things like that, the conclusion she'd already reached, though nobody but herself had been privy to the preceding discussion, the argument inside her head. As if he was supposed to miraculously fill in the missing paragraphs, reach consensus on things he didn't even know were under debate. Too much thinking, he said. Driving up and down those country roads from town to town and school to school. Staying alone in a hotel in the middle of the country, a woman alone with too much time, too much bloody *thinking*.

And now Frank Walsh knows that her *"So what will you do?"* is code for what she's already decided, back there at the seafood festival all afternoon, stewing around in her head. It means he's getting the boot, no playing house or keeping the best side out. Not even a move into the spare bedroom.

At last he says, "There's Vincent's house, I suppose."

Vincent is Frank's brother, a dentist in Sheffield, who built a sea-view holiday bungalow for himself out in Kinvara. Only uses it twice a year, once in summer, and sometimes in the spring when Vincent and his English wife come to trim the gardens and air out the place.

They are at another roundabout, then there's the wet-tyre swish as they drive along the dual carriageway, then exit for the village. Outside a stone-front pub, a few brave tourists are gathered around a picnic table, bicycles and yellow rain slickers.

Just after the village, they turn left up a side road, then left again up an even narrower road, the car labouring against the hill, then clang-clang over the Australian gateway, and up the steep driveway to their house.

She lets the front door slam behind her, so that he is left there on the front step, fumbling in his pockets for his house key. Inside, she takes a mad and aimless tour around the living room, the dining room, then down the hall to the kitchen, where she plugs in the kettle though she is neither hungry nor thirsty.

As the kettle boils, she hears him tromping between their master bedroom and the back spare room, dress shirts on a hanger, socks, shoes, toothbrush, cologne and shower gel. A familiar sound in their marriage, the declaration that the Walshes are officially at war. Again. Only this time, permanent.

She is sitting up in bed, the bedside lamp on, the television remote lost in the hammock of duvet between her propped knees, flicking through last month's issue of a glossy woman's magazine with its article "Make that tan last all summer long!"

Had the Powers actually gone away for their sun holiday? When she last saw Alan, in July, he was full of it, Sandie the little princess daughter combing the Internet for that perfect family holiday. Their last summer before she left home, as if the little princess were moving to China, not bloody Galway.

Moira forages for the remote, then clicks on the portable TV on the dressing table. It's some Californian comedy with its Californian girls prancing across the screen, heart-shaped faces and glittering teeth and every sentence ending on a question mark. Then canned laughter. Programme always gets on her nerves, but she can't be bothered to change it.

Stupid really, and certainly masochistic, but she makes herself imagine them, Alan and his wife and daughter. At this very moment they are probably strolling through a hot street, past noisy, smoky cafés, Sandie and Carolyn in strappy tops and swirly skirts; Alan in his signature white golf shirt (free samples from the sportswear company) and his dark, deep tan. Alan is not a handsome man, the pockmarks betray a once bad bout of teenage acne, but he is well presented, and, for a forty-seven-year-old, has a remarkably good physique.

The truth is, she rarely thinks of Alan in between their meetings, their *rendezvous* at the Shannonside. And she wouldn't think of him now, either, except . . .

She pulls the duvet up over her bare arms. Should really get up and turn on the heat—yeah, in the middle of August. The Californian girls are in some sort of a coffee shop now, joined by two Beatles-lookalike boys. A place with retro couches and coffee tables laden with magazines. She'd really like to strangle them, twist their scrawny little waists and wispy hair styles into one long, agonizing corkscrew.

Is Frank asleep already? She picks up the remote and clicks the mute button. From the guest room at the back of the house, she hears the Californian brigade twittering. Distant canned laughter. Duelling tellies. His 'n' hers.

It all started so simply, this business with Alan Power. Christmastime, five years ago, the last school sex workshop with a group of teachers who were far giddier, more anxious to vacate the school corridors and classrooms than their pupils. The Shannonside used to be hopping back then—sales representatives and business travellers, men and women who travelled east or west or south to consult or sell. The hotel was all decked out in faux Christmas garlands and red bows and gold balls, "Rudolf" and "Let it Snow, Let it Snow, Let it Snow" on the piped muzak.

That night, the twenty-third of December, there was that mood in the hotel lounge, everyone pulling up a stool, offering to buy each other after-dinner drinks. *Go on, 'tis the season.* And then, they were somehow all in this impromptu party, and it turned out that the young computer-guy from Tipperary had this stunning John McCormack voice.

After midnight, the barman herded them all into the residents' lounge, where the sing-song really took off. At last, some time after five o'clock, someone checked a watch, said, "Jesus, they'll skin me if I'm late for that meeting tomorrow," and retreated upstairs for a few hours' sleep. One by one, the others, stricken by giggly bouts of conscience and suddenly remembered work duties, went up too.

Alan Power and Moira Walsh were left sitting alone in a dark, shadowy bar. They did what, all evening, she knew they would do: moved into each other's arms, descended upon each other hungrily.

They made mad, greedy love that Christmas Eve morning in her hotel room with the paisley-pattern counterpane and the matching curtains, while underneath her window, the town in the middle of the country came alive with early morning cars and lorries.

After that, for their five years, it's always morning. So often, she's remarked to him that they must be the only illicit couple in Ireland who spend the night together but do little more than sit in bed watching telly, or he sits in her hotel bed watching silly sit-coms while she sits at the desk under the window, her laptop plugged into the hotel line, putting the finishing touches on tomorrow's school workshop. Sometimes he's already dozed off when she pads across the room to get into bed beside him. Until morning. When they have swift but quite good sex. Everything in that light, jocose vein, in the Alan-vein of everything being a bit of a lark.

Once, four years ago, he arrived at the Shannonside with a pale, sleepless look. Over their usual drinks and dinner she enquired, "You don't look yourself. Did something happen?" And without thinking, he told her, he hadn't had much sleep in the last two nights. Sandie, only thirteen then, was sent home from school with a blinding headache, the little girl screeching in pain. Paracetamol and drawn curtains, cold wash cloths on her forehead, the child calling for her Daddy. Alan summoned from his Clondalkin office. The awful, racing fear as he drove through Dublin's west-side traffic. Meningitis? Something worse?

When the doctor came, he said it was a viral thing, quite a few cases this past week, and in more than one school. Bed-rest and liquids and loads of sleep.

Moira watched that flicker of panic, that retrospective terror in Alan's face. A glimpse of the real Alan, what made him tick. As if, since their last meeting, he had aged from a precocious youngster to a rather haggard, middle-aged man—a much more likeable man. She reached across their hotel lounge table to pat his hand, to commiserate, to offer support.

And then she saw it, took note of it, and remembered. The deliberate switch, the purposeful resumption of his other persona, his chatter and his one-liners. *Don't get close here,* he was telling her. *Everything in my house in Dublin must stay intact, untouched by what we do here, in this town, this hotel. So don't get any foolish notions, issue any silly, your-wife-or-me ultimatums.*

So she didn't. Never.

For better or worse, however badly she and Frank were arguing, ignoring, he was—*they were*—her alibi. Mr. and Mrs. Frank and Moira Walsh—the names that were printed on wedding invitations to nieces' and nephews' weddings. The church collection envelope that was pushed through the front door. The names on mortgage, car loans, homeowners, life insurance. But not any more.

With Frank gone—his overcoats and mackintosh and umbrella permanently gone from the front hall stand—the rules of the affair have changed. And she, Moira Walsh, would *not* become an object of pity. A woman alone. Wanton and wanting.

So she would end it. And she has a whole month to concoct

some harmless excuse. God, she could even resort to good old-fashioned conscience, doing the right thing, if that's what it took. A clean break. The third Thursday in September when they meet again.

She clicks off the television, snuggles all the way under the duvet, and reaches a hand out for the bedside lamp.

"Hello, hello! Jesus, what d'ya have to do to get some service around here?" he says, laughing and swinging his garment bag down off his shoulder.

Louise, in her navy-blue receptionists' suit and her black ponytail, smiles primly at him and says in that customer-service voice, "Yes. Ah, *Mr.* Power. Back again to us."

"Howr'ya Louise? I thought you were gone off somewhere, working someplace else. Didn't see a sight of you all summer."

She is tapping his name into the computer. "God, that's a brilliant tan you have there; spent a while on the Med by the looks. Oh, now, must be nice for some!" She glances over the monitor at him, her made-up face and mascara eyes as impassive as they are trained to be. "The usual?"

Not that he's really given it much thought, but Alan knows that the Shannonside girls must know that he takes a business-class room for a total of half an hour—maximum, the time it takes him to freshen up, catch a little nap when he first arrives in off the road, and his shower the next morning after he leaves Moira's room.

He says, "Ah, Louise, *Louise,* you know me too well. Yeah. That'd be grand. Number 163. Away from the street and away from the kitchen and the rubbish tip." He winks at her. "Old fellas like me need our beauty sleep."

Louise shakes her head at him, rolls her eyes. He says the bit about old fellas and beauty sleep every time.

"Now. There you are, Mr. Power. Just have to sign as usual." She hands him the corporate reservation sheet.

He signs with a flourish—high, spiky letters. "Thanks, Louise." He nods to the double row of enlarged snapshots on the reception wall behind her. Employees of the month. "You're the one who should be up there. Permanently. Take the rest of that shower down."

In Number 163, the heavy, paisley-pattern curtains are half closed. In the white-tiled bathroom, there is the whiff of the hotel soap.

He unfolds the wash cloth, runs the hot water. Buries his face in the hot, steaming cloth, just like he used to when he was a teenager riddled with black-heads, willing them to just dislodge themselves, just levitate away. Now, every time he books into this and other hotels, he always makes a beeline for the bathroom and a hot wash cloth, as if the tar and teeth-clenching gridlock of early morning Dublin traffic and the M50 have somehow embedded themselves in his pores.

He pats his face dry, then loosens his tie, takes off his dress shirt and bundles it into the hotel's dry-cleaning bag. Steps out of his trousers, hangs them and the tie on the back of the door, then crosses to the bed and his garment bag for one of his white golf shirts (Adidas, free sample) and his nylon (Reebok) sports pants with the white stripe along the side.

Yeah. Much better. Lovely and comfy. He lies on the bed, hands straight down by his side, and shuts his eyes for his usual little nap.

The week before last they drove Sandie down there, across the country to a grey building beside a river in Galway. Student housing they called it. Said she was lucky to be selected for a place there. Better than hunting around *this* town for a student apartment.

Of course he couldn't say it, but the student-accommodation place gave him the bloody willies—more like an orphanage or some kind of mental institution with its metal windows and far too much grass and this walkway along the river with a smell of cow shit. But Carolyn and Sandie went plugging in CD players and putting up posters and fussing over Sandie's new duvet set that they bought her in Spain. Like two little girls playing house.

Then they drove away, all kisses and promises to ring home tonight before she goes to sleep in her new room. Around the city, past a shopping centre and out the Dublin road, past Oranmore where Moira Walsh lives (once, he even thought he saw her, a woman crossing from a shop to her car—ridiculous!). Alan's throat was tight. It was hitting him harder than he'd bargained for, his little girl, his little Sandie leaving them. But there was Carolyn, touching up her lipstick in the rear-view mirror, chattering away about how that college woman was right: it was the best, *by far* the best thing for their Sandie to live in that place for her first year. After that, well once she has new friends and everything, well . . . that's a *totally* different story. An apartment would be *no* problem then.

Some little viciousness in him wanted to challenge her, sitting there in her lipstick and her sun glasses in the passenger's seat. "How the hell would you know?" he wanted to spit at her. "Where did you ever live except your mother and father's house, then our house after we got married?"

Halfway back to Dublin, though it was not yet five o'clock, he was a little calmer, even contrite over his unspoken but poisonous thoughts. He said they'd stop for a nice meal somewhere, a drink and something really nice to mark the day, the occasion. Just the two of them now. Love-birds in the empty nest.

"Ach, All-ie"—he hated when she called him that—"Ach, no," she said, glancing at her watch. "Look, just something fast and we'll hit the road and then be home for *Coronation Street.*"

So they ate at a place just up the street from the Shannonside Hotel, a place with plastic-wrap sandwiches and sausage rolls in glass display cases. Dour-looking women with their after-shopping cups of tea, two men chain-smoking. Alan sat nibbling on a cream bun, seething over how the occasion, the day was completely lost on Carolyn. Oh, but if *he* forgot an anniversary, a birthday, a stupid Valentine's Day. Oh, well there was skin and hair flying then, wasn't there? But here *he's* stuck in a smelly café with her slurping her vegetable soup and going back up to the counter for extra napkins to protect her blue Capri trousers, the ones she'd bought for Spain.

Then, four days later, she comes home and announces *the job.* Shrieking around the kitchen as if she won the lottery. Tuesday, Wednesday and Thursday evenings, all day Saturdays as the receptionist at La Belle Femme, this spa and hairdresser place. Taking bookings over the phone, greeting customers and bringing them cups of herbal tea and coffee and magazines. She'd get commission for every jar of mud stuff and seaweed bath stuff that she sold at the counter. And look, she said, just look at the way it happened! Only in for her usual hair appointment, when André, that's the owner, he just mentioned that their receptionist was going out on maternity. Would she, Carolyn, happen to know of anyone? And so just like that, she takes the job, without even asking Alan's opinion, just arrives home full of it, and screeching how it was perfect, *perfect* timing with Sandie away now.

So, back there in Spain, he was right about their empty, silent house. Except that now, most evenings, it's just him and him alone: sitting in front of the living room telly with his microwave dinners. And when Carolyn *is* home, the smell of that place wafting around her, it's "down at the shop this" and "down at the shop that."

So for a week and a half now, ever since this Belle Femme business, he wondered if he shouldn't just let things go then, leave things as they are with Moira. Because there you are, trying to be the sensitive male, a male with a conscience, and well . . . all you get is . . .

Yeah, all you get is not able to take your afternoon nap in a hotel room, where you usually close your eyes and sleep like a baby. His nylon trousers crinkle as he rolls over to face the window, watches the swatch of blue sky between the half-pulled curtains. An Indian summer.

No. He'll do what he said he would. End the affair. I mean, Carolyn's bound to get over the novelty of this job and calm down and . . . maybe this André will just take the other one, the one with the new baby, back. And anyways, he's been rehearsing, practising his Moira speech. To tell Moira Walsh that he wants to really work on his marriage. Women love that kind of lingo— *"working on* things." He learned that once in a sales seminar: learn and then speak your clients' language and thought processes. Stay one step ahead.

A stiff "Thank you," to Louise the receptionist, then Moira Walsh heads with her little wheely-suitcase across the lobby, past the tourist brochures and the Ladies and Gents toilets, toward the lounge, where she sits at the third table down along the windows, orders sparkling water with ice and lemon, the suitcase and laptop tucked under the table. Waiting.

The familiar scent of Alan's cologne heralds his arrival. She stands, as usual, as if he is a business appointment, and they exchange something between a handshake and a grasping of the forearms, but no public collision of shoulders or cheeks.

Walls have eyes, ears. It is a pathetically small country.

"Howr'ya," he says, in that breathless, grinning way of his.

He is just as she pictured him, that night in her bedroom, the night of the Galway seafood festival when she imagined him in Spain: the tan under the white golf shirt, the nylon sports pants, the brand-new trainers.

He pulls out the lounge chair, looks around for the barman to order his usual pint of lager.

The words are out before she even decides to say it. She nods through the long, narrow windows, across the hotel lawn to the boats moored on the Shannon river, their masts against the blue September sky. "Alan, why don't we take a stroll?"

They have never left the hotel together, never gone to a restaurant in town, to a cinema, to a late-open shop. Everything between them—pints of lager and hotel dinners and morning sex—have been restricted to the inside of this hotel. Like people in a retirement home. Their whole world played out amidst polished wood, piped music and embossed wallpaper. Now, she watches the trepidation, the possibilities flicker across his features. But then, as if he remembers something, something that negates that fear, he shrugs and says, "Ah, yeah. Jesus, yeah. Why not?"

They have been walking for almost a mile along the narrow river path, first along the back of the hotel and its kitchens, bar, laundry, a church car park, then houses and their back-garden walls.

The path ends at a small park where young boys are kicking a football and people are sitting in gossipy twosomes on the riverfront benches.

Back on the path, he was telling her all about their holiday in Spain, how lucky they were to find this resort, last minute and on the Internet, but well, well worth it, every penny. Just before the park, they meet an approaching jogger, so Alan walks slightly on ahead.

He sprints to the last vacant bench along the river, where a young smoochy couple have just left. Grabs it before anyone else. Sits there waiting for her, one arm along the back for her to snuggle in, sit in the crook of his arm. Instead, she stands before him, arms folded, squinting into the sunlight on the river.

Now, here, she orders herself. In this wide open, fresh air, amidst the smell of freshly cut grass.

In the car she rehearsed it, the words growing smoothed and rounded as a well-chewed toffee. *Alan, we—can't go on like this.* Whizzing east along the motorway, she conjured his look, the sudden flash of alarm, his fear of the impending ultimatum, the *it's-me-or-your-wife* spiel. She decided that she would pause for effect, let him stew in it for a while before setting him straight, before offering deliverance: *It's just . . . well, it's just time, that's all. We've run our course.*

His voice is slightly raised above the screeching, cursing football players, the thuck-thuck of the football. He is telling about the night Sandie coaxed, dragged, the two of them (Jesus! At our age!) to the nightclub in the Cala d'Or resort. She studies his chin, his mouth, making the sounds. Flapping. Like a ventriloquist's dummy.

He shakes his head in reminiscence. "You shoulda seen it, Moira. Seen *us,* the three of us out on that dance floor, Sandie teaching us these mad dances."

He is already a stranger, she thinks. Some loud and silly stranger, telling a loud and silly story, a performance for everyone to overhear.

He stretches his legs, swish of nylon and flash of white trainers as he crosses his ankles, cracks his knuckles, presses his joined hands forward, then crooks his hands behind his head. "Aw, but great gas, though, and hey, that's what holidays are all about, letting the hair down, what?"

Standing there, the two places, countries, the past and the present fuse in her mind: strobe lights, wife's and daughter's arms raised, hips jiggling, Spanish music pulsing. And Alan here, on his river bench, the sun glinting behind him, stretched out like a cat. Always land on his feet. Lucky old Alan. Lucky old life of his. Always great gas.

Why should I tell him? Subject myself to an evening, a night of soporific talk and counter-talk and all those stupid ques-tions—*Look, is it me? Have I done something? Said? I thought we were snug as a bug in a rug.*

Her bitchy vindictiveness cheers her. I'll tell him absolutely nothing. Have the health board change my travel schedule, change my month or my territory. And that's the end of that.

They are walking back along the path, side by side but slightly apart, she avoiding the accidental brush of hips, hands, shoul-ders. She feels lighter, more buoyant than she has in days, weeks, since August and the seafood festival.

On the way back to the hotel it's more Spanish holiday stories, so she nods or laughs in appropriate places and says, "Really?" and "Oh, that sounds great." But her mind casts back over these past weeks, the solicitor's letters and separation agreements and the terse, businesslike phone calls from Frank's office. But these seem easier now, manageable, the seesaw tipping in her favour.

Their cutlery seems too loud in the almost empty dining room. Jesus, he could kick himself. They should have eaten in the lounge as usual. Me and my big idea that a proper dinner, a for-mal dining table is the place to break it off, to end the affair. But at least in the lounge there's a telly, a barman with comments about last Saturday's soccer match, things casual and no big deal. Not like this place. The last bleedin' supper.

And why have they dropped their voices like this, nearly to a whisper as if they're in a bloody church?

There are three other diners, men sitting alone at candlelit tables, newspapers propped against their water glasses, absently forking food into their mouths.

"How is it?" he asks about her monkfish dinner with braised vegetables and garlic mashed potatoes.

"Lovely," she says, smiling sweetly across at him.

She's been smiling like that all evening, ever since they came back from that stupid walk where he blathered his head off, couldn't bloody stop talking.

Yeah, there's really something different about her. Almost . . . almost as if he's just a snot-nose kid who has to be humoured, tolerated until the babysitter comes and she can escape.

"Mind you," he says, the words thudding across the air between them, "mind you, the steak is a bit tough-ish."

"Is it?" Another push-button smile.

"It is." (Shit. This is going worse than I thought.) "And you know, I never saw them to have tough steak here before."

"Didn't you?"

Yeah, there she is again, the tolerant mother saying, *That's lovely, darling. Yes, the sky is blue because God made it that way, darling.* Something distant and . . . well, *infuriating* about her. And none of the usual lads here tonight, nobody to distract, pull up a chair, swap a few yarns, take the pressure off.

"A chip?" he offers, mumbling through a particularly gristly piece. "I've more than . . . Really . . . I'll never . . . Well, just help yourself, love."

She shakes her head. Then, scraping back her chair, she nods behind towards the dining room door and the corridor and the Ladies. "Back in a minute."

When she's gone the dining room Muzak seems louder, this

Celtic mood stuff with those concocted sounds and those breathy words that everyone knows aren't real words. Has the maître d', that pimply faced little shit, suddenly turned up the stereo? Yeah, here's another blast of it, wafting out over the bamboo chairs and the candles and their dinners. Fal-dee-do, fal-dee-dee. Water down a waterfall. Make you want to run to the jacks all night. Probably just like the music they play in . . .

All his Thursday nights down here at the Shannonside, he has never imagined, pictured, Carolyn back up in Dublin. Yet in all these years she must have gone places, done things on Thursday nights—with her sister, Florrie, to a shopping centre or a cinema. But he has never wondered where or what she was doing as he sat in the Shannonside lounge or lay upstairs in Moira Walsh's bed.

But this evening, up in that park with all those shitting dogs and the panting joggers, he was tormented by images of her. There he was, talking, talking, talking to Moira, telling her any old thing just to chase Carolyn from his head.

Last night, she arrives home with shopping bags full of new shoes and trousers and a glittery top for a twenty-first birthday party she's going to tonight. A girl from work (*from work* as if the Belle Femme job is already a fixture). They're surprising the girl with a meal in a restaurant, then the whole gang are off to a party in a function room above a city centre pub.

Now he watches his own, blurry reflection in the darkened hotel window. There, he sees his wife and all those young girls and those androgynous-sounding men (Stewie and Jason and Joshua—I mean, did you ever?) getting rat-arsed and dancing and . . . Jesus, is there a stripper?

Moira is crossing towards their table, that fucking music still gusting through the room. Yeah, pimple face must've turned it up, just to cover up the shortage of customers. Moira seems miles

away—another planet. Almost at their table now, and she finally
meets his gaze, a placatory little grin, as if she's only just this second remembered him, remembered there was someone waiting
for her.

Feck her, he thinks, sawing at another piece of over-done
steak (he should have asked pimple face to take it back). *Feck her.*
More venom this time, and not really sure which woman—wife
or girlfriend—it's intended for. Or both. Because they both
deserve it, when you think about it. Need to be a bloody mind-
reader to know what they *really* want. Yeah, well, shag that for a
game of cowboys. And listen, why should I put myself in for all
this *it's-not-you-it's-me* speeches, all that sensitive-male shit when
all you get for it is a kick in the arse? No, one last little romp with
Moira here tomorrow morning, and then he'd just figure something out. Get Tony, his boss, to change his sales territory or
look, there were plenty of other hotels in this town. The easy exit.
Yeah, well, *Sayonara, senorita.*

"Everything all right?" he asks her just before popping the
piece of steak in his mouth.

"Lovely," she says.

Two months later, it is just gone half past four when Moira steps
through the doorway of her Galway solicitor's office. Down the
three front steps, buttoning up her wool coat against the damp,
chill breeze across Eyre Square. On the footpath, she stops, angles
back into the light from the office windows to fasten four shiny
new keys onto her key ring. Back door and front door, duplicates
of each—the keys to her new two-bedroom place out in Salthill
by the sea, walking distance to town, new town houses around a
small courtyard. She has just signed the final papers.

It is, in fact, her second visit to a solicitor's within a fortnight.
The Wednesday before yesterday, she sat in another office to sign

away her share of the bungalow on the hill in Oranmore. Frank even managed a smile for her.

It was always his dream, his hobby-horse, that ridiculously big house with the wind whistling around the chimneys, the foundations. A bank client once tipped him off on it, that hilltop land with the sweeping views. Well, Frank had it now, just him and little strawberry-blonde Fran. And tomorrow, Moira would start moving her things into the new town house by the sea, her car parked outside, the house number next to the doorbell, the shut-in anonymity of a middle-aged woman who, the neighbours might or might not notice, sometimes went away, went travelling for work.

The keys are heavy and clinking in her coat pocket as she walks briskly down the footpath. Across the street, people are trudging, winter caps and shoulders hunched, across the short-cut path that cuts diagonally across the green. A girl is lugging a huge suitcase, probably to the train station on the opposite side. Along the town end of the square, the sharp contours of the Galway Hooker monument stand silhouetted and pointed against the lit-up windows and shop fronts. Moira waits at the pedestrian crossing, the dome light flashing, the double lanes of headlights and tail lights all around the square.

On the other side, she walks along by the big hotel with the ivied front, the reflective, chandelier lights from the windows, the smell of roasted food, the air of waiters, chefs, maître d's bustling about their business. And then it occurs to her. Today is the third Thursday of November, and just about now, I am supposed to be driving towards the Shannonside Hotel.

It was easy, really. She just told her boss, Mrs. Fenton at the health board, that she'd like her November school appointments cancelled, deferred. She had . . . some changes to her personal life, but nothing to worry about, so if their secretary would ring the school principals and rearrange for after Christmas. Oh, and for the new year's schedule, please flip-flop the months, book the midland and border counties on the even-numbered months (February, April, June); the midwestern and southern counties on the odd-numbered (January, March, May). Mrs. Fenton said that, Galway being the small place it is and Frank Walsh being a well-known business figure, she wasn't exactly *unaware* of Moira's current *situation*. But rest assured that things would be taken care of. It was the least they could do.

Walking on past the opening to the train station with its buses and taxis ticking over, Moira pictures him, Alan Power, coming across the lobby at the Shannonside, all hand-rubbing and gusto and ordering his pint of lager while he waits for her, checking his watch and wondering.

She walks down Foster Street towards her car in the car park near the tourist office. Yes. Why not? She'd drive out there now, around the docks and out by the sea. Just for another little peek at her new place. Get a little takeaway and a nice bottle of champagne and enjoy a little din-dins at that new kitchen counter. Just her.

No. Not a patch, Alan thinks. Jesus, not even in the same league as the Shannonside. Not even a leisure centre or even a bit of an exercise room.

He is sitting alone at the counter of the Royal Hotel, sipping a pint of lager that tastes like the last one from the barrel. The barman, with a continuous cigarette smoking in an ashtray, sits opposite, across the horse-shoe bar, watching some moody film on UTV.

"Any chance of getting the Everton–Chelsea game on there?" Alan asks, nodding up towards the telly. It's his third attempt at conversation with this bloke.

The barman glances sourly across at him, winces, eyes narrowed as he takes another puff of his cigarette, then clicks through the channels until the screen is full of men in white shorts on a technicolour soccer pitch.

"Cheers," Alan says. But the man has already turned away, walked off into the back.

Born and brought up in County Mayo, **ÁINE GREANEY** now lives in Massachusetts, where she writes and teaches. She has published many features, essays, and award-winning short stories. Her first novel, *The Big House,* was published in 2003.

Photographs

Morag Prunty © Clodagh Moreland; Martina Devlin © Robert Doyle; Clare Dowling © Barry McCall; Suzanne Higgins © Orla Comerford; Sarah Webb © Margaret Moore (Photographic); Una Brankin © Fionn McCann; Cecelia Ahern © Robert Doyle; Julie Parsons © Maurice Rougemont/Opale; Joan O'Neill © Laura O'Neill; Annie Sparrow © Fionn McCann; Deirdre Purcell © RTÉ Stills; Mary Ryan © Norton Associates; Rosaleen Linehan © Colm Henry; Catherine Foley © Brenda Fitzsimons Gemma O'Connor © Barry Moore

Be the Next Downtown Girl
Contest Rules

NO PURCHASE NECESSARY TO ENTER.

1) ENTRY REQUIREMENTS:
Register to enter the contest on www.simonsaysthespot.com. Enter by submitting your story as specified below.

2) CONTEST ELIGIBILITY:
This contest is open to nonprofessional writers who are legal residents of the United States and Canada (excluding Quebec) over the age of 18 as of December 7, 2004. Entrant must not have published any more than two short stories on a professional basis or in paid professional venues. Employees (or relatives of employees living in the same household) of Simon & Schuster, VIACOM, or any of their affiliates are not eligible. This contest is void in Puerto Rico, Quebec, and wherever prohibited or restricted by law.

3) FORMAT:
Entries must not be more than 7,500 words long and must not have been previously published. Entries must be typed or printed by word processor, double spaced, on one side of noncorrasable paper. Do not justify right-side margins. Along with a cover letter, the author's name, address, email address, and phone number must appear on the first page of the entry. The author's name, the story title, and the page number should appear on every page. Electronic submissions will be accepted and must be sent to downtowngirl@simonandschuster.com. All electronic submissions must be sent as an attachment in a Microsoft Word document. All entries must be original and the sole work of the Entrant and the sole property of the Entrant.

All submissions must be in English. Entries are void if they are in whole or in part illegible, incomplete, or damaged or if they do not conform to any of the requirements specified herein. Sponsor reserves the right, in its absolute and sole discretion, to reject any entries for any reason, including but not limited to based on sexual content, vulgarity, and/or promotion of violence.

4) ADDRESS:
Entries submitted by mail must be postmarked by July 31, 2005 and sent to:

Be The Next Downtown Girl
Author Search

Downtown Press Editorial Department
Pocket Books
1230 Sixth Avenue, 13th floor
New York, NY 10020

Or Emailed By July 31, 2005 at 11:59 PM EST as a Microsoft Word document to:

downtowngirl@simonandschuster.com

Each entry may be submitted only once. Please retain a copy of your submission. You may submit more than one story, but each submission must be mailed or emailed, as applicable, separately. Entries must be received by July 31, 2005. Not responsible for lost, late, stolen, illegible, mutilated, postage due, garbled, or misdirected mail/entries.

5) PRIZES:
One Grand Prize winner will receive:

Simon & Schuster's Downtown Press Publishing Contract for Publication of Winning Entry in a future Downtown Press Anthology, Five Hundred U.S. Dollars ($500.00), and

Downtown Press Library
(20 books valued at $260.00)

Grand Prize winner must sign the Publishing contract which contains additional terms and conditions in order to be published in the anthology.

Ten Second Prize winners will receive:

A Downtown Press Collection
(10 books valued at $130.00)

No contestant can win more than one prize.

6) STORY THEME
We are not restricting stories to any specific topic, however they should embody what all of our Downtown Press authors encompass—they should be smart, savvy, sexy stories that any Downtown Girl can relate to. We all know what uptown girls are like, but girls of the new millennium prefer the Downtown Scene. That's where it happens. The music, the shopping, the sex, the dating, the heartbreak, the family squabbles, the marriage, and the divorce. You name it. Downtown Girls have done it. Twice. We encourage you to register for the contest at www.simonsaysthespot.com in order to receive our monthly emails and updates from our authors and read about our titles on www.downtownpress.com to give you a better idea of what types of books we publish.

7) JUDGING:
Submissions will be judged on the equally weighted criteria of (a) basis of writing ability and (b) the originality of the story (which can be set in any time frame or location). Judging will take place on or about October 1, 2005. The judges will include a freelance editor, the editor of the future Anthology, and 5 employees of Sponsor. The decisions of the judges shall be final.

8) NOTIFICATION:
The winners will be notified by mail or phone on or about October 1, 2005. The Grand Prize Winner must sign the publishing contract in order to be awarded the prize. All federal, local, and state taxes are the responsibility of the winner. A list of the winners will be available after October 20, 2005 on:

http://www.downtownpress.com

http://www.simonsaysthespot.com

The winners' list can also be obtained by sending a stamped self-addressed envelope to:

Be The Next Downtown Girl
Author Search
Downtown Press Editorial Department
Pocket Books
1230 Sixth Avenue, 13th floor
New York, NY 10020

9) PUBLICITY:
Each Winner grants to Sponsor the right to use his or her name, likeness, and entry for any advertising, promotion, and publicity purposes without further compensation to or permission from such winner, except where prohibited by law.

10) INTERNET:
If for any reason this Contest is not capable of running as planned due to an infection by a computer virus, bugs, tampering, unauthorized intervention, fraud, technical failures, or any other causes beyond the control of the Sponsor which corrupt or affect the administration, security, fairness, integrity, or proper conduct of this Contest, the Sponsor reserves the right in its sole discretion, to disqualify any individual who tampers with the entry process, and to cancel, terminate, modify, or suspend the Contest. The Sponsor assumes no responsibility for any error, omission, interruption, deletion, defect, delay in operation or transmission, communications line failure, theft or destruction or unauthorized access to, or alteration of, entries. The Sponsor is not responsible for any problems or technical malfunctions of any telephone network or telephone lines, computer on-line systems, servers, or providers, computer equipment, software, failure of any email or entry to be received by the Sponsor due to technical problems, human error or traffic congestion on the Internet or at any website, or any combination thereof, including any injury or damage to participant's or any other person's computer relating to or resulting from participating in this Contest or downloading any materials in this Contest. CAUTION: ANY ATTEMPT TO DELIBERATELY DAMAGE ANY WEBSITE OR UNDERMINE THE LEGITIMATE OPERATION OF THE CONTEST IS A VIOLATION OF CRIMINAL AND CIVIL LAWS AND SHOULD SUCH AN ATTEMPT BE MADE, THE SPONSOR RESERVES THE RIGHT TO SEEK DAMAGES OR OTHER REMEDIES FROM ANY SUCH PERSON(S) RESPONSIBLE FOR THE ATTEMPT TO THE FULLEST EXTENT PERMITTED BY LAW. In the event of a dispute as to the identity or eligibility of a winner based on an email address, the winning entry will be declared made by the "Authorized Account Holder" of the email address submitted at time of entry. "Authorized Account Holder" is defined as the natural person 18 years of age or older who is assigned to an email address by an Internet access provider, online service provider, or other organization (e.g., business, education institution, etc.) that is responsible for assigning email addresses for the domain associated with the submitted email address. Use of automated devices are not valid for entry.

11) LEGAL Information:
All submissions become sole property of Sponsor and will not be acknowledged or returned. By submitting an entry, all entrants grant Sponsor the absolute and unconditional right and authority to copy, edit, publish, promote, broadcast, or their entries, in perpetuity, in any manner without further permission, notice or compensation. Entries that contain copyrighted material must include a release from the copyright holder. Prizes are nontransferable. No substitutions or cash redemptions, except by Sponsor in the event of prize unavailability. Sponsor reserves the right at its sole discretion to not publish the winning entry for any reason whatsoever.

In the event that there is an insufficient number of entries received that meet the minimum standards determined by the judges, all prizes will not be awarded. Void in Quebec, Puerto Rico, and wherever prohibited or restricted by law. Winners will be required to complete and return an affidavit of eligibility and a liability/publicity release, within 15 days of winning notification, or an alternate winner will be selected. In the event any winner is considered a minor in his/her state of residence, such winner's parent/legal guardian will be required to sign and return all necessary paperwork.

By entering, entrants release the judges and Sponsor, and its parent company, subsidiaries, affiliates, divisions, advertising, production, and promotion agencies from any and all liability for any loss, harm, damages, costs, or expenses, including without limitation property damages, personal injury, and/or death arising out of participation in this contest, the acceptance, possession, use or misuse of any prize, claims based on publicity rights, defamation or invasion of privacy, merchandise delivery, or the violation of any intellectual property rights, including but not limited to copyright infringement and/or trademark infringement.

Sponsor:

Pocket Books,
an imprint of Simon & Schuster, Inc.
1230 Avenue of the Americas,
New York, NY 10020

1165